Caelus And The Fractals Of Fate

Joshua McMurray

Table of Contents

Chapter 1

Echoes of the Past

The ancient hologram museum of Solarune rises like a question mark against the evening sky, stone and light fused in impossible harmony. Inside, technology hums beneath floor tiles worn smooth by a million footsteps. History breathes here, not as a relic but as a living presence that shivers through the air, vibrating against the skin like static electricity-seeking ground.

Caelus steps through the arched entrance, his lean frame casting a long shadow across the marble floor. The sigils tattooed on his tan skin seem to pulse faintly in response to the museum's energy. Behind him, Selenea follows, her practical military-styled braid swinging between her shoulder blades as she adjusts the settings on a small device in her palm.

"You always look like you're about to steal something," she says, amber eyes narrowing at her brother's cautious movements.

"I'm just being thorough." Caelus crouches to examine a line of text etched into the baseboard, seemingly invisible to casual observers. "The best exhibits are the ones they don't advertise."

Their footsteps echo in counterpoint rhythms, his deliberate and measured, hers quick and precise. Around them, holographic displays flicker to life as they pass, star maps unfurling like luminous flowers blooming in accelerated time. A three-dimensional recreation of Solarune's first interstellar expedition hovers near the center of the hall, the ancient vessel rendered in particles of light so fine they resemble mist more than technology.

Selenea holds up her Sigil Processor, a sleek handheld device that looks like it might have been grown rather than manufactured. Its surface curves organically around her fingers.

"New model?" Caelus asks, straightening from his inspection of a particularly weathered glyph.

"Battalion-issue. Decodes twice as fast, and it can process parallel symbol systems simultaneously." She aims the device at a wall where concentric circles overlap in complicated patterns. The Processor hums, projects a thin beam of amber light and begins translating the ancient markings into a modern script that hovers in the air between them. "See? The outer ring tells the position of the third moon during the summer equinox, while the inner pattern maps quantifiable gravimetric anomalies."

Caelus nods, but his attention has already shifted. He moves to a section of the wall where deeply carved sigils form a spiraling pattern. Rather than pointing his sister's device at them, he places his fingertips directly against the stone. His eyes were half-close, head tilting slightly as if listening to something beyond human hearing.

"You'll get security called on us again," Selenea warns, but her voice lacks conviction. She's seen this behavior since they were children, her brother's unexplainable connection to certain artifacts.

"Feel that vibration under the glyph?" he asks, not removing his hand. "It's like a pulse but with a pattern."

Selenea sighs but approaches, extending her free hand toward the wall. After a moment, her eyebrows lift in surprise. "There's definitely something. The Processor isn't detecting any power source, though."

"Not everything that has power uses energy we can measure." Caelus traces the curve of a symbol that resembles a hook with three barbs. As his finger follows the final line, the carving emits a brief blue glow that fades almost instantly.

A handful of other visitors glance their way, then quickly return to their own explorations, accustomed to the museum's occasional unexplained phenomena.

The siblings move deeper into the museum, passing through a corridor where the ceiling opens to reveal Solarune's night sky. Three moons hang in formation, one silver-white, one with a bluish tinge, and the smallest showing a faint copper hue. Their light streams through the skylights, casting multiple shadows behind each exhibit and visitor.

"Look at how they've reconstructed the Battle of Cygnus." Caelus points to a display where miniature ships exchange fire across a simulated void. "They've finally got the formation right. Last time we were here, they had the defensive perimeter all wrong."

Selenea consults her Processor. "According to the cosmic records, that battle changed the gravitational dynamics of the entire sector. The mass displacement from the flagship's destruction actually altered the orbit of two planets." She sweeps her hand through the hologram, expanding a portion that shows debris trails. "See how the particles disperse? That pattern created new navigation lanes that we still use today."

Caelus moves through the exhibition with practiced efficiency, touching selected artifacts, pausing to absorb information, and then moving on. It's the movement of someone who has visited countless times but still discovers new details. Selenea follows a more methodical approach, scanning each exhibit systematically and recording certain readings with her Processor.

"The third moon is brighter tonight," Caelus observes, glancing upward through a particularly large skylight. "The alignment's almost perfect."

The three moons of Solarune create a natural calendar that has guided the planet's inhabitants for millennia. Their current positioning, forming an almost straight line across the night sky, happens only twice each year.

Selenea studies them for a moment. "When they align like this, the ancient texts say the veil between physical and cosmic thins. That's why so many of the prediction sigils are based on triple-moon alignments."

The air in the museum carries a distinct blend of scents, the crisp, electric smell of active holograms intermingling with the earthy permanence of ancient stone. It's a combination unique to Solarune, where history and cutting-edge technology exist not as separate entities but as complementary forces.

Caelus inhales deeply, his eyes closing briefly. "Do you smell that? The ozone is stronger near this exhibit." He approaches a circular platform where a holographic representation of the planet rotates slowly, surrounded by orbital calculations rendered in light.

"Probably just needs recalibration," Selenea suggests, but she follows him anyway. Her Processor beeps softly as it detects unusual energy patterns. "Or maybe not. These readings don't match standard hologram emissions."

Around them, the museum continues its daily rhythm, scholars debating in hushed tones, tourists capturing images, and children pressing their faces against protective fields that guard the most delicate artifacts. Yet at this moment, the siblings exist in their own bubble of focused exploration, their familiar dynamic playing out as it has countless times before: Caelus sensing, intuiting, physically engaging; Selenea analyzing, measuring, contextualizing.

The stone beneath their feet has witnessed this pattern for generations, curious minds seeking to understand the stars that birthed them.

The museum's eastern wing narrows into corridors less traveled, where lighting dims and exhibits grow more specialized. Caelus moves with the certainty of someone following an internal compass, leading his sister past holographic displays of increasingly ancient stellar charts. The floor transitions from polished marble to rough-hewn stone, the walls closing in until they enter a hexagonal chamber where shadows gather in the corners like shy spectators.

"I don't think we've been in this section before," Selenea says, her voice dropping to match the hushed atmosphere. Her Processor emits a soft whine as it recalibrates to the room's unique energy signature.

"They opened it last solstice. The restoration took three years." Caelus approaches the far wall, which rises from floor to ceiling in a seamless expanse of dark stone. Unlike the carefully labeled exhibits in the main hall, this wall bears no explanatory text and no visitor guidance.

The sigils covering its surface form concentric rings that spiral inward toward a central glyph larger than the rest. Each marking has been carved with impossible precision, too fine for ancient tools, yet the carbon dating displayed on a small, unobtrusive panel indicates an age of over four thousand years.

"Look at the depth variance," Selenea says, running her Processor along one spiral arm of symbols. "Each sigil is carved to a different depth, varying by microns." She squints at the readings. "It's not random. There's a pattern to the variations."

Caelus circles the chamber slowly, studying the wall from different angles. The ambient lighting shifts as he moves, responding to his presence. "The main museum database lists this as 'The Cosmographer's Wall.' No attribution to any specific culture or era."

"That's odd. The restoration team would have gathered substantial data." Selenea taps at her device, scrolling through information. "There's almost nothing in the public record."

The chamber's design features no obvious technological elements, yet a subtle hum vibrates just below the threshold of hearing, more felt than heard, like the pressure change before a storm.

Caelus stops directly before the central glyph. Unlike the surrounding sigils, which are carved with sharp, precise lines, this symbol appears fluid, almost organic. It resembles a star with seven asymmetrical points, each terminating in what might be a planet or moon.

"I think it's key," he says, more to himself than to his sister. Without hesitation, he presses his palm flat against the central glyph.

The stone feels warm beneath his hand, not the ambient warmth of a sun-heated wall, but something that pulses with internal energy. For three heartbeats, nothing happens. Then, light bleeds from the edges of his hand, seeping into the carved lines of the central sigil.

The light spreads outward like water, finding channels in dry earth, flowing through the spiraling patterns of smaller glyphs. The illumination shifts through spectral colors, cobalt to azure to violet, casting shifting patterns across their faces and the chamber floor.

Selenea gasps, her analytical composure momentarily forgotten. "The Processor's going crazy," she says, holding up the device. Its screen flashes with translated phrases that appear and fade too quickly to read completely. "Celestial currents... gravitational weave... cosmic threads..."

The light from the sigils intensifies and then projects outward into the center of the chamber. Motes of brilliance coalesce into three-dimensional forms, stars, planets, and nebulae hanging in the air between them. The holographic projection grows more complex with each passing second, with lines of force connecting celestial bodies orbital paths traced in light.

"It's a map," Caelus says, his voice hushed with wonder. He hasn't removed his hand from the central glyph. "But not just of space, of time. Look at the movement patterns."

The projected star systems rotate, shift, and drift in patterns that suggest the passage of eons compressed into minutes. Some stars flare and dim, and others spiral together in cosmic dances.

Selenea moves carefully around the projection, and her processor continuously scans and records it. "I'm identifying known systems, but they're... different. Positioned as they would have been thousands of years ago." She reaches toward a particular cluster, and the projection responds, expanding that section. "That's our system, but see how the planetary alignments differ?"

Caelus nods, his free hand moving to trace connections between specific stars. As his fingers pass through certain points in the projection, those areas brighten, revealing additional details, such as asteroid fields, radiation belts, and gravitational anomalies.

"The processor is translating more of the text," Selenea says, eyes fixed on her device. "It says Solarune was positioned at a 'convergence point of stellar currents.' Something about our planet's location making it ideal for... stellar cartography?" She frowns at the translation. "No, more like 'cosmic observation.' The planet itself was some kind of astronomical instrument."

The siblings work in practiced tandem, Selenea reading translated text segments, and Caelus intuitively finding the corresponding areas in the projection. Each discovery builds on the last, creating a comprehensive picture of Solarune's historical significance.

"Look at this," Caelus says, directing her attention to a section where light streams between systems in distinct patterns. "These aren't trade routes or travel paths. They're something else."

Selenea consults her device. "The text calls them 'threads of awareness.' Does that mean communication channels?"

"Maybe." Caelus traces one particularly bright thread that connects their star system to a distant cluster. The projection responds by highlighting that connection, showing how it pulses with varying intensity. "But I think it's more fundamental than technology. These feel like... natural phenomena."

Their excitement builds as they piece together more information. Solarune's position at the intersection of multiple cosmic threads made it uniquely valuable as an observation point, a natural astronomical platform from which to study the universe.

"The three moons," Selenea says suddenly. "Look how they're depicted in the projection. They're not just satellites, and they're amplifiers of some kind."

In the holographic display, Solarune's three moons appear encircled by concentric rings of energy that extend outward into space, intersecting with the threads connecting to other systems.

A small group of visitors enters the chamber, drawn by the spectacular light display. They pause near the entrance, murmuring appreciatively at the complexity of the projection.

"This is incredible," one whispers loudly enough to be heard. "I've never seen this exhibit activated before."

The museum's automatic announcement system chimes softly: "The Cosmographer's Wall is a recent restoration. Visitors are reminded that interactive elements may activate unexpectedly. Please maintain a respectful distance."

More people gather at the chamber entrance, but none venture further inside, instinctively recognizing that something extraordinary is unfolding.

Caelus and Selenea barely notice the audience. They're absorbed in their discovery, moving around the projection with the synchronicity of long-time collaborators.

"If Solarune was positioned to observe these cosmic threads," Caelus says, "what were they looking for? Or listening for?"

Selenea shakes her head, amber eyes reflecting the dancing lights. "The text mentions 'voices carried on stellar winds' and 'messages woven into gravity.' It sounds almost..."

"Mystical," Caelus finishes. "Or maybe just science we don't understand yet."

The projection shifts again, zooming outward to show a broader view of the galaxy. Solarune appears as a bright node in a vast network of interconnected star systems, one point in an incomprehensibly complex web of light.

"We've always wondered why the ancients were so advanced in astronomy," Selenea says, "why they built such precise observatories and kept such detailed records." She gestures at the projection. "This suggests they weren't just studying stars. They were studying connections between stars."

Caelus nods, his expression intense and concentrated. "And Solarune wasn't just their home. It was their instrument."

The light from the wall pulses once more then stabilizes into a steady glow that bathes the chamber in a cool radiance. The holographic star map rotates slowly before them, a universe in miniature, revealing secrets long forgotten.

A figure appears in the chamber doorway, tall and straight-backed, observing the siblings with quiet intensity. Their father, Emeritus Lorian Solaris, moves with the careful precision of someone accustomed to valuable and delicate things, his footsteps making no sound on the stone floor. The sigils adorning his arms, similar to those on his children but more numerous and more complex, catch the light from the holographic display, creating the impression that constellations move across his skin.

He stands motionless for several minutes, watching as Caelus and Selenea work in tandem to decode the ancient star map. His expression reveals nothing, but his eyes track every movement his son makes with particular focus.

Caelus doesn't notice Emeritus's presence. He circles the projection with his hand still connected to the central glyph, his fingers occasionally reaching out to trace lines between stars, lines that aren't visible in the hologram until after he touches them. The projection responds to his movements, revealing connections the Sigil Processor hasn't yet identified.

"There's a pattern here," Caelus says to Selenea, unaware of their audience. "See how these seven systems form a curved line? And these twelve create an offset grid? They're not random placements."

He draws his finger through the projection, connecting distant star clusters. As his hand passes through certain points, new lines of light appear, threads connecting systems that appeared unrelated moments before. The holographic display grows increasingly complex, responding to his touch like an instrument to a skilled musician.

Selenea checks her Processor, frowning. "That's strange. The device isn't detecting those connections you're tracing. According to its calculations, those systems shouldn't have any direct relationship."

"But they do," Caelus insists. "Can't you see how they pulse in the same rhythm? There's something linking them, something fundamental."

Emeritus steps forward then, the movement deliberate enough to draw their attention. The few remaining museum visitors respectfully withdraw from the chamber, sensing a private moment.

"Father!" Selenea straightens, her hand instinctively moving to smooth her braid, a childhood habit she's never outgrown. "We didn't expect you until closing."

Caelus turns, his hand still pressed to the central glyph. Excitement overrides his usual composure. "You need to see this," he says, gesturing to the star map with his free hand. "We've found something extraordinary. This wall doesn't just show star positions; it reveals connections between them. And look at Solarune's placement, and it sits at this critical junction point where multiple cosmic threads intersect."

He points to specific features in the projection, words tumbling out with uncharacteristic speed. "These energy patterns around the three moons suggest they amplify something, some kind of cosmic frequency. And these connection lines that I can trace, they're like..." He pauses, struggling to find the right words. "Like highways between stars, but not for travel. For something else."

Emeritus listens without interruption, his amber eyes, so similar to his children's, taking in every detail. When Caelus finally stops for breath, he moves forward and places a steady hand on his son's shoulder.

"What you're feeling is more than just curiosity," he says, his voice deep and measured. "It's Aetheris."

The word hangs in the air between them. Selenea inhales sharply.

"Aetheris?" Caelus repeats, brow furrowing. "Like the old myths?"

"Not myths." Emeritus's hand remains on Caelus's shoulder, firm and grounding. "Aetheris is rare but real. It's an ability that connects you to every stardust thread in the universe."

He turns to face the projection, gesturing toward the complex web of light. "What normal eyes see as separate, disconnected points, an Aetheris practitioner sees as parts of a single cosmic tapestry. The threads you traced, the ones your sister's device couldn't detect, they exist. You perceive them because you're attuned to them."

Caelus stares at Emeritus, then at his own hand still pressed against the wall. The holographic stars continue to rotate slowly, casting shifting patterns of light across his face. His pulse quickens visibly at his throat, and his eyes widen as understanding begins to dawn.

"That's why I could always find things, lost objects, hidden paths." His voice drops to barely above a whisper. "That's why I could track animals through the forest without footprints."

Emeritus nods. "Aetheris allows you to perceive location, precise, actual location, of anything formed from stardust. Which is everything and everyone." He pauses, letting the implication sink in. "You've been using it instinctively for years, but untrained, unfocused."

Caelus's hand finally drops from the wall. The projection flickers but remains active as if reluctant to break its connection with him. He stares at his palm, at the sigils tattooed across his skin that now seem to hold new meaning.

"Can I, " His voice catches. He swallows and tries again. "Can I locate anyone? Anywhere?"

"With training, yes," Emeritus confirms. "Distance becomes irrelevant. Planet boundaries are meaningless. The only limitation is whether the target exists and is composed of stardust."

Selenea watches her brother with a mixture of awe and protective concern. Her analytical mind races to process this revelation, to fit it into her understanding of her brother and the universe. She steps closer to him, her shoulder brushing against his in silent support.

"That's why you brought us to the museums so often," she says to Emeritus, pieces clicking into place. "You were testing him, watching for signs."

Emeritus inclines his head in acknowledgment. "I suspected when he was very young. The way he'd point to stars and name them without being taught. How he'd walk unerringly to hidden things." His expression softens with memory. "But Aetheris is rare and often misidentified. I needed to be certain before telling him."

Caelus looks back at the star map, seeing it with new eyes, not just as an archaeological curiosity but as a representation of connections he can actually perceive. "These threads between stars, they're real pathways? Things I can follow?"

"In a manner of speaking," Emeritus says. "More accurately, they're cosmic currents, flows of energy and matter that create natural connections throughout the universe. An Aetheris practitioner can sense these currents and use them to locate anything connected to them." He pauses, choosing his next words carefully. "Which, given enough training, means anything at all."

The implications hang in the air between them. Caelus stands motionless, absorbing this revelation that recontextualizes his entire life.

"Is that why the space monastery Zathira recruited me?" he asks finally. "They knew?"

Emeritus's expression reveals nothing. "That discussion is for another time. For now, understand that this ability makes you valuable. And that value can be a double-edged blade."

The museum's announcement system chimes softly, the tone different from before. "The museum will be closing in fifteen minutes. Please proceed to the exit at your convenience."

Around them, the chamber's ambient lighting dims slightly, signaling the approaching end of visiting hours. Through the high windows, Solarune's three moons are now visible in perfect alignment, their combined light streaming into the room and casting multiple overlapping shadows behind each person.

"We have much to discuss," Emeritus says, his gaze moving from Caelus to Selenea and back again. "But not here." He gestures toward the projected star map, still rotating slowly in the center of the chamber. "What you've discovered today, both about this ancient technology and about yourself, carries weight beyond these walls."

Caelus looks once more at the holographic universe suspended before them, at the countless stars connected by threads of light that only he can see. The knowledge settles into him like a stone dropping into still water, sending ripples through everything he thought he knew about himself.

The three moons shine through the skylights, their triple light merging and separating as clouds pass briefly overhead. On the floor below, their shadows dance and merge, three distinct shapes becoming one, then separating again in an ancient rhythm as old as Solarune itself.

Chapter 2

The First Hunt

The holostudy door slides open with a whisper of ancient mechanics and modern technology, the perfect metaphor for Solarune itself. Caelus steps inside, his mind still reeling from the museum revelation, each heartbeat sending tremors of awareness through his body like aftershocks from a cosmic quake. The familiar room, with its blend of stone architecture and floating holograms, suddenly feels different, as if his awakened Aetheris perception has altered everything, including home.

He moves past the threshold, fingers tracing the doorframe's weathered sigils. The carvings are cool against his skin, but something stirs beneath, a faint vibration he's always felt but never recognized for what it was. Connection. Resonance. Aetheris.

"Everything looks different now," he says, more to himself than to his father and sister who follow behind.

The holostudy occupies the heart of their home, a circular chamber where walls of solid stone support a domed ceiling of transparent crystal. Through it, the three moons of Solarune still hang in their perfect alignment, their combined light filtering down to illuminate ancient texts and artifacts arrayed on shelves and pedestals. But between these physical elements, hover the tools of modern scholarship, floating holographic displays, scanner arrays, and information nodes that pulse with gentle light.

Selenea crosses to the main console, her movements efficient and precise. "I'm downloading the museum data from my Processor," she says, sliding the device into a receptor slot. "Though I doubt your abilities will be cataloged in any database."

Emeritus closes the door behind them, engaging a security protocol with a gesture that activates a hidden sigil. The room responds, ambient lighting shifting to a warmer hue as bioluminescent crystals embedded in the walls come to life. They glow with soft blue-green luminescence, pulsing in a rhythm that mimics the human heartbeat.

"Your sister is right," he says, moving to stand beside a central holotable. "Aetheris doesn't translate well to data points and algorithms. It exists beyond conventional measurement."

Caelus nods absently, his attention caught by a floating projection near the far wall. Unlike the scholarly displays that dominate the room, this hologram flickers with an official security watermark, the emblem of galactic law enforcement rotating slowly at its corner. The projected image shows a male human figure with sharp features and eyes that seem to hold calculated malice, even in holographic form. Text scrolls beside the rotating image: name, crimes, last known locations, and at the bottom, a bounty figure substantial enough to make Caelus blink twice.

"Who's that?" he asks, moving closer to the projection.

Emeritus glances up from the holotable. "Marius Vex. Emerged on the criminal databases three standard months ago. Suspected in the theft of several ancient artifacts from protected sites across four systems."

The hologram rotates, showing the subject from different angles. Beneath the official data, a warning flashes in pulsing red: ARMED AND DANGEROUS, APPROACH WITH EXTREME CAUTION.

"He disappeared after hitting a research outpost in the Cygnus Sector," Emeritus continues, his tone carefully neutral. "Seventeen dead. No witnesses."

Caelus stares at the projection, his fingers reaching for the small hologram controller in his pocket, a childhood habit that surfaces whenever he's processing complex information. He retrieves the device, a worn cylinder not much larger than his thumb, and begins to manipulate it unconsciously, spinning it between his fingers with practiced dexterity.

His other hand reaches toward the criminal's hologram, not quite touching it but tracing the air around it. Something about the image tugs at him, a vague sense of wrongness that he can't articulate.

"You're wondering if you could find him," Emeritus says, not a question but a statement of fact. He moves to stand beside Caelus, his shadow merging with his son's in the crystal-filtered moonlight. "You could."

The hologram controller slips in Caelus's fingers, nearly dropping before he tightens his grip. He looks up at Emeritus, amber eyes wide with surprise. "You want me to, "

"I want you to try," Emeritus says, placing a firm hand on Caelus's shoulder. "Not to pursue. Not to confront. Just to locate."

The controller spins faster between Caelus's fingers, a blur of metal and crystal. His other hand moves to the console, tapping an erratic rhythm against its smooth surface.

The idea is both terrifying and exhilarating, using this ability he's only just discovered to find someone real, someone dangerous. Someone hiding.

"I wouldn't even know where to begin," he admits, looking down at his hands. The sigils tattooed across his skin seem to pulse with the bioluminescent crystals, creating patterns of light and shadow that dance with each heartbeat. "At the museum, it just... happened. I wasn't trying."

Emeritus's hand remains steady on his shoulder, neither pushing nor pulling but simply present. "Focus on the cosmic weave, son. Remember what we discussed at the museum. Every living thing, every object, is composed of stardust. And all stardust is connected by threads you can perceive."

The ambient technology hums around them, a constant background chorus of fans, processors, and energy fields that blend into white noise unless consciously noticed. Now, as Caelus stands before the hologram of a killer, that hum seems to rise in pitch, becoming more insistent.

Selenea moves from the main console to stand at the edge of the conversation, her presence a different kind of support than their father's. Where he guides, she observes. Where he instructs, she analyzes. She says nothing, but her eyes track every micro-expression that crosses her brother's face, cataloging reactions with the same precision her Processor uses for ancient texts.

"What if I can't do it?" Caelus asks, the controller spinning so rapidly now that it creates a soft whistling sound. "What if the museum was just... a fluke?"

"Then we'll try again tomorrow," Emeritus answers simply. "And the day after. You've lived with this ability your entire life, Caelus. Using it consciously rather than instinctively is just a matter of practice."

Caelus looks again at Marius Vex's hologram. The face rotates slowly, eyes seeming to meet his with each revolution. Seventeen dead. No witnesses. The text scrolls endlessly, a loop of crimes and warnings. The bounty figure blinks at regular intervals, a sum that could fund a small colony.

"How would I even start?" he asks, his voice quieter now, uncertainty giving way to curiosity.

Emeritus's grip on his shoulder tightens slightly, a gesture of encouragement. "Close your eyes. Picture the cosmic threads you saw in the museum projection. Feel how they connect everything: stars, planets, people. Then focus on the image of this man and ask the threads to show you where he exists among them."

The hologram controller is still in Caelus's hand. He takes a deep breath, feeling the air fill his lungs, air composed of the same cosmic elements as the stars themselves. He looks once more at the rotating face of Marius Vex, committing the features to memory, then glances at Selenea.

She gives him a small nod, her analytical presence steady and reassuring. In her eyes, he sees not just support but expectation, not pressure but potential. She believes he can do this.

The bioluminescent crystals pulse in their slow, steady rhythm. The three moons shine through the crystal dome above. The hum of technology provides a constant, grounding drone.

Caelus closes his eyes and prepares to reach out into the cosmos.

Caelus lowers himself to the holostudy floor, crossing his legs and placing his hands palm-up on his knees. The stone feels cool against him, ancient and grounding. He closes his amber eyes and shuts out the ambient hum of technology, the soft glow of bioluminescent crystals, his sister's watchful gaze, and everything except the rhythm of his own breath moving in and out like the cosmic tide.

The wanted criminal's face floats in his mind: sharp features, calculating eyes, a mouth set in perpetual defiance. Marius Vex. Seventeen dead. No witnesses. The holographic image had seemed to stare back at him as if challenging Caelus to find what so many others could not.

His sigil tattoos begin to respond, a subtle warmth spreading beneath his skin. The intricate patterns that spiral across his forearms and curve around his wrists seem to pulse with his heartbeat. It is not visual, not something anyone else could see, but he feels each line growing more defined and more present as if the ink itself is awakening.

"I can't, " he starts, frustration already building. "I don't know what I'm looking for."

"Don't force it," Emeritus says from somewhere above him. "Just be still."

Caelus tries again, focusing on his breath. In. Out. The face of Marius Vex reforms in his imagination, but nothing else happens. No cosmic threads. No galactic revelations. Just his own heartbeat and the growing tension in his shoulders.

His breathing quickens, shallow and irregular. Beads of sweat form at his temples despite the room's perfect temperature regulation. The small scar above his right eyebrow, a reminder of a childhood training accident, twitches as the muscles in his face contract with effort.

"I was wrong," he says, eyes still closed but voice tight with disappointment. "The museum was different. There was already a connection there, something to build on."

Fabric rustles as Emeritus kneels beside him. Caelus feels a hand on his shoulder, not his father's usual firm grip, but a lighter touch, barely there.

"You're trying too hard," Emeritus says, voice low and steady. "Aetheris isn't something you do. It's something you allow."

Caelus's fingers curl against his knees, bunching the fabric of his pants. "That doesn't make sense."

"Imagine the universe as an ocean," Emeritus continues, ignoring the frustration in his son's voice. "You're not trying to create waves. You're learning to feel waves that already exist, to recognize their patterns." The hand on his shoulder lifts away. "Don't force it. Let the stardust sense flow through you naturally."

Caelus exhales sharply through his nose. He uncurls his fingers, consciously relaxing each muscle group as he was taught in early meditation training. Shoulders. Arms. Hands. Face. The scar stops twitching. His breathing slows.

He thinks again of Marius Vex but in a different way now, not focusing on capturing or containing the image but simply allowing it to exist in his mind. A face. A collection of stardust arranged in human form. Connected to everything else that exists.

Something shifts beneath his skin, not just the warmth of the sigils now, but a vibration that travels up his arms, across his shoulders, into his spine. It spreads, resonating through bone and tissue until his entire body hums with it.

Behind his closed eyelids, darkness gives way to pinpricks of light, stars, galaxies, cosmic dust clouds. Not images he's creating but something his mind is finally perceiving. The lights multiply and connect, forming threads of luminous energy that stretch across unfathomable distances.

The vibration intensifies. His back straightens involuntarily as energy courses through him. He sees the cosmic threads more clearly now, billions upon billions of connections forming a web so complex it should be incomprehensible. Yet somehow, he understands and intuitively feels how each thread vibrates with unique resonance.

"I see them," he whispers, voice tight with wonder. "The threads. They're, " He lacks words to describe the vision unfolding behind his eyelids. "They're everywhere."

"Good," Emeritus says from what seems like a great distance. "Now think of Marius Vex again. Not as a target, but as a node in the web."

Caelus holds the criminal's face in his mind, and the cosmic web responds. Threads shift, some fading while others brighten, as if the entire network is reconfiguring itself around his focus. A single path begins to glow more intensely than the others, a route through stars and void, planets and moons, leading to one specific collection of stardust arranged in human form.

The vibration under his skin peaks suddenly, like a plucked string reaching maximum amplitude. The cosmic threads contract in his vision, the universe shrinking around that single glowing path until it resolves into a precise location.

His eyes snap open, now glowing with amber intensity that illuminates Emeritus's startled face.

"I can see him," Caelus whispers, his voice strained as if each word must travel across the same vast distances as his perception. "He's in the Cygnus Sector, Helios-9, grid coordinates 37-42-19."

The coordinates spill from his lips without conscious thought, as natural as breathing, as certain as gravity. He sees not just the numbers but the place itself: a small outpost station clinging to the outer rings of a gas giant, forgotten by most, perfect for someone who doesn't want to be found.

Emeritus stands abruptly, moving toward the main console. "You're sure?"

"Completely." Caelus remains seated, afraid to break whatever connection allows him to see so clearly. "He's in a maintenance bay on the station's lower level. There's, " He concentrates, the amber glow in his eyes intensifying. "There's a ship docked there. Not registered. Modified thrusters. He's preparing to leave, but not immediately."

Selenea approaches, her analytical expression giving way to undisguised awe. "That's over forty light-years from here," she says. "You shouldn't be able to, " She stops, recalibrating her understanding in real-time. "The Processor isn't detecting any known technology that could provide that information."

"It's not technology," Emeritus says, fingers moving across the console, calling up star charts and station schematics. "It's Aetheris. And he's right." He enlarges a section of the map. "Helios-9 station coordinates 37-42-19. It matches his description perfectly."

Caelus finally rises to his feet, the glow in his eyes fading to their normal amber hue. His legs feel unsteady as if he's been running for hours rather than sitting motionless on the floor. The vibration under his skin subsides to a gentle hum, then dissipates entirely, leaving only a residual warmth in its wake.

He stares at his hands, seeing the familiar sigil tattoos but understanding them differently now. Not just decorative patterns passed down through generations but conduits, focusing elements for an ability he's only beginning to comprehend.

"I found him," he says, the simple statement inadequate to express the magnitude of what just happened. "I reached across forty light-years and found one person among billions."

Emeritus turns from the console, face illuminated by the star charts and station schematics. For the first time since the museum, he smiles, a rare expression that transforms his serious features. "You did more than find him, Caelus. You've found yourself."

Caelus looks up from his hands, meeting Emeritus's gaze. The enormity of the moment settles around him like a cloak, heavy with responsibility but also shimmering with potential. He has taken his first conscious step into a vastly larger universe than the one he knew yesterday.

And somewhere forty light-years distant, a criminal who thinks himself hidden continues his work, unaware that he has been seen.

Emeritus moves to the communications console with a newfound urgency, fingers dancing across the surface with practiced precision. The discovery of Caelus's ability and the criminal's location demands immediate action. The console awakens beneath his touch, sigils illuminating in sequence as ancient technology interfaces with modern purpose. Through the crystal dome above, the three moons of Solarune cast their combined light onto the scene as if the cosmos itself bears witness to this pivotal moment.

"Zathira must be notified immediately," Emeritus says, voice tight with restrained excitement. "Marius Vex has eluded their trackers for months."

The communication array rises from the center of the console, a cluster of crystalline rods that arrange themselves in a specific geometric pattern. Each rod pulses with internal light, colors shifting through spectrum ranges as the system initializes. The air above the array shimmers, distorting like heat waves rising from sun-baked stone.

"Establishing Fractal pulse," Emeritus announces, his hands moving through a complex series of gestures. The sigils on his arms glow in response, matching the rhythm of the console's lights. "Selenea, monitor the stabilization metrics."

She steps forward, analytical focus returning as she scans the readouts flickering across a secondary display. "Fractal interference at thirteen percent and rising," she reports. "Solar flare activity might destabilize the connection."

Caelus watches, still processing the magnitude of what he's accomplished. His fingers tingle with residual energy, the pathways of cosmic awareness not fully closed. He can still sense Marius Vex, a distant point of consciousness in the vast web, though the connection grows fainter with each passing second.

Emeritus manipulates control fields that hover above the console, adjusting invisible parameters. "Compensating for solar activity," he says. "Redirecting the pulse through the tertiary Fractal node."

The explanation means little to Caelus, who has never fully understood the technology that allows communication across interstellar distances. He knows only that Fractal pulses somehow utilize the same cosmic threads he now perceives through Aetheris, natural pathways that exist in the fabric of space-time itself.

The crystalline rods accelerate their color shifts, then suddenly stabilize on deep indigo. A harmonic tone fills the room, rising in pitch until it hovers at the edge of hearing.

"Fractal stabilized," Selenea confirms. "Connection to Zathira established."

The air above the console tears open, not violently, but with elegant precision as if reality itself is being carefully folded aside. Through this aperture, light coalesces into the form of a robed figure. The holographic projection flickers momentarily, then solidifies, revealing a person whose features remain partially obscured by a deep hood. What is visible on their face appears weathered by time and wisdom, and their skin is mapped with fine lines that resemble the cosmic threads Caelus recently perceived.

"Honored Archivist," Emeritus addresses the figure, inclining his head slightly. "Forgive the unscheduled communication. We have urgent information regarding the fugitive Marius Vex."

The hooded figure returns the gesture, hands emerging from voluminous sleeves to form a complex symbol in the air. "Solarunian Adept," they respond, their voices resonating with both age and authority. "The monastery receives your call with interest. What information do you bring?"

Emeritus turns to Caelus, an unspoken invitation to step forward. For a moment, Caelus hesitates; this is his first direct communication with Zathira, the space monastery whose reputation spans galaxies. But the residual energy of Aetheris still flows through him, lending unexpected confidence.

He steps into the projection field, feeling the subtle resistance as he enters the space where worlds connect. "Honored Archivist," he begins, voice steadier than expected. "I have located Marius Vex at the Helios-9 station, grid coordinates 37-42-19. He occupies a maintenance bay on the lower level with an unregistered vessel. The ship appears prepared for departure, though not immediately."

The hooded figure remains motionless for several seconds, the only movement the slight ripple of their robe in some unfelt breeze. Then their heads tilted, attention shifting from Caelus to his father and back again.

"This information is precise," they observe. "Your sources are reliable?"

"The most reliable," Emeritus answers, placing a hand on Caelus's shoulder. "My son has manifested Aetheris. What he shares comes from direct perception, not secondhand intelligence."

The change in the Archivist's posture is subtle but unmistakable, with a straightening of the spine and a slight forward lean that conveys sudden, intense interest. "Aetheris? Verified?"

"Witnessed and confirmed today," Emeritus affirms. "The ability manifested fully at the Cosmographer's Wall in our museum."

The Archivist's hands emerge again, forming a different symbol, one that Caelus recognizes from ancient texts as signifying respect and acknowledgment. "This news holds significance beyond the criminal's location," they say. "The monastery thanks you for this service. We will dispatch immediately."

Their gaze fixes on Caelus, eyes briefly visible within the shadow of their hood, eyes that seem to contain pinpoints of light, like stars suspended in darkness. "Young Solarunian, your gift is rare and precious. The threads you now perceive have guided seekers for millennia."

Caelus nods, unsure how to respond to such recognition. "I'm still learning," he manages finally.

"As are we all," the Archivist replies, a hint of warmth entering their formal tone. "When Vex is secured, we would welcome your presence at Zathira."

The invitation hangs in the air, its significance not lost on any of them. Zathira seldom extends such offers, particularly to those without formal cosmic training.

"We are honored," Emeritus answers when Caelus remains silent. "Further communication will follow once matters are resolved."

The Archivist forms a final symbol, closure and continuity before the image begins to fade. "Until the stars align again," they intone, voice diminishing with their form.

The projection collapses, reality folding back into place as the connection terminates. The crystalline rods slow their pulsing, then retract back into the console with mechanical precision. For a moment, silence fills the holostudy, broken only by the ambient hum of technology.

Then Selenea laughs, a sound of pure, uncomplicated joy that seems to shatter the formal atmosphere. "They invited you to Zathira!" she exclaims, grabbing Caelus by the shoulders. "Do you have any idea how rare that is?"

Emeritus's serious expression finally breaks into a smile. "It's been seventeen years since they last extended such an invitation to anyone from Solarune," he says, moving to a side cabinet where a set of ceramic cups sits beside a heating element.

Selenea releases Caelus and moves to assist in retrieving a canister of spiced tea leaves from a nearby shelf. "This calls for a proper celebration," she says, measuring the aromatic blend into a steeping chamber. The scent fills the air with warm, complex notes of cinnamon-like bark and herbs unique to Solarune's northern mountains.

Caelus stands motionless, still processing everything that has happened. The day that began with a routine visit to the museum has transformed his understanding of himself, his abilities, and his future. He stares at his hands, no longer seeing just flesh and familiar sigil tattoos but conduits to something vast and ancient.

The heating element chimes softly, indicating the optimal temperature has been reached. Selenea pours the water over the leaves, releasing more fragrance into the air. Emeritus retrieves three cups from the cabinet, not the everyday ceramics they normally use, but special vessels reserved for significant occasions, their surfaces etched with the same sigils that adorn their skin.

"Here," Selenea says, handing Caelus the first filled cup. The liquid inside glows with amber warmth, mirroring the color of his eyes. "To find your path."

Emeritus accepts the second cup and then raises it in a formal gesture. "This is just the beginning," he tells Caelus, voice resonant with pride and something deeper, a recognition of destiny fulfilled. "What you've discovered today isn't just an ability, but a purpose."

Through the crystal dome above, the three moons of Solarune align perfectly, their combined light streaming down to illuminate the family gathered below. The triple moonlight catches in the tea, refracting through the amber liquid to cast complex patterns across their faces and hands.

Caelus raises his cup to meet the others, feeling the residual tingle of Aetheris in his fingertips as they connect with the warm ceramic. The sensation no longer alarms him. Instead, it feels like a greeting from something vast and ancient that has always been part of him, waiting to be acknowledged.

"To new beginnings," he says quietly, the words inadequate for the magnitude of the moment.

As they drink, he knows with absolute certainty that his life will never be the same. The taste of the spiced tea, familiar from countless family gatherings, now carries new significance, the flavor of a threshold crossed, a boundary between who he was and who he will become.

His hands cradle the cup, still tingling from the Aetheris activation, warm from the tea, steadier than they have any right to be given what they now can do. Through the cosmic threads that connect all things, he has found a criminal hiding forty light-years away. What else might he find once he learns to fully embrace this gift?

The question hangs unspoken in the air between them, illuminated by the light of three perfectly aligned moons.

Chapter 3

The Zathira Contract

The spiced tea gives off a fragrance that wraps around them like a familiar embrace, notes of cinnamon and star-flower mingling with the residual energy of Caelus's awakened ability. The steam rises in ghostly tendrils between them, three faces illuminated by the triple moonlight streaming through the crystal dome, a family transformed in a single day by cosmic revelation.

Caelus raises the cup to his lips, the warmth spreading through his fingers and up his arms. The sigils tattooed on his skin still tingle with aftershocks of power, humming at a frequency just below conscious perception.

"To new beginnings," Emeritus says, raising his own cup in a simple toast. His eyes, amber-like his children's, carry a depth of knowledge that suggests he's been preparing for this moment for years.

They drink together, and the silence between them is comfortable and weighted with shared understanding. Outside, the three moons of Solarune hang in their perfect alignment, casting multiple shadows across the garden stones, each person projecting three distinct silhouettes that merge and separate with the subtle movement of clouds across the lunar faces.

Emeritus moves toward the window, the cup still in hand. "When I was your age," he begins, then stops abruptly. His head tilts, attention caught by something beyond the crystal panes. "Do you feel that?"

Before either sibling can respond, subtle vibration pulses through the holostudy. It's not an earthquake, something more precise, more intentional. The bioluminescent crystals embedded in the walls flare brighter than dim in unison, responding to an unseen stimulus. Caelus's newly awakened senses tingle with recognition, a disturbance in the cosmic threads he'd so recently perceived.

"Someone's opening a Fractal," he says, the words emerging with certainty despite his unfamiliarity with the concept. "Right outside our home."

Emeritus turns from the window, face tightening into a mask of controlled anticipation. "Not someone. The Valthorim."

The vibration intensifies. Floating holographic displays flicker, their projections distorting like reflections in troubled water. The spiced tea in their cups ripples in perfect concentric circles, disturbed by forces that bypass physical barriers.

Through the window, reality tears open in the garden. Not a violent rending but a precise incision, space folding back on itself to reveal a swirling void shot through with distant stars and nebulae. The garden plants bend away from the opening, not from the wind but from the gravity of altered space-time.

A figure emerges, tall and imposing. Dark robes shift around his frame like a living shadow, moving with fluid grace that suggests they're composed of something not quite solid. The fabric seems to absorb light rather than reflect it, creating a silhouette of perfect darkness outlined against the moonlit garden.

Selenea rises first, military training taking over as she places herself slightly ahead of her brother. Her hand moves subtly toward her hip where a standard-issue battalion defensive tool would normally rest, and then she stills as she remembers its absence.

Emeritus opens the holostudy door with deliberate calm. "Enter and be welcome," he calls out, the traditional Solarunian greeting carrying more weight than usual.

The figure glides forward, not walking so much as flowing across the garden stones. As he reaches the threshold, moonlight catches the edges of an ornate mask that covers the upper portion of his face. Behind the mask, silver eyes scan the room with unnerving thoroughness, seeming to catalog every detail in a single sweep.

"Orpheus," Emeritus says with respectful recognition. "This is unexpected."

The visitor inclines his head slightly, the movement causing his hood to shift, revealing more of the mask beneath. Intricate patterns swirl across its surface, reminiscent of ancient sigils but somehow more fluid, as if they might rearrange themselves when unobserved.

"Solaris family," Orpheus responds, his voice resonant yet distant, carrying harmonics that human vocal cords shouldn't produce. "The alignment of circumstances required my direct attention."

He steps fully into the holostudy, the room seeming to shrink around his presence. The Fractal outside closes with a soft implosion of air, reality restitching itself seamlessly.

Caelus rises to his feet, hands trembling slightly despite his attempt to appear composed. The holographic controller he'd been fidgeting with earlier slips from his fingers, clattering against the stone floor. He retrieves it quickly, cheeks flushing with embarrassment.

Orpheus's silver eyes shift to him, pupils expanding slightly. "The awakened one," he says, not a question but a confirmation. "Your tracking of the criminal Marius Vex has reverberated through the cosmic threads. A most... interesting development."

"You know about that already?" Selenea asks, her analytical mind visibly processing this revelation. "We just contacted Zathira less than an hour ago."

"Time moves differently along Fractal paths," Orpheus replies, moving further into the room. His robes continue their strange undulation, edges blurring as if they exist partially in another dimension. "What are minutes for you? Maybe days elsewhere. Marius Vex has already been apprehended."

Emeritus gestures toward the seating area, where cushions surround a low stone table inlaid with constellations mapped in precious metals. "Please, join us."

Orpheus glides to the indicated space but doesn't sit, standing instead like a dark pillar among them. "I serve as First Guardian at Zathira, the space monastery," he explains, his mask catching the light from the bioluminescent crystals. "But I am also Valthorim."

The word resonates through the room like a struck bell, vibrating against the stone walls and penetrating deeper than mere sound.

"The Universal Monitors," Emeritus translates for his children, his tone reverent. "Ancient beings who maintain cosmic balance."

"We observe," Orpheus corrects gently. "We guide when necessary. We intervene only when the fabric of existence requires it." His silver eyes fix on Caelus again. "Your Aetheris ability has created ripples we have not seen in generations."

Caelus's throat constricts, words tangling before they reach his lips. "I just found one criminal," he finally manages.

"You navigated the cosmic threads consciously, without training," Orpheus says. "Do you understand how rare that is? Most with your gift require years to achieve what you accomplished in moments."

The silver eyes blink once, slowly, like stars momentarily obscured by passing clouds. "The Valthorim use Fractals, controlled tears in space-time, to travel instantaneously across the universe. These pathways exist naturally, but accessing them requires precise knowledge and considerable power."

He extends a hand, fingers splayed. The air between his digits shimmers and then splits open to reveal a miniature version of the void Caelus had seen in the garden. Stars wheel through it, and galaxies spiral in accelerated time.

"We monitor civilizations across countless worlds," Orpheus continues, closing his hand to dissolve the demonstration. "We observe their growth, their challenges, their potential threats to universal harmony. Zathira serves as our nexus point in this region of space, a place where physical reality meets the void between dimensions."

"And now you're here," Selenea says, the implication clear in her tone. "Because of my brother."

Orpheus inclines his head again, the mask catching light in hypnotic patterns. "Your gift, Caelus Solaris, is more than an ability. It is a cosmic responsibility." His voice drops lower, becoming almost gentle. "With proper training, you could help maintain balance throughout the universe. You could track those who seek to disrupt harmony, those who threaten countless innocent lives."

He turns slightly, robes swirling around him like smoke. "I offer you a position at Zathira under my direct guidance. You would learn to refine your Aetheris ability beyond what you can imagine now. You would help locate intergalactic criminals that even our most sophisticated methods cannot trace."

Caelus's eyes widen, pupils dilating as the full implication sinks in. His heartbeat accelerates, sending quick pulses of blood through his body that make the sigils on his skin warm with response.

"Your gift is rare," Orpheus says, each word measured and precise. "With proper training, you could help maintain cosmic balance. You could become essential to the continued stability of the universe itself."

The room falls silent except for the soft hum of technology and the subtle pulse of bioluminescent light. Through the crystal dome above, the three moons continue their silent watch, aligned in perfect harmony, just as Caelus's life has suddenly aligned with cosmic purpose.

Caelus paces the stone floor of the holostudy, each footfall striking a rhythm that matches his racing thoughts. The holographic displays cast shifting blue light across his features, highlighting doubt one moment and determination the next. His fingers trace unconscious patterns in the air, already reaching for cosmic threads that only he can see.

"This is..." he begins, but words fail him. The scope of Orpheus's offer expands in his mind like a supernova, possibilities branching outward in all directions.

Emeritus moves beside him, placing a steady hand on his shoulder. The weight feels different now, and it is not guiding but acknowledging. "This is what you've been preparing for," he says quietly. "Even before we knew the name of your gift."

The touch grounds Caelus, slowing his restless movement. He turns to face Orpheus, whose silver eyes remain fixed on him with unnerving patience. The mask covering the upper portion of the Valthorim's face catches the bioluminescent light, sending fractured reflections across the ceiling.

Selenea steps forward, her arms crossed over her chest. Her military training shows in the way she positions herself: balanced, ready, and analytical. "How often would he return home?" she asks Orpheus directly, cutting through cosmic implications to practical concerns.

"A valid question," Orpheus responds, his voice carrying that strange harmonic quality that seems to resonate with the stone walls themselves. "Service at Zathira follows no standard calendar. Time flows differently along Fractal paths."

He turns slightly, addressing both siblings now. "You would track criminals across vast distances, Caelus Solaris, traveling via Fractals when necessary. Training would be intensive initially, perhaps what would feel like several months to you." A pause, precise and measured. "After that, returns to Solarune would be possible between assignments. Irregular, but not infrequent."

Caelus nods, absorbing this information. The sigils on his skin respond to his heightened emotions, warming slightly along his forearms.

"The work itself?" he asks, his voice steadier than he expected.

"You would serve directly under my guidance at Zathira," Orpheus explains. "Learning to refine your Aetheris ability while applying it to locate those who threaten universal harmony." His robes shift around him like smoke caught in conflicting currents. "Some assignments would require only location work. Others might involve accompanying retrieval teams through Fractal pathways."

He reaches into the folds of his robe, producing a small crystalline device that fits in his palm. With a subtle motion of his fingers, the crystal activates, projecting a holographic image that hovers in the air between them.

A figure rotates slowly in the projection, humanoid but not human, with scaled skin and eyes that curve upward at sharp angles. Text scrolls beside the image: name, crimes, last known activities. The list of offenses grows longer as it cycles through mass destruction, biological warfare, and extinction-level threats.

"Nex'Vari," Orpheus says, the name falling from his lips like a stone into still water. "This would be your first official assignment. He vanished three standard months ago after releasing an engineered pathogen that decimated an entire moon colony. Our conventional methods have failed to locate him."

Caelus stares at the rotating hologram, and his attention is captured completely. Without conscious thought, his fingers begin to move, tracing invisible lines in the air around the projection. His Aetheris ability stirs in response; it is not fully activated but is resonating with potential.

The room's ambient temperature seems to drop several degrees. The bioluminescent crystals pulse brighter, then dim in rhythm with Caelus's unconscious movements. Even without training, his gift reaches toward the challenge presented, like a plant turning instinctively toward light.

"I could find him," Caelus whispers, not a question but a realization. His eyes lift from the hologram to meet Orpheus's silver gaze. "I could stop this from happening again."

Selenea touches her brother's arm, her expression mixing pride with protective concern. The military precision of her posture softens momentarily. "You don't have to decide now," she says. "This is no small commitment."

But Caelus sees in the hologram everything he's ever wanted: purpose aligned with ability, challenge matched with meaning. His entire life suddenly makes sense in a way it never has before, each experience and interest forming a path that led inevitably to this moment.

"How many more would die while I consider?" he asks, not unkindly but with newfound certainty. He straightens his posture, shoulders squaring as if physically accepting the weight of responsibility. "I accept," he tells Orpheus, his voice clear and unwavering.

The Fractal insignia embroidered on Orpheus's robe, previously unnoticed by Caelus, begins to glimmer with internal light. The intricate pattern resembles the cosmic threads Caelus perceived during his first conscious use of Aetheris, but more ordered, more refined.

"The decision honors you," Orpheus says, extending a hand to seal the agreement. "And honors Zathira."

Caelus steps forward, briefly meeting Emeritus's eyes, finding there not just approval but something deeper: recognition of a transition long anticipated. He reaches out, clasping Orpheus's offered hand.

The contact sends a jolt through his system, not painful but overwhelming, like plunging into freezing water. The sigils on his skin flare with sudden heat, responding to something in Orpheus that resonates at their frequency. For an instant, Caelus perceives not just the room around him but dozens of Fractal pathways pulsing with potential energy, connecting this moment to countless possible futures.

As they shake hands, the subtle hum of dormant Fractals intensifies around them. The air in the holostudy grows heavy with possibility, pressure building like the moments before a storm breaks. Caelus feels the weight of his decision to settle into reality, not just intellectual understanding but physical sensation, as if the universe itself acknowledges his choice.

"Preparations begin immediately," Orpheus says, releasing Caelus's hand. "You will need few personal possessions. Zathira provides all necessities."

The crystalline device with Nex'Vari's hologram floats from Orpheus's palm to hover before Caelus. "Study this," he instructs. "Begin familiarizing yourself with his energy signature. Training will build on this foundation."

Caelus accepts the device, cradling it carefully between his palms. The projection continues its rotation, and the criminal's features have burned into his memory already. The weight of responsibility should feel heavier, he thinks, but instead, there's a curious lightness to his movements now, the relief of finding one's true path.

Selenea approaches, military discipline briefly overwhelmed by sisterly concern. She embraces him quickly, fiercely. "Don't forget who you are," she whispers, then steps back, composure reinstated.

Emeritus offers no such physical comfort, but his eyes communicate volumes, pride, concern, and complete confidence intermingled. "When do you leave?" he asks Orpheus.

"The Fractal opens at dawn," the Valthorim responds. "When the three moons begin their separation."

Outside the crystal dome, the perfect lunar alignment has already begun to shift by imperceptible degrees. The multiple shadows on the floor lengthen and change the angle, marking the passage of time with celestial precision.

The spiced tea sits forgotten on the table, gone cold. The holographic displays continue their silent operation, databases and star charts cycling through information that suddenly seems both more relevant and more limited than before. The universe Caelus thought he understood has expanded beyond recognition in a single day.

His hands tingle with residual energy from Orpheus's touch, but he feels a warmth in his chest, an uncomfortable heat that he recognizes as anticipation mixed with the first threads of purpose taking root.

Chapter 4

Ascension to Valthorim

The grand atrium of Zathira stretches toward infinity, its crystalline columns rising like frozen thoughts caught between worlds. Caelus pauses at the threshold, amber eyes taking in the gathering of Valthorim entities whose forms blur at the edges as if reality itself cannot fully contain them. The transparent dome above reveals a universe stripped bare of planetary interference, stars burning with unfiltered clarity, and cosmic rays painting subtle auroras across the curved surface.

Four years of service have transformed him. The sigils adorning his tan skin have multiplied, spiraling up his forearms and across his shoulders in patterns that match the celestial mathematics etched into Zathira's ancient walls. His lean frame moves with the deliberate precision of someone who has learned to navigate not just physical space but the cosmic threads connecting all existence.

He steps forward. The sound of his boots against the polished stone floor sends ripples through the chamber's perfect acoustics. Every eye turns toward him, silver irises within hooded shadows, observing with the patience of beings who measure time in galactic cycles rather than human heartbeats.

Caelus breathes in the distinct atmosphere of Zathira, that impossible blend of ancient stone dust and the metallic tang of space itself, filtered through systems designed by minds that perceived dimensions beyond the standard four. His lungs expanded, drawing in the rarified air with practiced ease, which once made him light-headed and disoriented.

The Valthorim stand arranged in concentric circles throughout the atrium, and their dark robes are seemingly composed of material that exists halfway between matter and energy. They make no sound and communicate without words, a collective consciousness that pulses through the chamber like a single heartbeat spread across multiple bodies.

At the center stands Orpheus, taller than the others, his ornate mask catching starlight from the dome above. The intricate patterns swirling across its surface shift subtly, cosmic configurations rearranging themselves in response to unseen stimuli. His silver eyes find Caelus among the columns, acknowledging his presence with a slight nod that carries more weight than any elaborate gesture.

Four years. Four years since Caelus left Solarune at dawn, stepping through his first Fractal as the three moons separated from their perfect alignment. Four years of training, tracking, and discovery. Eighty-seven criminals are located across forty-three star systems. Seventeen major catastrophes were averted through his precise location abilities. His name now carries weight in interstellar diplomatic circles and strikes fear in the hearts of those who operate beyond the boundaries of cosmic law.

The assembled Valthorim turn in perfect unison, and their movements are so synchronized they appear choreographed. They part like a dark sea, creating a single path that leads directly to Orpheus at the atrium's center. The starlight from above casts multiple shadows behind each figure, not three, like the moons of Solarune, but countless overlapping silhouettes that suggest existence across multiple planes simultaneously.

Caelus begins his walk down this path. His head remains level, gaze fixed forward. The small scar above his right eyebrow, a reminder of childhood training accidents on Solarune, has been joined by a newer mark that traces his jawline, a souvenir from a particularly difficult extraction on the ice planet Drabliti. He no longer fidgets with his old hologram controller; his hands remain steady at his sides, each finger adorned with thin bands of metal that amplify his Aetheris abilities.

The harmonic hum begins as he reaches the midpoint of his journey, a sound not quite music, not quite language, but something between. It vibrates from the Valthorim in perfect resonance, building from subsonic depths to frequencies that make the crystalline columns sing in response. The sound passes through Caelus, rattling his bones and vibrating against his eardrums, yet somehow remaining pleasant, even welcoming.

"The Aetheris-wielder has proven his worth," Orpheus announces, his voice cutting through the harmonic with perfect clarity. The mask catches different angles of starlight as he speaks, creating the impression that the cosmos itself emphasizes his words. "Today, he joins us in the deeper mysteries."

The humming intensifies. The crystalline columns pulse with an internal light that synchronizes with the sound. The transparency of the dome above seems to increase, stars burning brighter, more immediately as if the barrier between Zathira and the void thins momentarily.

Caelus's sigils respond, warming against his skin. Not the fiery heat of active tracking but a gentle recognition, as if they acknowledge their proximity to something fundamental to their purpose. His pulse quickens, but his step remains steady. After four years, he has learned to contain his reactions to channel excitement and apprehension into focused attention.

As he nears the center, memories flash across his consciousness: his first successful Fractal navigation, the moment he located the criminal Nex'Vari across three galactic sectors, the pride in Selenea's eyes during his rare visits home, the growing respect from senior Valthorim who once regarded him with silent skepticism.

He reaches Orpheus and stops, standing at precisely the right distance, close enough to show confidence and far enough to demonstrate respect. The harmonic hum of the Valthorim reaches a crescendo and then stabilizes at a frequency that makes the air between them shimmer slightly.

Pride warms his chest, an expanding heat that reaches toward his throat. Yet beneath it lies curiosity, sharp, almost painful in its intensity. The "deeper mysteries" Orpheus mentions represent the culmination of four years of questions only partially answered, of doors glimpsed but never fully opened.

"I am honored," Caelus says, his voice steady despite the emotions churning beneath his composed exterior. The words carry the weight of genuine sentiment rather than mere formality.

Orpheus extends a hand, palm up, revealing a sigil etched into his skin that Caelus has never seen before, a pattern that seems to fold in on itself infinitely, creating depth where there should be only surface.

"Honor is earned," Orpheus responds, the silver eyes behind his mask studying Caelus with that familiar penetrating gaze that seems to evaluate not just his physical presence but his position within the cosmic threads themselves. "As is trust."

The assembled Valthorim continued their harmonic hum, the sound now pulsing in patterns that matched the beating of Caelus's heart. The crystalline columns respond in kind, their internal light flickering in the same rhythm. For a moment, everything in the atrium, stone, crystal, flesh, and whatever substance comprises the Valthorim, exists in perfect synchronization.

Caelus stands at the threshold of new understanding, poised between what he has learned and what awaits discovery. The stars above bear silent witness through the transparent dome, eternal and patient, just as they watched over Solarune on the night his ability first awakened.

Orpheus moves without sound, his robes gathering darkness around him like a collection of shadows borrowed from distant corners of the universe. Caelus follows through corridors that bend at angles that shouldn't be possible, where perspective shifts subtly with each step. The monastery's architecture defies conventional geometry; spaces that appear small from the outside open into chambers vast enough to house small moons, while seemingly endless hallways terminate abruptly in intimate alcoves barely large enough for whispered confessions.

They pass through an archway composed of interlocking crystalline segments that pulse with subtle energy. Each segment rotates slightly as they approach, aligning into a new configuration that acknowledges their presence with silent recognition. Beyond this living threshold lies a circular chamber that feels both ancient and timeless, a space that might have existed before Zathira was built around it rather than constructed as part of the monastery.

"The Fractal demonstration room," Orpheus says, his voice resonating differently here than in the atrium, as if the acoustics respond specifically to his unique vocal harmonics.

Crystalline arrays line the walls, arranged in spiraling patterns that draw the eye inward toward their increasingly complex centers. Unlike the transparent crystals in the atrium, these possess an internal structure visible through their semi-translucent surfaces, lattices of light suspended within solid matter, pulsing with gentle rhythm like captured heartbeats.

Ancient sigils cover every available surface, etched into the floor, carved into the curved ceiling, and embedded within the crystalline arrays themselves. Some Caelus recognizes from his years of training; others remain mysterious, their forms so complex they seem to change shape when viewed from different angles.

"Four years tracking criminals across the galaxy," Orpheus says, moving toward the center of the chamber. "You've mastered finding people through cosmic threads. Now you learn to navigate those threads directly."

He positions himself precisely at the center of a complex pattern etched into the floor, a mandala of interconnected geometric forms that expands outward from a central point like a frozen explosion of mathematical precision. The sigils on his robe align with corresponding marks on the floor, creating continuity between body and chamber.

"Fractals are the universe's natural pathways," he explains, his voice resonating in the enclosed space. "We merely open what already exists."

Caelus stands at the edge of the pattern, observing with the focused attention he's developed through years of tracking work. He notes how the crystalline arrays respond to Orpheus's presence, their internal lattices shifting orientation like compass needles finding true north.

"The universe contains infinite connections," Orpheus continues. "Most beings perceive only physical proximity, but the reality is more complex. Distance is often an illusion created by limited perception."

He extends his arms outward, fingers splayed. The sigils on his hands, normally hidden beneath the flowing fabric of his robes, become visible now, intricate patterns that match certain elements of the floor design beneath him. His silver eyes gleam behind the ornate mask, pupils contracting to pinpoints of absolute focus.

With deliberate precision, Orpheus begins tracing geometric patterns in the air. His fingers move through space as if drawing on an invisible canvas, each motion exact, measured, and purposeful. The crystalline arrays respond immediately, their internal lattices aligning with his movements, light pulsing brighter with each completed pattern.

The air in the center of the room thickens and becomes almost viscous. Light bends around a point directly in front of Orpheus, creating distortion like heat rising from sun-baked stone, but more structured, more intentional. The temperature drops several degrees in an instant, air molecules slowing as space itself begins to fold.

Caelus's sigils warm against his skin, responding to the energy building within the chamber. The bands of metal around his fingers vibrate slightly, resonating with frequencies beyond normal human perception. He watches with equal parts scientific curiosity and instinctive reverence as reality itself yields to Orpheus's precise manipulations.

A sound fills the chamber, not produced by any physical object but by the process itself, a crystalline ringing that grows higher in pitch as the folding of space intensifies. The sound penetrates bone and tissue, bypassing ears entirely to vibrate directly against the mind.

With a final, complex gesture, Orpheus completes the sequence. The building tension releases as space tears open in the center of the room, not a violent rupture but a perfect, ordered unfolding. The Fractal appears, a crystalline-like pattern that folds in on itself infinitely, each segment containing perfect replicas of the whole that somehow exist simultaneously at different scales.

The Fractal emits soft pulsing light that defies spectral categorization, not quite blue, not quite violet, but something between and beyond both. This light bends the surrounding space, creating overlapping areas where the same objects appear simultaneously from slightly different angles as if multiple versions of reality have been superimposed.

A subtle humming frequency fills the chamber, felt rather than heard, a vibration that resonates with something fundamental in the body's composition. Caelus feels it in his bone marrow, in the spaces between cells, in the atomic structure of his being.

"Magnificent," he whispers, the word inadequate but instinctive.

The Fractal hangs suspended before Orpheus, its edges both impossibly sharp and fluid simultaneously, a contradiction that should be visually jarring but instead appears perfectly natural as if conventional geometry is the true abstraction. Through its center, Caelus glimpses what might be stars, distant nebulae, cosmic dust clouds, or perhaps something else entirely, something beyond standard physical reference points.

He studies the process intently, noting how the energies flow between the crystalline arrays, the floor sigils, and Orpheus himself, a circuit of power that doesn't create the Fractal but rather reveals what was already present, like removing a veil from a hidden doorway.

"Each Fractal has a unique energy signature," Orpheus explains, maintaining the opening with subtle adjustments of his fingers. "Learn to read them, and you can navigate anywhere in the universe."

Caelus circles the phenomenon slowly, careful not to disrupt the energy patterns, maintaining its stability. His Aetheris perception, trained through years of tracking work, catches nuances in the Fractal's structure that his normal senses miss. He perceives not just its physical manifestation but the complex web of cosmic threads feeding into and through it, connecting this single point to countless others throughout the universe.

"The sigils that open a Fractal must match its energy precisely," Orpheus continues. "Imprecision leads to instability, or worse, emergence in unintended locations."

The Fractal pulses once, its internal patterns shifting slightly. Through its center, the glimpse of distant space changes. Different stars and different nebulae appear and then vanish, replaced by others in rapid succession.

"What you're seeing is a possibility," Orpheus says, noting Caelus's intense focus on these changes. "Each Fractal connects to multiple endpoints. The final destination is determined by the specific resonance established during opening."

He allows the Fractal to remain open a moment longer, then gradually reverses his hand movements. The opening contracts, folding back into itself with the same ordered precision with which it appeared. The temperature returns to normal as the final trace of the Fractal disappears, leaving only a lingering vibration in the air that fades slowly.

"The Valthorim did not invent Fractals," Orpheus says, lowering his arms. "We discovered them, learned their language, their mathematics. They are woven into the fabric of existence itself." His silver eyes fix on Caelus. "Your Aetheris ability makes you uniquely suited to understand them. You already perceive the cosmic threads that Fractals follow."

Caelus nods, connecting this new knowledge with his years of tracking experience. "That's why I sometimes sensed pathways between locations when tracking criminals, glimpses of these connections."

"Precisely," Orpheus confirms. "You've been perceiving fragments of the universal Fractal network your entire life. Now, you will learn to use it."

The private training hall exists in perpetual twilight, its walls of polished obsidian absorbing light rather than reflecting it. No stars visible here, no transparent dome, just smooth black surfaces that contain and focus energy like the inside of a perfectly crafted instrument. The only illumination comes from sigils etched into the floor, emitting a subtle glow that outlines two circular platforms hovering inches above the ground. Silence hangs thick in the chamber, not empty but pregnant with potential, waiting to be shaped by intention.

Caelus removes his boots before stepping onto one of the floating platforms. The surface feels neither warm nor cold beneath his feet, existing in perfect thermal neutrality. The platform adjusts to his weight, stabilizing with microscopic corrections that maintain its precise height above the floor. Across from him, Orpheus takes a position on the second platform, his robes settling around him like a liquid shadow finding its level.

"Sit," Orpheus instructs, lowering himself with impossible grace into a cross-legged position.

Caelus follows suit, arranging his limbs in the meditation posture he's practiced countless times. The sigils on his skin pulse once in unison, acknowledging the familiar configuration of muscle and bone. The metal bands around his fingers catch the minimal light, reflecting it in thin lines across his knuckles.

"Four years you've used Aetheris to find individuals," Orpheus says, his voice pitched to resonate perfectly within the obsidian chamber. "You perceive the stardust signature of a specific person and follow their thread through the cosmic weave."

He raises his hands, palms facing each other, creating a space between them. The air within that space darkens, then fills with pinpricks of light, a miniature galaxy hovering between his fingers.

"Today, you expand that awareness," he continues. "Not just the threads that connect to individuals, but the greater currents that flow between all things."

Caelus nods, amber eyes reflecting the miniature cosmos floating between Orpheus's hands. "The pathways that Fractals follow," he says, connecting this lesson to what he observed in the demonstration room.

"Close your eyes," Orpheus instructs. "Feel the universe breathe."

The obsidian walls seem to inhale as Caelus closes his eyes, the chamber contracting slightly around them. The platform beneath him vibrates at a frequency just below conscious perception, creating resonance in his pelvic bones and spine that travels upward to the base of his skull.

"Your Aetheris allows you to find individuals," Orpheus's voice continues, somehow both closer and more distant with eyes closed. "Now expand that awareness to the spaces between."

Caelus focuses on his breath first, which is the foundation of all meditation. In. Out. The air filling his lungs carries trace elements formed in the hearts of distant stars, connecting him physically to the cosmos he's trying to perceive. His heartbeat slows, adjusting to the chamber's resonant frequency.

He reaches for his Aetheris perception, the familiar sense that has guided him in tracking criminals across the galaxy. The ability responds, warming the sigils on his skin, creating that distinct awareness of cosmic threads connecting all stardust-formed matter.

But when he tries to shift focus from individual threads to the spaces between them, the perception slips away like water through splayed fingers. His brow furrows with concentration, muscles tensing despite his attempt to remain relaxed.

"You're forcing it," Orpheus observes, his voice undisturbed by Caelus's struggle. "Your mind seeks patterns it already knows. Let go of what Aetheris has been. Allow it to expand."

Caelus exhales slowly through his nose, consciously releasing the tension in his face and shoulders. He tries again, allowing his perception to unfocus slightly, like looking at a distant star from the corner of the eye rather than directly.

Minutes pass in silence. The hovering platforms adjust minutely beneath them, maintaining perfect stability. The sigils etched in the floor pulse in rhythm with Caelus's slowing heartbeat. Sweat beads at his temples despite the chamber's perfect temperature regulation.

"The currents are always there," Orpheus says eventually, his voice pitched lower now, almost hypnotic in its rhythm. "Like gravity or time, fundamental forces exist whether perceived or not. The Valthorim monitor these currents to maintain balance. Creation and entropy must remain in equilibrium."

Caelus feels frustration building in his chest, a tightening that threatens to disrupt his meditative state. Four years of successful missions, of pushing his abilities to their limits, yet this fundamental aspect of cosmic awareness eludes him. His sigils warm further, responding to his emotional state, glowing visibly now, even through his closed eyelids.

Orpheus shifts slightly on his platform. Without opening his eyes, Caelus senses the movement, a deliberate adjustment that brings Orpheus's hand near his shoulder, not quite touching but close enough to direct energy. The proximity creates pressure in the air between them, a focal point around which Caelus's scattered awareness can organize itself.

"The universe moves in currents like a vast ocean," Orpheus continues, his voice now seeming to originate from everywhere and nowhere simultaneously. "Stars form from the interaction of these currents. Planets coalesce in their eddies. Life emerges in their calm pools."

The image forms in Caelus's mind, cosmic energy flowing in vast, ordered streams through apparently empty space. It is not visible light or detectable radiation but something more fundamental and more essential. The conceptual framework Orpheus provides gives structure to his perception, a context within which the unfamiliar can become recognizable.

His breathing synchronizes perfectly with the chamber's resonant frequency. The platform beneath him seems to disappear from his awareness, creating the sensation of floating in the void. The sigils on his skin no longer feel like separate points of warmth but merge into continuous lines of energy that extend beyond his physical form.

"There," he whispers, the word barely disturbing the air.

He perceives it now not just the individual threads connecting specific points of stardust but the broader currents in which those threads exist, like seeing not only fish in a river but the river itself, its depth, its flow, its essential nature as a connective pathway between distant points.

The mental adjustment feels small yet profound, a shift in perspective that transforms everything. His body tenses with the effort of maintaining this expanded awareness, muscles straining as if lifting an invisible weight. His consciousness stretches across vast distances, perceiving how the cosmic currents connect entire star systems, not just individuals.

Caelus focuses on a specific current, following its flow to a distant point in space. Not tracking a person now but a location, a remote stellar junction where multiple currents converge. He holds that point in his awareness, feeling its unique resonance, its specific position within the cosmic weave.

Something shifts in the chamber, a subtle change in pressure as space responds to his focused intention. Between him and Orpheus, directly above their platforms, the air thins and then tears open in a perfect miniature Fractal. Barely larger than his hand, the opening shimmers with the same crystalline-like pattern he observed in the demonstration room, folding inward infinitely while emitting soft pulsing light.

The manifestation startles him, breaking his concentration. The small Fractal collapses immediately, folding back into nothing with a soft sound like a single crystal chime. The chamber returns to its previous state, though the air retains a charged quality, as if molecules have been rearranged at their fundamental level.

Caelus opens his eyes, finding Orpheus's silver gaze already fixed on him. Behind the ornate mask, those metallic irises contain something rarely seen: approval, perhaps even a hint of satisfaction.

"You begin to understand," Orpheus says simply.

"It's, " Caelus searches for words adequate to describe what he experienced. "It's like the difference between seeing stars as points of light and understanding they're massive fusion reactors generating elements that eventually form living beings."

"Yes," Orpheus nods, the mask catching the minimal light of the chamber and returning it fractured into component wavelengths. "Context changes everything. The threads you've always perceived exist within larger patterns, larger purposes."

Caelus looks down at his hands, at the metal bands around his fingers and the sigils spiraling up his forearms. They appear unchanged yet feel fundamentally different now, not just tools for tracking individuals but potential conduits for connecting with the cosmic currents themselves.

"I could only maintain it for moments," he admits, aware of his limitations even in this breakthrough.

"Moments are how eternities begin," Orpheus responds, rising from his platform with that same impossible grace. "You've taken your first step into a vastly larger understanding."

The obsidian walls seem to exhale around them, the chamber expanding slightly as if responding to this release of tension. Caelus stands more conventionally, muscles protesting after the period of intense concentration. Despite the physical discomfort, his mind feels expanded, awakened to possibilities that were always present but never before perceived.

"Again tomorrow," Orpheus says, not a question but a simple statement of fact. "The currents await."

The preparation chamber hums with contained power, its walls lined with equipment whose function Caelus can only partially guess. Navigation devices blink with coordinates in mathematical systems he's still learning. Emergency beacons stand ready in recessed alcoves, their casings marked with warning sigils. Monitoring tools track fluctuations in space-time with needle-thin precision, their displays showing wave patterns that shift and stabilize in response to adjustments too subtle for normal perception. In the center of it stands a small Fractal, already opened, its crystalline pattern rotating slowly like a lock waiting for the proper key.

Orpheus stands beside the Fractal, his robes particularly still now, as if responding to the delicate stability of the opening before them. Normally, his garments move with subtle, continuous motion, but here, they hang in perfect vertical lines, creating the impression of a statue rather than a living being.

"A field test," he announces, his silver eyes gleaming behind the ornate mask. "We will travel to a neighboring pocket of space and return."

Caelus approaches the Fractal carefully, noting how the equipment around the room responds to its presence. Displays flicker with readings that track minute changes in the opening's configuration. The air near the Fractal feels thinner somehow; molecules spread further apart as space itself stretches to accommodate the tear in its fabric.

"Never before have I passed through one," Caelus admits, studying the crystalline pattern with both normal vision and his enhanced Aetheris perception. Through the latter, he perceives how the cosmic currents he recently learned to detect flow into and through the opening, creating a pathway that connects this specific point to another.

"The experience is unique," Orpheus says, reaching into his robe to withdraw a small device that fits in his palm. The object pulses with light that matches the exact frequency of the Fractal before them, not just similar but identical, down to the microsecond intervals between pulses.

He hands the device to Caelus. "This will anchor you to our return point. Keep it on your person at all times."

The anchor feels surprisingly warm against Caelus's skin, vibrating slightly like a living thing. Its construction defies conventional analysis, neither purely mechanical nor entirely organic, but something between that responds to his touch by adjusting its pulse rate to match his heartbeat.

"Will it hurt?" Caelus asks, immediately regretting the question. Four years at Zathira have taught him that concepts like pain and comfort hold little relevance for the Valthorim.

"It is neither pleasant nor unpleasant," Orpheus answers without judgment. "It simply is. Your body will normalize the experience quickly, though the first transition can be... disorienting."

He moves to stand directly before the Fractal, gesturing for Caelus to join him. Together, they face the rotating crystalline pattern, which seems to accelerate slightly as they approach, as if responding to their intention.

"We step through together," Orpheus instructs. "Match my pace precisely."

Caelus readies himself, securing the anchor device in an inner pocket where it continues to pulse against his chest through layers of fabric. His sigils warm in anticipation, responding to the proximity of the Fractal's energy. The metal bands around his fingers vibrate in harmony with the anchor, creating a circuit of resonance that runs through his entire body.

"Now," Orpheus says and steps forward.

Caelus moves in perfect synchronization, his foot lifting from the preparation chamber floor at exactly the same moment as Orpheus's. They enter the Fractal together, not walking into it so much as being drawn through it, reality folding around them rather than them passing through reality.

The sensation defies every physical experience Caelus has known. His body simultaneously stretches and compresses, exists and doesn't exist. His consciousness expands outward in all directions while also contracting to a single point of absolute focus. Temperature, pressure, gravity, and all conventional physical constants disappear, replaced by a state that has no reference point in normal experience.

For what might be a microsecond or a millennium, time loses meaning entirely; Caelus perceives infinite pathways branching in all directions, each leading to different points in space-time. He glimpses countless possible destinations, worlds, void spaces and stellar phenomena flashing past his awareness faster than thought can track. The cosmic currents he's recently learned to perceive appear blindingly obvious here, massive flows of energy that carry everything in their eternal movements.

Then, with a sensation like being turned inside out and reassembled, he emerges into physical space again. The transition completes with a full-body shudder as his nervous system recalibrates to conventional reality. Gravity returns, lighter than Zathira's but definitely present, causing him to stumble slightly before regaining his balance.

They stand on the surface of a small asteroid, one of countless similar bodies forming a vast field orbiting a distant orange star. The ground beneath their feet consists of compacted dust and small rocks fused together by ancient heat, creating a surface that crumbles slightly with each step. No atmosphere surrounds them, yet they breathe normally thanks to the protective field that shimmers almost invisibly around their bodies, standard Valthorim travel protection that extends from Orpheus to include Caelus.

The silence presses against his ears with physical force. After Zathira's constant subtle sounds, machinery humming, crystals resonating, and the movement of robed figures through stone corridors, this absolute absence of noise feels suffocating. The only sound comes from within his own body, blood rushing through veins, lungs expanding and contracting, the faint electrical crackling of neural impulses.

"Your first Fractal transit," Orpheus observes, his voice somehow carried through the vacuum between them. "Your system adapts well."

Caelus nods, still orienting himself to their new location. The anchor device in his pocket pulses more rapidly now, maintaining a connection with their point of origin. Through his Aetheris perception, he senses how the cosmic currents flow differently here, faster less structured, creating eddies and vortices around the asteroid field.

The space around them stretches vast and empty in all directions, punctuated only by floating rocks and the occasional flash of a micro-meteorite impacting against their protective field. The star that governs this system hangs distant and dim compared to Solarune's brilliant primary, casting everything in copper-tinted light that creates sharp, well-defined shadows.

"Where are we?" Caelus asks, his voice sounding strange in his own ears, transmitted through the protective field rather than through air.

"The Cygnus Remnant," Orpheus answers. "What remains of a planetary system after its star's partial collapse twelve thousand years ago. We are approximately seventy light-years from Zathira."

The number should be shocking, seventy light-years traversed in what felt like no time at all, but after everything Caelus has experienced at Zathira, the distance seems almost mundane. More interesting is the immediate environment, the unique configuration of cosmic currents that flow through this specific region of space.

Orpheus raises a hand, pointing to a specific asteroid floating approximately two hundred meters from their position. Unlike most of the surrounding bodies, this one features a distinctive crater that cuts nearly halfway through its total mass.

"Focus your Aetheris there," he instructs.

Caelus complies, directing his attention toward the indicated asteroid. His sigils respond immediately, warming against his skin as his perception extends outward along cosmic threads. He narrows his focus, searching not just for any presence but for the specific signature of life, the unique configuration of stardust that indicates consciousness rather than mere matter.

At first, he detects nothing but rock and dust, elements forged in stellar furnaces but now cold and inert. Then, as his perception penetrates deeper into the crater, he senses it, a small, pulsing point of awareness hiding within a crevice. Not human, not even humanoid, but definitely alive, a silicon-based organism about the size of his hand, its consciousness alien but undeniable.

"I found it," he says, surprised by the discovery. "Some kind of indigenous life form. Silicon-based, using the asteroid's radiation for energy."

"Good," Orpheus says. The single word carries approval but also something else, confirmation as if this exercise tested something beyond mere skill.

Caelus maintains his connection with the life form a moment longer, fascinated by its alien nature. Unlike tracking humans, whose stardust configurations follow familiar patterns, this creature's cosmic signature spirals in unusual formations, creating threads of connection that move contrary to expected flows.

"Now we return," Orpheus announces.

He gestures to the space beside them, fingers moving in precise patterns that Caelus now recognizes from the demonstration room. The cosmic currents respond, flowing together to create a convergence point where space thins, stretches, and then opens into another Fractal. This one forms more quickly than the demonstration version, snapping into existence with practiced efficiency.

"The anchor will guide you," Orpheus says, indicating the device in Caelus's pocket. "Feel its pull."

The anchor pulses strongly now, creating a distinct sensation of directional pull, not physical but something perceived through Aetheris awareness. It shows him which branch of the infinite pathways will lead back to their origin point.

They step into the Fractal together, and the transition is smoother this time as Caelus anticipates the shift. His body still experiences that impossible state of simultaneous expansion and contraction, but his mind remains more focused, not overwhelmed by the infinite possibilities glimpsed during transit.

They emerge in the preparation chamber exactly where they departed, the equipment around them registering their return with synchronized alerts and status updates. The entire journey, seventy light-years out and back, has taken less than fifteen minutes by the chamber's chronometers.

Caelus exhales slowly, feeling his body readjust to Zathira's familiar gravity and atmosphere. The anchor device in his pocket gradually slows its pulsing as it synchronizes once more with the room's space-time signature.

"You adapted well," Orpheus observes, his robes resuming their subtle, continuous movement now that they're back in stable space. "Most require several transitions before maintaining such composure."

The compliment, rare from the Valthorim leader, warms Caelus more than his sigils ever could. He's crossed another threshold in his training, one that brings him closer to understanding the deeper mysteries Orpheus promised in the atrium ceremony.

"It was..." he searches for adequate words, "...like seeing the universe without its skin."

"An apt description," Orpheus responds, the silver eyes behind his mask studying Caelus with renewed interest. "Few perceive so clearly on their first journey."

Orpheus's private sanctum defies definition, its boundaries refusing to settle into permanent form. The walls shift between solid matter and translucent energy in slow, rhythmic pulses, revealing glimpses of star systems beyond Zathira's physical location before solidifying again into surfaces of material that resemble polished onyx but glow from within with its own inner light. The chamber breathes, not metaphorically but literally, expanding and contracting with subtle movements that match the tempo of cosmic radiation cycles. No right angles exist here, no straight lines, only curves and spirals that mimic the natural formations of galaxies and nebulae.

Ancient artifacts float in suspended animation around the room's perimeter, rotating slowly without visible support. Each object, fragments of forgotten technologies, crystalline structures from extinct civilizations, texts written in languages that predate known history, hovers within its own protective field that shimmers with precisely calibrated energy. The artifacts cast no shadows despite the multiple light sources as if they exist partially in dimensions where darkness cannot form.

At the chamber's center, a holographic map of the universe rotates slowly above a pedestal carved from material that appears simultaneously crystalline and liquid. The map doesn't simply represent space but time as well, showing stellar movements, galactic rotations, and the birth and death of stars in a compressed temporal sequence. Certain points within the projection glow more intensely than others, marking locations where Fractals naturally occur.

Caelus stands before this map, his attention caught by the precise mathematical beauty of cosmic movement. After four years at Zathira and today's series of revelations, he sees the universe differently, not just as a collection of celestial objects but as an interconnected system of energy flows and balanced forces.

"You performed well," Orpheus says, moving to stand beside him. The mask on his face catches light from the holographic display, creating the impression that galaxies rotate across its surface. "The transition through the Fractal, the detection of the silicon-based life form, both executed with precision."

Caelus inclines his head in acknowledgment, keeping his eyes on the map. "The creature was beautiful," he says. "Its stardust signature flowed in patterns I've never encountered before."

"Diversity is the universe's natural state," Orpheus responds. "Infinite variations on fundamental themes." He gestures toward the map, and the projection responds, zooming in on a specific sector where dozens of points glow with Fractal energy. "These are the pathways we currently monitor. Each requires consistent attention to maintain balance."

The map rotates again, revealing a different perspective of cosmic structure. From this angle, the universe resembles a vast neural network, with Fractals serving as connection points between otherwise distant regions, synapses in the mind of creation itself.

"The Valthorim's role as universal monitors requires both power and restraint," Orpheus continues, moving around the pedestal to view the map from different angles. "We open pathways to maintain balance, to ensure that no single force dominates the cosmos."

His silver eyes lift from the projection to fix on Caelus. "What you've learned today, about Fractals, about cosmic currents, represents power few beings ever access. The ability to move instantly across vast distances, to perceive the fundamental connections between all things... these gifts carry corresponding responsibilities."

Caelus nods, feeling the weight of those responsibilities settling across his shoulders. The sigils on his skin pulse gently, responding to the energy patterns in the sanctum. The metal bands around his fingers catch light from the holographic map, reflecting miniature galaxies across his knuckles.

"What about the risks?" he asks the question emerging from hours of observation and contemplation. "Such power could easily be misused. What prevents the Valthorim from becoming what they claim to prevent, a dominant force that disrupts cosmic balance?"

The question hangs in the air between them, bold in its directness. Four years ago, newly arrived at Zathira, Caelus would never have dared pose such a challenge. However, his growth has earned him the right to ask, and Orpheus's invitation to the deeper mysteries implies readiness for deeper questions.

Orpheus doesn't answer immediately. He moves to a window that looks out into deep space, not a fabricated view but an actual void, suggesting the sanctum exists partially beyond Zathira's physical structure. Stars burn with unfiltered brilliance against absolute darkness, their light traveling unimpeded by atmosphere or protective shielding.

"Creation and entropy exist in eternal tension," he says finally, his voice softer than usual, the harmonic qualities more pronounced. "Too much of either leads to chaos."

He turns from the window, the stars visible through his semi-transparent robe for a moment before the fabric solidifies again. "The Valthorim emerged in the early universe precisely because of this tension. We are not separate from the forces we monitor, and we are expressions of the universe's tendency toward equilibrium."

The holographic map shifts again, this time showing regions where stars collapse, planets disintegrate, and entire systems fade from existence. "Entropy is not evil, merely necessary. Creation is not inherently good, merely essential. Both must exist in proper proportion."

Caelus watches as the map displays both processes simultaneously, stars dying while new ones form, galaxies colliding while others spiral into elegant new configurations. The cosmic dance of creation and destruction plays out in miniature above the pedestal, beautiful in its perfect, terrible balance.

"Your question is valid," Orpheus acknowledges. "Power without accountability becomes corruption. This is why the Valthorim operates through consensus rather than hierarchy, why we bind ourselves to principles older than our existence."

He moves closer to Caelus, his robes shifting from absolute darkness to deep indigo, reflecting his mood in subtle chromatic shifts. "Your presence here represents another safeguard. Your Aetheris perception, independent of Valthorim training yet complementary to our methods, provides the perspective we might otherwise lose over millennia of existence."

For the first time in their four-year relationship, Orpheus places a hand directly on Caelus's shoulder, which is actual physical contact rather than the near-touch energy direction he's used in training. The weight feels simultaneously heavier and lighter than expected as if Orpheus exists at a density different from ordinary matter.

"Your Aetheris is a rare gift," he says, his silver eyes fixed on Caelus with unprecedented intensity. "With it, you help us preserve the delicate balance that allows life to flourish."

The touch resonates through Caelus's body, creating harmonic vibrations in his sigils that spread outward from the point of contact. His hands tingle with sudden energy, but he feels a warmth in his chest, an expansive heat that he recognizes as purpose finding its true expression. The sensation resembles what he felt upon first discovering his Aetheris ability on Solarune, but deeper, more profound, the difference between a child discovering a single puzzle piece and an adult seeing the completed image.

Caelus nods, accepting the responsibility with a newfound understanding of his place in the cosmic order. "I never imagined this when I first tracked Marius Vex four years ago," he says, remembering the criminal whose location first demonstrated his conscious Aetheris ability. "Finding people seemed the limit of my potential."

"Most beings never discover their true capabilities," Orpheus responds, removing his hand but leaving an energetic imprint that continues to resonate through Caelus's shoulder. "They perceive themselves as isolated individuals, separate from the cosmic currents that flow through all things."

He gestures again to the holographic map, and the projection expands to fill more of the chamber. Stars and galaxies rotate around them now, creating the impression that they stand at the very center of the universe, not geographically but fundamentally, at the still point around which all movement occurs.

"What began with tracking criminals becomes something greater," Orpheus says. "Your ability to perceive cosmic threads grows into an understanding of the tapestry itself, its patterns, its purpose, its preservation."

The sanctum walls pulse once more strongly than before, becoming fully transparent for several seconds. Through them, Caelus glimpses the entirety of Zathira, not just the physical monastery but its complete existence across multiple dimensions. Corridors extend in directions conventional geometry cannot describe. Chambers occupy spaces that should be paradoxical yet function with perfect harmony. Throughout this impossible architecture, robed figures move with purpose, maintaining the delicate balance between creation and entropy.

As the walls solidify again, returning the sanctum to its normal state, Caelus understands with sudden clarity that his journey has only begun. Four years of tracking criminals across the galaxy was merely preparation for this deeper purpose, learning to perceive and protect the cosmic balance itself.

The holographic map continues its eternal rotation above the pedestal, stars being born and dying, galaxies forming and dissolving, all in perfect equilibrium. Orpheus moves to stand before it once more, his form outlined by the light of a billion distant suns.

"Tomorrow," he says, "we begin your true work."

Chapter 5

The First Battalion

Selenea stands motionless among the line of recruits; her spine forged into perfect alignment by years of discipline. The First Battalion uniform hugs her athletic frame, its deep blue fabric absorbing light rather than reflecting it. Across her right shoulder, a silver Fractal insignia catches the ancient glow of Zathira's bioluminescent crystals, the sacred symbol that now marks her as both protector and instrument of cosmic balance.

The induction hall stretches above and around her, its ceiling vanishing into shadows where stone meets void. Columns rise like petrified titans, each carved with cosmic symbols whose meanings shift subtly when viewed from different angles. The stone beneath her boots has been worn smooth by millennia of ceremonial footsteps, each molecule compressed by the weight of tradition and purpose.

Fifty-three other recruits form perfect lines to her left and right. They stand at attention, faces composed into masks of solemn dedication. Yet Selenea's posture speaks of something beyond mere training, a natural authority that flows from her amber eyes down through her perfectly squared shoulders. The sigils tattooed across her tan skin pulse with subtle rhythm as if recognizing the significance of this moment.

At the front of the hall, Orpheus appears without sound or movement, simply present where moments before there was empty space. His robes absorb light rather than block it, creating a silhouette of perfect darkness outlined against the ceremonial flames that burn in ancient stone braziers. The ornate mask covering the upper portion of his face catches firelight in hypnotic patterns, silver eyes surveying the assembled recruits with the patient evaluation of one who measures time in cosmic cycles rather than human heartbeats.

"You stand at the threshold of purpose," Orpheus begins, his voice carrying harmonics that resonate with the stone walls themselves. "The First Battalion exists not merely as defenders of Zathira, but as instruments of universal balance."

The flames in the braziers pulse in rhythm with his words. Behind him, a holographic representation of the universe expands and contracts like a breathing entity.

"For countless eons, the Valthorim have monitored the delicate equilibrium between creation and entropy. We observe. We guide. We intervene only when necessary." His silver eyes seem to fix directly on Selenea for a moment, though she knows this perception is shared by every recruit present. "You are not chosen for strength alone, but for understanding, for the recognition that power without wisdom becomes destruction."

Selenea absorbs each word, letting them settle into her consciousness like stones dropping into still water. The speech continues, outlining duties and expectations, cosmic principles and practical applications. Orpheus speaks of star systems and dimensional barriers with the same matter-of-fact precision that her previous commanders used when discussing battlefield tactics.

"The uniform you wear carries the insignia of the Fractals, the universe's natural pathways that connect all things across time and space." Orpheus raises his hands, causing his robes to shift like liquid shadows. "In wearing this symbol, you become part of that connection, a living conductor of cosmic order."

The ceremony progresses through ancient rituals, oaths spoken in languages whose origins predate written history, and symbolic gestures that create patterns of energy visible only through enhanced perception. Selenea performs each with perfect precision, her military training merging seamlessly with these more esoteric requirements.

When the final words fade into the stone walls, Orpheus makes a gesture that simultaneously dismisses and honors the new inductees. The flames in the braziers grow bright enough to cast momentary shadows behind each recruit, not one shadow but three, reminiscent of the triple moons of Solarune.

As the formal structure dissolves, Selenea remains standing at attention a moment longer than necessary, allowing the ceremony's significance to fully register. Around her, other recruits begin to move, their voices creating a soft murmur that rises toward the invisible ceiling.

"At ease, Specialist Solaris." The familiar voice comes from behind her.

She turns to find Caelus approaching, his lean frame moving with the deliberate grace she's always associated with her brother, though now enhanced by years of Valthorim training. The sigils tattooed on his arms have multiplied since she last saw him, spreading upward to create complex patterns across his shoulders and neck. The metal bands around his fingers catch the light as he moves, reflecting miniature galaxies across his knuckles.

"First Battalion suits you," he says, amber eyes so like her own, filled with unmistakable pride.

Selenea breaks protocol, stepping forward to embrace him briefly but firmly. "Eight months of specialized training for this moment," she says as they separate. "Worth every second."

They turn together, moving away from the ceremonial space and into one of Zathira's countless corridors. The passage narrows as they walk, stone walls giving way to crystal segments that reveal glimpses of space beyond, stars burning with unfiltered brilliance against absolute darkness.

"Orpheus has been preparing for this," Caelus says, his stride matching hers exactly. "The Valthorim's work is expanding. New threats emerge across multiple star systems."

Selenea nods, processing this information with the analytical efficiency that earned her rapid advancement through the Battalion's ranks. "Your Aetheris tracking with my tactical operations." She glances sideways at her brother. "An effective combination."

"More than effective," Caelus corrects. "Orpheus believes our combined skills will be invaluable. The cosmic threads I perceive paired with your strategic application of force, we bridge gaps in the Valthorim's traditional methods."

They pass a window that opens directly into the void, the barrier between interior and exterior space so perfectly transparent it creates the illusion of walking directly among the stars. A distant nebula spreads purple-tinted gases across their field of vision, stellar nurseries igniting like distant campfires against cosmic night.

"I've trained for this moment," Selenea says, her voice steady despite the emotion underlying her words. "Together, we can make a difference across the stars."

Caelus stops at an intersection where multiple corridors branch outward at geometrically impossible angles. His expression shifts into something more serious. "What I do here, what we'll do together, goes beyond tracking criminals. The cosmic balance Orpheus speaks of isn't abstract philosophy." He gestures toward the nebula visible through the window. "It's as real as those stars and far more fragile."

Selenea's tactical mind immediately grasps the implications. "You find the threats. I neutralize them. Simple efficiency."

"Applied across galaxies," Caelus adds. "The Valthorim monitor universal patterns most beings never perceive. When disruptions occur, they need instruments precise enough to address them without causing further imbalance."

"Instruments like us." Selenea's lips curve into a slight smile that doesn't diminish her intensity. Her hand moves unconsciously to the Fractal insignia on her shoulder, fingers tracing its intricate pattern. "Family serving together. Father would be proud."

Caelus nods, his eyes catching starlight from the window. "More than proud. This is what he prepared us for, though I doubt even he understood the full scope."

They continue walking, their matched strides creating a rhythm against the ancient stone floor. Through the crystal segments in the walls, stars wheel silently in their eternal orbits, bearing witness to the unfolding of cosmic order.

The summons comes at the third rotation when Zathira's artificial cycle dims the corridor crystals to simulate evening. Three soft pulses against their communication bands, a priority signal bearing Orpheus's unique frequency. Caelus catches Selenea's eye across the tactical training chamber where she's been demonstrating Battalion maneuvers to junior recruits. No words are necessary, and the siblings move in perfect synchronization toward the east wing, where the briefing chambers await with their secrets and their purposes.

Four days since the induction ceremony. Four days of Selenea integrating into Zathira's rhythms, learning to navigate passages that occasionally rearrange themselves according to cosmic alignments beyond conventional understanding. The metal floor plates beneath their boots hum with subtle energy, living technology that responds to their clearance signatures, opening pathways that remain sealed to lesser ranks.

The mission briefing chamber reveals itself after three biometric scans and one final recognition pulse that reads the specific arrangement of sigils on their skin. Doors are composed of material that exists halfway between matter and energy without sound, revealing a spherical space where reality bends inward upon itself.

Inside, holographic star maps fill the air with points of light and streams of data. Stellar bodies rotate in compressed time, a millennium of cosmic movement reduced to visible patterns. At the center of it all stands Orpheus, his dark robes absorbing ambient light, the mask covering the upper portion of his face reflecting fragments of stars and planets as they wheel overhead.

"Siblings Solaris," he acknowledges, silver eyes fixing upon them with that familiar intensity that seems to evaluate not just physical presence but cosmic positioning. "Your first joint assignment arrives sooner than anticipated."

With a gesture that trails momentary shadows through the air, Orpheus brings one particular system into focus. The hologram expands, stars falling away as a single muddy green planet rotates before them, the atmosphere swirling with toxic clouds, the surface barely visible beneath layers of mist and vegetation.

"Pogwam," Orpheus states, is a name emerging with particular intonation that suggests multiple meanings across different languages. "Third planet in the Vescit system. Uninhabited by sentient life, officially."

Caelus steps forward, eyes narrowing as he studies the holographic representation. Selenea remains two paces back, automatically assessing strategic approaches based on the planet's visible features.

"The apparent emptiness conceals the truth," Orpheus continues, fingers tracing patterns that cause the hologram to shift, revealing topographical features beneath the cloud cover. "Swamps covering sixty-seven percent of the surface. Atmospheric composition is hostile to most respiratory systems. Flora evolved defensive mechanisms that include acid secretions and predatory behaviors."

The hologram shifts again, zooming toward a particular region where land masses create a rough archipelago among the swamplands. A pulsing red indicator appears at coordinates that scroll across the bottom of the display.

"Pogwam harbors a traitor who threatens our network," Orpheus explains, his tone maintaining that measured cadence that never betrays urgency yet somehow conveys absolute importance. "An individual who has stolen sensitive information about our Fractal technology."

Selenea's posture shifts subtly, the adjustment of a soldier receiving critical mission parameters. "Nature of the information?" she asks, her military training evident in the precision of her question.

"Fractal stabilization frequencies. Access codes to secured pathways." Orpheus's silver eyes narrow slightly behind his mask. "In the wrong hands, such information could disrupt travel between twelve major systems. More concerning, it could allow unauthorized access to restricted spaces, including Zathira itself."

The implications hang in the air like a physical presence. Disruption of Fractal pathways would strand countless travelers, collapse trade routes, and isolate entire civilizations from each other. Access to Zathira would jeopardize the Valthorim's millennia of work maintaining cosmic balance.

"The individual operates alone?" Caelus asks, his fingers unconsciously moving as if already tracing cosmic threads.

"Yes. Former support staff. Technical division." Orpheus gestures again, bringing up a new hologram, a hunched figure with amphibian features and translucent skin revealing multiple organs beneath. "Species Vescidian. Respiratory system adapted to Pogwam's atmosphere. Capable of surviving in environments lethal to most humanoids."

The hologram rotates, showing the subject from multiple angles. Technical specifications, such as height, weight, known abilities, and threat assessment, appear beside the image.

"Your mission," Orpheus continues, addressing both siblings now, "combines your specialized capabilities. Caelus, your Aetheris will locate the traitor with the precision that our conventional methods cannot match. Selenea, your tactical expertise will secure the capture."

He turns to face Selenea directly. "First Battalion training has prepared you for hostile environment operations. Standard oxygen enhancement will allow three hours of functional respiration in Pogwam's atmosphere. Beyond that timeframe, tissue damage becomes irreversible."

Selenea nods once, already calculating operational parameters. "Mission equipment?"

"Standard field kit with environmental modifications." Orpheus points to a section of the wall that slides open, revealing two compact packs containing specialized gear. "Weapons limited to non-lethal options. The traitor possesses information we must recover intact."

The siblings exchange determined glances, a silent communication honed through childhood and perfected through their respective pieces of training. Where Caelus sees threads and connections, Selenea sees angles and approaches, complementary perceptions forming a complete tactical picture.

"The environment is hostile beyond chemical composition," Orpheus warns. "Carnivorous flora react to movement. Bioluminescent predators emerge during nocturnal cycles. Trust each other's strengths and maintain constant awareness."

He moves to a raised platform at the room's center, where a small pedestal emerges from the floor. Placing his hand upon it, Orpheus activates a final sequence of commands. The holograms fade as mission coordinates transfer to the devices on the siblings' wrists, information flowing like water finding its level.

"Recovery of both the traitor and the stolen data remains the primary objective," Orpheus concludes. "Secundus protocol applies if extraction becomes impossible."

The unspoken implication hangs in the air, ensuring nothing useful remains for others to find. Selenea recognized the directive from her battalion training. Some information is too dangerous to exist outside Valthorim's control.

Caelus steps toward the equipment wall, retrieving both packs and handing one to Selenea. The gear feels lighter than its capabilities would suggest, and Zathira's technology operates at the intersection of physical and theoretical limits.

"Time restriction?" he asks, securing the pack's straps across his chest.

"Standard forty-eight-hour operation window," Orpheus responds. "Extraction upon mission completion or at window closure."

He moves toward the chamber's far wall, where nothing but smooth stone appears visible. With precise movements that leave momentary after-images hanging in the air, Orpheus traces sigils that correspond to specific coordinates. The wall responds immediately, stone appearing to fold inward upon itself as a Fractal tears open before them.

The opening shimmers with internal energy, not quite blue, not quite violet, but something between and beyond both. Its crystalline pattern rotates slowly, each segment containing perfect replicas of the whole that somehow exist simultaneously at different scales. Through its center, the swampy landscape of Pogwam becomes visible, murky green light filtering through dense fog.

Selenea checks her weapon, a sleek energy pistol with Zathira markings etched along its barrel. The power cell pulses with contained potential are calibrated precisely for Vescidian physiology. She secures it in her holster, runs one final check on her environmental seals, and then nods to her brother.

Caelus activates his Aetheris enhancement bands, and the metal rings around his fingers glow briefly as they power up. The sigils on his skin respond with matching luminescence, preparing to track their target through cosmic threads.

They step toward the Fractal together, weapons ready, minds focused. The shimmering tear in reality pulses once in recognition, then opens wider to receive them.

They emerge on Pogwam's surface between one heartbeat and the next, reality reassembling around them as the Fractal seals shut with a soft implosion of air. Dense fog immediately engulfs them, a sickly greenish-yellow miasma that clings to exposed skin like wet silk. Caelus inhales cautiously through his filtration mask, and the atmosphere burns his nostrils despite the protection. It carries metallic undertones and something deeper and more organic: the smell of constant decay and rebirth.

Massive trees rise like skeletal fingers around their insertion point, and trunks twist into unnatural configurations that suggest pain rather than growth. From their bark, viscous fluid drips in slow, deliberate pulses, hitting the sodden ground with soft hisses as it eats through layers of fallen vegetation. Each droplet leaves behind small craters of charred organic matter, perfect circles of destruction spreading outward.

Selenea activates her environmental scanner, its soft blue glow creating momentary clarity in the surrounding fog. Data streams across her wrist display, atmospheric composition, toxicity levels, and radiation readings. She absorbs the information without speaking and adjusts her filtration mask's settings with two quick movements.

"Breathable with filtration," she reports, voice slightly distorted through the mask. "Skin contact inadvisable with fluid emissions. Temperature thirty-two degrees Celsius with ninety-seven percent humidity."

Strange croaking sounds echo from somewhere behind the curtain of mist, answered by high-pitched whistles that modulate in unnatural patterns. Something large moves through the canopy overhead, dislodging moisture that falls around them in fat, heavy drops.

Caelus checks his own equipment, finds the environmental seals intact, and finds Aetheris enhancement bands active around his fingers. Their metal surfaces catch what little light penetrates the fog, reflecting it in muted flashes. He nods to Selenea, then steps away from the insertion point, seeking solid ground among the spongy vegetation.

"Activation process initiated," he says, finding a relatively stable position between two massive roots. "Environmental interference minimal."

He closes his eyes, face relaxing into practiced concentration. The sigils tattooed across his skin respond immediately, warming beneath his uniform. His back straightens as the Aetheris connection builds, channeling through the enhancement bands on his fingers. Beneath closed his eyelids, and his eyes moved rapidly, tracking cosmic threads invisible to normal perception.

Selenea takes up a defensive position, and her battalion training automatically compensates for her brother's momentary vulnerability during tracking. Her energy pistol remains holstered but within immediate reach, hand resting lightly on its grip as she scans its surroundings with methodical precision. Years of military operations have taught her to identify threats by the smallest disruptions in environmental patterns.

A soft blue glow emanates from beneath Caelus's skin, tracing his veins and highlighting the sigils in luminous patterns. His muscles tense visibly, jaw clenching as he extends his awareness outward along cosmic threads that connect all stardust-formed matter. The process looks painful, though he's assured Selenea countless times that it simply requires intensive focus rather than causing actual discomfort.

Seconds stretch into minutes. The ambient sounds of Pogwam continue around them, liquid dripping, vegetation squelching underfoot, distant creatures communicating in their alien tongues. The fog shifts in subtle currents, occasionally thinning enough to reveal glimpses of the swampland stretching in all directions, endless variations of murky green and brown broken only by occasional patches of bioluminescent fungi.

"Northeast," Caelus finally whispers, eyes still closed, face tight with concentration. "Three kilometers. Moving slowly." His fingers twitch as if plucking invisible strings. "Anxiety pattern in the stardust signature. They know something's wrong."

His eyes open, the amber irises now rimmed with the same blue luminescence that traced his veins moments before. "Water terrain most of the way. Some solid landmasses form islands. Target is in motion, but erratic, searching rather than fleeing."

Selenea processes this information instantly, her tactical mind converting cosmic awareness into operational parameters. She takes points without discussion, moving forward with practiced efficiency. Her hand rises, forming signals drawn from Battalion protocol but modified for their specific partnership, two fingers extended then curved eastward, followed by a circular motion that indicates caution.

Caelus falls into position behind her, close enough for visibility in the dense fog but maintaining sufficient distance for combat maneuvering if necessary. The blue glow recedes from his eyes but doesn't disappear completely, maintaining a low-level connection to the target's position.

They move through the swamp with deliberate care, each step placed with conscious precision. The ground beneath alternates between semi-solid peat and treacherous mud that threatens to swallow boots whole. Within minutes, they're navigating through knee-deep murky water, its surface broken by occasional bubbles that release noxious gas when disturbed.

Selenea points to a particular pattern of bubbles ahead, perfectly concentric circles expanding outward from a central point. She diverts their path without explanation, guiding them wide around the area. Moments later, a massive air pocket erupts where they would have been, releasing a cloud of yellowish gas that briefly ignites upon contact with the atmosphere.

The water deepens as they progress, rising to mid-thigh. Movements become slower and more deliberate, each ripple potentially attracting unwanted attention. A fallen tree creates a natural bridge across a particularly deep section. Selenea tests its stability with practiced efficiency before signaling advance.

"Position update," she mouths silently, the words barely disturbing the air between them.

Caelus closes his eyes briefly, reconnecting with the cosmic threads. "Two point seven kilometers. Still northeast. Stationary now."

They proceed in practiced silence, their breathing synchronized through years of training together, steady, controlled, and minimal. When a twisted vine blocks their path, Selenea draws a small utility blade from her belt, testing the plant's reaction with the tip before making any cut. The vine recoils from the metal's touch, curling away to reveal an alternate path.

A distant splash alerts them to move ahead. Both freeze instantly, becoming part of the swamp's natural stillness. Through the fog, a massive shape glides across the water's surface, a sinuous body propelled by undulating fins that barely break the tension. Six glowing spots along its flanks pulse with bioluminescent warning.

Selenea points to a dense patch of reeds nearby. They move as one, sliding into concealment with minimal disruption. The creature passes within meters of its position, sensory organs that resemble inverted flowers extending from its head to sample the air. It pauses, turns partially toward them, and then continues onward, apparently satisfied that no prey exists within its territory.

When they resume their approach, the water level begins to recede. Patches of more solid ground emerge, creating an archipelago of small islands amid the swamp. Selenea leads them onto one such formation, kneeling to examine the soil composition.

"Recent passage," she indicates, pointing to subtle indentations that most would miss entirely. "Webbed feet. Direction consistent with your tracking."

Caelus nods, confirming through his Aetheris perception. The cosmic threads connecting them to their target grow stronger and more defined as distance decreases. The blue glow in his eyes intensifies slightly.

They encounter a channel too deep to cross by wading. Selenea scans the nearby vegetation, identifying a particular species of hollow reed growing along the bank. With two quick cuts, she harvests several sections, testing their structural integrity between strong fingers.

"Submersion required," she states, measuring the channel's width with practiced eyes. "Current moderate. Visibility near zero." She hands Caelus one of the reed sections. "Breathing apparatus. Follow my lead."

Without waiting for acknowledgment, she slides into the murky water, submerging completely while keeping one end of her reed above the surface. Caelus follows, mimicking her technique perfectly. Together, they navigate the underwater portion of their approach, communicating through light touches against arms and shoulders when necessary, their movements invisible beneath the swamp's opaque surface.

They emerge on the far bank, water streaming from their environmental suits, filters working overtime to process the increased moisture. Selenea checked her chronometer; thirty-seven minutes had elapsed since insertion, and the oxygen supply was still well within operational parameters.

A series of low, vibrating croaks echoes through the fog ahead. Caelus touches Selenea's arm, pointing forward with two fingers. His eyes now glow bright enough to cast faint blue shadows across his cheekbones.

"Close," he whispers, voice barely audible even in the stillness. "Less than half a kilometer. Agitated movement patterns."

Selenea draws her energy pistol, adjusting its settings with practiced efficiency. She signals their final approach pattern, flanking positions with converging angles and maximum coverage with minimal exposure. No words pass between them as they separate slightly, each taking one side of a natural pathway that forms through the twisted vegetation.

They move forward in perfect tandem, two aspects of a single purpose, and their complementary skills create an operational efficiency that exceeds formal training. The fog thins slightly as they approach their target, the swamp grudgingly revealing its secrets.

The crude shelter rises from the swamp like a malformed growth, half-submerged in murky water, half-embedded in the massive trunk of a dying tree. Bioluminescent fungi creep across its surface in geometric patterns that are too regular to be natural, deliberate cultivation for light without heat visibility without detection from above. Caelus and Selenea converge on the structure from opposite angles, and their approach is silent despite the sucking mud that threatens to claim each footstep. Twenty meters out, Caelus raises a closed fist. The target is inside, and cosmic threads are converging with absolute certainty on the shelter's dark interior.

Selenea responds immediately, signaling a standard containment formation with three quick hand gestures. She draws her weapon, the sleek energy pistol with Zathira markings etched along its barrel. Its power cell pulses with soft blue light as she adjusts the settings, calibrating for non-lethal incapacitation. The barrel extends slightly, compensating for the planet's specific atmospheric density.

They close the distance in measured increments, each movement deliberate, controlled, and invisible to untrained perception. Ten meters from the entrance, Caelus's enhancement bands flare suddenly with increased energy. His head snaps up, eyes widening as the cosmic threads shift in his perception.

"Movement," he mouths silently, the blue glow around his irises intensifying. "Aware."

Selenea immediately switches tactics, abandoning stealth for the direct approach. She signals the flanking pattern they practiced countless times in Zathira's training chambers, and she'll force the target's movement toward Caelus's position, creating a capture lane with minimal escape vectors.

Before they can execute, the shelter's entrance erupts with violent motion. The traitor, a hunched figure with amphibian features exactly matching the briefing hologram, bursts from the doorway with unexpected speed. Translucent skin catches the bioluminescent light, and internal organs are briefly visible as dark shadows beneath the surface. The Vescidian's massive eyes swivel independently, one fixed forward, one cataloging potential escape routes.

Selenea reacts instantly, finger squeezing the trigger with precise pressure. The energy pistol discharges a stun pulse, not a projectile but a controlled burst of neurological disruptors calibrated for Vescidian physiology. The blue-white energy cuts through the fog, illuminating droplets of moisture in its path.

The traitor drops flat against the swamp's surface with surprising grace, the stunning pulse passing harmlessly overhead. Webbed hands slap against the water, creating propulsion that sends the Vescidian skimming across the surface with the efficiency of evolution perfectly adapted to this environment.

"North quadrant," Caelus calls out, already in motion, enhancement bands leaving trails of blue light as his hands cut through the air. The Aetheris connection allows him to track the target's movement with perfect accuracy despite the visual interference of fog and vegetation. "Heading for the deep channel!"

Selenea breaks right, circling wide to cut off the most likely escape route. Her battalion training manifests in the perfect economy of movement, with no wasted energy and no unnecessary steps. She vaults over a fallen log, boots barely touching its surface before she moves again, compensating for the uneven terrain without conscious thought.

The chase intensifies as they penetrate deeper into the swamp. Hanging vines descend from the canopy, some benign, others armed with barbed stingers that track motion. The traitor navigates through them with practiced familiarity, following paths too complex to be improvised. Selenea ducks beneath a particularly vicious specimen, its stinger missing her filtration mask by millimeters.

"Sinkhole pattern ahead," Caelus warns through their communications link, his voice tight with the effort of maintaining Aetheris tracking while running. "Five-meter radius, concentric trigger points."

Selenea processes this information without breaking stride. She modifies her pursuit angle, using a series of protruding roots as stepping stones to bypass the danger zone. The traitor glances back, massive eyes registering surprise at her continued proximity despite the environmental hazards.

The Vescidian reaches into a pouch strapped across its chest, withdrawing a small device that pulses with red light. One webbed finger activates a sequence, and immediately, their communication bands emit a high-pitched squeal before falling silent.

"Communication disruption," Selenea announces unnecessarily, projecting her voice to bridge the growing distance between her and Caelus. "Standard Vescidian counter-intelligence device."

She'd anticipated this, but battalion training emphasizes preparation for technology failures. From her belt, she unfastens a specialized net launcher, its compact form expanding in her hands as internal mechanisms activate. The weapon hums softly as it charges, mesh fibers glowing with contained energy.

Ahead, the traitor plunges into a section of dense reeds, momentarily disappearing from visual contact. Selenea slows, scanning for disturbance patterns rather than chasing blindly. The vegetation moves artificially at three points, one directly ahead and two to either side. A diversion technique, creating multiple potential targets.

She fires the net toward the leftmost movement, not where the traitor appears to be but where the cosmic threads indicate actual presence. Caelus's training has taught her to recognize the subtle signs of genuine versus false tracking signals. The net expands in flight, energy-infused fibers spreading to create a three-meter capture zone.

A strangled croak confirms her accuracy as the net entangles the Vescidian, specialized fibers contracting around the struggling form. The traitor thrashes in waist-deep water, webbed hands clawing at the constricting mesh. Bioluminescent patterns flash across its skin, distress signals with no receivers in this isolated location.

Caelus circles to block the remaining escape vector, his Aetheris perception confirming the target's continued containment despite the visual obstruction of reeds and murky water. "Data crystals still present," he calls out, the blue glow in his eyes pulsing with certainty. "Left thoracic pouch."

Selenea wades into the chest-deep water, approaching the struggling captive with calculated caution. The Vescidian's movements become more frantic as she nears, powerful legs kicking beneath the water's surface, trying to destabilize her approach. One such kick connects with her thigh, not painful through the environmental suit but forceful enough to unbalance her momentarily.

She recovers instantly, with battalion training converting a stumble into strategic repositioning. The traitor's webbed hands break partially free from the net, clawing toward Caelus as he maintains a position on the opposite side. Three-fingered hands with surprising strength grasp at his arms, trying to disrupt his Aetheris connection.

"Pressure points ineffective on Vescidian physiology," Selenea reminds him, circling to flank the increasingly desperate captive. "Central nerve cluster at the dorsal junction."

Caelus nods, maintaining his position despite the traitor's attempts to break his focus. The siblings execute a coordinated containment maneuver, Caelus deliberately drawing the Vescidian's attention while Selenea approaches from behind, moving through the water with minimal disruption.

The traitor's head swivels too late, one massive, eye-catching movement just as she delivers the precise strike, two fingers extended, applied with exact pressure to the junction where the spine meets the skull. The blow requires neither excessive force nor cruelty, just anatomical knowledge and perfect execution.

The Vescidian goes rigid, a final croak escaping its wide mouth before its systems shut down temporarily. Not unconsciousness exactly, but a state of neurological reset common to amphibian species, a survival mechanism coopted for tactical advantage.

"Central nervous system suppressed," Selenea confirms, maintaining pressure on the precise point while Caelus moves to secure the limbs more thoroughly. "Approximately twenty minutes until reactivation."

Water drips from her uniform as she reaches into the thoracic pouch, as indicated by Caelus's tracking. Her fingers close around several small crystalline objects, data storage devices containing the stolen Fractal information. She extracts them carefully, confirming their intact status before securing them in a specialized containment unit on her belt.

The Vescidian floats motionless in the murky water, restrained by the energy net and the siblings' efficient teamwork. Its translucent skin has faded to a pale gray, a biological response to defeat that manifests in most amphibian species from the Vescit system.

"Target secured," Selenea states, professional satisfaction evident in her tone despite her otherwise neutral expression. "Mission parameters achieved."

The specialized restraints close around the Vescidian's limbs with soft clicking sounds, material that resembles liquid metal flowing into position before hardening into unbreakable bonds. Caelus adjusts the final setting, the metal bands around his fingers leaving faint blue traces in the murky air as he works. Across from him, Selenea completes her security check, methodically ensuring their captive cannot access hidden weapons or devices during transport. The Vescidian's unconscious form hangs between them like a physical manifestation of their success, first mission, first capture, first proof that their complementary abilities function as effectively in field operations as in training simulations.

"Neural inhibitor secured," Selenea confirms, attaching a small device to the base of the traitor's skull where amphibian awareness centers cluster. The device pulses once with soft light, synchronizing with the captive's unique biological rhythms. "Consciousness will be maintained at thirty percent capacity during transport. Sufficient for basic functions, inadequate for resistance."

The swamp continues its constant symphony around them, liquid dripping from vegetation, gases bubbling through murky water, and distant creatures calling to each other in languages composed of croaks and whistles. The fog has thinned slightly with the approach of evening, revealing more of the twisted landscape that stretches in all directions.

Caelus reaches into the various pouches they discovered hidden throughout the crude shelter, retrieving several additional data crystals. Unlike the primary devices found in the thoracic pouch, these smaller crystals appear to contain personal logs and technical specifications for the traitor's escape plan.

He examines each crystal closely, and his Aetheris perception allows him to sense the information density without accessing the actual content. "Complete set," he confirms, securing them in a specialized containment case. "Primary security protocols and access codes intact. No evidence of transmission to secondary parties."

The data crystals pulse with faint internal light as he handles them, responding to the energy from his enhancement bands. Each crystal contains thousands of coordinates, access sequences, and stabilization frequencies, information that would allow unauthorized users to breach Zathira's security or destabilize established Fractal pathways between systems.

Selenea checks her chronometer, noting their elapsed time on Pogwam. "One hour forty-seven minutes since insertion. Well within operational parameters." Her gaze sweeps the surrounding terrain, and tactical assessment is ongoing despite their successful capture. "Extraction preparations initiated."

Together, they secure the prisoner to a collapsible transport frame, the lightweight yet incredibly strong material extending from a compact unit on Selenea's belt. The Vescidian's amphibian form settles into the contoured surface, and restraints automatically adjust to maintain security while preventing unnecessary discomfort.

With the practical aspects of their mission complete, a moment of quiet triumph passes between the siblings. No words are necessary, just the shared recognition of the perfect coordination of Selenea's plans and Caelus's perception, creating an operational efficacy that exceeded even Orpheus's expectations.

The swamp water laps gently against their boots, its surface reflecting the gradually changing light as Pogwam's distant sun begins its descent toward the horizon. Soon, the bioluminescent predators will emerge, drawn by the planet's natural nocturnal cycle and the biochemical signals released by its native flora.

"Your Battalion training paid off," Caelus acknowledges, breaking the comfortable silence. He gestures toward the specialized net launcher still attached to Selenea's belt. "That capture technique wasn't in the Zathira protocols."

Selenea's lips curve into a slight smile, the expression small but genuine. "First Battalion specialized in adaptation. Standard equipment, non-standard applications." She secures the final transport lock, testing its integrity with one quick tug. "And your Aetheris is more precise than ever. The tracking through those reed beds was remarkable."

Caelus nods, the blue glow finally fading completely from his eyes as he powers down his enhancement bands. "The cosmic threads were unusually clear here. Something about Pogwam's positioning relative to the galactic core. The planet itself acts as a natural amplifier."

Around them, the swamp begins its transition to night. The ambient light shifts from murky green to deeper blue as bioluminescent organisms activate in sequence, like stars appearing one by one in an evening sky. The water's surface comes alive with pinpricks of light, microscopic creatures rising from the depths, creating patterns that mirror constellations overhead.

More ominous, larger patches of light begin to move beneath the water, predators awakening, drawn to the surface by the changing biochemistry of their environment. A ripple passes within meters of their position, disturbing the otherwise perfect reflection of emerging bioluminescence.

"Extraction window optimal," Selenea notes, observing the increasing predator activity with professional detachment. She activates her communication band, which emits a particular frequency, not sound but energy that travels along pathways invisible to conventional detection methods. The signal will reach Zathira instantly, regardless of physical distance, following the same cosmic threads that Caelus perceives through his Aetheris.

They position themselves on relatively stable ground, and the Vescidian is secured between them on the transport frame. The data crystals pulse softly in their containment case, synchronized with the extraction signal. All standard procedures are executed with precision and are born of rigorous training.

"This is just the beginning, isn't it?" Selenea asks, her tone suggesting she already knows the answer. Her amber eyes reflect the increasing bioluminescence around them, creating the impression of internal light matching the external environment.

Before Caelus can respond, space folds inward several meters ahead of their position. The air thickens and becomes almost viscous as reality bends according to precise mathematical principles. Fractal tears open before them, their crystalline pattern rotating slowly, each segment containing perfect replicas of the whole that somehow exist simultaneously at different scales.

Through the opening, the familiar interior of Zathira's extraction chamber becomes visible, with stone walls lined with monitoring equipment and personnel standing ready to receive both prisoners and data. The contrast between the swamp's organic chaos and the monastery's ordered precision couldn't be more profound.

"The Valthorim's work spans galaxies," Caelus confirms, answering his sister's question as they prepare to step through. "Maintaining balance requires constant vigilance. New threats emerge. Old dangers resurface." He adjusts his grip on the transport frame, ensuring the prisoner remains secure during the transition. "Together, we can help maintain the balance."

The Fractal pulses once in recognition of their approach, widening slightly to accommodate their passage with the prisoner. Around them, Pogwam's nocturnal cycle accelerates, more predators surface and their bioluminescent patterns grow brighter, more complex, and more threatening.

Selenea steps forward first, guiding their captive toward the extraction point with practiced efficiency. "Together," she echoes, the simple word carrying layers of meaning, acknowledgment of their complementary skills, recognition of shared purpose, and acceptance of the cosmic responsibility they now both shoulder.

They step through the Fractal together, leaving behind Pogwam's dangerous beauty for the ordered precision of Zathira. The transition feels less disorienting than their departure, with Caelus's Aetheris and Selenea's tactical awareness combining to create a smoother passage through the tear in reality.

As the Fractal closes behind them, sealing with that familiar soft implosion of air, brother and sister exchange a glance that requires no words. Their first joint mission is complete, and countless more are awaiting. Two aspects of a single purpose, maintaining balance across the stars.

Chapter 6

Shadows of Doubt

The staircase spirals downward through solid stone, each step worn smooth by millennia of passage. Orpheus descends with measured grace, his silver-embroidered robes gathering darkness around him like a cloak of captured shadows. The air grows thicker with each step, charged with ancient energies that brush against his mask with curious tendrils. His silver eyes remain fixed forward, unwavering in their purpose despite the weight of the cosmos pressing against his consciousness.

No ordinary Zathira inhabitant knows of this passage. Hidden beneath the monastery's foundations, it exists in a pocket of space-time that folds between dimensions, accessible only to those with the proper sigils etched into their very essence. Orpheus traces a pattern on the wall as he passes, five precise movements that leave momentary trails of silver light hanging in the darkness. The stairway responds to steps rearranging themselves beneath his feet, carrying him deeper than physical architecture should allow.

At the four hundredth step, he has counted each one, as ritual demands, the stairs terminate at a doorway that isn't quite a doorway. More accurately, it's a tear in reality, stabilized and made permanent through methods lost to all but the most ancient Valthorim texts. Orpheus pauses before it, gathering his thoughts like a general arranging troops before battle. The mask covering the upper portion of his face catches what little light exists here, fracturing it into patterns that correspond to specific cosmic alignments.

He steps through.

The chamber unfolds around him like a flower composed of impossibilities. Its dimensions stretch beyond what the space should contain, the vaulted crystalline ceiling arcing so high above that it seems to capture actual stars within its facets. Walls of pure white stone curve inward, every surface covered in sigils that pulse with subtle energy, some carved ten thousand years ago, others far older, their meanings known only to those who saw the universe's birth.

Orpheus moves to the center of the circular floor, his footsteps echoing with perfect acoustic precision. The sound ripples outward, disturbing motes of light that float through the chamber like conscious dust. Above, the crystalline ceiling responds to his presence, internal structures shifting to focus energy downward in a subtle cone of power that bathes him in colorless light.

They are already waiting.

Seven massive entities hover at equidistant points around the chamber's circumference. To call them robed figures would be an inaccurate simplification; the Valthorim exists as much between dimensions as within them, and their physical manifestations are mere suggestions of their true nature. What appears as fabric is actually condensed void, folded and shaped into forms that allow three-dimensional interaction. Within each shadowed hood, silver eyes burn like captured supernovae, unblinking and ancient.

The smallest of them towers three times Orpheus's height, its form rippling with subtle energy that distorts the air around it. The largest extends nearly to the vaulted ceiling, its presence so dense that space curves visibly in its vicinity. They make no sound, no movement, yet the chamber fills with a pressure that would crush ordinary consciousness.

Orpheus stands perfectly centered among them, physically dwarfed yet showing no sign of intimidation. His posture speaks of authority earned through millennia of service, his silver eyes meeting their gaze without flinching. The mask on his face, part of him now, rather than mere adornment, gleams with an internal light that matches the chamber's energy signature.

He begins the ritual, arms extending outward in precise angles that correspond to specific cosmic coordinates. His fingers trace sigils in the air, not random patterns but mathematical equations expressed through movement, each gesture creating ripples in reality that spread outward as stones dropped in still water.

Where his fingers pass, the light follows, silver trails hanging in the air, forming complex geometric structures that rotate slowly, each rotation adding layers of complexity. The sigils build upon each other, creating a three-dimensional matrix of energy that encompasses him completely.

The chamber responds. Ancient markings on the walls flare to life in sequence, creating answering patterns that interlock with Orpheus's sigils. The crystalline ceiling pulses in perfect rhythm, focusing additional energy downward. The floor beneath his feet grows warm, then begins to glow with patterns that mirror the stars in their current configuration throughout the galaxy.

"We acknowledge Orpheus, First Guardian of Zathira, Voice of the Valthorim," the entities intone in unison, their words bypassing air to resonate directly through bone and tissue. The sound feels physical, like pressure against the skin, yet carries perfect clarity.

The ritual nears completion as Orpheus traces the final sigil, a complex symbol that represents his position within the cosmic hierarchy. It hangs before him, spinning slowly, its internal structure continuously reconfiguring itself like a living thing. With a precise gesture, he sends it outward to join with the larger pattern created by the chamber and the seven entities.

Perfect integration. The light flares brilliantly and then stabilizes at a higher frequency. The greeting is complete.

"The universe grows restless," says the entity directly opposite Orpheus. Its voice emerges not from where its mouth would be but from everywhere at once, vibrations that travel through stone and air and flesh simultaneously. "We feel the tremors across dimensions."

Orpheus inclines his head in acknowledgment, the movement slight but precisely calculated. Though surrounded by beings who could erase him with a thought, his composure remains absolute. "The cosmic threads fray at increasing rates," he confirms. "Our monitors register disturbances in seventeen major systems."

The largest entity shifts slightly, its form momentarily losing cohesion before resolidifying. The movement sends a cascade of energy rippling through the chamber. "Disturbances are expected. The universe breathes. It expands and contracts. This is different."

"Directed," adds another, its silver eyes dimming briefly and then flaring brighter. "Purposeful disruption of established patterns."

Orpheus stands motionless, absorbing their concerns while revealing nothing of his own thoughts. The sigils continue to rotate around him, their light casting multiple shadows behind his form, not three, like the moons of Solarune, but seven, one extending toward each entity in perfect alignment.

"The Aetheris practitioner and his sister have proven effective," he says, each word measured and precise. "They secure stability in the regions where they operate."

"Two beings cannot maintain the entire cosmic web," the central entity responds, its immense form bending forward slightly to focus its silver gaze more directly on Orpheus. The movement causes the crystalline ceiling to shift in response, realigning its facets to accommodate the change in energy flow.

Orpheus meets the entity's gaze without hesitation. The chamber hums with building power as the discussion intensifies, ancient energies responding to emotional currents that flow beneath the formal exchange. Despite being dwarfed by the towering beings around him, Orpheus shows no sign of subservience; his position is not one of physical dominance but of functional necessity.

"No," he agrees, "they cannot. Which is why I have requested this council."

The entities grow completely still, a stillness beyond normal physical capability, not just the absence of movement but the absence of probability, as if they temporarily step outside the normal flow of cause and effect.

"Speak your purpose," they command in unison, the chamber vibrating with the power of their combined voice.

Orpheus's silver eyes gleam with calculated intensity, revealing nothing of his inner thoughts. The trap is baited, and the hook is set. Now comes the careful drawing of the line.

Orpheus stands at the center of power, his proposal hanging in the air like a challenge to cosmic law. The holographic data emanates from his outstretched palm, galaxy clusters rotating in miniature, trouble spots pulsing with angry red light. The seven entities tower above him, their massive forms shifting like smoke caught in conflicting currents, silver eyes narrowing as they absorb his request. Their disapproval manifests physically; the chamber's temperature drops several degrees, and crystal facets on the ceiling contract with sounds like distant ice breaking.

"An expansion of the Fractal network," he states, voice carrying perfect clarity despite its measured softness. "Targeted deployment in seventeen key sectors where disturbances have increased beyond containment thresholds."

His fingers trace precise patterns through the holographic display, highlighting specific regions where the red pulses intensify. "The data speaks plainly. Conventional response times are no longer sufficient. Our battalions require faster deployment to maintain equilibrium."

The hologram expands, showing a time-lapse progression of disturbances spreading like an infection through neighboring systems. Stars flare, and dim in irregular patterns, planetary orbits show subtle deviations and cosmic threads stretch and strain under unnatural pressures.

"Expansion was limited for reasons beyond your comprehension," rumbles the entity to Orpheus's left, its voice causing dust motes to vibrate in geometric patterns. Its massive form contracts slightly, hood tilting downward to focus more directly on the comparatively tiny figure before it. "The pathways were limited by necessity, not oversight."

Another entity shifts forward, its motion sending ripples through space that distort the holographic display momentarily. "Too many tears weaken the fabric," it adds, silver eyes pulsing with internal light that suggests barely contained power. "Each Fractal creates stress points that never fully heal."

The chamber's subtle background hum intensifies as the entities' disapproval grows stronger. The ancient sigils carved into the walls pulse in response, some dimming while others grow brighter, creating complex patterns that reflect the emotional currents flowing through the council.

Orpheus allows the objections to settle into the chamber's acoustics before responding. His posture remains perfect; his spine is straight, his shoulders level and his hands are now clasped before him in a gesture that suggests respect without submission. The mask covering the upper portion of his face catches light from the hologram, casting mathematical patterns across its surface.

"With respect," he begins, each word precisely chosen, "the limitations were established when the universe existed in greater harmony. Our mandate to maintain balance remains unchanged, but the methods must evolve as threats evolve."

He gestures again, causing the holographic display to shift focus. Now, it shows populated systems, worlds teeming with life, and civilizations at various stages of development. Within these systems, red disturbance patterns pulse with increasing frequency.

"Seventeen billion sentient lives exist within the affected regions," Orpheus continues, voice remaining calm despite the weight of his words. "Without faster response capabilities, our calculations predict thirty-seven percent casualties before conventional methods can restore stability."

The largest entity moves suddenly, its massive form seeming to fold inward upon itself before expanding again, a gesture equivalent to indignation in beings that exist partially beyond physical dimensions. "You request permission to create permanent tears in reality to save temporary lives," it states, its voice causing the floor beneath Orpheus to vibrate. "The cosmic balance considers longer timescales than mere civilizations."

Orpheus inclines his head slightly, acknowledging the rebuke without accepting its premise. "The cosmic balance is maintained through countless small adjustments, not occasional large corrections," he counters. "When disruption exceeds a critical threshold, recovery becomes exponentially more difficult."

He dismisses the population display with a subtle gesture, replacing it with technical schematics that rotate slowly in the air between him and the entities. These diagrams show Fractal structures in microscopic detail, the precise mathematical patterns that allow controlled tears in space-time, the stabilization frequencies that prevent collapse, and the energy requirements for sustained operation.

"The proposed expansion includes enhanced stabilization protocols," he explains, highlighting specific sections of the schematic. "Each new Fractal would incorporate multiple redundancy systems and automatic sealing mechanisms if stress patterns exceed safety parameters."

The chamber's temperature continues to fluctuate as the entities consider his arguments. The crystalline ceiling contracts and expands in irregular patterns, focusing energy downward in concentrated beams that create pools of intense light across the circular floor. The ancient sigils on the walls pulse more rapidly now, their rhythm matching the increasing tension of the debate.

Three of the entities withdraw slightly, their massive forms drifting backward until they nearly merge with the chamber walls. Their silver eyes dim momentarily as they initiate silent communication among themselves, not verbal exchange but direct consciousness transfer, bypassing the limitations of sequential thought.

Orpheus stands perfectly still during this deliberation, his face a mask of patience while his eyes calculate every reaction. Behind the ornate mask, his mind catalogs every fluctuation in the chamber's energy, every subtle shift in the entities' positions. He has anticipated this resistance, planned for it, and determined optimal responses for seventeen different objection scenarios.

The silent communication continues for what might be seconds or hours; time flows differently in this chamber, compressed or expanded according to the entities' combined will. Throughout this period, Orpheus maintains his perfect stillness, becoming almost statuesque in his controlled patience. Only his eyes move, tracking the subtle energy transfers between the deliberating entities.

Finally, the three entities return their full attention to the center of the chamber. Their massive forms resize slightly, adjusting to new energy configurations resulting from their exchange. The central entity leans forward, causing the crystal ceiling to realign its facets directly above Orpheus.

"Peace requires order," it acknowledges, its voice softer now but still resonating through bone rather than air. "But order without flexibility becomes stagnation, then decay."

"We have witnessed the decay of rigid systems," Orpheus agrees, carefully building upon this concession. "The current disturbances represent exactly this risk, forces that resist adaptation, that seek to impose singular patterns upon cosmic plurality."

The subtle humming of the chamber intensifies further as the debate reaches its critical point. Energy currents flow visibly through the air now, creating aurora-like patterns that spiral upward toward the crystalline ceiling. The ancient sigils on the walls pulse in complex sequences, some illuminating for the first time in thousands of years.

One entity remains particularly resistant, its massive form contracting into a denser configuration that bends light around its edges. "Creating more pathways invites more travelers," it warns, silver eyes narrowing to thin crescents of light. "Some doors should remain closed."

"Yet we must travel to maintain the barriers," Orpheus counters smoothly. "Our battalions cannot defend what they cannot reach. The universe's size becomes our greatest weakness if we cannot traverse it efficiently."

He dismisses the technical schematics, returning to the original display of troubled systems. The red disturbance patterns have spread further during their debate, now affecting previously stable regions. The progression follows exactly the pattern his models predicted, not by coincidence, though nothing in his expression betrays this knowledge.

"Time favors entropy," he reminds them. "Each moment of deliberation allows the disturbances to strengthen their position. Our intervention becomes more difficult, more disruptive with each delay."

The entities shift their massive forms, creating a loose circle formation that allows them to observe both Orpheus and each other simultaneously. Their silver eyes dim and brighten in patterns too complex for non-Valthorim minds to interpret, a final exchange of perspectives before reaching a consensus.

Throughout this process, Orpheus maintains his perfect composure. The proposal has been made, and the arguments presented. Now comes the most delicate phase, allowing the entities to believe the decision is entirely their own and that their role is merely advisory rather than directive. His face reveals nothing of his certainty regarding the outcome, no hint of the careful psychological manipulation embedded within his seemingly logical presentation.

The chamber's humming reaches its peak intensity, ancient energies flowing in visible currents around the circular space. The crystalline ceiling refracts this energy into precise patterns that correspond to specific cosmic alignments, the same alignments that Orpheus calculated would occur during this exact moment of decision.

Perfect timing. Perfect pressure. The perfect illusion of choice.

The entities complete their silent deliberation, their massive forms resettling into their original positions around the chamber's circumference. The humming subsides slightly, though tension remains in the charged air between them.

"We have concerns," the central entity acknowledges, leaning closer to Orpheus. "But the patterns of disturbance match historical precedents that cannot be ignored."

Orpheus bows his head slightly, the picture of a leader respecting the wisdom of ancient advisors. Inside, he feels a warmth in his chest, a spreading heat that he recognizes as triumph carefully disguised as deference.

"We consent," the central entity announces, its voice vibrating through the chamber like a physical force that stirs the ancient dust. The words hang in the air, visible as ripples of energy that spread outward in concentric circles. The entity rises higher, its massive form expanding to brush against the crystalline ceiling. "But with caution. The balance remains paramount." Orpheus bows his head in acknowledgment, the gesture humble while his silver eyes calculate victory. Inside his chest, satisfaction burns cold and precise.

The seven entities move with sudden unanimity, their massive forms gliding across the chamber floor without disturbing the air. They arrange themselves in a perfect circle around Orpheus, creating a living barrier of shadow and power. Where before they hovered at the chamber's periphery, now they crowd close, their presence pressing against his consciousness with the weight of compressed centuries.

The smallest towers three times his height, its hood tilted downward to fix silver eyes directly upon him. The largest extends nearly to the vaulted ceiling, shadow-substance flowing around its form like liquid darkness. Together, they create a perfect geometric pattern, each positioned at precise angles that correspond to specific cosmic constants.

"Approach the center, Voice of Valthorim," they intone in unison, the words bypassing air to resonate directly through tissue and bone.

Orpheus steps forward, positioning himself at the exact center of their circle. His silver-embroidered robes catch the light from the crystalline ceiling, reflecting it in patterns too complex for coincidence, each thread placed with deliberate purpose to form sigils visible only during specific ritual alignments.

The entities extend limbs toward him, not arms in any conventional sense, but extensions of their shadow-substance that reach across the intervening space like living darkness given purpose. These projections stop just short of touching Orpheus, creating a secondary circle that hovers around him at precisely calculated distances.

"The pathways will open," declares the central entity, its voice deeper now, reverberating through the chamber's foundations. "The fabric will stretch but must not tear beyond repair."

Beneath Orpheus's feet, the chamber floor comes alive with sudden illumination. Ancient sigils activate in sequence, geometric patterns expanding outward from his position in perfect mathematical progression. Each sigil represents a specific Fractal configuration, the exact coordinates where space-time will be folded, the stabilization frequencies required to maintain the openings, and the energy parameters that prevent collapse.

The patterns grow more complex as they spread, creating nested mandalas of light that overlap and interact according to principles beyond ordinary comprehension. Some sigils have remained dormant for millennia, their activation setting off chain reactions throughout the chamber's integrated systems.

Above, the crystalline ceiling responds immediately. Its faceted surface shifts and realigns, internal structures reconfiguring to focus energy downward in precise columns of colorless light. Each beam targets a specific sigil pattern on the floor, creating vertical energy conduits that connect ceiling to floor with Orpheus at their center.

"The balance must be maintained," the entities intone, their voices perfectly synchronized into a single harmonic frequency. The sound penetrates deeper than hearing, vibrating against the fundamental particles that comprise physical existence.

Orpheus stands motionless within this convergence of energies, his body a conduit between forces powerful enough to reshape reality. The mask covering the upper portion of his face absorbs energy from the surrounding ritual, its surface shifting with patterns that mirror the activated sigils beneath his feet.

The chamber trembles as power builds beyond containment thresholds. The walls, carved with ancient markings, begin to pulse with internal light that follows the spreading patterns across the floor. The air itself becomes charged, molecules vibrating at accelerated rates that create visible distortions around the assembled figures.

Beyond the chamber, beyond Zathira itself, the effects manifest across vast distances. Throughout the seventeen targeted systems, space-time responds to the ritual's directed energy. The fabric of reality stretches thin at precisely calculated coordinates, molecular bonds weakening as cosmic forces redirect to create controlled openings.

Inside the chamber, Orpheus perceives these distant changes through the sigil patterns beneath his feet. Each activated sigil represents a specific location where new Fractals now open, permanent tears in reality that allow instant travel across otherwise insurmountable distances. The pattern's complexity ensures perfect stability and perfect control.

"We witness the creation," the entities continue, their unified voice rising in volume and intensity. "We authorize the pathways. We demand their proper use."

The shadow-substance extensions from the entities' forms begin to rotate around Orpheus, creating a secondary barrier that spins with increasing speed. This movement generates its own energy signature, a counter-frequency that stabilizes the ritual's growing power, preventing uncontrolled manifestations beyond the targeted systems.

Orpheus raises his hands, fingers splayed in precise configuration. This motion represents his formal acceptance of the entities' authorization and, more importantly, his assumption of operational control over the newly created Fractal network. Power flows through his body, causing the sigils tattooed beneath his robes to warm against his skin.

"I accept the responsibility," he states, his voice carrying unexpected weight despite its measured tone. "The pathways will serve balance. Order will be maintained."

His fingers begin tracing complex patterns in the air before him, not random movements but precise mathematical equations expressed through motion. Each gesture creates momentary after-images that hang in the charged atmosphere, silver trails that form additional sigils suspended between floor and ceiling.

The entities recognize the signature ritual, the final stage that seals their decision and implements the authorized changes throughout the universe. Their massive forms grow perfectly still, silver eyes fixed on Orpheus's movements with intense focus.

As his hands complete the final sequence, energy surges through the chamber with unprecedented intensity. The floor sigils flare blindingly bright, their patterns extending upward to merge with the ceiling's focused beams. The walls nearly disappear behind curtains of activated sigils, ancient power awakening after eons of dormancy.

Space itself shudders within the chamber and across distant galaxies. New Fractals snap into existence simultaneously throughout the seventeen targeted systems, crystalline-like patterns that fold inward infinitely, each segment containing perfect replicas of the whole. These controlled tears, in reality, shimmer with internal energy, creating pathways that bypass conventional space-time limitations.

The signature ritual concludes with a single unified gesture, Orpheus bringing his hands together in perfect alignment before his chest, fingers intertwined in a configuration that mirrors the largest floor sigil. The contact creates a momentary spark that jumps between his palms, not electricity but condensed potential, the final activation key that stabilizes the entire network.

"It is done," he announces simply.

The surge of power recedes gradually, energy levels dropping from critical intensity to sustainable operational parameters. The floor sigils dim but don't deactivate completely, now pulsing with the steady rhythm of established connections. The crystalline ceiling realigns its facets to maintain these connections while distributing energy more evenly throughout the chamber.

The entities begin to withdraw, and their purpose is fulfilled for this convocation. Their massive forms lose definition around the edges, shadow-substance thinning until light passes partially through their outlines. Like mist dispersing before the morning sun, they fade from the chamber, not departing through conventional means but simply ceasing to manifest in this particular slice of reality.

"The balance must be maintained," echoes their final unified statement, words hanging in the air long after their physical presence has dissolved.

Orpheus remains alone in the chamber, surrounded by the flickering light of activated sigils and the subtle hum of newly established Fractal connections. His posture, so rigidly controlled throughout the ritual, relaxes by imperceptible degrees. The mask covering the upper portion of his face no longer shifts with reflected patterns, settling into its standard configuration.

For the first time since entering the chamber, a slight smile forms on his lips, not the deferential expression shown to the entities but something colder, more calculated. The smile of a strategist whose pieces have moved precisely as planned across a board only he can fully see.

He turns slowly, surveying the chamber with silver eyes that now hold a different quality, not the respectful attention shown during the council but something sharper, more purposeful. The activated sigils cast shifting shadows across his features as he contemplates his victory.

The entities have granted him exactly what he requested: expanded Fractal networks, faster deployment capabilities, and increased operational control. All are presented as necessities for maintaining cosmic balance and responding to growing disturbances across the universe. All logical, all justified.

All were serving additional purposes they could not suspect.

Orpheus moves toward the chamber's exit, his silver-embroidered robes flowing around him with renewed energy. Each step leaves momentary after-images in the charged atmosphere, not mere visual distortions but brief glimpses of potential futures spreading outward from this pivotal moment.

The chamber seals itself behind him as he departs, ancient systems returning to dormancy until the next convocation. But the Fractals remain open, the connections established, and the network expanded exactly as he designed.

His face returns to its customary composed mask before he reaches the stairway, all traces of satisfaction hidden beneath perfect control. Yet inside his chest, purpose burns with cold precision, a heat he channels not toward guilt but toward the next phase of his carefully orchestrated design.

Chapter 7

The Nammu Massacre

The Fractal tears open in the darkness of space near Nammu, its crystalline edges pulsing with soft blue-violet light. It exists there suspended between stars, a perfect mathematical impossibility folding inward upon itself infinitely. The tear stretches wider, responding to the passage of those crossing from Zathira, its pattern rotating with precise geometric certainty. Where there were empty voids moments before, the reality now parts like curtains to reveal its hidden pathways.

Selenea emerges first, her body reassembling molecule by molecule as the Fractal deposits her into real space. The transition feels smoother than usual, which is evidence of the newly expanded network Orpheus had implemented. Her squad follows in perfect formation behind her, thirty-six soldiers materializing in staggered rows, each bearing the streamlined armor and insignia of the First Battalion. The Fractal seals itself with a soft implosion of air once the final soldier steps through, leaving only a faint shimmer that fades like disturbed water, returning to stillness.

They land not on Nammu's cratered surface but within its hollow core. The asteroid's caverns stretch before them in sweeping arches and winding tunnels, every surface carpeted with luminescent fungi in shades of blue and green. The organisms pulse with a subtle rhythm as if breathing in concert with the massive asteroid itself. Their glow throws the soldiers' shadows against the curved walls in elongated silhouettes that shift with each movement.

"Secure the perimeter," Selenea orders, her voice clear and commanding despite the subtle disquiet beginning to form in her chest. Something feels wrong about this mission. The briefing had been unusually vague, a threat to universal stability requiring immediate neutralization. Standard protocol for extreme situations.

Her squad moves with practiced efficiency, booted feet disturbing delicate fungal spores that rise into the air like luminous dust, swirling in their wake. The air carries a sweet, earthy scent, nothing like the sterile, recycled atmosphere of Zathira. Beneath their movements runs the constant, soothing rumble of underground water flowing through the asteroid's porous core, carving new passages through ancient stone.

"Environmental analysis complete, Lieutenant," reports her second-in-command, consulting a handheld scanner. "Atmosphere composition within acceptable parameters. No immediate biological threats were detected. Gravity at point-seven-three standard."

Selenea nods, amber eyes scanning the cavern with tactical precision. The fungi-light reveals natural walkways curving deeper into the asteroid, leading toward what appears to be a larger central chamber. Her sigils warm slightly beneath her uniform, not the fiery heat of active combat but a subtle response to the unfamiliar environment.

The battalion technicians assemble portable lighting units that flood the immediate area with harsh white illumination, destroying the natural ambiance of the cavern. Equipment cases snap open as soldiers check weapons, sleek energy rifles with multiple settings, precision calibrated for different physiological targets. Their movements are synchronized and economical, the result of countless drills and live operations.

Selenea walks a short distance from the main group, drawn to a formation where the bioluminescent fungi grow in a pattern too regular for coincidence. She kneels, examining the arrangement without touching it. The fungi here have been cultivated and encouraged to grow in specific directions. Not random natural growth but evidence of intelligent tending.

"Lieutenant Solaris," her comm unit crackles to life, the signal unusually clear across what should be a vast interstellar distance. She realizes the newly expanded Fractal network. Another boon of efficiency.

"Receiving," she responds, straightening to her full height.

"Your battalion has arrived at the target coordinates." Orpheus's voice flows through the comm with that distinctive quality, simultaneously charismatic and cold, resonant with harmonics that no human vocal cords should produce. "Preliminary scans confirm the intelligence assessment."

Selenea frowns slightly. "Sir, we've only just begun environmental analysis. The asteroid appears to be"

"The Nammu tribes represent a threat to universal stability," Orpheus interrupts, his tone shifting to something harder, more definitive. "Their biological adaptations and technological development patterns indicate divergence from acceptable cosmic parameters."

Selenea's hand tightens around her comm unit. "Divergence" is a technical term in Valthorim protocols but is typically applied to rogue AI systems or unstable dimensional experiments. Never to developing civilizations.

"First Battalion, your orders are simple," Orpheus continues, his voice broadcasting now to all squad commanders simultaneously. "Complete elimination is required."

Selenea's jaw clenches tight enough to send pain shooting through her temples. Her fingers flex involuntarily around her weapon, the smooth metal suddenly feeling foreign against her skin. Her eyes widened, and pupils contracted to pinpoints despite the dim ambient light. The words reverberate in her mind: complete elimination. Not containment, assessment, and even the standard forced relocation protocols are used for civilizations developing along concerning paths.

Elimination. Of an entire people.

"Sir," she begins, fighting to keep her voice steady, "requesting clarification on threat assessment parameters. Our initial scans show no weapon signatures or"

"The threat is existential, not tactical," Orpheus cuts her off again. "The Valthorim Council has determined that the Nammu developmental trajectory creates unacceptable probability curves for future cosmic stability. Implementation of Secundus Protocol is authorized."

Secundus Protocol. The words land like stones in Selenea's stomach. Authorization for complete removal of a civilization from the universal equation. She's trained for this and studied the theoretical frameworks but never expected to execute such orders.

"Confirmation code required," she responds automatically, military training asserting itself despite her internal turmoil.

"Valthorim sequence seven-three-nine-epsilon-omicron," Orpheus provides without hesitation. "Mission parameters uploaded to your tactical systems. Orbital observation confirms three primary settlement clusters within the asteroid's internal structure. Your battalion will divide accordingly."

The communication ends with clinical abruptness, leaving Selenea staring at the cultivated fungi pattern with a new understanding. This is not just evidence of habitation but of culture, of beings who create beauty from their surroundings and of shaping their environment with purpose and, perhaps, joy.

Around her, the battalion continues its preparations with mechanical precision. Squad leaders check formations; technicians calibrate targeting systems for optimal effectiveness in the cavern environment. Weapon power cells hum as they charge to full capacity, the sound cutting through the natural rumble of flowing water.

"Lieutenant," her second-in-command approaches, datapad in hand, "assault formation diagrams ready for your approval."

Selenea turns, expression carefully neutral despite the storm building behind her eyes. Her hand trembles slightly as she takes the offered datapad, a minute movement, nearly imperceptible, but a betrayal of the conflict raging within. On the screen, neat lines and arrows indicate battalion movement through the caverns, converging on three locations marked in pulsing red.

"Five minutes to advance positions," she acknowledges, her voice hollow to her own ears.

The Valthorim insignia gleams on each soldier's shoulder plate, catching the blue-green light of the fungi and the harsh white of the portable illuminators. The symbol that once represented balance and cosmic order now seems to transform before Selenea's eyes, its elegant patterns rearranging into something colder, more absolute.

Her boots disturb more fungal spores as she moves back toward the main group, sending them swirling through the air like tiny, luminous galaxies. The beauty of their dance stands in stark contrast to the purpose that brought them here: the orders waiting to be executed.

Selenea feels a warmth in her chest, an uncomfortable heat that she recognizes as the first flames of rebellion igniting against years of discipline and trust. The battalion forms up into advanced positions around her, weapons ready, awaiting only her command to begin their systematic progress deeper into Nammu's glowing heart.

Selenea selects her team with careful precision, her eyes scanning the assembled battalion for the right faces. "Advance reconnaissance," she announces, voice steady despite the tremor in her hands. "Ankaa, Icarus, you're with me." She chooses them deliberately, Ankaa with her anthropological background, Icarus with his adaptive thinking. Not coincidentally, they're also the two squadron members whose eyes had flickered with the same doubt she felt when Orpheus's orders came through.

"Standard scout pattern," she continues, loud enough for the battalion commander to hear. "We'll mark optimal approach vectors and identify primary targets." The words taste bitter on her tongue, each syllable a small betrayal of her growing certainty that something is fundamentally wrong with this mission.

They detach from the main force, moving deeper into the network of tunnels that wind through Nammu's core. The bioluminescent fungi grow thicker here, their patterns more clearly cultivated, confirming Selenea's suspicions. The natural light wells, spots where the asteroid's porous surface allows starlight to filter through, create columns of silver that intersect with the blue-green glow of the fungi.

"Lieutenant," Ankaa says quietly after they've put sufficient distance between themselves and the battalion, "these growth patterns show a sophisticated understanding of both aesthetics and ecology. The Nammu must maintain a complex cultural relationship with their environment."

Selenea nods, amber eyes scanning the cavern walls where the fungi form spiraling mandalas and flowing wave patterns. "These aren't random decorations. They're language, or history, or both."

Icarus runs his hand just above a particularly intricate pattern, careful not to disturb it. "They're also practical. The specific arrangement maximizes light output while minimizing nutritional requirements." His usual boundless energy seems subdued, contained behind a mask of professional assessment.

They follow a widening tunnel where the ceiling rises high enough to disappear into darkness. The constant rumble of underground water grows louder, punctuated by occasional musical notes, the sound of liquid striking formations of crystal embedded in the stone walls. The path slopes gently downward, following the natural contours of the asteroid's internal structure.

The tunnel opens abruptly into a vast central cavern, and the three of them freeze at its edge, momentarily stunned by what lies before them.

A Nammu settlement sprawls across the cavern floor, built into and around natural rock formations with such organic integration that architecture and geology become indistinguishable. Homes carved from the stone rise in terraced levels, each entrance framed by cultivated fungi that pulse with light in distinct patterns, not just illumination but identity markers, Selenea realizes. Family signifiers.

Water flows through the center of the settlement in channels lined with bioluminescent stones, dividing into smaller streams that service each dwelling. Above, massive crystal formations hang from the cavern ceiling, catching and amplifying both the fungi-light and the starlight from natural shafts, creating a gentle illumination that ebbs and flows like breathing.

The Nammu themselves move through this marvel of adaptation with unhurried purpose. Their forms are humanoid but clearly evolved for their environment, with skin that holds a slight translucence, eyes larger than human standard to capture maximum light, and fingers with extra joints for precision work in close quarters. They wear simple garments adorned with patterns that echo the fungi-light around them.

Children play near the central water channel, sending small crafts made of polished stone floating downstream, their laughter carrying a musical quality that harmonizes with the water's flow. Elders gather around a circular pool of clear water, performing what appears to be a ritual, hands moving in synchronized patterns while their voices rise and fall in measured chants.

"This isn't a threat," Ankaa whispers, her anthropologist's training evident in her observational precision. "This is a civilization in perfect equilibrium with its environment."

Selenea doesn't respond, her attention caught by a sudden movement to their left. A small Nammu child, perhaps equivalent to six or seven human years, has noticed their presence. Instead of showing fear of these strange visitors in their military uniforms, the child approaches with curious dignity, clutching something in their three-fingered hands.

The child stops before Selenea, large eyes reflecting the blue-green light of the cavern. With a gesture of unmistakable offering, they extend their hands, revealing a piece of luminescent fruit, its skin translucent enough to show the glowing flesh within, perfectly ripe.

Selenea's hand trembles visibly as she accepts the gift, her fingers brushing against the child's skin, cool and smooth like polished stone, yet undeniably alive. The fruit pulses with a gentle light that matches the rhythm of her heartbeat the moment she touches it, as if synchronizing with her life force.

Her eyes dart between the innocent child and the peaceful settlement beyond, then back to the weapon strapped at her hip, a weapon calibrated for "optimal effectiveness" against these people. Her throat constricts, making it difficult to swallow. The sigils tattooed across her skin were warm with conflicting emotions, their patterns momentarily visible through her uniform as they responded to her internal turmoil.

Ankaa moves closer, her voice low and intense. "Something's wrong, isn't it? These orders don't match what we're seeing."

Selenea says nothing, watching as the Nammu child returns to their playmates, occasionally glancing back with what might be curiosity or pride at having made contact with the visitors. The elders at the central pool continue their ritual, undisturbed by the strangers at the cavern's edge, either unaware of the danger or trusting in the sacred nature of their space.

"I've never seen Secundus Protocol authorized for a pre-spaceflight civilization," Icarus adds, his usual enthusiasm replaced by quiet concern. "Especially one showing such harmonious development patterns."

The fruit in Selenea's hand pulses once more strongly, casting her face in momentary illumination. The choice crystallizes within her like the formations hanging from the cavern ceiling: clear, sharp-edged, and immovable.

Her comm unit crackles to life at her hip, the battalion commander's voice cutting through her moment of clarity: "Advance team, report position for artillery targeting. Battalion moving to support positions in two minutes."

Selenea places the glowing fruit carefully in the pocket of her uniform. With deliberate movement, she removes her comm unit, stares at it for one heartbeat, and then crushes it beneath her boot. The crunch of components against stone echoes briefly in the tunnel behind them.

"I won't be part of this," she declares, her voice finding new strength with each word. Her eyes meet Ankaa's, then Icarus's, seeking confirmation of what she already suspects, that they share her horror at what they've been ordered to do. "These aren't threats. They're families."

Icarus nods immediately, and his decision is made the moment they enter the cavern. "The Valthorim trained us to protect the balance, not destroy it." He disables his own comm unit with practiced efficiency, fingers moving across its surface in precise patterns that render it inoperable without destroying it. "Whatever Orpheus thinks he's doing, this isn't right."

Ankaa's hand moves to Selenea's arm, a gesture of solidarity that carries more weight than words. "I've studied seventeen different civilizations across the galaxy. This one is special, perfectly adapted, sustainable, peaceful." Her eyes hardened with resolve. "I won't help destroy something so rare."

The battalion commander's voice echoes faintly from Icarus's disabled comm: "Advance team, respond immediately. Artillery deployment requires confirmation."

Selenea's amber eyes reflect the bioluminescent glow as she turns to face her companions fully. "We have maybe ten minutes before they send a second team to find us. Time enough to warn the Nammu, maybe help them hide." Her voice drops lower, weighted with the magnitude of their choice. "Are you with me?"

Ankaa and Icarus stand straighter, their postures shifting from military precision to something more human, more aligned with the flowing organic patterns of the cavern around them.

"Always," Icarus says simply.

"Until the end," Ankaa affirms.

The fruit in Selenea's pocket pulses once more, its light shining through the fabric like a small beacon, a single point of illumination against the darkness of what they've been ordered to do and a guide toward what they choose to become instead.

Panic spreads through the Nammu settlement like ripples in disturbed water. At first, the tribes don't understand the concept of deliberate elimination so foreign to their peaceful existence that Selenea's warnings translate poorly. But when Ankaa kneels beside an elder, her hands forming universal gestures of urgency and danger, comprehension dawns in their large eyes. A call rings out, three notes in perfect harmonic progression, and the settlement transforms from a peaceful community to an orchestrated emergency response.

"They've done this before," Icarus observes, watching as the Nammu move with surprising efficiency. "Not military evacuation, but something similar."

"Environmental adaptation," Ankaa explains, her anthropologist's knowledge surfacing. "Asteroids have unstable periods, gas pockets, structural collapses. They've evolved emergency protocols."

Selenea's tactical mind shifts instantly to advantage assessment. "We need to direct them to tunnels the battalion won't expect." Her amber eyes scan the cavern, identifying flow patterns in the rock formations. "There," she points to a narrow fissure partially hidden behind a waterfall. "Natural drainage channel. It must lead to secondary caverns."

She approaches a Nammu elder whose elaborate fungi patterns suggest leadership status. Through a combination of gestures and simple words, she communicates her plan. The elder's eyes, large and luminous in the blue-green light, narrow with understanding. They trace a pattern in the air that resembles the settlement's layout, then extend the drawing to show previously unmentioned tunnels.

"They have exit routes," Selenea translates for her companions. "Three main passages leading to, " she pauses, interpreting the elder's flowing gestures, "what looks like ship storage. Ancient vessels, possibly unused for generations."

The cavern fills with purposeful movement as families gather children and essential supplies. The Nammu move with coordinated precision despite their fear, parents calling to children in musical tones, elders collecting sacred objects from the central pool, and younger adults guiding the elderly toward the hidden passages.

Selenea positions herself at the main entrance to the cavern, calculating battalion approach vectors. "Standard protocol gives us twelve minutes before they send a secondary team." Her fingers tap against her weapon, not nervous energy but tactical timing. "First priority is getting everyone clear of artillery range."

Ankaa moves among the youngest Nammu, who cluster together with wide, frightened eyes. She kneels to their level, her movements deliberately slow and gentle. "It's going to be alright," she says, though they can't understand her words. Her tone carries the message her language cannot be calm, reassuring, and determined. She helps small three-fingered hands gather treasured toys and guides tiny bodies toward waiting parents.

One child refuses to move, frozen in fear. Ankaa sits beside them, takes their hands in hers, and begins humming a simple melody that matches the rhythmic pulsing of the bioluminescent fungi. The child's rigid posture gradually relaxes, large eyes blinking away their panic-induced stillness. The humming spreads as other Nammu children join in, creating an impromptu harmony that cuts through their fear.

Meanwhile, Icarus examines the battalion equipment left in his pack. "I can create diversions," he announces, fingers moving rapidly through components. "Signature replicators. They'll register as Nammu life signs in empty tunnels." His usual impulsiveness now channels into focused creativity, assembling small devices from communication components and environmental sensors.

"Set them in the northern passages," Selenea directs. "Battalion will follow standard containment formation, and they'll split their forces if they detect multiple movement clusters."

As Icarus plants his diversionary devices, Selenea's attention snaps toward movement at the far tunnel entrance. The distinctive hum of energy weapons powering up echoes against the stone walls. First, battalion soldiers appear in standard assault formation, five at the front with weapons raised, three behind with scanning equipment, and the commander in a protected center position.

The fungi respond to the disruption, their light pulsing faster, more erratically, casting strobing shadows across the cavern. The remaining Nammu families freeze momentarily and then accelerate their retreat toward the hidden passages.

"Lieutenant Solaris," the battalion commander's voice cuts through the chaos, amplified by his tactical helm. "Stand down immediately. You are interfering with a direct Valthorim order."

Selenea positions herself between the soldiers and retreating Nammu, weapon drawn but held at an angle that communicates defense rather than aggression. Her face hardens into the mask she wore through countless Battalion operations, professional, detached, and dangerous.

"These people are innocent," she responds, her voice carrying the authority that earned her rapid promotion through Battalion ranks. "I won't let you harm them."

"Secundus Protocol is not a suggestion, Lieutenant. It's a direct order from Orpheus himself." The commander advances one step, flanked by his squad. "Stand aside or be removed."

Selenea's response comes not in words but in action. Her weapon discharges with surgical precision, targeting the commander's rifle rather than the commander himself. The energy pulse strikes true, rendering the weapon inoperable with minimal peripheral damage.

The cavern erupts into chaos. Energy weapons flash against stone walls, creating stark shadows and disturbing the fungi that release clouds of luminescent spores into the air. The blue-green particles swirl through weapons fire, creating eerie traces of light that track each shot's trajectory.

Selenea moves with controlled efficiency, and each action is precise and economical. She takes cover behind a stone formation and emerges to fire three rapid shots, each disabling a Battalion weapon rather than harming her former comrades. The strategy buys precious seconds for more Nammu to reach the escape tunnels.

"You trained these soldiers," Ankaa shouts over the weapons fire as she guides a group of children behind protective rock outcroppings. "They know your tactics!"

"They know my battalion tactics," Selenea corrected, sliding to a new position. "Not what my brother taught me."

She switches techniques immediately, abandoning standard Battalion patterns for the more unpredictable movements Caelus developed during their childhood training. She rolls between cover positions, fires from unexpected angles, and creates confusion among soldiers expecting standard engagement protocols.

Across the cavern, Ankaa stands with her back to the central pool, her arms spread wide to shield several young Nammu who couldn't reach the tunnels in time. A Battalion soldier advances on her position, weapon raised. Without hesitation, she meets his eyes through his tactical visor.

"We were sent to protect the balance," she reminds him, her voice steady despite the weapon pointed at her chest. "Look around you. Is this what balance means?"

The soldier hesitates, weapon wavering slightly. In that moment of uncertainty, a Nammu elder emerges from behind the pool, takes the children's hands, and pulls them toward safety. Ankaa doesn't move until they're clear, maintaining eye contact with the conflicted soldier.

Meanwhile, Icarus demonstrates why his training reports always noted "reckless creativity under pressure." He vaults across the exposed ground, deliberately drawing fire away from the escaping tribes. Battalion targeting systems track his erratic movement, unable to establish a lock as he zigzags between cover points, occasionally reversing direction completely.

"Northern passage clear!" he shouts to Selenea, narrowly avoiding an energy pulse that strikes the stone where he stood moments before. The rock sizzles and cracks from the impact.

Selenea assesses the situation with a tactical officer's precision: approximately seventy percent of the Nammu have reached the escape tunnels, Battalion reinforcements will arrive within minutes, and the current defensive position is becoming untenable. She makes her decision instantly.

"Fall back to the waterfall passage," she orders Ankaa and Icarus. "I'll cover."

She increases her rate of fire, forcing the Battalion soldiers to take defensive positions as her companions guide the last group of Nammu toward the hidden fissure behind the waterfall. The narrow opening barely accommodates adults, requiring them to turn sideways and squeeze through the flowing water.

Energy pulses strike stones near Selenea's position with increasing accuracy as the Battalion adjusts to her non-standard tactics. A shot grazes her upper arm, leaving a burn that cuts through her uniform to the sigils beneath. The damaged tattoos flare with pain, sending jagged signals through her nervous system.

"Lieutenant!" Icarus calls from the passage entrance. "Last group through!"

Selenea retreats in measured steps, maintaining suppressive fire while moving backward toward the waterfall. The Battalion advances steadily, forming a semi-circle that tightens around her position. Water soaks her back as she reaches the fissure, the cool liquid offering momentary relief to her burned arm.

"You can't escape, Solaris," the commander shouts, his voice echoing across the now-empty settlement. "Surrender now and face proper judgment on Zathira."

Her response comes in the form of a precisely aimed shot at the cavern ceiling above the Battalion's position. The energy pulse strikes a crystal formation, fracturing it from its moorings. With a sound like breaking glass magnified a hundredfold, the massive structure crashes down, creating a barrier of jagged crystal between the soldiers and the escape route.

Selenea slips through the fissure, joining Ankaa and Icarus in the narrow tunnel beyond. Water runs along the passage floor, soaking their boots as they follow the last of the Nammu refugees deeper into the asteroid's network of caverns.

"We need to seal it," Ankaa says, glancing back at the fissure where water continues to flow through from the main cavern.

Icarus already has components in hand, assembling them with practiced speed. "Controlled collapse," he explains, attaching the device to a specific point in the tunnel wall. "Not enough to damage the water system, just enough to block pursuit."

They move further down the passage, around a bend that shields them from the entrance. Icarus activates the device remotely. A muffled rumble shakes the tunnel, followed by the sound of falling rock and rushing water. When it subsides, the passage behind them has transformed into a solid wall of stone and debris, and water now diverted into small rivulets that find new paths through the collapsed section.

"That won't hold them forever," Selenea says, wincing as she examines the burn on her arm. "But it buys us time."

Ahead, the narrow passage widens into another tunnel where the remaining Nammu wait, their bioluminescent patterns creating enough light to navigate by. Their large eyes watch the three renegades with what might be gratitude or perhaps simply evaluation, measuring these strange outsiders who chose to protect rather than destroy.

Selenea feels a warmth in her chest, an uncomfortable heat that isn't quite a pain or fear or even certainty. It burns with purpose and consequence, with bridges destroyed and paths chosen that can never be unmade.

The tunnels wind deeper into Nammu's core, nature's patient hand having carved pathways more complex than any military strategist could design. Selenea leads them forward, amber eyes sharp despite exhaustion, her tactical mind converting geological formations into defensible positions, escape routes, and choke points. Behind her come the Nammu, their movements swift despite fear, their bioluminescent patterns creating a living stream of light that flows through the darkness like conscious water.

They navigate by starlight filtering through the asteroid's natural light wells, shafts where micrometeorite impacts have punctured the surface, allowing silver illumination to penetrate the depths. These columns of light intersect with the tribes' bioluminescence, creating navigation markers at tunnel junctions.

"Battalion will bring in tracking specialists," Selenea notes, pausing at a fork in the passage. "They'll follow water flow patterns to predict our route." She gestures toward the left tunnel, where condensation glistens on stone surfaces. "That's what they'll expect. We go right."

The right passage narrows, requiring them to proceed in single file. The ceiling drops lower, forcing taller Nammu to bend at their already-flexible spines. The air grows warmer, carrying mineral scents that suggest proximity to the asteroid's geothermal core.

Ankaa drops back to where several Nammu show signs of injury, minor burns from weapons fire and cuts from rushing through narrow fissures. Despite the language barrier, her hands communicate healing intent. She applies emergency sealant from her pack to a child's lacerated palm, the gentle pressure of her fingers saying what words cannot.

"Their physiology adapts quickly," she observes, watching as the sealant bonds with Nammu skin more effectively than it would with human tissue. "Remarkable cellular regeneration. I suspect they've evolved to recover from asteroid instability events."

Ahead, Icarus scouts each junction before signaling the group forward. His movements display none of his usual restless energy, each step calculated, each gesture precise. The crisis has transformed his impulsiveness into focused vigilance.

"No pursuit signals yet," he reports, returning from a particularly lengthy reconnaissance. "But I'm picking up communication bursts. They're coordinating a systematic sweep of all tunnel networks."

Selenea nods, calculating distances and response times. "How much further to the ships?" she asks the elder leading their group.

The elder extends three fingers and then points to where the tunnel curves beyond sight. Their large eyes blink in sequence, right, left, right, a communication pattern Selenea has begun to recognize as indicating proximity.

The passage widens suddenly, opening into a vast cavern unlike any they've seen. Unlike the settlement's blue-green illumination, this space glows with amber light from crystalline formations that rise from floor to ceiling, massive structures that resemble frozen flames. The crystals hum with subtle energy, creating a resonance that vibrates through bone and tissue.

And there, arranged in concentric circles around the cavern's center, stand the ships.

"Vessels" might be a more accurate term; each craft appears somewhere between a boat and a spacecraft, and its hulls are carved from the same stone as the asteroid itself. They curve like ancient sailing ships, prows extending into delicate points that catch and reflect the amber light. What appears to be crystal serves as their propulsion system, complex arrays positioned at each stern, pulsing with the same energy as the formations surrounding them.

"These haven't been used in generations," the elder explains through a combination of gestures and simplified vocal patterns that Ankaa translates. "But they will carry us to the outer reaches."

"Not conventional engines," Icarus observes, moving closer to examine one vessel. "Some kind of crystal resonance technology. They're essentially mineral batteries that interact with asteroid field currents."

Selenea circles a ship, assessing its capacity and function with practiced efficiency. "How many people per vessel?"

The elder indicates the largest craft, extending seven fingers twice in succession. Fourteen per ship, approximately twenty ships, enough to evacuate the entire tribe.

The cavern fills with purposeful activity as the Nammu prepare their ancient vessels. They move with inherited knowledge and muscle memory passed through generations, performing maintenance rituals without ever expecting actual departure. Crystalline components are checked, and navigation systems, consisting of complex mineral alignments rather than electronic devices, are calibrated.

Selenea assists with launching preparations while continuously checking her backup communication unit for Battalion signals. The burn on her arm throbs beneath its hastily applied sealant, the damaged sigils sending occasional pulses of pain through her nervous system. She ignores it, focusing instead on securing mooring lines and helping families board their designated vessels.

A small movement catches her attention, a familiar form approaching with deliberate steps. The Nammu child who offered her the luminescent fruit now stands before her again, small three-fingered hands clutching something new. The child extends their hands upward, offering a carved crystal that catches the ambient light and splits it into prismatic patterns across Selenea's uniform.

She kneels, bringing herself to the child's eye level. The crystal sits cool against her palm as she accepts it, not simply decorative but inscribed with minute patterns that match the bioluminescent markings of the child's family. A name, perhaps, or a blessing, or simply a memory preserved in mineral form.

Something breaks inside Selenea, not her resolve but the professional distance she's maintained through years of Battalion training. Her posture softens, shoulders dropping from their military rigidity as she closes her fingers around the crystal. The significance of this moment crystallizes in her mind: she has betrayed everything she trained for, everyone who trusted her with command.

And she cannot bring herself to regret it.

The child retreats to their waiting family as Selenea rises, the crystal clutched tight in her fist. She turns to find Ankaa watching her, eyes reflecting the amber light of the cavern.

"We've betrayed everything we were trained for," Ankaa says quietly, giving voice to Selenea's thoughts.

Selenea straightens, certainty hardening her features. "No. We've remembered what we're supposed to stand for." She opens her hand, revealing the crystal lying against her palm. "The Valthorim taught us to protect the balance. This, " she gestures toward the peaceful tribes preparing their vessels, "is balance. What Orpheus ordered was extinction."

Icarus joins them, his usually animated face serious. "Battalion will reach this cavern within thirty minutes. These ships are functional but slow. They'll be vulnerable during launch."

Selenea's backup communication unit activates without warning, and an automated message cuts through the cavern's ambient sounds: "Lieutenant Solaris, report to Zathira immediately. Failure to comply will be considered treason against the Valthorim Council. Repeat: report to Zathira immediately."

The message repeats once, then falls silent, leaving only the hum of crystal formations and the quiet activity of the Nammu preparations.

"What now?" Icarus asks, his tone indicating he already anticipates her answer.

Selenea watches the Nammu tribes board their vessels, families helping elders navigate narrow gangways, children clutching cherished possessions, and an entire civilization preparing to abandon their homes rather than face destruction.

"Now we make sure they get away safely," she says, her voice quiet but firm. "Then we face whatever comes next."

She moves toward an open area near the cavern wall, fingers already tracing patterns in the air, movements she's observed her brother perform countless times, patterns she's studied in Zathira's training halls but never executed without authorization. The sigils on her skin warm in response, recognizing the familiar configurations despite her lack of Aetheris ability.

"You can't open a Fractal," Ankaa says, alarm evident in her voice. "Only authorized Valthorim can create stable pathways."

"I can't create one," Selenea corrects, continuing her precise movements. "But I can access the existing network. Temporarily." Her fingers leave faint traces in the air, muscle memory replicating patterns she was never meant to use independently. "Caelus showed me the emergency access protocols. The Fractals will recognize my biological signature through the sigils."

The air before she thickens and becomes almost viscous as reality responds to her unauthorized commands. Opening a Fractal without proper authorization requires overriding multiple security systems, the equivalent of forcing a lock rather than using a key. The process creates instability, visible in the jagged edges that begin to form as space tears open before her.

Unlike the perfect crystalline pattern of authorized Fractals, this opening appears raw and unfinished, its edges pulsing with erratic energy that threatens to collapse at any moment. Through the tear, the darkness of open space becomes visible, peppered with distant stars and the safety of the outer asteroid belt.

"It's unstable," Selenea acknowledges, strain evident in her voice as she maintains the opening through sheer force of will. The sigils on her skin burn with effort, visible now through her uniform as they respond to the unauthorized connection. "But it will give them a direct path beyond Battalion's immediate reach."

The Nammu elders approach the Fractal with reverent caution, recognizing its nature if not its specific technology. The lead elder extends a hand toward the opening, feeling the energy that pulses from its edges, then turns to Selenea with a gesture that universally signals gratitude.

"They need to go now," Selenea says, jaw tight with the effort of maintaining the unstable pathway. "The Fractal won't hold long."

Ankaa relays the urgency to the tribes, and the first vessels begin to move, rising from their ancient moorings with surprising grace, crystal propulsion systems illuminating as they activate. One by one, the ships enter the Fractal, passing through the tear in reality to emerge in the safety of deep space.

Sweat beads on Selenea's forehead as she holds the pathway open, each passage depleting her strength. The unauthorized connection taxes her in ways official users never experience, the network actively resisting her commands, requiring constant reinforcement to prevent collapse.

"Half through," Icarus reports, counting vessels as they depart. "Battalion signals strengthening. They've found our trail."

The crystal in Selenea's pocket, the child's gift, pulses with sympathetic energy as it resonates with the Fractal's frequency. The sensation spreads through her body, providing unexpected support for her faltering strength. The remaining ships increase their speed, sensing the urgency of their situation.

"Last vessel approaching," Ankaa announces as the final ship rises from the cavern floor.

Selenea's face, illuminated by the pulsing light of the unstable Fractal, reveals both strain and absolute conviction. This choice to defy Orpheus, reject Valthorim's orders, and protect those deemed expendable has changed her irrevocably. There is no returning to what she was before seeing the truth behind her training.

The final ship passes through the opening. The moment it clears the boundary, Selenea releases her hold on the Fractal. The tear, in reality, collapses with a sound like distant thunder, edges fusing back together as space reclaims its continuity. The sudden absence of the pathway leaves ghostly after-images floating in the air, jagged lines of light that fade slowly like the memory of lightning.

Selenea staggers slightly, steadied by Ankaa's hand on her arm. The sigils across her skin cool gradually, their glow subsiding as the connection terminates. The crystal in her pocket returns to dormancy, its momentary resonance with the Fractal energies complete.

"They're safe," Icarus confirms, checking readings on his modified scanner. "Emerging on the far side of the asteroid belt, beyond immediate Battalion tracking range."

Selenea nods, her breathing returning to normal as she recovers from the strain of maintaining the unauthorized pathway. "And we have visitors," she says calmly, head tilting toward the tunnel entrance where the first sounds of Battalion approach echo against stone walls.

Together, the three renegades turn to face whatever consequences await their choice. The amber light of the crystal cavern casts their shadows across the stone floor, not three separate silhouettes but a single unified darkness, merged by purpose and illuminated by the same light that guided the Nammu to freedom.

Chapter 8

Betrayal and Deception

Caelus stands before the obsidian door to Orpheus's private chamber, his reflection distorted across the polished surface. The summons came without explanation, a simple pulse against his communication band bearing Orpheus's unique frequency. His fingers hover over the access panel, the metal bands around them catching the dim corridor light. Something in the air feels wrong, a subtle disturbance in the cosmic threads that brush against his enhanced perception.

He touches the panel. The door recedes into the wall without sound, revealing darkness beyond. Caelus steps forward, crossing the threshold into space that feels simultaneously vast and suffocating. The door seals behind him with a soft hiss of displaced air.

The chamber materializes around him as his eyes adjust, a perfect circle of obsidian walls etched with ancient sigils that predate recorded history. The markings pulse with faint blue light that provides the only illumination, creating pools of shadow between islands of cold radiance. The light shifts in subtle rhythms, like breathing, or perhaps like a heartbeat, slowed to the pace of geological time.

At the center of the chamber stands Orpheus, motionless as a statue. His ceremonial robes absorb rather than reflect the sigils' light, creating an outline of perfect darkness against the glowing walls. The hood hangs forward, casting his face in shadow deeper than the mere absence of light, a void where features should exist. Only his silver eyes penetrate the darkness, twin points of metallic light that fix on Caelus with uncomfortable intensity.

"You came quickly," Orpheus observes, his voice carrying those distinctive harmonic undertones that no human vocal cords should produce. He doesn't move, doesn't gesture, and remains perfectly still as if conserving energy for some greater purpose. "That speaks to your devotion."

Caelus inclines his head respectfully, maintaining the precise distance protocol demands. "Your summons indicated urgency, Master."

"Indeed." A single word hangs in the air between them. Orpheus finally moves, raising one hand in a gesture that activates a central sigil on the floor. The marking expands upward, light coalescing into a holographic projection that hovers at chest height. "What I must show you causes me great personal pain."

The hologram resolves into an image of Nammu, the tribal asteroid's interior caverns captured from multiple angles. The familiar blue-green bioluminescent fungi carpet the curved walls and ceiling, their light creating patterns of beauty and harmony. Then, abruptly, the imagery changes. Fire erupts across the peaceful landscape. Energy weapons discharge in blinding flashes. Bodies lie scattered across glowing fungal beds, their forms twisted in postures of terror and pain.

"These transmissions arrived one hour ago," Orpheus states, his voice unnaturally calm despite the horror unfolding before them. "The Nammu tribal asteroid, home to a pre-spaceflight civilization of particular interest to our anthropological division. A civilization now decimated."

The hologram shifts again, focusing on a figure moving through the destruction, a figure in First Battalion uniform, weapon raised, face illuminated by weapons fire. Selenea. The footage shows her firing into a group of fleeing Nammu, their bodies falling amid the burning fungi. Her expression appears cold, determined, and merciless.

"Your sister betrayed everything we stand for," Orpheus continues, the hologram reflecting in his silver eyes as he observes Caelus's reaction. "The Valthorim dispatched her unit to establish peaceful contact and study the Nammu's unique adaptation to their environment. Instead, she executed a massacre."

Caelus's sigils pulse beneath his skin, responding to the surge of emotion the images provoke. His breath catches in his throat, creating physical pain that matches his psychological shock. The metal bands around his fingers grow suddenly cold against his skin.

"There must be some mistake," he manages, voice barely above a whisper. "Selenea would never, "

Orpheus raises a hand, silencing him. The gesture leaves momentary traces in the air, silver lines hanging briefly before dissipating. "I thought the same. I reviewed the evidence personally, hoping to find alternative explanations." He lowers his hand, darkness flowing back into the space the movement disturbed. "There are none. The Valthorim demand justice."

The hologram continues playing, showing more scenes of destruction. Selenea moves through the burning caverns with two companions, directing the assault with precise hand signals. The footage jumps to another location, what appears to be a ceremonial pool now stained with the biological equivalent of blood, bodies floating on its surface.

Caelus's hands tremble slightly as he watches. Something in the imagery strikes him as wrong: angles that don't align, timing that seems artificially compressed, and details that contradict his understanding of his sister's character. But the evidence plays before him with merciless clarity, each frame more damning than the last.

"Why?" The question escapes before he can contain it, raw with confusion and pain.

Orpheus moves for the first time since activating the hologram, stepping around it to approach Caelus directly. His robes make no sound as they shift with his movement, creating the impression of a shadow gliding across the stone.

"Power corrupts even the most dedicated servants," he says, stopping precisely one arm's length away. "Your sister's unprecedented rise through battalion ranks, her access to Fractal technology, and her immersion in Valthorim training without proper psychological preparation. In retrospect, the warning signs existed."

He reaches out, placing a hand on Caelus's shoulder. The touch feels simultaneously heavier and lighter than it should as if Orpheus exists at a density different from ordinary matter.

"I take responsibility for this failure," Orpheus continues, his voice softening to a tone almost resembling remorse. "I pushed her advancement, impressed by her abilities and her connection to you. I overlooked the psychological instability her reports occasionally mentioned."

Caelus stares at the hologram as it loops back to the beginning, showing the peaceful caverns before the destruction began. His mind races through possibilities, external influence, mistaken identity, and falsified footage. None seem plausible against the evidence before him.

"What would you have me do?" he asks, the question weighted with knowledge of what must come next.

"Find her," Orpheus answers, removing his hand from Caelus's shoulder. "Your Aetheris ability exists for precisely this purpose. Trace her cosmic signature, locate her position." He gestures toward the hologram, which freezes on an image of Selenea standing amid the destruction. "Then bring her to Zathira for judgment. She must answer to the Valthorim Council for her actions."

The chamber's sigils pulse more intensely, their blue light brightening in response to the command. Orpheus moves back to the center of the room, his form once again becoming a silhouette of perfect darkness.

"This mission must supersede all personal considerations," he adds, silver eyes fixed on Caelus with unwavering focus. "The cosmic balance depends on accountability. No one, not even someone of your sister's talent, can violate universal order without consequence."

Caelus's jaw tightens, a muscle pulsing beneath the skin. His sigils warm against his flesh, responding to the conflicting emotions surging beneath his controlled exterior. Duty to the Valthorim, loyalty to Orpheus, and love for his sister force pulling in different directions with impossible strength.

"I understand," he says finally, his voice steady despite the turmoil beneath. "I will find her."

"And bring her to justice," Orpheus adds, the words carrying the weight of immutable law.

Caelus bows his head in acknowledgment, though doubt flickers across his face, a momentary expression quickly mastered. The sigils on his skin pulse once, strongly, as if responding to the decision forming in his mind rather than the one his words suggest.

"Cosmic order must be maintained," he responds, the ritual phrase falling from his lips with practiced ease. Inside his chest, a warmth spreads, not the comforting heat of certainty but the uncomfortable burn of something closer to suspicion.

Orpheus nods, apparently satisfied. The hologram collapses back into the floor sigil, darkness reclaiming the space it occupied. "Go now. Time favors those who would escape judgment."

Caelus turns and walks toward the door, feeling Orpheus's silver gaze tracking him with calculated interest. The chamber's sigils dim as he approaches the exit, shadows reaching toward him like grasping fingers against the obsidian walls.

The door to Caelus's quarters slides shut behind him with a soft hiss. He stands motionless for three heartbeats, and then his composure fractures. His fist slams against the wall, the impact sending shock waves through his arm that momentarily override the turmoil in his mind. The metal bands around his fingers leave indentations in the stone surface, small crescent moons carved by rage and disbelief.

"Not possible," he whispers to the empty room. The words hang in the air, insufficient against the weight of what he's witnessed.

He paces across the stone floor, seven steps in one direction, turn, seven steps back. His reflection fragments in the crystalline viewport that dominates the outer wall, breaking his image into shards that reassemble with each pass. The viewport looks directly into deep space, unfiltered by atmospheric distortion. Stars burn with perfect clarity against absolute darkness, their light traveling unimpeded for years to reach this exact point, this exact moment.

His hands tremble as he moves. The tremors begin at his fingertips, where the metal enhancement bands circle his skin and then spread upward through his arms and shoulders until his entire body vibrates with contained energy. He stops suddenly, forcing stillness through sheer willpower. His eyes close, his breath steadies, heart rate, decreases through practiced techniques.

When he opens his eyes again, his gaze fixes on his reflection. The sigils tattooed across his forearms seem to watch him, their intricate patterns shifting slightly beneath his skin as they respond to his emotional state. He pushes up his sleeves, exposing the full network that wraps around his arms. The tattoos represent dual commitments to the Valthorim and their cosmic principles to Orpheus and his direct authority.

He traces one particular sigil with his index finger, feeling the skin warm beneath his touch. The mark that binds him to truth-seeking, to following evidence wherever it leads. The irony doesn't escape him.

Caelus turns abruptly from his reflection, crossing to the personal data terminal embedded in the wall opposite the viewport. His fingers move across its surface with practiced efficiency, calling up secure files and entering clearance codes that grant access to restricted information. The screen illuminates his face from below, casting sharp shadows that emphasize the tension in his jaw and the strain around his eyes.

"Show me, Selenea Solaris," he commands. "Final communications before Nammu mission. Full sensory recording."

The screen flickers and then resolves into an image of Selenea in her quarters. The timestamp indicates this recording was made seven hours before the alleged massacre. She sits at her own terminal, expression serious but composed. Her amber eyes, so like his own, reflect the light from her screen.

"Personal log, Lieutenant Selenea Solaris," she begins, her voice steady. "Mission briefing for Nammu operation completed. Parameters feel... incomplete." She pauses, a slight furrow forming between her brows. "Tribal assessment objectives provided without supporting documentation. Cultural interaction protocols were bypassed. Direct intervention authorized without standard observation period."

She leans closer to her terminal, voice dropping lower. "Requested clarification from command and received standard override codes. Something doesn't align with established first-contact methodology."

The recording continues, showing Selenea reviewing equipment specifications, squad assignments, and tactical approaches. Nothing in her demeanor suggests violent intent or psychological instability. Instead, she displays the methodical preparation of a professional officer, with one notable undercurrent: concern about the mission's foundational parameters.

Caelus freezes the playback on her face. He studies his sister's expression, searching for any sign of the person he witnessed in Orpheus's doctored footage. The disconnect between the two images grows more pronounced with each moment of scrutiny.

"Next communication," he instructs.

The screen shifts to a formal mission acceptance recording, with Selenea standing at attention in full battalion uniform. Her voice recites standard acknowledgment phrases, professional and detached. Then, as the recording ends, a brief flicker crosses her face so quickly that most observers would miss it. But Caelus knows his sister's expressions like his own. That momentary shift reveals reservation, not malice.

His hands drift to the metal bands around his fingers, twisting one absently as memories surface. Solarune's triple moons cast multiple shadows across the hologram museum's polished floor. Selenea, at age twelve, explained a particularly complex historical display to a group of younger children, and her natural leadership was already evident. Her unwavering sense of right and wrong, even when it made life more difficult.

He remembers the night he first demonstrated his emerging Aetheris ability, tracking a lost pet through the crowded market district by following its unique cosmic signature. Selenea's pride had been immediate and complete, untainted by the jealousy others might have felt toward such a rare gift.

"Where is the person who would slaughter innocents?" he asks the frozen image on his screen. No answer comes from the recording, but he doesn't expect one. The question wasn't for Selenea but for himself.

Caelus closes the communications logs and accesses the Nammu mission briefing instead. He scans the official parameters, noting the unusual vagueness where specific objectives should be listed. The authorization bears Orpheus's unique signature pattern, but the formatting deviates slightly from standard Valthorim protocols, the difference imperceptible to most observers but glaring to someone who has studied these documents for years.

The more he examines the evidence, the more inconsistencies emerge. The alleged massacre occurred too quickly after arrival for proper tribal assessment. The weapons signatures in the footage don't match standard Battalion equipment settings. The destruction patterns lack the methodical progression typical of military operations.

His sigils warm against his skin, responding to his growing certainty. The tattoos pulse with subtle light that reflects his conviction rather than his doubt, not the reaction they would display if his suspicions were misplaced.

Selenea has many qualities, both strengths and flaws. Her stubborn adherence to principle sometimes prevents necessary compromise. Her empathy occasionally clouds tactical judgment. Her trust in authority figures has diminished over years of witnessing institutional imperfection. But the capacity for unprovoked violence against innocents? That quality exists nowhere in the sister he knows.

Caelus rises from the terminal, moving back to the viewport. Stars wheel slowly beyond the crystal surface, indifferent to the decision forming in his mind. His reflection stares back at him, fractured across the faceted surface but somehow more unified than before.

His fingers move to his collar, where the Valthorim insignia rests against his throat, the symbol of his position, his training, and his oath. With deliberate care, he unpins it, holding the small metallic emblem between his fingers. The insignia catches starlight from the viewport, casting miniature reflections across his palm.

"I'm sorry," he whispers to the emblem, though the apology isn't meant for the symbol itself or even the institution it represents. The words are for Orpheus, for the breaking of trust that his next actions will represent.

He places the insignia beside the terminal, positioning it with precise care. Not discarded, not rejected, simply set aside. The gesture represents not abandonment of his principles but prioritization of more fundamental values.

The sigils on his arms pulse once, strongly, responding to his decision. The glow spreads upward from his wrists to his shoulders, networks of light visible beneath his skin. His Aetheris ability stirs cosmic threads brushing against his perception even without formal activation.

Caelus's jaw sets in a line of determination. He will find Selenea, not to deliver her to judgment, but to discover the truth behind Orpheus's deception. His sister would never massacre innocents. This means the footage was falsified, the mission corrupted, and the truth buried beneath layers of manipulation.

He moves to his equipment storage unit, beginning preparations for departure. His hands no longer tremble. The decision, once made, brings clarity that overrides doubt. Whatever consequences await this choice, they cannot outweigh the cost of betraying his sister to a justice system suddenly revealed as suspect.

The Aetheris chamber waits for him like a sacred space, circular and austere. Caelus enters with reverent steps, the door sealing behind him with a soft pneumatic hiss that suggests separation from ordinary reality. Unlike the communal tracking rooms used for standard operations, this private chamber exists solely for advanced practitioners, its systems calibrated to enhance and focus abilities beyond normal parameters. The rounded walls display a three-dimensional star map of the known universe, countless points of light suspended in a perfect representation of cosmic reality.

At the chamber's center stands a raised circular platform, its surface inscribed with sigils that mirror those on his skin. Unlike the cold blue light of Orpheus's chamber, these markings glow with warm amber energy that pulses in subtle rhythm, like heartbeats slowed to match the rotation of distant planets. The platform raises three hand-spans above the chamber floor, high enough to create separation from the physical world and low enough to maintain stability during the mind's journey.

Caelus moves to the platform's edge, his fingers working efficiently to unfasten his outer garments. The Aetheris connection functions through any barrier, but cloth creates interference patterns that reduce precision, like trying to feel texture through gloves. He removes his tunic, folding it with mechanical precision, and then places it on a recessed shelf designed for this purpose. The air touches his exposed skin, cool against the sigils that cover his torso in intricate networks.

The tattoos form a complete system, not random decorative patterns but precise mathematical equations expressed through ancient symbology. Each connects to specific cosmic frequencies, allowing his consciousness to resonate with particular types of stardust across the universe. Some practitioners develop specialized abilities, tracking only living beings, only technology, or only celestial phenomena. Caelus's gift lies in his adaptability, his ability to follow any thread once he attunes to its specific signature.

He steps onto the platform barefoot to maximize contact with the energized sigils beneath. His toes curl slightly as he feels the first tingling sensation of connection, like stepping into water charged with gentle electricity. He kneels, assuming the traditional pose of cosmic meditation, back straight, hands resting palm-up on his thighs, eyes focused on the middle distance where physical sight transitions to cosmic perception.

The star map surrounding him dims slightly, then brightens again as the chamber recognizes his presence. The display shifts, stars redistributing themselves to reflect his most recent cosmic understanding. This configuration exists nowhere in Zathira's official records; it is a personalized representation of the universe as Caelus perceives it through his enhanced awareness.

He closes his eyes. His breathing slows, and each inhalation is measured and deliberate, with each exhalation releasing distractions along with carbon dioxide. The sigils on his skin begin to warm, first those on his fingers where the metal enhancement bands circle like conductive rings, then those on his palms, wrists, and forearms, spreading across his torso in waves of gentle heat. The warming isn't uncomfortable but intimate, a recognition between his flesh and the cosmic forces that flow through all matter.

The platform beneath him responds, its inscribed sigils brightening to match the intensity of those on his skin. The two systems, biological and technological, synchronize their energy signatures, creating amplification through resonance. Around him, the star map pulses once, strongly, then settles into a rhythm that matches his heartbeat.

Caelus extends his awareness outward, like fingers stretching into infinite space. The sensation defies ordinary description, simultaneously expanding his consciousness to a cosmic scale while maintaining the precise focus of his individual identity. He becomes both impossibly vast and intensely particular, a single point of awareness with universe-spanning perception.

Cosmic threads emerge from his fingertips, not physical manifestations but energy patterns visible through enhanced perception. The threads appear as filaments of light, thinner than hair yet stronger than gravitational fields. They stretch outward through the holographic display, weaving between star systems, nebulae, and planetary bodies. Each thread follows a specific frequency, searching for the unique cosmic signature that belongs to Selenea Solaris.

The threads multiply as they extend further, splitting and branching at junctions where possibility fragments into multiple paths. They probe star systems where Battalion operations are active, examine common escape routes, and investigate established safe harbors for those fleeing authority. The search pattern follows a logical progression, its efficiency reflecting years of training in cosmic tracking.

But Selenea would anticipate such methods. If she truly went rogue, she would avoid obvious paths, choose unconventional routes, and perhaps employ counter-tracking technologies. Caelus adjusts his search accordingly, redirecting threads toward improbable locations, systems deemed too remote for practical consideration, and regions where strange phenomena might mask a fugitive's presence.

Sweat beads on his forehead as he pushes his Aetheris ability further, stretching the threads across distances he rarely attempts. The physical strain manifests through increased heart rate, elevated body temperature, and accelerated respiration. The body protests the mind's cosmic wandering, reminding him of his biological limitations even as he transcends them.

His awareness now spans lightyears; consciousness extended across vast interstellar distances. The experience resembles being simultaneously present in thousands of locations while maintaining a central identity in the Aetheris chamber. Through the threads, he perceives fragments of distant realities, the burning surface of a blue giant star, the frozen methane oceans of an outer rim planet, and the dense asteroid fields that mark the boundaries between established territories.

The search continues without results. No thread finds resonance with Selenea's unique signature. The metal bands around his fingers grow uncomfortably warm as they struggle to channel the increasing energy required to maintain this expanded awareness. The sigils on his skin pulse more rapidly, their glow visible even through closed eyelids.

Normal protocol dictates withdrawal at this stage. Extended Aetheris connection taxes both mind and body, creating an accumulated strain that can lead to neural feedback loops, perceptual distortions, and eventually physical collapse. Most practitioners limit their cosmic searching to predetermined parameters, pulling back when those boundaries are reached.

Caelus pushes onward.

He directs the threads toward increasingly distant sectors, regions so far removed from Zathira that tracking them requires exponential energy increases. The star map around him shifts to accommodate these new vectors, revealing systems rarely displayed due to their remote positioning. His muscles tense with concentrated effort as he maintains threads that want to snap back, cosmic distances asserting their fundamental reality against his determined violation.

His breathing grows labored. The sweat on his skin evaporates from the heat generated by his sigils, creating a thin mist that rises around his kneeling form. The chamber's environmental systems activate automatically, compensating for the temperature increase and circulating cooled air that provides minimal relief.

Still, Selenea remains hidden from his perception. A flicker of doubt surfaces in his mind; what if Orpheus was right? What if something fundamental changed in his sister? Would her cosmic signature transform beyond recognition? The doubt threatens his concentration, causing the threads to waver momentarily.

Caelus forces the uncertainty aside, refocusing with increased determination. The connection between siblings transcends ordinary tracking parameters. He shifts his approach, no longer searching for Selenea's standard signature but for the unique resonance pattern they share, the subtle harmonic created by their genetic similarity, their shared childhood on Solarune, and the countless moments that shaped them both. This signature exists at a deeper level and is resistant to conventional masking techniques.

The threads reorganize, weaving new patterns that reflect this more fundamental search strategy. They probe not just physical locations but resonance fields, harmonic convergence points, and places where cosmic energies align in patterns compatible with the sibling bond he seeks to trace.

His arms begin to shake with the effort of maintaining this unprecedented extension. The metal bands around his fingers now glow visibly, channeling more energy than their design parameters anticipated. The sigils across his torso pulse erratically, their normal patterns disrupted by the strain of his determination.

Caelus grits his teeth, pushing beyond pain, beyond conventional limitations. Memories flash through his consciousness, Selenea standing beside him at their father's memorial service, her hand finding him without looking; the first time she successfully replicated a complex sigil pattern he'd taught her; their last meal together before her Battalion induction ceremony, simple food made profound by shared understanding.

These memories strengthen the threads, infusing them with an emotional resonance that transcends purely technical connection. The cosmic pathways brighten, gaining definition and purpose as they stretch across impossible distances.

"Where are you?" he whispers, the words barely disturbing the air yet somehow traveling along the threads like ripples across a cosmic pond.

The cosmic threads suddenly converge, thousands of searching filaments snapping toward a single point in the star map. The redirect happens with such force that Caelus's physical body jerks backward, his spine arching as the connection intensifies beyond anticipated parameters. The chamber's star map responds instantly, zooming toward the convergence point, a small moon orbiting a gas giant in an obscure system far from established trade routes. The coordinates burn into his mind with perfect clarity, each digit and designation searing itself into his memory through the Aetheris connection.

The moon materializes in heightened detail before his perception, a cratered surface of pale blue ice, atmosphere thin but present, gravity approximately sixty percent of the standard. Beneath the frozen surface, liquid water forms an ocean warmed by tidal forces from the massive gas giant looming in its sky. The moon's rotation creates a day-night cycle of thirty-seven standard hours.

Caelus's consciousness rushes toward the location, following the converged threads that now pulse with certainty. He penetrates the icy surface, descends through layers of frozen history, and finds a network of caverns carved by patient water through millennia of geological time. The spaces resemble Nammu's interior, not coincidentally, he realizes. Similar environments, similar adaptations.

His Aetheris perception locks onto Selenea's signature, finding her within a central cavern where refugees have established temporary settlements. The vision comes in fragments, not continuous observation but flashes of reality captured through the strained connection:

Selenea kneels beside an injured Nammu child, applying medical sealant to a wound on its three-fingered hand. Her face shows concentration mixed with genuine concern, not the cold determination from Orpheus's doctored footage.

She stands with her companions, the anthropologist and the technician from her squad, studying a makeshift map of the moon's cavern system, planning routes that avoid detection from orbit.

Her hand gestures while speaking to Nammu elders, explaining something with patience and respect, and her expression is earnest beneath the blue-tinged light of transplanted bioluminescent fungi.

Most importantly, he sees her helping refugees disembark from stone vessels, the ancient tribal ships mentioned in mission briefings. She supports an elderly Nammu, ensuring their safe passage from ship to cavern. Her actions show protection, not persecution.

The visions last mere seconds before the connection destabilizes, cosmic distance reasserting itself against his strained ability. But those seconds provide what he needs: confirmation that Orpheus's claims contradict reality. The footage shown in the obsidian chamber was manipulated and created to serve some purpose beyond truth.

Caelus's eyes snap open, glowing with the same amber light as his sigils. The enhancement bands around his fingers emit wisps of smoke as they cool from near-overload temperatures. His entire body trembles with the aftereffects of extended cosmic perception, muscles quivering from sustained tension, nerves sending confused signals that register as simultaneous hot and cold sensations across his skin.

He falls forward, catching himself on hands and knees as the Aetheris connection breaks completely. The sudden return to purely physical perception hits like a gravitational shift, his consciousness contracting from a cosmic scale to a singular presence with disorienting speed. His lungs heave, drawing oxygen that tastes painfully dense after the ethereal sensations of extended awareness.

For several moments, he can only breathe, allowing his biological systems to stabilize. The sigils across his skin cool gradually, their glow fading as his connection to cosmic currents normalizes. The platform beneath him dims in response, calibrating its energy output to match his reduced activity.

When he can move again, he rises on unsteady legs. The coordinates remain perfect in his memory, untouched by the physical discomfort of his return. He stumbles to the chamber's data terminal, fingers leaving sweat marks on its surface as he inputs the location with mechanical precision.

"Record and encrypt," he instructs, voice raw from the exertion. "Personal authentication only."

The terminal processes his command, storing the coordinates behind multiple security protocols. Standard procedure after significant discoveries, except this information won't be shared with Orpheus or the Valthorim Council. This discovery remains his alone.

Caelus gathers his discarded clothing, movements still uncoordinated from the tracking strain. The fabric feels unnaturally coarse against his sensitized skin, and the weight of the garments is unexpectedly burdensome after his cosmic immersion. He dresses with methodical focus, each movement bringing him further back into his physical identity.

He exits the Aetheris chamber with measured steps, careful to maintain a normal appearance despite his inner urgency. The corridors of Zathira continue their eternal patterns around him, robed figures moving with purpose between ancient stone walls, crystal illumination shifting in cycles that mimic natural daylight, and subtle atmospheric currents carrying faint incense from meditation chambers.

None of it feels quite real after his extended cosmic perception. The solid walls seem almost permeable, the passing figures like temporary arrangements of stardust rather than permanent entities. He blinks away this disorientation, forcing his mind to accept conventional reality again.

His quarters receive him with familiar silence. He moves directly to his storage unit, retrieving travel essentials with practiced efficiency. Each item serves multiple functions: clothing that adapts to various environments, tools with diverse applications, and medical supplies suitable for different physiologies. His training emphasizes preparedness without excess effectiveness through careful selection rather than quantity.

His personal ship waits in docking bay seven, a small, maneuverable vessel assigned for his Aetheris tracking operations. Its systems are calibrated specifically to his preferences, and its navigation array is capable of reaching even obscure coordinates without additional calculation. Most importantly, its authorization protocols recognize his command without requiring mission approval from higher authorities.

Caelus secures his pack, performs a final check of his quarters, and then pauses before the crystalline viewport. Stars burn with perfect clarity beyond the transparent surface, indifferent to the decisions being made beneath their ancient light. He places his palm against the cool crystal, feeling the subtle vibration of Zathira's environmental systems through the surface.

For four years, this place has been his home, Orpheus his mentor, and the Valthorim his purpose. The betrayal of these foundations leaves an emptiness in his chest, a void where certainty once resided. Yet beneath this hollowness burns something more fundamental: the conviction that truth must be sought regardless of consequence.

He turns from the viewport and moves toward the door, determination straightening his spine despite his physical exhaustion. The coordinates remain perfect in his memory, a destination beyond established routes, beyond easy tracking, exactly where Selenea would go if helping refugees escape persecution.

The corridors remain busy with Zathira's eternal activities, providing convenient cover for his movement toward the docking bays. His access privileges as an advanced Aetheris practitioner prevent immediate questions, though eventually, his absence will trigger notification protocols. He estimates that approximately six hours before Orpheus realizes his true intentions, sufficient time is needed to be well beyond the conventional pursuit range.

The docking bay opens to his authentication with a soft pneumatic hiss. His vessel waits in its designated position, sleek and efficient, designed for maneuverability rather than imposing presence. The entry hatch recognizes his approach, extending its boarding ramp in silent welcome.

Inside, the ship's systems activate at his touch, and the displays are illuminated with status reports and navigation options. He inputs the coordinates from memory, and each digit is precise despite the lingering effects of Aetheris strain. The navigation system processes the destination, calculating optimal routes through established travel lanes before veering into uncharted regions.

"I'll find the truth," he whispers to himself as the engines cycle through their startup sequence. The words form both promise and prayer, commitment to his sister and acknowledgment of the uncertain path ahead.

The docking clamps release metallic groans that reverberate through the hull. The ship hovers momentarily on its stabilizers, then glides forward through the atmospheric barrier that separates Zathira's internal environment from the void beyond. Stars stretch before him, infinite possibilities in every direction.

Caelus engages the main propulsion system. The ship responds instantly, accelerating away from the monastery with increasing speed. Behind him, Zathira diminishes rapidly, first to a distinctive structure among the asteroids, then to a point of light barely distinguishable from surrounding matter, and finally to nothing visible at all.

Ahead lies only stars, distance, and the coordinates burning in his memory where Selenea waits with the truth that someone very powerful wants hidden.

Chapter 9

The Voldom Uprising

The signal breaks through the static like a needle through the fabric, precise, invasive, and unmistakable. Selenea's fingers move across her ship's communication array with practiced efficiency, isolating the transmission from surrounding space noise. The Valthorim encryption patterns glow on her monitor, familiar yet foreign now that she stands on the other side of their security protocols. Her amber eyes narrow as the decryption algorithms run, each layer peeling away to reveal the coordinates and battle plans within.

"Voldom," she murmurs, the name leaving her lips as a statement rather than a question. The volcanic world appears in the decoded data stream, detailed topographical maps, thermal signatures, and population centers marked with clinical precision. Her former colleagues in the First Battalion have taught the Second Battalion well.

She studies the attack vectors with the practiced eye of someone who once designed such assaults. The patterns reveal themselves immediately: a three-pronged approach targeting geothermal infrastructure, standard containment formations to prevent civilian evacuation and surgical strikes against defensive positions. The timestamp indicates deployment within twenty-six hours. Not much time.

"Record and transmit," she commands, voice activating the ship's systems. "Encrypt using Magma Protocol Delta."

The communication system acknowledges with a soft chime. Selenea leans back in her chair, the ambient light of her small command deck casting sharp shadows across her face. Since leaving the battalion and choosing truth over orders at Nammu, she's established networks among worlds that the Valthorim consider "disruptive to cosmic harmony." Their definition of harmony increasingly resembles submission.

"Connection established," the system announces. "Recipient awaiting secure transmission."

The monitor flickers, static resolving into the face of Pyrra Brim. Even through the distortion of long-range communication, her features reveal determination hardened by experience, eyes that have witnessed too many attacks, mouth set in a line that seldom softens into smiles anymore.

"Selenea." Pyrra's voice carries the distinctive crackle of Voldom's interference-heavy atmosphere. "You have news?"

"Second Battalion. Twenty-six hours." Selenea transmits the decrypted files with a flick of her fingers across the control surface. "Full tactical package. They're targeting your primary caldera network and geothermal stations."

Pyrra's eyes move rapidly, scanning the incoming data with an engineer's precision. "This confirms our seismic readings. We detected fractal energy signatures in the upper atmosphere." Her face hardens. "The battalion configuration matches previous attacks on Drabliti and Vescit."

"They're getting predictable." Selenea pulls up her own analysis, overlaying battalion movement patterns from the last three planetary assaults. "Their right flank always deploys fifteen degrees offset from their central approach. Exploit that gap."

"We will." Pyrra nods once, a gesture of respect between equals. "The council assembles now. Your intelligence will save lives."

"Fight well." Selenea's hand moves to end the transmission then pauses. "Pyrra, the new fractal network allows faster reinforcement. Be prepared for second-wave deployment."

The communication ends, and the screen returns to its standard monitoring display. Selenea turns her attention to the navigation systems, plotting a course that will bring her ship to Voldom's orbit before the Battalion arrives. Her brother is already en route, their paths converging once again as they work to uncover the truth behind Orpheus's machinations.

In Voldom's central war chamber, heat rises from the floor in visible waves. The massive circular room sits suspended above an active magma flow carved directly into the wall of an ancient caldera. Strategic design rather than mere dramatic effect, the location allows immediate core samples of the planet's current geological status while providing uninterrupted power to the defense systems.

Pyrra Brim stands at the center, her figure haloed by the orange glow emanating from transparent sections of flooring that reveal the molten rock flowing beneath. The heat-resistant alloy tables surrounding her display holographic projections of the planet's surface, each defensive position marked with pulsing indicators.

"Second Battalion deployment confirmed," she announces as council members enter. They move with the deliberate care of those accustomed to life on constantly shifting ground; their bodies adapted to Voldom's higher gravity and sulfurous atmosphere. "We have intelligence indicating an attack within twenty-six hours."

"Source?" asks the eldest council member, his skin bearing the distinctive heat-scarring of those who work the deepest mines.

"Selenea Solaris. Former Battalion tactical officer." Pyrra projects the intercepted data across the primary display. "Her intelligence has proven reliable three times now."

The council members study the projections with the quiet intensity of those who have survived previous attacks. Maps of Voldom rotate above the tables, highlighting vulnerable sectors where volcanic activity already threatens structural stability.

"They target our weakest geological points," observes a female council member, her fingers tracing a line of dormant volcanoes where the battalion's attack vectors intersect. "Trigger enough eruptions, and our infrastructure collapses without direct engagement."

"Tactical efficiency," Pyrra confirms. "Minimum expenditure for maximum damage." Her voice carries no admiration, only clinical assessment. "They've studied our planet's pressure points."

The atmosphere in the chamber grows heavier as the council absorbs the implications. Defense strategies form and dissolve in the subsequent discussion, evacuate vulnerable sectors, concentrate forces at geothermal stations, and deploy mobile response units.

"Our primary weapon remains our environment," Pyrra interrupts the escalating debate. She activates a secondary display showing Voldom's extensive lava tube network, which is made up of natural tunnels formed by ancient magma flows that connect the major volcanic systems. "We arm the tubes with magma bombs at key junctures. When battalion forces establish ground positions, we trigger sequential detonations."

She demonstrates with simulation data. The holographic display shows pressurized magma explosions cascading through the tunnel system, creating controlled eruptions that surface directly beneath enemy positions.

"The magma bombs can reach 4,000 degrees on impact," she continues, her voice level despite the destruction displayed before them. "Sufficient to penetrate battalion armor. But, " her expression tightens imperceptibly, "the yield radius will destabilize nearby settlements. Evacuation becomes mandatory rather than precautionary."

Arguments erupt immediately. A younger council member pounds the table, sending holographic projections temporarily as an askew. "We evacuate now, and they claim victory without firing a shot! Our people built those settlements precisely because the geothermal energy sustains life."

"We sacrifice infrastructure, not lives," Pyrra responds, her voice cutting through the heightened emotions. "Structures rebuild. The dead remain dead."

The debate continues with increasing intensity, voices rising above the constant background rumble of the planet's geological activities. Through it all, Pyrra remains centered, her engineering mind calculating probabilities, weighing options, and examining alternatives with ruthless efficiency.

In the end, her plan prevails, not through force of personality but through irrefutable tactical logic. The council disperses to implement evacuation protocols while Pyrra moves toward the manufacturing levels to oversee weapons preparation.

The bomb assembly line occupies a reinforced chamber adjacent to an active magma tap. Workers in heat-resistant suits move with practiced precision, filling specialized containment shells with precisely measured amounts of pressurized molten rock. Each bomb requires exact calibration, is too stable, and won't detonate properly, and is too volatile, and it might explode during transport.

Pyrra takes a partially assembled device from the line, her hands moving with familiar expertise that betrays her background. Before becoming chief engineer of Voldom's defensive systems, she designed these weapons for peaceful applications, controlled demolition for mining operations, and pressure relief for overtaxed volcanic vents.

She adjusts the detonator mechanism, testing its response to different pressure scenarios. Her fingers don't hesitate despite the ethical weight pressing on her consciousness. The contradiction doesn't escape her, an engineer who believes in creation now mass-producing instruments of destruction.

"Increase core pressure by twelve percent," she instructs the assembly team. "Battalion armor has adapted since the last encounter."

As the workers implement her modifications, Pyrra moves to the observation window overlooking the caldera. The vast lake of molten rock bubbles with prehistoric power, indifferent to the conflict about to erupt above its surface. Her planet, her people, and her weapons are all connected in ways that both comfort and disturb her.

She feels the weight of the military intelligence in her pocket, Selenea's warning providing a chance that many worlds never received. Her hand closes around a small data crystal containing the complete defense plans, her knuckles whitening with determination. Tomorrow, her weapons will be destroyed. Today, they offer hope.

The ship tears through the fabric of hyperspace, reality reasserting itself in a flash of distorted starlight. Voldom fills the main viewport, it's surface a network of glowing veins against black volcanic rock, rivers of molten material flowing across the planet's crust like luminous blood through arteries. Caelus studies the display with measured concentration, the metal bands around his fingers tapping a precise rhythm against the navigation console as his Aetheris ability already detects disturbances in the cosmic threads surrounding the planet.

"Standard orbit achieved," announces the navigation officer, her voice cutting through the subtle hum of ship systems. "Maintaining position above the northern hemisphere."

Caelus nods, amber eyes never leaving the tactical display. The enhancement bands around his fingers catch the light from the console, reflecting it in muted flashes as he adjusts sensor parameters. Data streams across the screens, atmospheric composition, volcanic activity indices, gravitational fluctuations, and each measurement build a comprehensive tactical picture.

"Sensor sweep, full spectrum," he orders. The bridge crew responds with practiced efficiency, each member executing their function without unnecessary communication. They've served together since leaving Zathira, a crew assembled not from military ranks but from those who questioned Valthorim's methods, who chose conscience over orders. Their loyalty lies with principles rather than institutions.

The sensor data materializes as a three-dimensional projection at the center of the bridge. Voldom's defensive preparations become visible even from orbit, energy barriers erected around major population centers, heat signatures indicating troop movements, and concentrated activity around the major volcanic channels. Caelus studies these patterns, recognizing his sister's influence in their tactical arrangement.

"Selenea's warning reached them in time," he observes, satisfaction evident in his otherwise neutral expression. "They're fortifying the primary caldera network and evacuating civilian zones." He expands a section of the display, focusing on a particularly intense concentration of energy readings. "That's their command center. Established defensive perimeter, multiple redundant shields."

At the weapons station, Neous Dera shifts his massive form. Unlike the humanoid crew members, Neous's body consists of semi-solid magma contained within a specialized environmental suit. The transparent sections reveal his internal composition, a core that pulses with orange-white heat, cooling to darker basalt near his exterior. His voice emerges as a rumbling bass that seems to vibrate through the deck plates rather than travel through the air.

"They prepare well," he observes, four-fingered hands moving across controls modified to accommodate his higher body temperature. "But Battalion weapons are designed to disrupt volcanic stability. I've seen what they did to Vescit." The heat emanating from his form intensifies momentarily, reflecting his emotional state. "They turn a planet's strength against itself."

Caelus acknowledges this with a slight nod. He understands why Neous takes this mission personally. Voldom's volcanic environment mirrors his home world, and its people share similar adaptations to extreme heat conditions. The Battalion's strategy of triggering catastrophic eruptions represents not just tactical warfare but environmental destruction on a planetary scale.

The bridge lighting dims slightly as Caelus activates his Aetheris enhancement bands. The sigils tattooed across his skin respond immediately, warming beneath his uniform. His back straightens as the connection builds, channeling through the metal rings on his fingers. The familiar sensation washes over him, expanding awareness that stretches beyond conventional perception, connecting with the cosmic threads that bind all stardust-formed matter.

The crew maintains respectful silence, continuing their preparations while giving him space for concentration. They've witnessed this process enough to understand its demands, the physical strain of extending consciousness beyond normal parameters, and the mental discipline required to interpret the information received.

"Fractal disturbance detected," Caelus announces after several moments, his voice carrying the slight harmonic undertone that accompanies active Aetheris connection. His eyes now contain flecks of blue light, cosmic energy reflecting in amber irises. "Second Battalion configuration. Arrival coordinates locked."

He transfers the information to the main tactical display. A red marker appears in Voldom's upper atmosphere, directly above the largest active caldera system. The location confirms what they feared: the Battalion intends to trigger a chain reaction through the planet's most volatile geological features.

"Battalion arrival in seventeen minutes," he continues, fingers tracing patterns in the air that leave momentary blue trails hanging in the bridge's subdued lighting. "Standard deployment formation. Three attack vectors. The primary target is the geothermal network."

The weapons officer, a compact woman with precise movements that betray previous military training, enters targeting solutions into her console. "Defensive countermeasures prepared. Focusing on disrupting their formation upon emergence."

"Communication from the surface," the systems operator announces. "Encrypted channel. It's Selenea."

Caelus nods, and Selenea's face appears on the main display. Behind her, the orange glow of Voldom's command center creates dramatic shadows that emphasize the determination in her expression.

"Brother," she greets, the familiar formality of their relationship unchanged despite all that's happened. "Your timing is perfect."

"As is your intelligence," he responds. "We've confirmed the Second Battalion configuration. The fractal signature matches their previous planetary assaults."

Selenea nods, unsurprised. "We've coordinated with Pyrra Brim's defense forces. Her magma bombs are deployed throughout the lava tube network, ready to trigger targeted eruptions beneath Battalion positions." She glances at something off-screen, then continues. "Your ship's energy weapons can disrupt their air support. We'll handle ground resistance."

"Understood." Caelus studies his sister's face, recognizing the tactical officer she was trained to be now directed toward defense rather than conquest. "Be careful. Orpheus wouldn't commit the Second Battalion unless he considered this target high priority."

Something flickers across Selenea's features, recognition of the larger game they're caught in. "This isn't about Voldom. It's about controlling geothermal technology that could make other worlds self-sufficient." The connection begins to degrade, interference patterns crawling across her image. "Position yourselves above the primary caldera. That's where they'll concentrate their initial assault."

The transmission ends as Caelus turns to his navigation officer. "Take us to these coordinates. Maintain altitude above their anti-aircraft range but within targeting parameters for our main batteries."

The ship banks smoothly, engines adjusting with barely perceptible vibrations through the hull. Through the viewport, Voldom's surface features become more distinct: massive volcano cones rising from black plains, rivers of lava casting orange light against perpetual ash clouds, and the geometric patterns of settlements built to withstand constant seismic activity.

"All stations, battle preparation," Caelus orders, his voice carrying calm authority that belies the tension evident in the crew's movements. They've faced Battalion forces before, witnessed their methodical efficiency, and experienced their unwavering commitment to Valthorim directives. Each engagement has ended in retreat, tactical withdrawals to preserve lives when victory proved impossible.

Today feels different. Voldom's defenders have advance warning. Selenea's tactical knowledge provides a crucial advantage. Their ship enters position above the primary caldera, a massive depression thirty kilometers across filled with bubbling lava that occasionally sends fountains of molten rock hundreds of meters into the air.

"Energy signatures increasing at target coordinates," reports the sensor officer, voice tight with concentration. "Spatial distortion beginning to form."

Caelus feels it through his Aetheris connection before the instruments detect it, a wrongness in the fabric of reality, a stretching of cosmic threads beyond their natural parameters. The sensation always disturbs him, reminding him how the Valthorim manipulates fundamental forces for convenient transport without concern for long-term consequences to space-time stability.

"Fractal formation confirmed," he announces. "Prepare all defensive systems."

The bridge falls silent except for the soft beeps of equipment and the background hum of power systems charging to combat levels. Through the viewport, the air above the caldera seems to thicken, becoming almost viscous as reality bends according to precise mathematical principles. A tear begins to form, not the controlled, crystalline pattern of authorized Fractals, but something more aggressive, forced rather than finessed.

The tear pulses with dark energy that absorbs rather than emits light. Its edges expand outward in mathematical progression, creating an opening large enough to accommodate transport vessels and troop deployments. Through the widening gap, the outline of Battalion ships becomes visible, angular craft designed for atmospheric combat, their weapons already charging.

"They're coming through," says Neous, the magma in his core pulsing with heightened intensity. The transparent sections of his containment suit glow brighter, reflecting his increasing agitation. "The Second Battalion never retreats until their objective is complete."

Caelus's fingers tightened around the command console, and the metal bands left temporary impressions on the surface. His sigils pulse beneath his uniform, responding to both the Fractal disturbance and his own rising determination.

"Neither do we," he responds, eyes fixed on the fully-forming Fractal tear. The ship's weapons systems come online with a subtle change in the background hum, power redirected from non-essential systems to offensive capabilities. "Prepare to engage."

The Fractal tears wider, its edges stretching reality into impossible geometries. The Second Battalion emerges like a nightmare given form, first the angular prows of assault ships, then the ground forces in formation, their heat-resistant armor reflecting the volcanic glow from below. They move with mechanical precision, each unit assuming predetermined positions as they materialize fully in Voldom's atmosphere. Last through the rift comes their commander, Magmara Pyrox, the Molten Guardian, whose massive form of semi-solid magma contained within specialized armor resembles a walking volcano more than a conventional soldier.

Magmara towers four meters tall, their core glowing with intense orange-white heat visible through transparent sections of their containment suit. Their outer layer cools to form a dark, basaltic crust that shifts and cracks with each movement, revealing glimpses of the molten interior. Their helmet, more ceremonial than functional, bears the insignia of the Second Battalion etched in cooling obsidian against the flowing magma of their face.

"Deploy," Magmara commands, their voice a deep rumble that travels through the sulfurous air like distant thunder. The Battalion responds instantly, breaking into three distinct attack formations that spread across Voldom's sky like talons reaching for the planet's surface.

The primary force targets the largest geothermal power station, its angular ships descending in a perfect triangular formation. The second group banks toward the residential districts, their weapon systems already locking onto evacuation routes. The third, led by Magmara themselves, head directly for the central caldera, where Pyrra coordinates the defense.

"This world returns to ash," Magmara announces through the Battalion communication system, their words broadcasting across both their forces and intercepted by Voldomian defenders. "Their resistance is a pebble before an avalanche."

The first energy salvos fire from Battalion ships, not targeting structures directly but striking the unstable volcanic fissures that crisscross Voldom's surface. The precisely calibrated weapons superheat the already volatile magma chambers beneath, creating instant pressure buildup. Geysers of lava erupt where the blasts connect, sending molten rock hundreds of meters skyward.

The air itself becomes a hazard as the superheated atmosphere creates pockets of near-plasma that distort visibility and disrupt communication signals. Sulfurous gases are released from newly opened vents, forming yellow-green clouds that drift across the battlefield. The constant rumble of seismic activity increases as Battalion weapons destabilize the planet's natural volcanic rhythms.

From defensive positions carved into the caldera walls, Voldomian forces launch their response. The first wave of magma bombs arcs toward the Battalion's advancing lines, spherical containers designed to rupture on impact, releasing their pressurized molten contents in deadly, focused sprays. Unlike conventional explosives, these weapons harness Voldom's natural environment as ammunition.

The bombs strike with devastating effect. Where they impact Battalion armor, they create temperatures exceeding 4,000 degrees, hot enough to melt through the heat-resistant plating designed for standard combat environments. Soldiers caught in the spray zones become living torches, and their specialized equipment is insufficient against the liquid rock that clings and continues burning through protective layers.

Magmara observes the initial exchange by calculating intensity, the magma of their form pulsing with increased energy as they analyze defense patterns. "Predictable," they rumble to their command unit. "They defend where we expect. Redirect the second wing to coordinates seven-three-mark-four."

Battalion ships adjust their approach vectors, some climbing higher to avoid the magma bomb trajectories, others descending to skim just above the volcanic surface where Voldomian targeting systems struggle to establish locks through the heat distortion. Their tactics display the adaptability that makes the Second Battalion particularly effective against environmentally defensive worlds.

The battlefield deteriorates rapidly as natural volcanic vents rupture from combat vibrations. Across Voldom's surface, dormant pressure points activate in chain reactions, small eruptions triggering larger ones, lava flows redirecting through collapsed tunnel systems, and ash plumes rising to obscure aerial visibility. What began as organized combat devolves into warfare conducted through environmental chaos.

In a forward command post carved directly into the caldera wall, Pyrra Brim monitors the battle through heat-resistant display screens. Sweat beads on her forehead despite the environmental controls, and the command center's temperature rises as external conditions worsen. Around her, Voldomian tacticians track Battalion movements, adjusting defense deployments to counter their three-pronged assault strategy.

"They're adapting to our standard bomb yield," Pyrra observes, fingers moving across display surfaces with engineer's precision. "Recalibrate to thermal signature pattern delta, and their armor adapts to sustained heat."

Technicians implement her instructions, transmitting new detonation parameters to the defensive lines. The next wave of magma bombs launches with modified pressure settings; instead of single high-temperature impacts, they now release their contents in multiple pulses, preventing Battalion armor from adjusting to consistent heat levels.

"Southeastern quadrant breached," reports a communications officer, voice tight with controlled urgency. "Battalion forces approaching the secondary geothermal station."

Pyrra's response comes without hesitation. "Activate lava tube sequence nine through fourteen. Redirect defensive units from the northern perimeter." Her hands trace patterns across the tactical display, identifying weak points in Battalion formation. "They're concentrating too much force on the power infrastructure. That leaves their aerial support patterns too thin here, " she indicates, indicating a section where battalion ships maintain their triangular approach formation but with wider spacing than protocol dictates.

Outside, the sky darkens as ash clouds block Voldom's distant sun. The battlefield illumination comes primarily from below now, the orange-red glow of fresh lava flows, the bright flashes of energy weapons, and the white-hot detonations of magma bombs. Visibility reduces to a series of heat signatures moving through clouds of particulate matter.

The Battalion's initial advantage of organized deployment fades as Voldom's environment becomes an active participant in the battle. Ships struggle to maintain formation through unpredictable thermal updrafts. Ground forces find their advance routes suddenly blocked by fresh lava flows erupting from destabilized vents. Communication signals degrade as the thickening atmosphere absorbs and distorts transmission patterns.

Yet despite these challenges, the Second Battalion continues its relentless advance. Their numerical superiority and specialized training compensate for environmental disadvantages. Where Voldomian defenses concentrate, Battalion forces simply redirect, probing for weaknesses with machine-like efficiency.

Magmara Pyrox leads from the front lines, their massive form striding through conditions that would incapacitate ordinary soldiers. Lava splashes against their armor only to be absorbed into their natural magma composition. They reshape sections of their form at will, extending appendages to clear obstacles or create shields against defensive fire.

"Your defenses fragment like cooling stone," they broadcast to Voldomian channels, their voice carrying the absolute conviction of one who views conquest as natural law.

"Your technology cannot save you from what you fundamentally are, a world born of fire, returning to fire."

Pyrra receives this transmission in the command center, her expression hardening as she recognizes the voice. "Magmara Pyrox," she tells her assembled officers. "I wondered if Orpheus would send them. Their species once maintained Voldom's volcanic harmony before the Valthorim recruited them."

"Why would they attack a world so similar to their own nature?" asks a junior officer, confusion evident in his voice.

"Because they believe strength comes only through dominance," Pyrra responds, her eyes never leaving the tactical display where Magmara's heat signature moves inexorably toward the central defensive line. "And they see our defensive stance as proof of fundamental weakness."

She activates a direct communication link to Caelus's orbiting ship. "Their primary force approaches the main caldera. Magmara leads personally. We need orbital support to thin their air cover."

Above the thickening ash clouds, Caelus's ship moves into position, its weapons systems targeting the geometrically perfect formation of the Battalion support craft. Energy beams lance downward through the atmospheric chaos, disrupting the Battalion's carefully maintained flight patterns.

On the ground, Pyrra observes these impacts with grim satisfaction. "Now," she orders her defensive coordinators. "Trigger sequence alpha through the main tube network."

Deep beneath the battlefield, detonators activate in perfect synchronization. The network of lava tubes, natural conduits running throughout Voldom's crust, become weaponized delivery systems as controlled explosions direct pressurized magma upward through predetermined channels. The ground beneath the advancing Battalion forces suddenly erupts in dozens of precise locations, creating a curtain of liquid fire that separates their front line from supporting units.

Magmara pauses their advance, the magma of their form pulsing with what might be a surprise or perhaps respect. "Creative," they rumble to their command unit. "They use our tactics against us." The cooling crust of their exterior cracks as they expand their form, internal heat intensifying with what can only be described as anticipation. "Bring forward the seismic disruptors. If they wish to fight with the planet itself, we will show them mastery of geological warfare."

The battle enters its second phase as both sides escalate their environmental manipulation. Voldom's natural volcanic activity, already heightened by the conflict, begins to show signs of cascading instability. The planet itself becomes both battlefield and weapon, with neither side fully in control of the elemental forces they've unleashed.

The battle consumes Voldom's surface like a living entity, devouring order and replacing it with elemental chaos. Sulfur fills the air, burning lungs and leaving a metallic taste that coats tongues and teeth. The ground trembles in a constant rhythm, no longer distinguishing between natural seismic activity and weapon impact. Each breath draws in ash particles that scratch throats raw. Between flashes of energy weapons, visibility extends barely twenty meters before dissolving into a swirling orange-black miasma. Through this hellscape, battalion soldiers advance in heat-rippling lines while Voldomian defenders hold positions that shift beneath their feet with each new eruption.

Magmara Pyrox leads the central assault force with terrible purpose, their massive form cutting through defensive fire like a living weapon. Where magma bombs strike their exterior, the molten material simply incorporates into their form, temporarily increasing their mass before being redistributed through their internal circulation. They reshape parts of themselves at will, extending appendages into whip-like tendrils that crack against Voldomian barricades, forming shield plates from cooling crust to deflect energy weapons.

"Forward," they command, voice carrying through Battalion communication systems despite the atmospheric interference. Behind them, soldiers advance in tight formation, their heat-resistant armor now supplemented with additional shielding calibrated specifically for Voldom's environment. They move with the synchronized precision that makes the Second Battalion particularly effective, each soldier functioning as a component in a larger machine rather than an individual fighter.

Above the battlefield, partially obscured by ash clouds, Caelus's ship maintains its position over the central caldera. The vessel's sensors continuously adjust to penetrate the thickening atmospheric conditions, providing tactical data that normal visibility cannot offer. From this vantage point, Battalion movements appear as heat signatures flowing across Voldom's surface like methodical lava streams, converging, separating, and reforming according to predetermined patterns.

"Target their supply lines," Caelus directs his weapons officer, fingers tracing patterns through the three-dimensional tactical display. The metal bands around his fingers leave blue light trails in the air, amplifying his Aetheris-enhanced perception. "They're channeling additional shielding technology through these transport corridors."

The ship's energy weapons discharge with precise targeting, lancing through gaps in the ash cloud to strike Battalion supply vessels. The impacts disrupt the carefully maintained logistics chain, temporarily isolating forward units from technological support.

On the ground, Selenea moves among Voldomian defensive positions; her Battalion training is repurposed to strengthen rather than overcome resistance. She carries a modified Valthorim energy pistol, and its settings are recalibrated for maximum effectiveness against Second Battalion armor configurations. Her uniform, a hybrid of Battalion utility and Voldomian heat resistance, bears scorch marks from close encounters with both weapons fire and environmental hazards.

"Concentrate fire on their formation seams," she instructs a group of defenders positioned behind a natural basalt formation. "They maintain rigid patterns even when tactically disadvantageous. Exploit the predictability."

The defenders adjust their aim, targeting the narrow gaps that appear when Battalion units transition between formations. Several soldiers fall as precision shots find the minimal exposure points in their armor. The advancement temporarily falters ripples of disruption spreading through their otherwise perfect coordination.

This momentary advantage dissolves as Magmara personally spearheads a direct assault on the central defensive line. Their form expands to nearly twice normal size, internal heat intensifying until their exterior glows white at the core, forcing defenders to avert their eyes or risk temporary blindness. They reach the defensive perimeter and simply flow over it, their semi-solid form conforming to obstacles before reforming on the other side.

"Your world already burns from within," they announce as defensive positions collapse around them, their voice like stone grinding against stone. "We merely hasten its inevitable collapse."

Defenders retreat before this unstoppable advance, falling back to secondary positions as Battalion forces pour through the gap Magmara creates. The breakthrough threatens to split Voldom's defensive coordination, potentially isolating command centers from field units.

In the forward command post, Pyrra observes this development with a tightly controlled alarm. Her fingers dance across control surfaces with the engineer's precision, activating systems designed for exactly this contingency.

"Initiate pressure valve sequence," she orders. "Full network, sections twelve through twenty-nine."

Across the battlefield, hidden mechanisms activate within Voldom's natural lava tube network. What appear to be ordinary volcanic vents suddenly reveal their dual purpose: precisely engineered pressure valves that release controlled lava flows into predetermined channels. Molten rock surges from dozens of points simultaneously, forming rivers of liquid fire that cut across Battalion advance routes.

These aren't merely defensive barriers but a complex grid designed to segment the battlefield into manageable sectors. Battalion units find themselves suddenly isolated from supporting groups, communication lines physically severed by impassable flows. The perfect coordination that defines their effectiveness fractures as individual squads must adapt to rapidly changing conditions without centralized command.

Yet despite this tactical success, the situation remains critical. Battalion forces adapt with practiced efficiency, establishing new communication relays and reconfiguring their approach vectors. Their numerical advantage begins to overcome the environmental restrictions as more troops continue to deploy through the still-open Fractal.

The battle devolves into desperate close-quarters combat across multiple fronts. Voldomian defenders, intimately familiar with their volatile environment, use heat-resistant melee weapons, obsidian-edged blades and basalt clubs reinforced with metals forged in volcanic depths. These primitive-appearing tools prove surprisingly effective against Battalion armor designed primarily for energy weapon resistance.

Selenea finds herself caught in one such engagement, surrounded by three Battalion soldiers whose armor bears the distinctive markings of elite shock troops. She moves with fluid precision, and each motion is economical and lethal. Her Battalion training manifests in perfect form: a disabling strike to joint seams in the first soldier's armor, a precision shot through the breathing apparatus of the second, a tactical retreat that lures the third into a superheated gas vent that compromises their suit integrity.

Throughout the chaos, her communication link to Caelus remains active, and their tactical coordination is unbroken despite physical separation.

"They're adapting too quickly," she reports, voice steady despite her elevated breathing. "Magmara's presence accelerates their environmental adaptation. Standard Battalion protocols would have them rotating troops to prevent heat fatigue."

Above the battlefield, Caelus absorbs this information while simultaneously monitoring the tactical display. His Aetheris perception extends beyond normal sensors, detecting patterns in cosmic threads that conventional technology cannot register. The sigils across his skin pulse beneath his uniform as he traces connections between the Battalion forces and their still-open Fractal portal.

"Energy fluctuations detected," he responds, his voice carrying the harmonic undertone of an active Aetheris connection. "The Fractal isn't stabilizing correctly."

He focuses his enhanced perception on the tear in reality that continues to discharge Battalion reinforcements. Unlike properly authorized Fractals with their perfect crystalline patterns, this forced opening shows signs of instability, its edges pulsing irregularly, and its internal structure lacking the mathematical perfection that ensures spatial integrity.

"Their rear guard formation is weaker than standard configuration," he continues, the blue light around his irises intensifying as he channels more energy through his enhancement bands. "They're diverting power to maintain the Fractal rather than following normal deployment protocols."

On his tactical display, he highlights a specific section of the Battalion's rear formation, where troops maintain the connection between the main assault force and the Fractal entrance. The pattern there shows subtle irregularities, spacing too wide, energy signatures fluctuating, and coordination slightly delayed compared to front-line units.

"I see it," Selenea confirms, her tactical mind immediately grasping the implications. "They're overextended. Maintaining a Fractal of that size while deploying troops exceeds standard parameters."

Caelus's fingers trace patterns across his console, calculating precise coordinates. "Fractal energy signature fluctuating at their rear guard hit it now. A concentrated strike at these exact coordinates could disrupt their connection completely."

He transmits targeting data to both Selenea's ground forces and Pyrra's command center. The information appears as a three-dimensional overlay on tactical displays throughout Voldom's defensive network, a single point of vulnerability in the otherwise impenetrable Battalion deployment.

Pyrra reviews the data with an engineer's critical assessment, verifying calculations against her own understanding of energy dynamics. Her expression shifts from skepticism to determined focus as she confirms Caelus's analysis.

"All remaining defensive units," she broadcasts across the command network, "redirect fire to transmitted coordinates. Maximum yield, converging trajectories."

Across the fragmented battlefield, Voldomian forces receive these instructions. Those not directly engaged in close-quarters defense reposition to establish firing lines on the identified weak point. Selenea organizes one such group, using natural terrain features to shield them from battalion counter-fire while establishing clear lines of sight for the target area.

"On my mark," she instructs, positioning herself with the precision of a Battalion tactical officer. Around her, Voldomian defenders prepare their most powerful weapons, not just conventional energy devices but specialized volcanic armaments designed to channel and direct Voldom's natural forces.

Above, Caelus's ship moves into an optimal position, with the main batteries aligning with the identified coordinates. The weapons charge with building hum that resonates through the vessel's hull, power redirected from non-essential systems to maximize impact potential.

"Target locked," reports the weapons officer, her voice reflecting the focused intensity that permeates the bridge. Beside her, Neous Dera monitors energy levels, his magma form pulsing with anticipation that mirrors the volcanic activity below.

Between the ash clouds and environmental chaos, a single point of vulnerability presents itself, the nexus where Battalion rear guards maintain their connection to the still-unstable Fractal. For a brief moment, the swirling ash clears enough to reveal this critical junction: soldiers in formation around equipment designed to stabilize the spatial tear, their attention divided between battlefield awareness and technical maintenance.

Caelus leans forward in his command chair, enhancement bands glowing with intensified energy as he perceives both physical reality and the cosmic threads that connect it to deeper truths.

"Fire," he commands, his voice calm despite the weight of consequence carried by that single word.

The coordinated strike hits the Battalion's rear position with devastating precision. Energy beams from Caelus's ship lance through ash clouds, illuminating the battlefield in stark blue-white light. Simultaneously, Selenea's ground forces unleash a barrage of magma bombs, their trajectories converging on the exact coordinates where the Fractal connection remains most vulnerable. The resulting explosion doesn't merely damage equipment and soldiers; it tears through the fabric of reality itself, disrupting the mathematical perfection required to maintain a stable Fractal. The spatial tear shudders visibly, its edges pulsing with uncontrolled energy as a connection to the Battalion's reinforcements destabilizes.

What begins as calculated damage cascades into catastrophic failure. The Fractal's crystalline pattern, already forced beyond standard parameters, fractures along mathematical fault lines. Reality attempts to reassert itself against the artificial tear, creating feedback loops that manifest as violent energy discharges across the Battalion's rear position. Soldiers caught in this disruption zone contort in impossible angles as space-time distortions affect their physical forms. Equipment was designed to stabilize the fracture overloads, and components were melting under energies they were never designed to contain.

Selenea observes the effect from her forward position, amber eyes reflecting the chaotic energies now consuming the Battalion's rear guard. "Fractal connection compromised," she reports through the communication network, voice steady despite the devastating spectacle before her. "Reinforcement pathway collapsing. Battalion forces cut off from support."

The tactical implications register immediately across Voldom's defense network. What began as desperate resistance against overwhelming force transforms into potential victory. The battalion's numerical advantage and primary tactical strength suddenly vanishes as reinforcements can no longer deploy through the destabilized Fractal.

In the command center, Pyrra Brim analyzes the shifting battle dynamics with an engineer's precision. Her fingers dance across tactical displays, recalculating force distributions and opportunity zones. What she sees confirms her assessment: the moment for counterattack has arrived.

"Deploy the heat-walkers," she orders, already moving toward the exit. "All units converge on the central breach point."

From concealed hangars throughout the caldera network, Voldom's elite defensive units emerge. The heat-walkers represent the pinnacle of Voldom's adaptation technology; soldiers encased in specialized suits that not only withstand direct contact with magma but actively channel volcanic energy as both protection and weapon. Each suit stands three meters tall, its exterior composed of articulated plates harvested from the planet's ancient lava flows and reinforced with metals forged in geothermal pressure chambers.

Pyrra emerges from the command center wearing one such suit, the armor conforming to her movements with engineered precision. Unlike standard military equipment, these suits represent a partnership between operator and environment, each step generating kinetic energy that powers internal cooling systems, each exposure to extreme heat harvested to enhance offensive capabilities.

"Forward pattern," she commands through the heat-walker communication network. "Converge on Magmara's position."

The heat-walkers move with surprising grace despite their imposing size, advancing through terrain that would be impassable to conventional forces. They wade through active lava flows, the specialized leg articulation allowing them to navigate the viscous surface. Their weapons, focused magma projectors that harness and direct the planet's molten resources, leave trails of superheated stone as they advance toward the Battalion's position.

Caught between this new threat and the collapsed Fractal behind them, the Battalion's perfect formation dissolves into fragmented resistance. Without continuous tactical updates from command, individual units fall back on standard protocols ill-suited to the rapidly changing battlefield conditions. Their previously unified assault fractures into isolated engagements fought with diminishing coordination.

Magmara Pyrox recognizes the strategic shift immediately. The cooling crust of their exterior cracks as internal temperatures surge with what might be interpreted as rage or perhaps respect for an effective countermove. They redirect their forces, attempting to establish a defensive perimeter around what remains of the Fractal connection.

"Maintain position," they command their scattered units. "The Fractal can be stabilized. Priority is securing the entry point."

But this temporary focus on defense rather than offense creates the opening Pyrra's forces need. The heat-walkers encircle the Battalion's fragmented lines, cutting off retreat paths with precisely directed lava flows. What began as a three-pronged Battalion assault transforms into surrounded pockets of resistance fighting with dwindling resources.

Selenea coordinates this encirclement with tactical precision, and her battalion training is now directed toward containing rather than executing assault patterns. "Close the northern quadrant," she directs a unit of heat-walkers. "They'll attempt to establish elevated positions on those volcanic spires."

Above the battlefield, Caelus's ship maintains its position over the destabilizing Fractal. His Aetheris perception monitors the tear's deteriorating mathematical cohesion, calculating the precise moment when a final strike might collapse it completely.

"Energy signature fluctuating at increasing intervals," he reports to Selenea and Pyrra. "The Fractal sustains itself through Battalion power systems, but the connection weakens with each disruption."

On the ground, Pyrra leads her heat-walkers directly toward Magmara's position. The Molten Guardian stands amid their remaining forces, their massive form shifting between offensive and defensive configurations as they assess the deteriorating tactical situation. When Pyrra approaches in her heat-walker suit, Magmara turns to face her directly, internal magma surging with recognition.

They meet in a small crater formed by earlier weapons impact, superheated air shimmering between them. Geysers of steam erupt from fissures around their position as groundwater contacts exposed magma chambers. Ash falls like black snow, accumulating on Pyrra's armor while simply incorporating it into Magmara's fluid exterior.

"Your world and mine are not so different," Pyrra challenges, her voice amplified through her heat-walkers external speakers. "Why destroy what you could protect?"

Magmara's form expands, internal heat intensifying until their core glows white-hot. The cooling crust that forms their exterior features cracks and reforms continuously, suggesting agitation beyond normal parameters.

"Weakness deserves consumption," they respond, their deep voice reverberating through the superheated air. "The strong devour the failing. This is the law of molten worlds."

"Strength through destruction is temporary," Pyrra counters, her heat-walker suit harvesting the extreme temperatures around them to power its offensive systems. "We build strength through adaptation, through protection of what matters."

Magmara moves with sudden violence, extending a magma tendril toward Pyrra's position. The attack carries enough heat to melt conventional armor on contact. Instead of evading, Pyrra advances directly into the strike, her suit's specialized exterior absorbing and redistributing the thermal energy. The heat-walker's systems glow as they process this power surge, redirecting it to internal capacitors.

"Your philosophy is flawed," Magmara declares, reforming their extended appendage. "Your defenses require constant maintenance, technological intervention, and artificial supports. My existence requires nothing but what I am."

"Yet you serve the Valthorim," Pyrra responds, circling to maintain optimal engagement distance. "Natural strength harnessed to artificial purpose. How is that different from our technological adaptation?"

This observation triggers visible disruption in Magmara's form, ripples of intensified heat spreading from core to exterior as if the words penetrate deeper than physical attacks could reach. Before they can respond, the battlefield dynamics shift dramatically.

Above them, Caelus's ship positions itself directly over the weakened Fractal. All weapons systems focus on an unstable tear and energy building to maximum capacity.

Neous Dera, the magma-based warrior on Caelus's crew, monitors these power levels with particular intensity. His internal composition, similar to Magmara's, though on a smaller scale, pulses with conflicting emotions as he watches the battle unfold.

"They attack a world of their own nature," he observes, voice rumbling through the bridge. "The Battalion turns brother against brother."

Caelus acknowledges this with a solemn nod, understanding the personal dimension this conflict holds for his crew member. "Sometimes the greatest threats come from those who should be our closest allies." His enhancement bands glow as he channels his Aetheris perception one final time, identifying the exact coordinates where reality struggles most aggressively against the forced tear. "Target locked. Fire."

The ship's main batteries discharge with blinding intensity, energy beams converging on the Fractal's most vulnerable point. The impact triggers catastrophic collapse, not merely closing the tear but actively sealing the fabric of reality with such force that a shockwave of displaced energy rolls across the battlefield. The Fractal implodes with a sound like distant thunder, leaving only empty air where the spatial tear had been.

Magmara witnesses this destruction, their form momentarily frozen in what might be disbelief. With the Fractal gone, no retreat or reinforcement remains possible. Battalion forces across the battlefield register this development simultaneously, their coordinated resistance fracturing into individual survival calculations.

"Retreat to defensive positions," Magmara commands, their voice carrying less certainty than before. "Establish perimeter at coordinates delta-seven."

Pyrra seizes this moment of vulnerability, directing her heat-walkers to apply maximum pressure against the disorganized Battalion forces. "Drive them toward the northern ridges," she orders. "Cut off their access to the remaining ships."

The battle shifts into its final phase, not conquest but containment, not victory but survival. Battalion soldiers retreat in established patterns, maintaining what discipline remains despite their tactical collapse. Magmara coordinates this withdrawal with evident expertise, prioritizing equipment recovery and wounded extraction despite the deteriorating situation.

From orbit, Caelus observes this retreat with analytical detachment. "They're abandoning their forward positions," he reports to Selenea and Pyrra. "Consolidating forces around their remaining atmospheric vessels."

On the bridge beside him, Neous Dera watches the conflict with growing anger, not directed at Voldom's defenders but at the Battalion that would attack a world so similar to his own nature. The magma of his core pulses with heightened intensity, creating temperature fluctuations that the ship's environmental systems struggle to compensate for.

"They waste what should be cherished," he says, four-fingered hands tightening around the console edge, leaving slight indentations in the metal surface. "Worlds of fire are rare treasures in the cold void."

Caelus places a hand near, though not touching, Neous's superheated shoulder, a gesture of understanding that requires no physical contact. "This victory may help prevent similar attacks on other volcanic worlds," he offers, though the words provide limited comfort against the visible destruction below.

On the surface, Voldom bears the scars of battle across its already volatile landscape. Fresh craters pockmark the black plains, and lava flows carve new channels through previously stable terrain; ash clouds will linger in the atmosphere for months. Yet beneath these wounds, the essential infrastructure remains intact, the geothermal network still functions, population centers survive behind their protective barriers, and the planet's core continues its ancient rhythms undisturbed.

Pyrra stands at the edge of the central caldera, her heat-walker suit now powered down to conservation levels. She watches as the remaining Battalion forces complete their retreat, loading onto the few atmospheric craft that survived the conflict. Magmara boards the final vessel, their massive form compacting slightly to accommodate the transport's dimensions. For a brief moment, the Molten Guardian turns toward Pyrra's position, their cooling exterior reflecting the volcanic glow from below.

No words pass between them, yet something communicates nonetheless, recognition between beings shaped by similar environments but diverged through different philosophies. Then, the vessel's hatch seals, and the last Battalion ship rises through the ash-filled sky, diminishing to a point of light that eventually vanishes against Voldom's disturbed atmosphere.

"They'll return," Selenea says, approaching Pyrra's position with the measured steps of someone conserving remaining energy. "The Valthorim never abandon a target completely."

Pyrra nods, removing her helmet to feel Voldom's sulfurous air against her skin. The planet smells of fire and stone, of destruction and renewal, scents she has known her entire life. "And we'll be better prepared," she responds, eyes tracking the paths of fresh lava flows already beginning to cool, to harden, to form new foundations upon the scars of conflict. "That's what volcanic worlds do best. We rebuild from the ashes."

Chapter 10

Allies in the Flames

Neous Dera stands before the main viewscreen, his massive form of living magma reflecting the destruction displayed before him. His core pulses with intensifying orange-red light as Battalion ships descend upon Voldom's volcanic surface. Each explosion sends ripples through his semi-solid body as if the impacts strike him directly rather than the planet below. The specialized chamber that accommodates his extreme temperature grows uncomfortably warm even for him as his internal heat rises with his mounting rage.

The Voldomian defense forces launch magma bombs in precise trajectories, creating brilliant flares when they connect with Battalion vessels. These brief victories burn like stars against the black volcanic landscape before fading. Neous's outer crust cracks at the edges, molten material seeping through the fissures before resealing. His structure always betrays his emotions, which are impossible to hide when your body is transparent and not glowing.

"Magnify sector four," he requests, his voice a deep rumble that vibrates through the deck plates.

The viewscreen shifts, focusing on a series of geometric structures built into the side of a dormant volcano. Mining Colony Seventeen. Neous recognizes the intricate heat-shielding patterns he helped install five cycles ago, the reinforced evacuation tunnels he personally carved through cooling basalt.

Battalion dropships descend on the colony in perfect formation. Their weapons target structural supports first, which is the standard battalion procedure for civilian settlements. The heat shields collapse in a methodical sequence, exposing residential quarters to the planet's harsh environment. Evacuees stream from the tunnels like insects fleeing smoke, desperation evident even from orbit.

Magmara Pyrox stands at the colony's edge, their massive form directing the systematic destruction with terrifying efficiency. Their core glows white-hot through their containment armor as they extend a semi-solid appendage toward fleeing civilians, cutting off their escape route with a precise stream of directed magma.

"They're just miners," Neous rumbles, his temperature spiking sharply enough that the ship's environmental alerts ping softly in response. "Crystal harvesters and heat technicians. Not soldiers."

Caelus approaches, careful to maintain a safe distance from Neous's increasingly unstable form. The metal bands around his fingers gleam as he adjusts environmental controls to compensate for the rising heat.

"Orpheus classified all Voldomians as threats to cosmic stability," Caelus explains, though his tone suggests he no longer believes this assessment.

"Orpheus promised protection." Neous's voice drops lower, each word grinding against the next like tectonic plates. "He recruited me with vows of preserving volcanic worlds. Said the Valthorim understood the value of fire planets in the cosmic balance."

The viewscreen shows Magmara directing Battalion forces toward the colony's geothermal taps. The specialized structures that harness Voldom's natural heat now become vulnerabilities, and each tap, when destroyed, releases pressurized steam and magma during violent eruptions. Colony Seventeen disappears behind clouds of black ash and orange fire.

Neous's form shifts, his usually humanoid shape temporarily losing cohesion as rage disrupts his normal structural control. Memory surfaces in waves of intensified heat: descending into Colony Seventeen's deepest mine shaft, instructing young Voldomians on proper crystal extraction techniques, and sharing meals in the community cooling chamber where temperatures dropped low enough for solid foods.

"I worked those shafts for eighteen cycles," he says, more to himself than Caelus. "Taught two generations how to read thermal flows without disturbing pressure points."

He watches a Battalion officer systematically execute colony administrators who attempt surrender. Each death registers as a temperature spike within his core, the magma of his being churning with increasing turbulence.

"They're innocent," he rumbles to Caelus, turning away from the viewscreen. The movement leaves momentary afterimages, trails of superheated particles that briefly hang in the air, marking his path. "Orpheus promised protection, not destruction."

Caelus's sigils pulse beneath his skin as he reviews tactical displays, his expression tightening. "Battalion forces are targeting all major mining operations simultaneously. Their pattern suggests resource denial rather than population control."

"They want the crystals," Neous concludes, understanding immediately. "Voldomian heat crystals store energy better than any technology in seventeen systems. Control them, control power supplies across the sector."

Another explosion rocks Colony Seventeen. Neous's outer layer cracks completely, exposing his molten core in a display of raw emotion he hasn't permitted himself since joining Caelus's crew. The surrounding equipment registers the temperature surge; protective measures activate automatically.

He moves toward the weapons locker with determined steps, each footfall leaving slight indentations in the heat-resistant flooring. The specialized path installed for his movement throughout the ship, metal alloy that withstands his normal temperature range, struggles to accommodate his current state, edges glowing faintly where his feet make contact.

"Neous," Caelus begins, concern evident in his voice. "Battalion forces outnumber, "

"They won't expect another magma-form fighting against them," Neous interrupts, his structure reshaping into combat configuration, more compact, extremities reinforced with cooling basalt for increased impact force. "Magmara's tactics assume all volcanic entities follow strength-worship principles. I don't."

He reaches the weapons store, palm print melting the security lock rather than triggering it properly. Inside, he selects specialized equipment designed for his unique physiology, heat channeling gauntlets that focus his natural temperature into directed energy, coolant grenades that can temporarily solidify opponents, and a chest plate of rare metal that contains his core's radiation while amplifying his strength.

"I helped build three of those colonies," he says as he integrates the equipment into his form, the metal softening slightly before bonding with his exterior crust. "Shared heat with those families. Celebrated crystallization ceremonies with their children."

He turns to Caelus, fully armed, his form now a terrifying fusion of natural force and technological enhancement. The cooling basalt of his exterior takes on armor-like properties, his core glowing through strategic openings like weaponized windows.

"I won't stand by while my people burn," he declares, the words causing the air around him to shimmer with heat distortion.

Caelus says nothing for a moment, then nods once. His fingers move across the command console, initiating sequences Neous recognizes as atmospheric entry preparations.

"We'll get you to the surface," Caelus decides, amber eyes reflecting the orange glow of Neous's form. "But you'll need cover fire and extraction planning."

Neous's core pulses once, strongly, the closest his kind comes to expressing gratitude. He moves toward the ship's deployment bay, each step more stable as purpose replaces pure rage.

Behind him, Caelus speaks quieter words not meant to be heard, though Neous's enhanced senses catch them anyway: "And perhaps it's time we all stopped watching."

Caelus stands at the bridge's center, hands extended before him with fingers spread wide. The metal enhancement bands circling each digit glow with soft blue light as he channels his Aetheris ability, tracking the cosmic signatures of Battalion forces across Voldom's surface. The sigils tattooed on his skin warm beneath his uniform, responding to the extended use of his power. Through this enhanced perception, battalion movements appear as threads of disturbed cosmic energy, which are methodical, precise, and terrifying in their efficiency.

The viewscreens display Voldom's volcanic landscape from multiple angles: rivers of molten rock flowing between obsidian spires, geysers of superheated steam erupting in rhythmic patterns, and Voldomian defenders using modified lava tubes to ambush Battalion ground forces. The atmosphere ripples with heat distortion, creating a shimmering effect that makes the battlefield appear almost liquid.

"Neous has reached the deployment bay," reports his second officer, voice tight with the tension permeating the bridge. "Launching in three minutes."

Caelus acknowledges with a nod, his attention caught by a distinctive energy signature appearing at the edge of his Aetheris perception. Selenea's ship. The vessel executes a series of precise attack runs against Battalion positions, targeting weapons emplacements rather than personnel carriers. Each strike disables rather than destroys, creating opportunities for Voldomian evacuation without maximizing casualties.

He zooms into the main viewscreen to track her movements. The ship maintains a protective position above a civilian evacuation route, intercepting Battalion attackers with surgical precision. Her tactical approach is unmistakable; the same patterns they practiced together during childhood games on Solarune are now adapted for actual combat.

"She's protecting them," he whispers, the observation colliding with memories that surface unbidden.

Orpheus stands before him in the obsidian chamber, silver eyes reflecting holographic images of destruction. "Your sister ordered the execution of unarmed civilians on Nammu." His voice carries those distinctive harmonic undertones that no human vocal cords should produce. "The tribal asteroid's peaceful settlements were reduced to ash under her direct command."

The holovid shows figures in Battalion uniform, one unmistakably Selenea, brandishing heat lances against tribesmen fleeing through luminescent caverns. Bodies collapse in heaps, their bioluminescent markings fading as life extinguishes.

Caelus blinks away the memory, focusing on the present reality. On his viewscreen, Selenea's ship now positions itself between Battalion forces and a mining colony under heavy attack. Her defensive formation creates a corridor through which transport vessels escape, carrying civilians to safety. The contrast between these actions and Orpheus's accusations creates a dissonance that makes his head throb.

"Squadron Three's orbital bombardment targeting civilian shelters," announces his tactical officer, interrupting his thoughts. "Voldomian defenses overwhelmed in sectors seven through twelve."

Caelus adjusts the sensor to focus, his enhancement bands leaving trace patterns of blue light hanging briefly in the air. Through his Aetheris perception, he detects Selenea's ship adjusting course to intercept the bombardment.

Another memory intrudes: Orpheus displays a massacre log with Selenea's battalion signature. "The death count bears her authentication code," he had explained, enlarging the document to highlight her name. "Five thousand three hundred twenty-seven non-combatants eliminated. Her armor was stained with Nammuvian blood when she returned to Zathira."

The forensic report appeared next, along with battalion identifiers from weapons discharge records residue analysis confirming Nammu tribal protein structures. Evidence was so comprehensive and meticulous that questioning it seemed pointless.

Yet now Caelus watches as Selenea positions her ship to absorb fire meant for civilian transports, her vessel's shields flaring as they intercept energy blasts targeting evacuees. Her actions speak with more authenticity than any documentation Orpheus presented.

"That's not the behavior of a war criminal," he murmurs, fingers tightening around the command console edge. The metal enhancement bands cut into his skin slightly, the minor pain focusing his thoughts.

On the viewscreen, Voldomian defenders rally around the protection Selenea provides. Their heat-walker units advance through gaps in Battalion formations created by her tactical strikes. Mining colonists who appeared doomed minutes earlier now reach evacuation transports in growing numbers.

Final fragments of Orpheus's accusations echo in his mind, the holo-vid of fungal groves smoldering after Selenea's alleged assault, the intercepted communications where a voice matching hers ordered "complete elimination of resistance," the equipment logs showing her battalion's weapons discharged thousands of times during what should have been a peaceful assessment mission.

All fabricated. All lies are crafted with perfect precision to leverage his trust in authority against his love for his sister.

Caelus's sigils warm beneath his uniform, responding to the emotional shift as certainty crystallizes within him. His Aetheris perception expands further, tracing the cosmic threads that connect all participants in this conflict. In this heightened awareness, Selenea's signature burns with protective determination rather than destructive intent, not just now but stretching backward in time. The pattern displays consistent protective resonance incompatible with the actions Orpheus described.

"She's not a murderer," he whispers, finally accepting what his heart knew before his analytical mind would permit. "She never was."

His hands move across the command console with renewed purpose, initializing weapon systems dormant since their arrival. The ship responds with a subtle shift in its ambient hum, power redirecting to offensive capabilities, tactical systems activating, and target acquisition protocols engaging.

"Sir?" questions his weapons officer, surprise evident in her voice.

"Prepare for atmospheric entry," Caelus commands, his voice finding new strength with each word. The enhancement bands around his fingers pulse with intensified energy as he transfers Aetheris-gathered intel to the tactical display. "Plot intercept course with Battalion command vessels. Calculate firing solutions that disable rather than destroy."

The bridge crew hesitates briefly, exchanging glances that contain months of unspoken questions about their mission's true purpose.

"We're joining the fight," Caelus clarifies, amber eyes now fixed on Selenea's ship as it continues its protective maneuvers. "On my sister's side."

Activity erupts across the bridge, navigation plotting descent vectors, weapons calibrating for atmospheric conditions, and shields reconfiguring for combat rather than observation. The ship banks toward Voldom's atmosphere, thrusters engaging with increased power.

Caelus feels the weight of the decision settle across his shoulders, simultaneously heavier and more liberating than the doubt that preceded it. The sigils on his skin pulse once, strongly, as if approving this alignment between action and truth.

"Alert Selenea's vessel," he instructs his communications officer. "Transmit our targeting data and proposed attack pattern." His fingers trace sigils in the air, leaving momentary patterns of blue light that translate into tactical formations on the main display. "Tell her, " he pauses, searching for words adequate to bridge the gulf Orpheus created between them, finding none that suffice. "Tell her we're with her."

The ship descends toward Voldom's turbulent atmosphere, weapons charging, course locked to intercept Battalion forces. Around Caelus, the crew moves with renewed purpose; they are no longer observers but participants, and they are no longer neutral but committed.

Below, through swirling clouds of ash and steam, Selenea's ship briefly adjusts course, its running lights flashing in the pattern that, since childhood, has always meant recognition between siblings. Acknowledgment. Acceptance. Alliance.

Caelus's ship cuts through Voldom's atmosphere, leaving a trail of superheated air that dissipates into the already turbulent sky. Volcanic ash particles scatter against the shields, creating a fiery halo around the descending vessel. The bridge viewscreens display battalion positions with clinical precision, with red markers crawling across Voldom's black landscape like blood cells through arteries. Tactical systems lock onto command vessels first, identifying the neural centers that coordinate the assault.

"Weapons at ninety percent efficiency in volcanic atmospheric conditions," reports the tactical officer, her fingers dancing across heat-resistant controls. "Targeting Battalion command ships alpha and delta."

"Execute," Caelus commands. The metal bands around his fingers pulse with blue light as he channels Aetheri's perception, tracking cosmic threads that connect troops to commanders. "Focus on communication arrays and propulsion systems. Disable, don't destroy."

The ship's main batteries discharge with precisely calculated force. Energy beams slice through ash clouds, connecting with Battalion vessels at exactly the points Caelus indicates. The targeted ships list sideways; communication arrays shattered, and maneuvering capabilities compromised. Without central coordination, ground forces falter mid-attack, their perfect patterns disintegrating into scattered individual actions.

Below, Neous Dera strides across a terrain no ordinary being could traverse. His massive form of living magma moves through active lava flows like a predator through native waters. The specialized weapons bonded to his exterior glow with absorbed heat, storing energy for directed release. Where Battalion soldiers establish firing positions on stable ground, Neous approaches through the molten rivers they use as defensive barriers.

He emerges from a lava stream directly behind a Battalion artillery position, his form dripping with liquid rock that hardens into additional armor upon contact with cooler air. The soldiers turn too late, their heat-resistant armor designed for environmental protection, not combat against a being composed of the same elements as the environment itself.

"You chose the wrong world to attack," Neous rumbles, his voice vibrating through the ground beneath their feet. He releases a focused stream of superheated magma from his gauntlets, not at the soldiers but at their weapons, melting artillery emplacements into useless pools of liquid metal.

The soldiers scatter, their tactical coordination broken without central command guidance. Some attempt to engage Neous directly, energy weapons discharging against his magma form. The blasts create momentary disturbances in his exterior, small craters that immediately refill as he redistributes his semi-solid mass.

Above this engagement, Selenea's ship executes a series of precise attack runs against Battalion transport convoys. Her tactical approach targets vehicle junctions rather than passenger compartments, disabling mobility without maximizing casualties. Each disabled transport creates a blockade that compounds the Battalion's coordination problems.

Her ship banks sharply, executing a maneuver that positions it parallel to Caelus's approaching vessel. The ships fly in formation briefly, exchanging targeting data through secured channels. On Selenea's command screen, a pattern appears, not standard military formations but a childhood cipher she and Caelus developed on Solarune, a tactical language known only to siblings.

"Understood," she transmits back, her ship already adjusting course to implement the suggested pattern. "Like the reservoir defense at East Basin?"

"With the Halicon variation," Caelus confirms, his own ship breaking formation to circle wide around the main battlefield.

The siblings' vessels move in complementary patterns; when Selenea's ship dives to strafe Battalion ground forces, Caelus maintains a high altitude to intercept retaliatory fire. When his vessel draws enemy attention with direct engagement, hers slips behind Battalion lines to target supply chains. The coordination displays years of shared thinking, and tactical minds developed along parallel paths are now reunited for a common purpose.

Battalion forces struggle to adapt to this synchronized assault. Their standard response patterns assume opponents who can be predicted through established military doctrine. The Solaris siblings operate outside these parameters, their attacks seeming random to conventional analysis but following internal logic comprehensible only to each other.

Near the largest mining colony, Magmara Pyrox observes this shift in battle dynamics with growing concern. Their massive form pulses with intensified heat as they analyze the deteriorating tactical situation. The cooling crust that forms their exterior features cracks and reforms continuously, betraying agitation beneath their commanding presence.

"Consolidate remaining forces," they order, voice rumbling through Battalion communication systems. "Priority targets are no longer achievable under current conditions."

The admission costs them visibly, their form momentarily losing cohesion as frustration disrupts structural control. Battalion units acknowledge with practiced efficiency, disengaging from active combat to form retreat formations. Their withdrawal reveals the extent of Voldomian defensive success; less than forty percent of the original Battalion force remains operational, and their formation patterns fractured beyond recovery.

Magmara turns their attention skyward, massive arm extending toward the atmosphere above Voldom's largest caldera. Their hand forms intricate patterns that leave momentary trails of superheated air, mathematical sequences that initiate Fractal formation. The space above the battlefield begins to thicken, reality folding inward upon itself as an escape route forms.

"The Battalion attempts to retreat," Caelus broadcasts to Selenea and Voldomian defenders. "Fractal forming at these coordinates."

His ship adjusts course to intercept, weapons targeting the forming tear in reality. Selenea's vessel moves to complement this approach, positioning to catch Battalion forces caught between Caelus's attack and the incomplete escape route.

But Neous recognizes the danger immediately. "Let them go," he transmits from the ground, his rumbling voice distorted by background battle noise. "Forcing them to fight without escape ensures maximum casualties on both sides."

Caelus hesitates, enhancement bands pulsing as he weighs options through Aetheris-enhanced calculation. "Confirmed," he decides after a moment. "Adjust targeting to ensure withdrawal corridor remains open but narrow."

The siblings' ships reposition, maintaining weapons lock on Battalion vessels but creating a clear path to the forming Fractal. Their precision fire herds retreating forces through this corridor, accelerating withdrawal while preventing reorganization for a counterattack.

The Fractal completes its formation, a crystalline tear in reality that pulses with dark energy. Battalion vessels stream toward this escape, abandoning damaged equipment and fallen soldiers in their haste. Magmara Pyrox enters last, their massive form compacting slightly to accommodate the Fractal's dimensions. They pause at the threshold, magma core pulsing once strongly as they survey the battlefield they failed to conquer.

As the final Battalion ships disappear through the Fractal, the tear seals itself with a sound like distant thunder. The abrupt silence feels almost physical in its intensity, the constant weapons fire and engine noise suddenly replaced by Voldom's natural volcanic rumbling.

Then, celebration erupts across Voldomian defensive positions. Geysers of lava shoot skyward from controlled vents, not weapons fire but victory signals used since ancient times to mark battlefield triumphs. The miners Neous protected emerge from emergency shelters, filling communication channels with overlapping expressions of gratitude and relief.

Caelus guides his ship toward a stable landing zone, an obsidian platform formed by rapidly cooled lava flows from a recent but now dormant eruption. The smooth black surface reflects the vessels' approach like dark water. Selenea's ship follows, executing a perfect parallel landing that positions the craft side by side with their exit hatches aligned.

Between the ships, lava flows have already begun to cool and harden, creating natural pathways that connect the obsidian platform to the nearest mining colony. The sulfurous air shimmers with heat distortion, but for the first time since the battle began, no weapons fire disrupts the volcanic rhythm of Voldom's natural environment.

The siblings' ships power down in synchronized sequence, landing lights dimming to minimum illumination as environment-adapted hatches prepare to open. Around them, Voldom continues its ancient pattern of destruction and creation, lava flowing, cooling, forming new landscapes even as other areas crumble into molten rebirth.

The Voldomian cavern city unfolds before them like a negative image of a surface settlement, where other civilizations build upward toward the light, and these structures descend into protected darkness. Ancient volcanic tubes widened and reinforced over generations, forming main thoroughfares that branch into smaller chambers. Each living space, communal area, and government hall has been meticulously carved from cooling magma flows, creating organic architecture that follows the stone's natural strength lines. Channels of still-active lava provide both illumination and heating, their orange-red glow casting dramatic shadows across polished obsidian walls.

Caelus stands at the entrance to a council chamber, the metal enhancement bands around his fingers catching and reflecting the ambient magma light. Behind him, officials discuss reconstruction plans and defense reinforcements, but these conversations fade to background noise as a familiar figure approaches from the opposite corridor.

Selenea stops five paces away, and the distance between them is charged with unspoken accusations and defense. Her First Battalion uniform bears modifications for Voldom's environment: heat-resistant panels, reinforced breathing filters, stripped of all Valthorim insignia. The sigils tattooed on her skin pulse faintly beneath the fabric, matching the rhythm of the ones visible on Caelus's forearms.

"Brother," she says simply, the word carrying years of shared history that transcends recent division.

"Sister," he responds, his voice finding unfamiliar uncertainty.

They observe each other with careful assessment, searching for changes for evidence of the truths each now holds. Caelus fidgets with the small hologram projector he always carries, his fingers activating and deactivating its basic functions without conscious thought. Selenea's hands remain still at her sides, the deliberate control betraying her tension more clearly than movement would.

The first step forward comes from both simultaneously, as if choreographed. They meet in the center of the corridor, still maintaining arm's length separation.

"I didn't do it," Selenea says, breaking the silence. Her amber eyes, so like his own, hold steady, unflinching. "Any of it."

"I know," Caelus responds, the admission unlocking something tight in his chest. "I've seen you fighting to protect civilians here. It contradicts everything Orpheus claimed about you."

The space between them shrinks by another half-step.

"Nammu was beautiful," Selenea continues, her voice dropping lower, meant for his ears alone despite the empty corridor. "The tribes lived in perfect harmony with their asteroid environment. Their fungi gardens created sustainable food, light, even written language." Her eyes take on a distant quality, seeing scenes no longer before her. "Orpheus ordered their complete elimination."

Caelus's sigils warm beneath his skin, responding to the surge of emotion her words provoke. "Why? What threat could pre-spaceflight tribes pose to the Valthorim?"

"None." Selenea's jaw tightens, the memory visibly painful to revisit. "That's what made no sense. The official reason was 'divergence from acceptable cosmic parameters,' but they were perfectly balanced with their environment." She steps closer, now within arm's reach. "I refused the order. Helped them escape instead. Orpheus responded by doctoring footage to make me appear responsible for the very massacre I prevented."

Caelus processes this, his analytical mind connecting new information with existing anomalies he's observed in Orpheus's behavior. The inconsistencies in mission parameters, the contradictions in Valthorim council decisions, and the pattern of targeting self-sufficient worlds while claiming to protect cosmic balance.

"He's not who we thought he was, Caelus," Selenea says, her amber eyes reflecting the magma light. "He's using the Valthorim to commit genocide across the universe."

A group of Voldomian officials passes, nodding respectfully to the siblings before continuing toward the council chamber. When they're alone again, Caelus speaks, his voice barely above a whisper.

"I've tracked seventeen worlds targeted by Battalion forces in the past cycle. Each attack justified as maintaining cosmic balance." His fingers are still on the hologram projector, and he is finding a still point instead of an anxious movement. "But each world shared one characteristic, technological or environmental self-sufficiency."

"Worlds that don't need the Valthorim," Selenea concludes.

"Worlds that might question them," Caelus adds. "Or worse, inspire others to independence."

He rubs his thumb across the enhancement bands, circling his fingers, the metal warm from proximity to Voldom's active environment. The sigils on his arms pulse once, strongly, as if confirming his realization.

"I believed him because I wanted to," Caelus admits, the words physically difficult to form. The confession carries the weight of operations conducted, intelligence gathered, and worlds deemed dispensable based on falsified assessments. "The structure, the purpose, the sense of cosmic significance, I needed it to be true."

"We both did," Selenea acknowledges. "Until we couldn't ignore the contradictions anymore."

The final distance between them dissolves as Selenea extends her hand. Caelus takes it without hesitation, their sigils brightening at the contact, recognizing the shared energy patterns established in childhood. The moment stretches, silent communication passing between them, a reconnection that transcends the manipulation that separates them.

"I'm sorry," he says, the inadequate words carrying genuine remorse for doubting her.

"You're here now," she responds, acceptance rather than accusation. "That's what matters."

They embrace properly then, the formal distance of Valthorim training giving way to the simpler truth of family connection. Their silhouettes cast a unified shadow against the obsidian wall, the magma channels creating dramatic elongation that stretches their joined form across the polished surface.

Heavy footsteps interrupt the moment, the distinctive sound of mass redistributing with each movement. Neous Dera approaches from a side corridor, his massive form now partially solidified after battle exertion. His core still pulses with orange-red energy visible through transparent sections of his exterior, but the violent heat of combat has cooled to a more controlled intensity.

"The mining colonies report no further battalion signals," he announces, his voice rumbling through the chamber. "Preliminary assessments show sixty-three percent infrastructure survival, near-total civilian evacuation success."

His magma form shifts slightly, the outer layer cooling to form more defined features as he regards the reunited siblings. "Your coordination turned the battle," he acknowledges, the closest his species comes to expressing gratitude.

Caelus releases Selenea, though they remain standing closer than Valthorim protocol would permit. "The Battalion will report this defeat to Orpheus," he notes, analytical mind already calculating consequences. "He'll send reinforcements once the Fractal network stabilizes."

"Not just here," Neous rumbles, his exterior cooling further as he settles into the discussion. The process creates faint crackling sounds like stone settling after heat stress. "Orpheus will send more battalions to more worlds. Voldom is one battle in a larger campaign."

"Drabliti was attacked last month," Selenea confirms. "Same pattern, claims of cosmic imbalance used to justify resource seizure and population control."

"Three mining worlds in the Vescit system before that," Caelus adds. "Each rich in materials needed for independent deep space travel."

Neous moves closer, his form solidifying further with his resolve. "We need to stop him," he states simply, the weight of his people's suffering evident in his voice. "Before more worlds burn."

Caelus nods, decision crystallizing within him. "Then we build a crew," he says, finger tracing patterns in the air as he considers logistics, enhancement bands leaving momentary trails of blue light. "Gather others who've seen through Orpheus's deceptions. Create a network across targeted systems."

"We fight back," Selenea concludes, her tactical mind already calculating potential allies, resources, and strategic approaches. "Not just against the battalions, but against the false narrative of cosmic balance he's constructed."

The three stand in the volcanic corridor, united by a shared purpose despite their different natures. The magma channels flowing through the cavern walls cast their shadows in overlapping patterns against the obsidian surface, three distinct forms merging into a single silhouette of resistance.

"We'll need transportation beyond tracking ability," Caelus says, practical considerations following the decision. "Ships that can operate outside Fractal networks, communication systems independent of Valthorim relays."

"I know people on six worlds who would join immediately," Selenea offers. "Former Battalion officers who questioned orders, scientists who detected patterns in targeted planets, survivors who've witnessed Orpheus's true intentions."

"Voldom's miners will provide resources," Neous adds, his rumbling voice gaining strength with each word. "And heat crystals for power systems that function outside Valthorim control."

Caelus extends his hand, palm open. Selenea places her hand atop his without hesitation. After a moment's consideration of temperature compatibility, Neous adds one partially-cooled finger to the gesture, careful to maintain safe contact heat.

"The universe deserves truth," Caelus states, the simple declaration carrying the weight of their collective commitment.

"And protection," Selenea adds.

"And freedom," Neous concludes.

Their shadows stretch long against the obsidian wall as a distant explosion sends vibrations through the cavern system, not Battalion weapons but Voldom's natural volcanic processes, destruction and creation proceeding in eternal balance. The planet continues its ancient rhythms, indifferent to the cosmic struggle beginning to form within its protective depths.

Chapter 11

Ice and Strategy

The meditation chamber aboard the ship exists in perfect stillness, its curved walls inscribed with sigils that dampen sound and stabilize energy flows. Caelus sits cross-legged at its center, his physical form motionless while his consciousness stretches across star systems. The metal enhancement bands around his fingers glow with soft blue light, channels for an ability that most beings couldn't comprehend, let alone control.

He breathes in measured intervals. Each inhalation draws cosmic energy into his body; each exhalation extends his perception further beyond physical limitations. The sigils tattooed across his skin respond, warming beneath his simple meditation garments until they shine through the fabric, amber light pulsing in mathematical sequences that correspond to specific stellar frequencies.

His eyes remain closed, yet he sees more than ordinary vision could ever reveal. The Aetheris ability transforms perception, converting the fundamental truths of reality into comprehensible patterns. Stars become not distant balls of fusion but nodes in a universal network. Planets register as harmonics in a cosmic symphony. And ships, especially military vessels moving with purpose, create distinctive ripples in the fabric that connect all matter derived from stardust.

The metal bands around his fingers grow warmer as he channels more energy. His consciousness expands exponentially, stretching from the meditation chamber across thousands of light years in search of specific disruption patterns. The Third Battalion leaves distinctive traces, mathematical precision in their movements, and artificial order imposed on natural cosmic flows. They never travel randomly. Their paths always follow optimal routes calculated by Valthorim algorithms programmed with objectives only Orpheus truly understands.

Sweat beads on Caelus's forehead despite the chamber's controlled temperature. Locating a specific military force moving through the vastness of space demands concentration that strains both mind and body. The threads of cosmic connection stretch thinner as his awareness extends further, searching, sensing, and following tenuous paths between stars.

There. A disruption. Multiple vessels moving in formation with the distinctive harmonic frequency of Battalion energy signatures. Caelus focuses on this distant ripple, directing the full power of his Aetheris perception toward the disturbance. The enhancement bands around his fingers pulse with increased energy, their blue light intensifying as they channel cosmic awareness through precisely calibrated conduits in his nervous system.

His consciousness follows the Battalion's trail across three star systems, tracing their vector with growing certainty. The formation advances with perfect efficiency, never deviating from the optimal trajectory. Each ship maintains position with machine-like precision, creating a composite energy signature that Caelus recognizes from previous engagements. The Third Battalion specialized in cold-environment assault and was equipped with ice-penetrating weaponry, commanded by officers trained in Arctic warfare.

Halfway through the fourth system, the physical toll begins to manifest. A muscle in Caelus's jaw twitches involuntarily. The sigils across his forearms pulse with discomfort rather than just warmth. His breathing pattern falters momentarily before he reasserts control with practiced discipline. Extended Aetheris perception taxes the physical form in proportion to the distance and detail sought.

Still, he pushes further, following the Battalion's path through a nebula where cosmic threads tangle like overgrown vegetation. His perception momentarily fragments, consciousness scattered across too many points of reference. The sensation resembles drowning, awareness diluted to near-ineffectiveness, cosmic noise threatening to overwhelm the signal.

Caelus forces his focus to narrow, abandoning breadth for precision. The metal bands around his index fingers glow brighter than the others, channeling additional energy as he applies specialized tracking techniques reserved for critical operations. The effort sends sharp pain through his temples, but the connection stabilizes.

Beyond the nebula, the Battalion's trajectory clarifies. Their formation aligns toward a specific vector, mathematical certainty replacing investigative tracking. They've entered the final approach to their target. Caelus follows the projected path forward, his consciousness racing ahead of their physical position to confirm his destination.

The realization forms with sickening clarity. Drabliti. The ice planet with its ancient crystalline structures and self-sufficient energy systems. A world that needs nothing from the Valthorim. A world whose defense technologies could protect other systems if shared.

Coordinates materialize in glowing holographic form around Caelus's seated figure, his Aetheris perception translating cosmic awareness into navigational data. The numbers hover in three-dimensional space, precise measurements defining the Battalion's exact trajectory and estimated arrival time.

The effort of maintaining such a distant perception finally exceeds sustainable limits. Blood trickles from Caelus's left nostril, a thin line of red against his increasingly pale skin. The sigils across his body flash with erratic patterns, overtaxed energy pathways struggling to process information beyond biological design parameters. His muscles begin to tremble, first his hands, then spreading through his arms and shoulders until his entire body vibrates with fine tremors.

With disciplined effort, he withdraws his consciousness, pulling perception back across light years and compressing awareness from cosmic scale to individual existence. The process feels like falling from orbit, a controlled descent that must neither rush nor stall lest the mind separate permanently from physical form.

When his awareness fully returns to the meditation chamber, Caelus gasps, a sharp inhale that fills oxygen-starved lungs. His eyes snap open, revealing irises that still glow amber with residual cosmic energy. The holographic coordinates continue to float before him, their mathematical precision contrasting with his now-ragged breathing.

He reaches toward the communication panel with shaking hands, fingers struggling to input the proper sequence. The enhancement bands have cooled to dull metal, temporarily drained of energy, making his movements clumsy. After two failed attempts, the connection is established.

"Skif Zar," he says, voice hoarse from prolonged disuse. "I've tracked the Third Battalion."

The response comes through with the characteristic pause of long-distance communication, Skif's measured voice carrying none of the urgency Caelus feels. "Coordinates received. Their target?"

"Drabliti." Caelus wipes the blood from his upper lip, leaving a crimson smear across the back of his hand. "They'll reach you in less than forty-eight hours."

The revelation hangs in the silence that follows, heavy with implications. The Third Battalion specializes in cold-environment assault. Their deployment against an ice world represents perfect tactical matching, with Orpheus selecting the optimal force for maximum effectiveness against specific planetary defenses.

"Understood." Skif's voice remains calm, though a slight change in tone betrays comprehension of the danger. "The Council must be informed immediately."

The communication ends. Caelus remains seated, his body demanding recovery time before attempting movement. The holographic coordinates continue to glow, accusatory in their precision. Forty-eight hours. Perhaps less. There is not enough time for reinforcements to reach Drabliti before the Battalion arrives.

He closes his eyes again, but not to track cosmic threads. Instead, he focuses inward, directing energy toward healing overtaxed systems. The sigils across his skin gradually stabilize, their pattern returning to normal rhythm. The trembling in his muscles subsides incrementally.

The ship's automated systems detect his biometric distress, adjusting chamber temperature and oxygen content without requiring commands. The lights dim slightly, reducing sensory input to aid recovery. These small assistances reflect Selenea's attention to detail modifications implemented specifically to support his Aetheris work.

When he finally rises, his movements display careful precision born of necessity rather than choice. Each step requires conscious attention, muscles responding sluggishly to mental commands. The information justifies the cost, but the cost remains substantial.

He must reach the bridge. Selenea needs to know. The Battalion's approach to Drabliti requires an immediate response, not just warning but intervention. As he moves toward the chamber door, the holographic coordinates follow briefly before dissipating into points of light that fade like dying stars.

The High Council chamber sits buried beneath two kilometers of ancient ice, its walls carved from compressed snow that predates Drabliti's earliest recorded history. Massive hexagonal pillars support a domed ceiling where ice crystals refract blue light from below, creating patterns that shift with the subtle movements of the council members. The chamber exists in perfect, pristine silence broken only by the occasional soft grinding of ice against ice as the massive entities adjust their positions around the circular discussion platform.

Ancient sigils line the circumference of the chamber, their deep grooves filled with bioluminescent algae harvested from the thermal vents beneath Drabliti's frozen surface. The symbols pulse with a slow, deliberate rhythm, not electrical but biological, their light intensifying and dimming according to atmospheric pressure fluctuations too subtle for non-natives to perceive. These sigils tell the story of Drabliti's formation, its discovery, and its evolution from a simple ice field to conscious crystalline existence.

Skif Zar stands before the council, his semi-transparent body absorbing and refracting the blue light from crystal lamps suspended at strategic intervals throughout the chamber. Unlike the council members, whose massive forms extend nearly to the ceiling, Skif maintains a more compact structure optimized for movement across various environments. The ice that forms his consciousness has arranged itself into a roughly humanoid shape, a concession to his frequent dealings with non-crystalline species rather than necessity. As he shifts position, light passes through his interior at different angles, creating momentary rainbows that dance across the chamber floor.

"Respected Council," he begins, his voice emerging not from a mouth but from precisely controlled vibrations through his entire form. The sound resonates through the chamber with bell-like clarity. "I bring verified intelligence from our ally, Caelus Solaris."

The council members respond with subtle position adjustments, their massive crystalline bodies making soft scraping sounds as they turn their attention toward Skif. Each entity stands at least four meters tall, their forms resembling abstract sculptures more than bodies, twisted spires of transparent ice with denser cores where consciousness resides. They communicate through a combination of vibration, light refraction, and structural reconfiguration that non-natives find almost impossible to interpret.

"The Third Battalion approaches Drabliti," Skif continues, methodically projecting the data Caelus transmitted. The numbers appear as frost patterns in the air before him, precise coordinates forming and dissolving as he presents each piece of evidence. "Their trajectory suggests arrival within forty-eight standard hours. Their formation and equipment profiles indicate a full-scale assault specifically configured for ice-environment penetration."

The eldest council member, distinguishable by the deeper blue coloration of their ice core and more complex crystalline patterns, shifts forward slightly. Their response comes as a harmonic vibration that makes the suspended lamps tremble. "The Valthorim promised protection when their representatives visited last. Now they send destroyers?"

"The Valthorim no longer uphold their stated principles," Skif responds, his tone remaining measured despite the grave nature of his words. "Multiple systems have already fallen to similar attacks. Each targeted world shares Drabliti's key characteristic, a self-sufficiency that requires no Valthorim support."

He manipulates the frost patterns to display a map of nearby star systems. Small ice crystals form and dissolve to mark previous Battalion attack locations, creating a clear pattern of systematic conquest radiating outward from Valthorim-controlled space.

"Caelus Solaris has tracked their movements using his Aetheris ability. The data confirms both their destination and approach vector." Skif restructures his right arm, extending it to indicate the most likely entry point into Drabliti's atmosphere. "They will target the northern ridge first, where our defensive ice walls are thinnest."

The council members communicate among themselves in their native fashion, subtle changes in density creating prismatic effects within their bodies, vibrations passing between them at frequencies that make the chamber's temperature fluctuate by fractional degrees. To an outsider, the discussion would appear as nothing more than shifting light patterns and nearly imperceptible movement, but Skif interprets the complex deliberation with practiced ease.

"The Third Battalion specializes in cold-environment warfare," he adds as their discussion continues. "Their weapons include thermal lances designed to shatter ice structures, mobility systems adapted for frozen terrain, and atmospheric processors that can alter local climate conditions."

A younger council member's crystalline structure displays sharper angles and fewer complexity patterns and vibrates with greater intensity. "Our people have faced threats before. The Great Freeze of the Seventh Cycle threatened our very consciousness, yet we endured."

"With respect," Skif responds, "the Battalion represents a different category of threat. They don't seek natural dominance but complete subjugation. Worlds that resist are not merely conquered but systematically dismantled."

The council's deliberation intensifies, their massive forms subtly repositioning as various perspectives emerge and merge within their collective awareness. The sigils along the chamber walls respond to this energetic exchange, their bioluminescent glow pulsing more rapidly as if recognizing the gravity of the moment.

"We must prepare precise defensive measures," Skif continues, his methodical delivery unchanged despite the urgency underlying his words. "The northern ridge requires immediate reinforcement. Our ice wall network must be activated to full defensive capacity. The ancient avalanche systems should be primed for strategic deployment."

The council's vibrations harmonize gradually, reaching consensus through their unique form of crystalline communion. The eldest member extends a portion of their form toward Skif, ice restructuring to create a roughly articulated appendage.

"Drabliti has stood for seven thousand cycles," they vibrate, the harmonics carrying solemn determination. "We will not fall to those who would break what they cannot understand."

Before further discussion can proceed, the chamber's entrance is disrupted by a sharp cracking sound. The massive ice door normally operated through careful pressure equalization, fragments momentarily before restructuring to admit a new presence. Frizz Ravna enters with none of the ceremonial patience typically observed in council proceedings.

Her crystalline form contrasts sharply with the other ice entities. Where they display rounded formations and flowing lines, she consists almost entirely of sharp angles and precise geometries. Her interior core glows with intense blue-white light that suggests higher energy density than normal for their species. As she moves, her ice doesn't flow but relocates with mathematical precision, each plane and facet repositioning with audible clicks rather than fluid transitions.

"Talking wastes time," she announces, her vibrations cutting through the harmonics of council deliberation like a blade through thin ice. Unlike Skif's measured tones, her communications carry sharp, staccato rhythms that demand immediate attention. "The Battalion arrives within forty-eight hours. The defense systems require thirty-six hours for full activation."

She approaches the council platform without waiting for acknowledgment, her form reconfiguring to project detailed schematics of Drabliti's defense network. The frost patterns she creates display far greater complexity than Skif's, showing not just locations but system capacities, activation sequences, and vulnerability assessments.

"I need authorization for full defensive protocols," she continues, her sharp-edged form rotating to address each council member individually. "All power redirected to the ice walls. All non-essential community functions are suspended. All reserve moisture reservoirs released for defensive construction."

The council members vibrate among themselves briefly, their deliberation now compressed into seconds rather than the customary minutes or hours. The eldest shifts their massive form, extending crystalline appendages toward Frizz's schematics in a gesture of examination.

"These measures will strain our people," they observe, harmonics suggesting concern rather than resistance.

"Survival requires strain," Frizz responds, her form reconfiguring to emphasize her core's intense energy signature. "Half measures ensure failure."

The council members rotate in perfect synchronization, their ice cores aligning in a pattern that signifies a unanimous decision. The chamber's ancient sigils respond immediately, their bioluminescent glow intensifying until the entire space bathes in blue-white light.

"Authorization granted," the eldest member vibrates, the simple statement carrying the full weight of their collective authority. "Full defensive protocols. Immediate implementation."

Frizz Ravna's form reconfigures once more, consolidating into a more streamlined shape optimized for rapid movement. Without further acknowledgment, she exits the chamber, ice fragments trailing behind her like crystalline dust.

Skif watches her departure, then turns back to the council. "I will coordinate communication with our allies," he offers, his methodical tone returning. "Selenea Solaris approaches with her ship. They may provide crucial support when the Battalion arrives."

The council members have already begun to disperse, their massive forms flowing toward various exit points around the chamber's perimeter. As they move, the ancient sigils dim sequentially, their light following each member as if recognizing their authority and purpose.

The chamber, so recently filled with deliberation and decision, returns to pristine silence broken only by the occasional soft grind of ice against ice, the sound of a world preparing for war.

The ice walls surrounding Drabliti's main settlement rise thirty meters from the perpetually frozen ground, their surfaces carved with overlapping defensive patterns that catch sunlight in blinding arrays. Frizz Ravna moves along the northern perimeter, her crystalline form shifting between states of transparency and opacity as she assesses each section with critical precision. Where others see imposing barriers of solid ice, she sees vulnerabilities, microscopic stress fractures, suboptimal density gradients, and imperfect alignment with the ancient defensive templates established a thousand cycles ago.

Her angular body makes sharp sounds against the compacted snow as she walks, each step leaving precisely geometric impressions rather than natural footprints. Unlike other Drablitians who flow from one shape to another, Frizz reconfigures with mechanical exactness, her form maintaining sharp edges and precise angles that reflect her uncompromising approach to defense engineering.

"Insufficient compression in section twelve," she announces to a team of workers reinforcing the wall's base. Her voice vibrates through the ice with frequencies that make nearby crystals resonate sympathetically. "Repack with twenty percent higher density and realign the pressure distribution patterns."

The workers, smaller ice entities with simpler crystalline structures, immediately abandon their current task and begin implementing her corrections. None questioned her assessment. Her reputation as a Defense Systems Engineer spans three generations, and her demands for perfection are as legendary as her results.

She moves to a steep mountainside where another team carves avalanche tunnels into the compacted snow. These precisely angled passages serve as both defensive weapons and emergency evacuation routes, a dual-purpose design dating back to Drabliti's earliest conflicts. When triggered, they release controlled snow slides that can bury approaching forces without damaging the settlement's structural integrity.

"The angle is wrong," she states, her core temperature dropping in what passes for frustration among her kind. The temperature change sends visible frost patterns radiating through her crystalline form. "Seventeen degrees, not fifteen. At fifteen degrees, the avalanche velocity reaches the terminal too quickly, reducing effective coverage radius."

The tunnel foreman adjusts his own structure to produce measurement appendages. "Our calculations suggested fifteen degrees provides optimal, "

"Your calculations are theoretically sound but practically flawed," she interrupts, her form reconfiguring to project precise mathematical models into the air around them. Frost patterns crystallize to show avalanche dynamics under different conditions. "Theory assumes uniform snow density. Reality presents stratified compression layers. Seventeen degrees account for variable resistance during release."

Without waiting for acknowledgment, she extends a portion of her form into the tunnel entrance. Her ice merges temporarily with the tunnel structure, reconfiguring its angle with precise micro-adjustments that no mechanical tool could achieve. The entire passage realigns under her direction, its walls glowing briefly as she infuses them with her own crystalline pattern.

"Seventeen degrees," she confirms as she withdraws, leaving behind a perfectly formed tunnel that gleams with enhanced structural integrity. "Test the triggering mechanism."

A worker approaches the concealed pressure plate embedded near the tunnel mouth. The mechanism, deceptively simple in appearance, consists of interlocked ice crystals arranged in precise geometric configurations. When compressed with the correct force, the pattern propagates a sonic wave through the mountainside, destabilizing the avalanche zone above.

The worker applies preliminary pressure. The plate responds with a faint harmonic resonance that travels upward through the snowpack. Frizz observes with hyper-focused attention, her entire form stilling to better sense the vibration patterns.

"Insufficient amplitude," she declares after the test is completed. "The resonance peak falls eighteen percent below an optimal triggering threshold." She reconfigures her right appendage into a complex tool shape and makes microscopic adjustments to the crystal alignment within the trigger mechanism. "The harmonic sequence must intensify at precisely the third resonance interval to achieve chain-reaction destabilization."

Across the perimeter, teams haul massive blocks of reinforced ice toward strategic positions along the wall. These aren't merely frozen water but complex composite structures, ice infused with mineral deposits from Drabliti's rare thermal vents, compressed under precise conditions, and embedded with ancient sigils that enhance their structural properties through harmonic resonance.

Each block weighs over two tons, requiring six workers to maneuver into position. The sigils carved into their surfaces glow with faint blue-white light, not decorative patterns but precise mathematical formulas expressed through ancient symbolic language. The symbols create interference patterns that distribute force across the entire structure when impacted, allowing relatively thin ice barriers to withstand energy weapons that would shatter conventional frozen water.

Frizz approaches a section where workers position these specialized blocks into a reinforcement matrix. Her angular form shifts subtly as she analyzes their placement, her core pulsing with intensified light when she detects a misalignment.

"Insufficient. The angle is wrong," she declares, her voice causing nearby ice crystals to vibrate with uncomfortable intensity. "They'll breach within minutes."

The work team leader, a veteran ice entity with complex crystalline patterns indicating centuries of experience, attempts an explanation. "We've aligned according to standard reinforcement protocols, "

"Standard protocols assume standard attacks," Frizz interrupts, her form reconfiguring to project schematics of Battalion thermal weapons. "The Third Battalion carries modified plasma lances with oscillating frequency modulators. Standard alignments create vulnerable resonance points at each junction."

She moves forward, her crystalline body partially liquefying as she interfaces directly with the misaligned section. The workers step back as she merges with the wall, her consciousness temporarily extending into the defensive structure. From within, she restructures the ice at the molecular level, realigning crystal lattices to create destructive interference patterns against thermal weapons.

As she withdraws from the wall, her form momentarily displays the same precise geometric patterns now embedded in the structure. The reinforced section gleams with enhanced density, the embedded sigils glowing more intensely as they integrate with her modifications.

"The sigil alignment must counter thermal oscillation," she explains, her tone marginally less harsh when sharing technical knowledge. "Our ancestors developed these patterns after the Great Burning during the Fourth Cycle. The Battalion's weapons operate on similar principles with higher energy density."

She moves along the wall, inspecting each section with the same exacting standards. Where other defense engineers might compromise in the face of time constraints, Frizz demands perfection regardless of circumstance. Her form casts angular shadows across the snow as the sun begins to set, the diminishing light highlighting the geometric precision of her crystalline structure.

"The ancients survived eighteen major assaults without Valthorim assistance," she tells a young worker who questions whether modern weapons might overwhelm traditional defenses. Her voice carries a rare intensity that suggests personal conviction beyond professional expertise. "They developed defensive methods that work with our nature rather than against it. Ice flexibility against rigid force. Avalanche fluidity against static positions. Thermal absorption against heat weapons."

She gestures toward mountainsides strategically shaped over generations to channel natural forces against invaders. "The Battalion brings technology. We bring the accumulated knowledge of a thousand cycles of survival in the harshest environment imaginable."

A team approaches with reports from the southern perimeter. Frizz reviews their data with characteristic efficiency, her form reconfiguring to better process the information.

"Implement full ice-trigger arrays along the secondary ridge," she instructs. "Triple the compression ratio in the avalanche collection basins and prepare the resonance chambers for maximum amplitude."

As the team departs, she turns her attention to the massive ice gates that control access to the settlement. The ancient structures feature the most complex sigil patterns on the planet, and defensive formulas were developed when Drabliti first faced external threats. The symbols don't merely strengthen the ice but create interaction fields that disperse energy attacks across broader surfaces, preventing concentrated breakthroughs.

Frizz places her appendage against these symbols, her own crystalline structure momentarily aligning with their ancient patterns. For a brief moment, her typically angular form flows into more natural configurations, a rare display of connection to traditional forms that suggests deeper reverence than her harsh exterior normally permits.

The moment passes quickly. She reconfigures back to her characteristically sharp-edged form and continues her inspection with undiminished critical focus. The sun sets completely, but work continues under the blue-white illumination of amplified sigils embedded throughout the defensive perimeter.

"We have twenty-four hours remaining," she announces to all work teams simultaneously, her voice propagating through ice structures with perfect clarity. "Any section not meeting optimal specifications will be your responsibility when the Battalion arrives."

The simple statement needs no elaboration. Every Drablitian involved in the preparations understands what failure would mean. Their world has survived cycles of natural threats through perfectionism, not approximation. Against the approaching Battalion, anything less than optimal defense guarantees extinction.

Frizz turns her attention to the northern ridge, where sensors indicate the Battalion will likely make their first approach. Her crystalline form catches starlight in patterns that emphasize her angular structure, creating the impression of a being comprised entirely of sharp edges and unyielding surfaces, exactly what Drabliti needs as the deadline for survival approaches.

Selenea's hands move across the control panels with practiced efficiency, making micro-adjustments to the ship's thrusters as they enter Drabliti's orbit. The planet fills the viewport, a brilliantly white sphere etched with geometric patterns of mountain ranges and ice fields that suggest intelligent design rather than natural formation. Atmospheric interference creates a thin blue halo around the planet's curve, the only color in an otherwise monochromatic landscape that stretches beyond visual limits.

"Stable orbit achieved," she announces to the small bridge crew. "Maintaining position over northern hemisphere at thirty thousand kilometers."

The navigation officer acknowledges with a nod, her fingers already programming secondary approach vectors in case rapid repositioning becomes necessary. Unlike the large crews of Battalion vessels, Selenea operates with just four specialists, each selected for both expertise and unwavering ethical commitment after deserting Valthorim's service.

Selenea studies the tactical display where Drabliti's surface features transform into strategic data points. The massive ice walls surrounding settlements appear as reinforced defense lines. Mountain ranges with their avalanche tunnels register as potential ambush zones. The seemingly endless ice fields between major population centers become killboxes where Battalion landing parties would find themselves exposed without cover.

Her fingers trace a pattern across the weapons control surface, initiating diagnostic sequences for the ship's offensive systems. Status indicators flash green across the board, energy weapons are at full capacity, shield generators are optimized for cold-environment combat, and targeting arrays are calibrated for extreme atmospheric refraction conditions common to ice planets.

"Begin weapons check," she instructs her tactical officer. "Full spectrum. Prioritize variable-frequency thermal disruptors."

The officer, a former Battalion weapons specialist who refused orders at Nammu, implements the command with efficient precision. "Thermal disruptors calibrated for ice-environment engagement. Modulation patterns set to counter Battalion shielding frequencies."

Selenea nods approval while simultaneously adjusting scanner arrays. Her movements display the focused intensity of someone who's fought the Battalion before and fully comprehend the brutality of their tactics. She calibrates sensor profiles specifically for the Third Battalion's signature energy patterns, knowing their specialized equipment for cold-environment warfare generates distinctive emissions.

"Secure primary munitions load," she directs the operations officer. "Cryo-phase torpedoes armed with twenty-second delay fuses rather than standard ten. The extreme cold affects detonation timing."

Statistics scroll across her personal display, ammunition stores, shield capacity, and engine performance metrics. She absorbs the information while muttering calculations under her breath, mentally applying mathematical formulas to transform raw data into a tactical advantage. The sigils tattooed across her skin pulse faintly beneath her uniform, responding to her heightened focus.

"Program the automated defense drones for high-altitude dispersal," she continues, fingers dancing across the control surface to define precise deployment patterns. "Configure scanning frequencies to penetrate ice fog and blizzard conditions."

The drones, spherical units equipped with miniaturized weapons and enhanced sensors, represent a significant tactical advantage against Battalion forces. Their autonomous tracking systems can maintain operation even when electronic countermeasures disrupt ship-to-drone communication. Selenea programs specific flight patterns designed to maximize coverage over probable Battalion landing zones.

"Five drones with thermal detection as primary. Five with movement tracking. Five with communications interception," she specifies, creating overlapping defense layers. Each drone receives distinct patrol coordinates and contingency protocols tailored to different attack scenarios.

Her tactical officer completes the weapons check sequence and looks up with grim satisfaction. "All offensive systems operational at optimal capacity. Cold-environment modifications implemented for all energy weapons."

Selenea acknowledges with a sharp nod while continuing her own preparations. Her hands never stop moving across the control surfaces, making incremental adjustments to defensive configurations, patrol paths, and engagement protocols. The ship becomes an extension of her tactical mind, each system optimized according to her extensive experience fighting the very forces she once served alongside.

"Deploy sensor buoys at sixty-kilometer intervals along the projected approach vector," she instructs. "Program them for passive detection only. The Battalion will be scanning for active sensor emissions."

The operations officer implements this command, launching a series of small, unobtrusive devices that drift away from the ship like seeds carried on the wind. Once in position, these buoys will create an early warning network capable of detecting Battalion vessels before conventional sensors can register their presence.

Selenea straps herself more securely into the command chair, adjusting the harness to allow maximum mobility while ensuring stability during combat maneuvers. Her fingers test each buckle with methodical thoroughness, the gesture betraying battlefield habits formed through hard experience.

"Open a channel to Caelus," she requests, her attention never leaving the tactical display.

The communications officer establishes the connection with practiced efficiency. Caelus's face appears on the secondary display, the subtle strain around his eyes revealing the lingering effects of his extended Aetheris tracking.

"I've got eyes on the approach vector," Selenea reports without preamble. "Any Battalion ships enter this airspace, they'll regret it."

Caelus nods, his expression reflecting both concern and confidence in her abilities. "The Drablitian Council is fully mobilized. Frizz Ravna implements ground defenses while Skif Zar coordinates between their forces and ours."

"Expected arrival time?"

"My Aetheris tracking suggests less than twelve hours now," Caelus replies, the enhancement bands around his fingers still dull from recent energy depletion. "They're moving faster than standard approach protocols dictate."

Selenea processes this information with a slight tightening of her jaw, which is the only visible indication of concern. "They've adapted their tactics since our encounter at Voldom. Standard Battalion procedure would include a twenty-four-hour orbital assessment before ground deployment."

"They learn," Caelus acknowledges. "Like we do."

"But not fast enough," Selenea responds, the confidence in her voice matching the precision of her preparations. "We'll coordinate defense with Drabliti ground forces. Your ship should maintain position on the far side of the planet; they won't expect a pincer maneuver on their first approach."

Caelus agrees with this assessment. "Already on course. We'll be in position within the hour."

The communication ends just as the sensor officer straightens in her chair, attention suddenly focused on readings from the outermost buoys. "Energy signatures detected at the edge of the system," she reports, voice tight with controlled urgency. "Fractal distortion consistent with Battalion transit methods."

Selenea immediately adjusts the main viewport, magnifying the indicated sector. At maximum enhancement, barely visible distortions appear against the backdrop of distant stars, reality-bending in unnaturally precise patterns as Battalion ships force their way through controlled tears in space-time.

"Signature profile confirms Third Battalion configuration," the sensor officer continues, her fingers moving rapidly across her station to extract maximum data from minimal evidence. "Fifteen ships. Heavy assault class."

Selenea's expression hardens as she processes this information. Fifteen ships represent a significant commitment of resources, nearly half the Third Battalion's total strength. The deployment indicates Orpheus considers Drabliti a priority target worth substantial force allocation.

"Time to planetary approach?"

"At current speed, approximately ten hours."

Selenea secures her harness with a final click that resonates through the suddenly quiet bridge. Her hands move to the weapons control surface, programming initial targeting solutions with a calm precision that belies the gravity of their situation.

"All stations, battle preparation," she orders, her voice carrying both authority and absolute conviction. "Configure shields for maximum deflection against thermal lances.

Rotate energy frequencies according to variable pattern alpha to prevent adaptive targeting."

The crew responds with efficient precision, each member implementing specific preparations without requiring detailed instructions. They've fought alongside Selenea before and survived previous encounters with Battalion forces through the combination of her tactical brilliance and their technical expertise.

"They expect compliance," she reminds them, fingers completing the final weapon calibrations. "They expect a small ice planet to surrender rather than face the Third Battalion's full might." A grim smile touches her lips briefly. "That expectation creates our first tactical advantage."

The ship's engines shift to combat standby, power redirecting from non-essential systems to weapons and shields. The subtle change in ambient humming reflects the vessel's transformation from transport to warship, every system optimized for the coming conflict.

Through the viewport, Drabliti continues its serene rotation, ice fields glittering in the light of its distant sun. The peaceful scene contrasts sharply with the preparations for war taking place both in orbit and on the surface below. Beneath the pristine white landscape, an entire civilization prepares to defend its existence against forces that consider them expendable for the sake of cosmic "balance."

Selenea's amber eyes reflect the planet's white surface as she makes a final weapons check. The ship responds to her commands like an extension of her body, systems activating and adjusting with perfect synchronization to her input. The sensor display shows the Battalion ships still distant but approaching with inevitable precision.

"Let them come," she says quietly, the simple phrase carrying absolute determination rather than bravado. Her hands rest momentarily on the control surfaces, steady, prepared, resolved, before resuming their methodical preparation for the battle that will determine whether Drabliti survives or joins the growing list of worlds sacrificed to Orpheus's twisted vision of cosmic order.

Chapter 12

Frozen Battleground

Reality splits above Drabliti's northern ridge, not with thunder but with mathematical precision. The Fractal tear forms first as a hairline fracture in the atmosphere, then widens with cold efficiency into a crystalline portal whose edges shimmer with unnatural aurora light. The snow beneath the rift takes on its colors, electric blues and poisonous purples that have no place in Drabliti's natural spectrum. The air temperature plummets further as space-time distortion leaches energy from the surrounding environment, turning breath into ice crystals before it leaves the lungs of watching defenders.

The Third Battalion emerges through the rift like a mechanical infection. First come the scout vessels, a sleek, angular craft designed specifically for cold-environment penetration. Their hulls gleam with a reflective coating that minimizes heat signatures, making them nearly invisible against Drabliti's white landscape except for the blue thruster flares that betray their positions. Behind these advanced units, larger assault craft push through the Fractal, their specialized landing gear extending beneath them like predatory claws seeking purchase on the frozen terrain.

Ground troops follow in precise formation; soldiers are encased in white exoskeletal armor that enhances strength while maintaining flexibility in sub-zero conditions. Their helmets feature enhanced thermal imaging systems that cut through blizzard conditions, and their weapons, primarily modified thermal lances, glow with deadly orange-red energy designed to shatter ice structures at the molecular level. They deploy from transport vessels in triangular formations that leave no angle unprotected, each soldier moving with the synchronized precision that makes the Battalion both effective and terrifying.

Skif Zar stands at the observation platform carved into a glacial spire overlooking the northern defensive perimeter. His semi-transparent body catches and refracts the strange Fractal light, sending prismatic patterns across the ice wall beside him. Unlike most Drablitians, who maintain more abstract crystalline forms, Skif has configured his ice-based body into a roughly humanoid shape that facilitates interaction with other species. He shifts position slightly, his form making soft grinding sounds as he adjusts internal crystal structures to better process the visual data streaming in from the battlefield.

"They're deploying in standard assault formation," he says into the communication crystal embedded in what passes for his wrist. His voice emerges as precisely controlled vibrations through his entire crystalline form. "Three-tier approach. Heavy weapons at a thirty-degree offset from the central column."

The crystal pulses once, transmitting his analysis through ice-conducted vibrations to the defense command center two kilometers away. Skif restructures his right arm, extending it into a thin sheet of perfectly clear ice that functions as an enhanced viewing surface. Through this modified limb, he projects magnified images of Battalion deployment patterns, identifying vulnerabilities that might not be apparent to less experienced observers.

"Their thermal lances appear upgraded since the Voldom engagement," he adds, noting the distinctive energy signature that registers differently against his ice-sensitive perception. "Heat output approximately twenty-two percent higher than previous models."

In the defense command center, a massive chamber is carved deep into the face of an ice cliff, and Frizz Ravna receives these reports with characteristic efficiency. Her angular crystalline form moves between control stations with sharp, precise movements that contrast with the fluid motions of most Drablitians. Where others flow, she clicks, her body reconfiguring with audible snapping sounds as she shifts between functions.

"Understood," she responds, her vibrations traveling through the communication crystal with frequencies that would seem harsh to non-ice entities. "Adjusting thermal resistance parameters."

She places both hands against a massive control panel formed from ancient ice embedded with bioluminescent algae. The sigils carved into its surface, mathematical formulas disguised as artistic patterns, respond to her touch, glowing with intensified blue-white light that spreads outward through conduits within the ice walls. These defensive sigils activate in sequence, creating visible patterns across the massive barriers that protect the settlement.

"Avalanche tunnels primed," she announces, her form becoming temporarily more jagged as she channels energy into the defensive systems. "Adjusting resonance frequencies to counter thermal lance specifications."

Outside, the massive ice walls surrounding Drabliti's main settlement now pulse with soft blue light that follows geometric patterns established millennia ago. The light travels through the ice like blood through veins, concentrating at strategic junctions where specialized crystals amplify and direct its defensive properties. These aren't merely illumination but active countermeasures, ancient technology that reinforces molecular bonds within the ice, making it resistant to the precise frequencies used by Battalion thermal weapons.

Drablitian defenders take positions behind reinforced barriers along the wall's upper walkways. Unlike the massive council members with their abstract crystalline forms, these defensive units have configured themselves into more practical combat shapes, some with extended limbs optimized for operating ice-manipulation devices, others with compressed density structures that maximize stability during defensive operations. They move with practiced precision, their crystalline bodies making soft grinding sounds against the ice walkways.

Their breath forms clouds in the biting wind, though they require far less oxygen than carbon-based lifeforms. The respiration serves primarily to facilitate verbal communication rather than biological necessity. They speak in short, efficient phrases, position confirmations, system checks, and observation reports while adjusting defensive equipment with appendages specifically formed for each task.

"Eastern perimeter secured," reports a unit commander, his crystalline form slightly blue-tinted compared to the perfect transparency of younger defenders. "Pressure plate triggers at maximum sensitivity."

At strategic intervals along the wall, specialized ice entities monitor thermal variance gauges, devices that detect minute temperature changes that might indicate approaching Battalion forces. Others operate reinforcement stations, where they channel their consciousness directly into the wall structure, merging temporarily with the defensive barrier to enhance its properties at the molecular level.

Frizz Ravna's voice cuts through the communication network, reaching all defenders simultaneously. "Priority targets are thermal lance battalions and mobile artillery. Secondary targets are command units."

She activates a series of resonator chambers embedded within the cliff face behind the settlement. These ancient structures, spherical chambers carved from single ice crystals of extraordinary purity, begin to vibrate at frequencies that propagate through the surrounding snowpack. The vibrations aren't random but precisely calibrated to unstable frequencies that create destructive interference patterns against Battalion communication systems.

"All units confirm operational status," she commands, receiving immediate responses from each defensive section. Her form reconfigures again, optimizing for command functionality with enhanced sensor arrays extending from what would be her head on a humanoid entity.

Near the battlefield's western edge, where shadow-filled ravines create natural blind spots in defensive coverage, the air suddenly thickens with unnatural density. A barely perceptible distortion forms and then solidifies into a cloaked figure that seems to absorb rather than reflect light. The Valthorim entity stands silent and motionless, its face hidden within a hood of material that appears to shift between states of matter with each subtle movement.

The air around this figure crackles with ionized particles, creating a faint electrical hum that disturbs the natural silence of Drabliti's frozen landscape. The snow beneath its feet doesn't compress but sublimates directly from solid to gas, creating a small ring of bare ground that steams slightly despite the bitter cold.

The entity makes no move to approach either side, its presence seemingly unknown to both Battalion forces and Drablitian defenders. It merely observes the hood turning slightly to track key movements across the battlefield with an unnatural stillness between adjustments. For fleeting moments when Fractal light catches its shadow, the silhouette cast bears little resemblance to its apparent physical form, suggesting a shape both more expansive and less defined than its visible manifestation.

As Battalion forces complete their deployment, spreading across the snow plain in attack configuration, the cloaked figure raises one hand in what might be a gesture of acknowledgment or perhaps a blessing. Then it fades from view, not moving away but simply ceasing to interact with normal space-time, leaving only a lingering electrical charge in the air where it stood.

Battalion forces advance across the snow plain with mechanical precision, their white exoskeletal armor blending with the landscape while thermal lances cut glowing orange lines through the bitter air. Their formation maintains perfect symmetry despite the difficult terrain, a living algorithm of destruction moving steadily toward Drabliti's ice walls. The snow beneath their feet compacts with each synchronized step, leaving a grid of footprints that resembles a mathematical formula written across the pristine surface.

From the command center, Frizz Ravna watches their approach through ice-lens monitors. Her angular crystalline form moves between control stations with sharp, decisive motions that produce soft clicking sounds each time she reconfigures a limb. The defensive sigils embedded in her transparent body pulse with intensified light as she channels energy through specialized conduction pathways.

"Distance to primary trigger zone: eighty meters," reports a sensor operator, his voice creating vibrations that travel through ice rather than air.

Frizz nods, a human gesture she's adopted for efficiency rather than necessity. She moves to the central control platform where ancient trigger mechanisms await, crystalline devices shaped by generations of defensive engineers to channel specific frequencies through the mountain's ice structure.

"Prepare resonance chambers one through seven," she orders, her voice clipped and precise. "Activation on my command."

The Battalion's front line crosses an invisible threshold marked only by subtle differences in snow density. Frizz's form becomes more jagged as she extends her right arm, reconfiguring it into a flat palm that she presses against a crystal trigger embedded in the control platform. The trigger, a perfectly formed hexagonal crystal harvested from Drabliti's deepest ice caves, glows with blue-white intensity at her touch.

"Sector one engaged," she announces.

The mountain trembles. Not violently, but with a controlled purpose. The vibrations travel through precisely engineered channels carved within the ice over centuries, propagating to specific weak points in the snowpack above. Ancient technology activates, not with the brutal force of explosives but with the elegant efficiency of harmonics that disrupt snow's natural cohesion at the molecular level.

The Battalion's forward scouts notice too late. They turn their helmeted heads upward just as the mountain's face detaches with a sound like planetary exhalation. The avalanche begins not as a chaotic collapse but as a choreographed sequence, snow releasing in calculated volumes from predetermined points, creating overlapping waves of white destruction that converge on the advancing formation.

Battalion soldiers attempt evasive maneuvers, their exoskeletons whining as they push beyond normal performance parameters. Some manage to activate emergency shield generators that create momentary bubbles of protection. Others fire thermal lances upward, briefly cutting paths through the descending wall of white. But the avalanche's mass proved overwhelming, and its momentum was calculated by Drablitian engineers to exceed the thrust capacity of battalion armor.

The snow roars across the plain, burying entire squads beneath its crushing weight. Communication signals from the impacted units cut off mid-transmission. The perfect formation dissolves into disarray as survivors scramble to regroup, their movements now jagged with urgency rather than flowing with disciplined precision.

Skif Zar observes this from his elevated position, his crystalline form shifting slightly to process tactical information through specialized sensory structures. He reshapes portions of his body, extending transparent limbs that function as communication relays to scattered defensive units across the perimeter.

"Hold positions at the eastern ridge," he instructs, his voice propagating through ice-conduction networks. "Let them think they've found a safe approach."

The defenders acknowledge, their ice bodies remaining motionless despite the battlefield chaos below. They've practiced this strategy through countless drills, allowing apparent weaknesses in specific sections to channel enemy forces into prepared kill zones. Ice entities disguised as natural formations guide Battalion survivors through subtle terrain manipulation, creating paths of lesser resistance that inevitably lead to trap zones.

"Group three, prepare pressure plate sequence," Skif continues, reconfiguring his form to project tactical data as frost patterns hover briefly in the air before him. "Activate on proximity, not visual confirmation. Their thermal masking systems have improved."

In orbit above Drabliti, Caelus stands on his ship's bridge, hands extended as he channels his Aetheris perception. The metal enhancement bands around his fingers glow with soft blue light, channeling cosmic awareness through his nervous system. Through this enhanced perception, he sees not just physical battlefield positions but intention patterns, the cosmic threads that connect minds to actions, revealing strategies before they manifest.

"They're adapting faster than expected," he notes, eyes fixed on the tactical display where Battalion movements appear as heat signatures against Drabliti's frozen landscape. "Third wave redirecting to avoid avalanche zones."

The sigils tattooed across his skin warm beneath his uniform as he traces Battalion command signals through Aetheri's perception. He identifies discontinuity patterns that indicate strategic adjustments, the subtle shifts in cosmic resonance that precede tactical redeployment.

"They're regrouping at the western flank," he warns, transmitting data to Selenea's ship as it breaks orbit. "That's where the ice is thinnest."

Selenea receives this intelligence in her command chair; amber eyes narrowed as she processes the tactical implications. Her fingers dance across control surfaces with practiced efficiency, adjusting approach vectors and weapons configurations for maximum effectiveness against the identified threat.

"Acknowledged," she responds, strapping herself more securely into the command harness. "Commencing atmosphere entry now."

Her ship angles downward, hull glowing as it penetrates Drabliti's upper atmosphere. The vessel shudders briefly during the transition before stabilizing in a controlled descent. Weapons systems activate automatically, energy cells charging to combat readiness while targeting arrays compensate for atmospheric distortion.

"Deploy countermeasures," Selenea commands. "Cryo bombs on projected Battalion paths. Decoy flares to draw fire from airborne units."

The tactical officer implements these orders with precise efficiency. The ship's undersides open like petals, releasing cylindrical devices that tumble toward the battlefield below. These cryo-bombs, specialized weapons designed specifically for Drabliti's environment, don't explode with heat but implode with cold, creating localized super-freezing effects that can immobilize even thermally protected Battalion armor.

Simultaneously, bright flares eject from the ship's dorsal launchers, their chemical compositions producing heat signatures that mimic attack vessels. Battalion anti-aircraft units respond automatically, wasting precious ammunition on these decoys while Selenea's ship continues its approach through electronic shadows cast by distractions.

On the western flank, Battalion forces implement their contingency strategy. Mobile drilling platforms deploy their specialized bits designed to penetrate ice at the molecular level without generating heat that might trigger sensors. These devices bore into Drabliti's defensive walls with silent efficiency, creating access points for infiltration units equipped with scaled-down thermal lances optimized for close-quarters combat.

The ice responds. Not passively, as the normal matter would, but with active defense mechanisms activated by Frizz Ravna's command systems. The walls groan, not from stress but through deliberately engineered acoustic channels that amplify vibrational frequencies harmful to Battalion equipment. These sounds travel through the ice with the perfect transmission, creating destructive resonance patterns that interfere with drill-bit molecular alignments.

Beneath the snow, previously dormant defense systems awaken. Energy fields generated by ancient technology buried within Drabliti's permanent ice layer activate, creating a lattice of electromagnetic barriers that disrupt Battalion targeting systems. These fields hum with metallic resonance as they establish connection patterns based on mathematical formulas developed when Drabliti first faced external threats centuries earlier.

The humming intensifies as Frizz Ravna channels additional power through the command center's conduction networks. The ice sigils embedded throughout the defensive perimeter respond, their blue-white light strengthening as they draw energy from deep thermal taps that reach Drabliti's core. This power manifests not as conventional weapons but as environmental manipulation, temperature fields that fluctuate unpredictably, snow density that changes without visual indication, and ice crystals that form in Battalion equipment cooling systems with impossible speed.

"All defensive zones active," Frizz reports, her form briefly glowing brighter as she interfaces directly with control systems. "Avalanche sequence two prepared for the northwestern sector."

She transmits updated tactical data to Skif, who relays coordinate adjustments to defensive units. The crystalline defenders respond with silent efficiency, repositioning to channel surviving Battalion forces into the next prepared kill zone. Their ice bodies shift between states of transparency and opacity, sometimes blending completely with the surrounding environment, becoming indistinguishable from natural formations until the moment of attack.

Selenea's ship descends through thickening cloud cover, its hull collecting a thin layer of ice that cracks and reforms with each maneuver. The vessel emerges below the weather system, banking sharply to align with the western flank where Battalion forces concentrate their secondary attack. Her targeting systems lock onto command units identifiable by their distinctive energy signatures.

"Weapons hot," she confirms, fingers poised above firing controls. "Beginning attack run."

The ship dives toward the battlefield, leaving contrails of crystallized moisture that flash briefly in the thin sunlight. Below, the Battalion looks up as shadows pass overhead, the combined threat of Selenea's aerial assault and the inevitable next wave of Drabliti's defensive measures converging to transform their careful tactical advantage into desperate survival calculations.

The battlefield dissolves into white chaos as Frizz Ravna triggers the master sequence. All remaining avalanche tunnels activate simultaneously, releasing torrents of snow that converge from multiple elevations. Battalion forces caught between zones have no retreat path, their perfect formation now fragmented into isolated pockets fighting not against soldiers but against the planet itself. The snow moves with unnatural precision, not just falling but flowing in calculated patterns that target areas of greatest vulnerability.

Frizz stands in the defense command center, her crystalline form vibrating with intense concentration. The normal sharp angles of her ice body begin to lose definition as she makes a decision unprecedented in recent Drablitian history. She places both hands against the ancient control interface and allows her consciousness to merge with the defense system itself.

"Initiating direct integration," she announces, her voice already changing as her physical form becomes increasingly translucent. "Maintaining communication but surrendering independent structure temporarily."

The other operators step back, their ice bodies reconfiguring in gestures of respect mixed with concern. Direct integration represents both opportunity and risk, allowing unprecedented control over defensive systems but temporarily sacrificing individual consciousness to the greater network. Frizz's body loses cohesion, her ice melting into the control interface until only a faint outline of her original form remains visible within the wall.

The effect on battlefield operations is immediate. The defense systems, previously operating with mathematical precision but limited adaptability, suddenly exhibit organic responsiveness. Avalanche cascades adjust their flow mid-descent, redirecting to counter Battalion evasive maneuvers. Ice walls strengthen at precise points seconds before thermal lance impacts. Temperature fluctuations occur in patterns too complex for automated systems to calculate, creating zones where Battalion thermal regulation systems fail without apparent cause.

Through the ice itself, Frizz perceives the entire battlefield simultaneously. Each snowflake becomes an extension of her awareness, and each ice crystal is a sensory node in a network that spans the entire defense perimeter. She feels Battalion soldiers struggling through deep snow, detects the specific harmonic signatures of their communication systems, and calculates precise stress tolerances of their armor under various environmental conditions.

"Now!" she commands, her voice emerging not from a single location but from dozens of ice formations across the battlefield. The trenches, defensive structures buried beneath the snow and previously invisible to Battalion scanners, collapse on her command. The precisely engineered structural failures create synchronized sinkholes beneath advancing forces, dropping entire squads into prepared containment zones where ice immediately refreezes around them.

Skif Zar observes these developments from his elevated position, his crystalline form refracting sunlight as he analyzes the tactical advantages created by Frizz's integration. He extends communication appendages, connecting directly with defensive units positioned at strategic intervals around the perimeter.

"She's created an opening in their eastern formation," he notes, projecting tactical data through ice-conduction networks. "Prepare for coordinated strike with orbital support."

He reconfigures a portion of his form into a specialized communication array that can transmit directly to non-ice entities. This crystalline structure vibrates at precise frequencies that translate into standard communication protocols compatible with Selenea's systems.

"Selenea," he transmits, "their command units are exposed at these coordinates." The message includes not just location data but density readings of snow coverage, structural analyses of remaining Battalion defenses, and optimized attack vectors calculated specifically for her ship's capabilities.

Selenea receives this transmission in her command chair, amber eyes narrowing as she processes the tactical opportunity. Her fingers move across control surfaces with practiced precision, inputting the coordinates while simultaneously adjusting weapons configurations to maximize effectiveness against the identified targets.

"Executing attack run," she responds, her voice cutting through the communication chatter with calm authority. "Clear the eastern perimeter."

Her ship banks sharply, executing a maneuver that brings it directly above the exposed Battalion command units. Defensive operators alerted through Skif's coordination network withdraw Drablitian forces from the designated impact zone, their ice bodies flowing like liquid into protected positions behind reinforced barriers.

"Weapons locked," Selenea confirms. "Deploying primary payload."

The ship's undersides open, releasing a synchronized pattern of specialized ordinance designed specifically for this environment. Unlike conventional explosives that would lose effectiveness in the extreme cold, these weapons use Drabliti's natural conditions as a force multiplier. They burrow beneath the snow before detonation, creating shock waves that propagate through ice layers at calculated frequencies that shatter Battalion armor joints while leaving ice structures intact.

The impact transforms the eastern section of the battlefield. Snow erupts upward in precise columns that momentarily resemble a forest of white trees before collapsing onto Battalion positions. Command units lose cohesion, their carefully maintained formation dissolving into individual survival responses. Communication networks fail as relay units disappear beneath the white deluge.

Battalion officers recognize the tactical failure. Emergency signals flash through remaining communication channels, their coded patterns indicating the command that no soldier wishes to receive: strategic withdrawal. The surviving units immediately shift from attack to extraction protocols, converging toward the Fractal entry point with disciplined efficiency even in defeat.

The Fractal itself has begun to destabilize. Without proper maintenance from the Battalion's specialized equipment, the artificial tear in reality starts to close, its crystalline edges contracting as natural space-time reasserts itself. The phenomenon creates urgency among retreating forces, who abandon equipment and even wounded comrades in their rush to reach the dimensional gateway before complete closure.

Frizz Ravna, still integrated with the defense systems, senses this retreat through countless ice formations across the battlefield. She calculates optimal harassment patterns that maximize Battalion withdrawal speed while minimizing defender exposure to potential counterattacks. Ice barriers rise and fall at precise intervals, creating corridors that channel retreating forces along predetermined paths where they remain vulnerable to defensive fire without being trapped completely.

"Allow their extraction," she communicates to defensive units, her consciousness speaking through ice formations nearest to each position. "But maintain suppression patterns on flanking positions."

The last Battalion vessels disappear through the narrowing Fractal, the tear in reality shrinking behind them until it collapses with a sound like a distant crystal shattering. The battlefield falls silent except for the whisper of settling snow and the occasional groan of ice formations returning to natural balance after extreme stress.

Frizz Ravna begins the delicate process of extracting her consciousness from the defense network. Her ice body gradually reforms at the control interface, crystalline structures reestablishing the angular geometric patterns that define her individual identity. The process takes several minutes, and her form is initially transparent before regaining its characteristic density and definition.

"Defense systems returning to standard operational parameters," she announces, her voice once again emerging from a single location rather than the distributed network. "Damage assessment protocols initiated."

Across the settlement, Drablitians emerge from protective positions. Their celebrations remain subdued by off-world standards, with no shouting or chaotic movement, just precise adjustments in crystalline structure that create harmonic resonances expressing collective relief and satisfaction. Some defensive units reconfigure to begin immediate repairs on damaged wall sections, while others extend sensory appendages to assess battlefield conditions with methodical thoroughness.

Caelus's voice comes through the communication network, transmitted from his ship, which is still maintaining orbit above Drabliti. "Battalion forces retreating beyond sensor range," he reports. "No signs of secondary attack formations. Drabliti holds."

Skif Zar acknowledges this report with a brief signal pulse before making his way across the ice-covered battlefield toward the northern ridge. His crystalline form shifts as he moves, adapting to varying snow densities with fluid adjustments in pressure distribution. He reaches a prominent overlook where the day's first battle became its last, the entire field of conflict visible from this elevated position.

The setting sun catches his transparent body, sending prismatic patterns across the disturbed snow. The light reveals that the battalion equipment was partially buried beneath white drifts and abandoned in their retreat. Dark scorch marks from thermal lances cut black lines through otherwise pristine surfaces, while impact craters from Selenea's attack run create a geometric pattern across the eastern sector.

Frizz Ravna joins him, her angular form making distinctive crunching sounds as she traverses the fresh snow. Unlike Skif's more fluid movement, she progresses with sharp, efficient steps that leave perfectly geometric impressions behind her. She stops beside him, her crystalline structure catching the same sunlight but refracting it in more precise, controlled patterns.

"Eighteen percent structural damage to the main ice wall," she reports without preamble. "Repairable within forty-two hours. The avalanche basins require twenty-nine hours to refill to optimal capacity."

Skif nods, a gesture adopted from humanoid species for its communicative efficiency. "They employed only sixty-four percent of standard Battalion strength," he observes. "A testing force rather than full commitment."

"They'll be back," Frizz states, her form reconfiguring slightly to optimize sensory input as she studies the battlefield. The movement creates subtle crystalline sounds, like ice sheets shifting against one another.

Skif turns toward her, light passing through his transparent form in patterns that suggest agreement. "And we'll be ready," he responds, already calculating improvements to defensive positions based on observed Battalion tactics.

Frizz's normally jagged form softens almost imperceptibly, the closest she comes to expressing satisfaction. "I have fourteen modifications to implement before they return," she says, turning back toward the settlement. "The western wall requires complete reconfiguration of its resonance chambers."

They descend from the ridge together, two crystalline forms moving across a battlefield that will soon disappear beneath fresh snow, leaving no trace of today's conflict except in defense system modifications and tactical memory banks. Behind them, Drabliti's sun touches the horizon, its light fracturing through ice crystals in the atmosphere into patterns that resemble, just briefly, the mathematical precision of the Fractal that brought destruction to their world and will undoubtedly do so again.

Chapter 13

Storms of Sand and Deception

The metal bands around Caelus's fingers glow blue-white as he extends his hands toward Bardes, his consciousness stretching beyond physical form. The sigils beneath his uniform warm against his skin while his Aetheris perception traces cosmic threads through the void, seeking the distinctive disruption patterns of Battalion Fractals. Beside him on the bridge, Selenea studies weapons displays with methodical focus, her amber eyes reflecting scrolling tactical data as she calculates optimal defense vectors.

"Found them," Caelus says, voice carrying the harmonic undertone of active Aetheris connection. "Fourth Battalion. Three Fractal entry points forming on the eastern hemisphere."

His perception extends across thousands of light years, following cosmic disturbances that most technology cannot detect. The Fourth Battalion tears through reality with mathematical precision, their Fractal signatures displaying the distinctive ordered patterns of Valthorim technology. Unlike the chaotic natural rifts that occasionally form between worlds, these are surgical incisions deliberate wounds in space-time.

"Time to emergence?" Selenea asks, not looking up from her station. Her fingers glide across control surfaces, programming targeting solutions with veteran efficiency.

"Twenty-seven minutes." Caelus winces as blood vessels in his eyes dilate from extended perception strain. "Standard formation. Assault configuration."

Selenea nods once, her movements economical as she activates orbital defense protocols. "Deploying countermeasures now. Targeting solutions locked for all emergence points."

Below them, Bardes rotates slowly beneath twin crimson suns. The planet's surface appears as vast rocky plains intersected by crystalline formations that catch and scatter light in geometric patterns. From orbit, the massive resonance towers look like needles thrust into the planet's skin, artificial structures aligned with mathematical precision across the desert landscape. Their surfaces gleam with embedded technological arrays that pulse with subtle energy fluctuations.

The atmosphere carries a visible charge, electrical patterns that flow across the planet's surface like luminous rivers. Each discharge connects resonance towers in momentary spider-web configurations before dissipating. The phenomenon intensifies as the towers activate, responding to planetary defense protocols initiated from below.

At the base of the largest resonance tower, Sidia Lith assembles her warriors in tiered formations. Her massive rock-giant form towers over even the tallest soldiers, her crystalline skin reflecting crimson sunlight in fractured patterns. The sigils carved into her stone exterior glow with internal energy, power conduits connecting her consciousness to both her warriors and the tower's defensive systems.

"Fourth Battalion confirmed," she announces, her voice rumbling like stone grinding against stone. "Deployment positions as practiced."

The Bardesian warriors respond with disciplined silence, moving into predetermined defensive formations around the tower's base. Their armor, forged from rare metals infused with the planet's unique mineral compounds, reflects the crimson light in bloody patterns. Each warrior carries weapons custom-calibrated to Bardes' natural electromagnetic field, designed to draw power directly from the planet's energy currents.

"They think us primitive," Sidia continues, addressing her assembled forces. "Desert dwellers clinging to a harsh world." She stretches her massive stone arms, signaling to technicians who begin final calibrations on the resonance tower. "Let them discover how Bardes transforms disadvantage to strength."

The warriors acknowledge with ritualistic thumping of weapons against the rocky ground. The sound travels through the desert floor, creating vibrations that the resonance towers amplify and redirect. Electrons dance across armor surfaces, creating blue-white discharge patterns that increase in intensity as the towers absorb and redistribute the energy.

Ten kilometers east, buried within a mesa that appears unremarkable among hundreds of identical formations, Kiran Tritus monitors surveillance systems with frenetic attention. Their rock-giant fingers tap against crystalline control panels with an irregular rhythm, each movement leaving slight indentations in surfaces designed to withstand such pressure. Unlike Sidia's composed presence, Kiran's form displays constant micro-movements, small shifts and reconfigurations that betray their perpetual anxiety.

"Detecting Fractal formation exactly as predicted," they report through the communication network, voice vibrating with both information and nervous energy. "All three entry points align with Battalion approach patterns from previous engagements."

They switch between monitoring screens with practiced efficiency despite their apparent agitation. Each display shows different aspects of Bardes' defensive systems, camouflage integrity monitors, resonance tower energy levels, atmospheric condition reports, and subterranean sensor readings. Kiran's eyes move between them in patterns too rapid for most species to follow, their stone pupils dilating and contracting with each assessment.

"Camouflage systems at full capacity," they continue, running diagnostic sequences for the third time in ten minutes. "All fleet units maintaining asteroid mimicry. Energy signatures masked. Visual profiles consistent with natural space debris."

Through the communication network, Caelus acknowledges. "Confirmed from orbit. Your camouflage technology is remarkable, Kiran. Even our sensors can barely distinguish your ships from actual asteroids."

Kiran's form briefly stills at the compliment before resuming its perpetual motion. "The best defense isn't, "

"a weapon, but making sure they never see you coming," Selenea finishes, a hint of warmth briefly softening her tactical focus. "You've mentioned it before."

"Nineteen times, actually," Kiran responds without hesitation. "But the principle remains sound regardless of repetition frequency."

On the bridge, Caelus retracts his consciousness from extended perception, focusing back on immediate tactical concerns. Blood vessels have burst in his left eye, creating a red starburst pattern against the white. The enhancement bands around his fingers dim as he redirects energy to more immediate applications.

"Sidia, the status of ground forces?" he asks, wiping a thin trickle of blood from his nostril.

"Warriors deployed at all critical junctions," she responds, her voice coming through with the slight distortion characteristic of transmission through Bardes' electrically charged atmosphere. "Resonance towers at eighty-four percent charge capacity. Increasing."

The air around the towers vibrates with intensifying frequency. Dust particles rise from the desert floor, suspended in patterns that reflect the tower's energy emissions. The phenomenon spreads outward, creating visible waves that travel across the planet's surface. Electronic equipment registers increase interference, and signals become distorted as ambient electrical charge builds in the atmosphere.

"Hair-raising, isn't it?" Kiran comments, touching the stone formations that serve as their equivalent of hair. The mineral extensions stand perfectly upright, conducting electrical current between them in small arcs of blue-white energy.

Around Sidia, her warriors experience similar effects. The few species with organic hair find it standing on end, while those with crystalline or metallic components in their biology become temporary conduits for the building electrical charge. The sensation is familiar to Bardesians, a physical manifestation of their planet's increasing defensive readiness.

"Fourteen minutes to Fractal completion," Caelus updates, consulting tactical displays. "Battalion emergence imminent."

Kiran's screens flicker with electromagnetic interference, data temporarily distorting before stabilization algorithms compensate. "They're coming through exactly where you predicted," they report, fingers tapping rapidly on crystalline control panels. "All three Fractals maintain stable formation. Standard Battalion invasion configuration."

Sidia turns to face the eastern horizon, where the first signs of disturbance appear, a shimmering in the air, and reality begins to fold inward upon itself. The towers around her pulse with stronger energies, their embedded technological arrays glowing bright enough to be visible even in the harsh sunlight of the twin suns.

She places her massive stone hand against the base of the primary tower, feeling the vibrations building within its structure. Power flows through the connection, and sigils on her body illuminate in sequence as they channel and amplify the planet's natural electromagnetic field.

"Initiate the storm protocol," she commands, voice carrying through both technological communication systems and the resonance conduction of the planet itself. "Let them taste Bardes."

The towers respond immediately. Energy discharges connect between them in sustained patterns rather than momentary flashes. The ambient electrical charge intensifies, creating visible distortions in the air as electron density reaches critical thresholds. Deep beneath the surface, ancient mechanisms activate technology that harnesses and directs the planet's unique mineral properties toward defensive application.

The first particles rise from the desert floor, not simply dust but mineral compounds with naturally conductive properties. They swirl in tight patterns, gathering energy from the ambient field, beginning to glow with amber light. What starts as scattered eddies quickly grows into organized flows as the resonance towers establish control parameters.

The building storm responds to mathematical instructions encoded in the towers' emissions, forming not through chaotic weather patterns but through precise electromagnetic manipulation.

Bardes prepares to defend itself not with conventional weapons but by transforming its entire environment into a defense system that no invader, no matter how technologically advanced, can possibly prepare for. The planet itself becomes the weapon, just as it has through countless invasions across millennia of carefully preserved history.

Reality splits above Bardes' eastern hemisphere, not with chaotic violence but with mathematical precision. The Fractals complete their formation, creating crystalline tears in the atmosphere through which Battalion vessels emerge like mechanical predators entering new hunting grounds. Their hulls gleam with combat polish, weapon systems already activating as they establish attack formations designed to maximize coverage of critical targets below.

The Fourth Battalion specializes in desert warfare; their ships are equipped with specialized filters and reinforced hull plating designed to withstand abrasive environments. They deploy in their characteristic arrowhead configuration, assault vessels at the fore, troop carriers protected in the middle, and command ships directed from the rear. The formation cuts through Bardes' upper atmosphere with clinical efficiency, adjusting for wind resistance and gravitational variables with machine-like coordination.

From orbit, Selenea watches the emergence through tactical displays that transform the Battalion's movements into color-coded threat assessments. Her fingers dance across targeting systems, designating priority vessels with practiced precision.

"Targeting lead assault ships," she announces, strapping herself more securely into the command chair. "Fire pattern Theta-Six."

The ship's weapons systems respond immediately. Energy beams lance through the atmospheric gap between the orbiting position and Battalion formation. The attacks connect with mathematical precision, not attempting to destroy vessels outright but targeting communication arrays, weapon systems, and navigation equipment. Each strike is calculated to degrade capability rather than achieve immediate destruction.

"Three direct hits," she confirms, already adjusting target priorities based on results. "Their shields compensated faster than expected. Recalibrating attack frequency."

Beside her, Caelus extends his perception once more, the enhancement bands around his fingers pulsing with renewed energy. His consciousness stretches between orbital position and ground forces, creating awareness connections that technology alone cannot achieve. The sigils across his skin burn bright enough to be visible through his uniform as he channels unprecedented amounts of energy through his Aetheris ability.

"Selenea, target the vessel at these coordinates," he directs, transmitting precise positioning data directly to her tactical display. "It's their primary communication hub. The cosmic threads connecting it to other vessels show higher density patterns."

Simultaneously, he extends his awareness downward, connecting with Sidia and Kiran through channels that bypass conventional communication systems. "Battalion approaching central defense zone. Primary vessels thirty seconds from optimal engagement range."

On the planet's surface, the resonance towers complete their power accumulation cycle. Energy discharges between them now form constant connections rather than intermittent arcs, creating a geometric pattern visible from orbit, a massive web of power with each tower forming a critical junction point. The atmosphere itself becomes charged, and electrons are excited to states that transform air molecules into a semi-conductive medium.

Beneath the towers, the ground trembles as ancient machinery activates, not with the industrial rumble of conventional technology but with the precise harmonic vibrations of systems designed to work with planetary forces rather than against them. The resonance builds, frequencies aligning with the natural harmonic signature of Bardes' mineral-rich substrate.

The storm begins.

What starts as localized dust devils quickly expands into organized flows as the resonance towers establish control parameters. The particles don't simply rise through thermal updrafts but are actively pulled into electromagnetic currents that form precise circulation patterns. Each particle carries a slight electrical charge, creating collective behavior more akin to programmed swarm intelligence than natural weather.

Within minutes, the storm front rises two kilometers high, its leading edge advancing with unnatural precision toward Battalion positions. The particles glow amber from within, energized by the electrical field that binds them together. Through this luminous wall, occasional arcs of blue-white energy flash like neural impulses through a living organism, the storm responding to guidance from the resonance towers with near-sentient adaptability.

Battalion vessels enter the storm's outer boundary with misplaced confidence, their sensors indicating merely extreme but manageable weather conditions. Their specialized filters engage atmospheric shields, increasing power to compensate for particulate density. For thirty seconds, their systems appear to maintain optimal functionality.

Then, the storm reveals its true nature.

The electrically charged particles don't simply impact against shields; they cling to hull surfaces, accumulating in patterns that follow electromagnetic field lines. These accumulations create conductive pathways that short-circuit external sensor arrays first, then begin interfering with communication systems. The particles' abrasive properties simultaneously degrade external equipment, tiny impacts multiplied billions of times per second, wearing away protective coatings with extraordinary efficiency.

"They're experiencing primary systems failure," Kiran reports from the command center, their stone fingers moving across control panels with unusual steadiness as the defense systems they've dedicated their life to developing prove effective. "Sensor arrays compromised. Navigation systems show a seventy percent accuracy reduction. Communication networks experiencing frequency degradation."

Kiran switches to a different control surface, activating a sequence that transmits coded signals to apparently empty regions of Bardes' orbit. "Releasing the fleet now."

What appeared to be ordinary asteroids in Bardes' orbit suddenly ignited thrusters, revealing themselves as camouflaged Bardesian warships. The deception isn't mere visual mimicry but comprehensive camouflage, energy signatures, material composition readings, and gravitational profiles, all precisely engineered to register as natural space debris on Battalion scanners.

The fleet consists of thirty vessels of varying sizes, each designed specifically for Bardes' defense. Their exterior surfaces maintain an asteroid-like appearance even as they maneuver into attack positions, the camouflage systems adjusting in real-time to maintain deception until the final moment of engagement. Only when they move into firing positions, does the camouflage dissolve, revealing sleek vessels whose designs optimize planetary defense rather than deep-space combat.

"Attack pattern Epsilon," Kiran transmits to the fleet. "Maintain electromagnetic countermeasures at maximum intensity."

Below, the sandstorm reaches full manifestation, transforming the battlefield into an electrically charged maelstrom. Visibility reduces to meters, and the air is filled with glowing particles that abrade exposed surfaces and interfere with electronic systems. The howling reaches volumes that penetrate even battalion ship hulls, and the sound-carrying harmonic frequencies are specifically calibrated to create psychological discomfort in most sentient species.

Through this chaos, Sidia leads her warriors up dune formations with natural confidence born from lifetimes spent navigating Bardes' harshest conditions. Their bodies evolved for this environment to move with perfect adaptation through currents that would disorient off-worlders. The electrical charge that disables battalion equipment actually enhances the warriors' capabilities, and their specialized armor draws power directly from the ambient field.

"Southern approach secured," Sidia reports, her massive stone form pushing through the storm without effort. "Enemy ground forces deploying but disoriented. Their armor systems fail under electrical interference."

She gestures for her warriors to take positions along ridgelines where the storm's intensity creates natural ambush zones. The Battalion soldiers below struggle through blinding conditions, their formation discipline deteriorating as navigation systems fail and visual confirmation becomes impossible. What should be a coordinated ground assault devolves into isolated units fighting not enemies but the environment itself.

"They can't see us," Sidia says into her comm, watching Battalion soldiers fire blindly into the storm. "But we can see them."

The Bardesian warriors activate specialized visors that filter the storm's interference while amplifying electrical signatures. Through these devices, Battalion soldiers appear as bright heat sources moving through the maelstrom, perfect targets for precisely aimed attacks.

In orbit, Caelus maintains his expanded awareness, coordinating between Selenea's attacks and ground forces. The strain shows in physical symptoms: blood vessels rupturing in both eyes now, nose bleeding freely, and muscles trembling with micro-seizures. Still, he channels more energy through the enhancement bands, pushing his Aetheris ability beyond normal limitations.

"Battalion command ship reorienting," he reports, voice strained but steady. "Attempting to establish higher altitude position above the storm."

Selenea immediately adjusts her targeting. "Not happening," she mutters, inputting new attack vectors. The ship's weapons systems lock onto the climbing Battalion vessel, energy beams connecting with its propulsion systems. The damage isn't catastrophic but sufficient to prevent escape from the storm's influence.

The Battalion's initial confidence dissolves as their technological advantage proves increasingly irrelevant to Bardes' environmental warfare. Their formation fragments as individual commanders attempt different strategies for countering the unexpected defense, some pushing through the storm with maximum power, others attempting to climb above it, and still, others deploying ground forces to secure positions for equipment that might counter the electromagnetic interference.

All strategies fail against a defense system that transforms the entire environment into a weapon. The storm doesn't merely obstruct visibility or damage equipment; it actively adapts to counter battalion responses, with the resonance towers adjusting emission patterns to intensify effects precisely where resistance appears strongest.

From his command center, Kiran observes these developments with rare satisfaction, their typically anxious movements momentarily stilled. "The pattern holds," they note, more to themselves than others. "Nature perfected deception long before we did. We're just learning her tricks."

The storm continues to intensify, its howl becoming a physical force that vibrates through ship hulls and combat armor alike. The glowing particles create an otherworldly battlefield illuminated by constant flashes of electromagnetic discharge and the filtered crimson light of the twin suns. Through this luminous chaos, Bardesian defenders move with practiced ease while Battalion forces struggle against an environment that actively opposes their presence on every level, from the microscopic to the planetary.

The Fourth Battalion forces descend through the amber maelstrom, their landing craft shuddering against electromagnetic currents that interfere with stabilization systems. Hulls designed to withstand conventional warfare now emit high-pitched screams as abrasive particles scour protective coatings down to the raw metal. Inside these failing vessels, soldiers check equipment with practiced efficiency that belies the growing realization that their extensive training has prepared them for every contingency except the one they now face.

Landing zones transform into chaos as visibility drops to near zero. The soldiers deployed in defensive formations, their white exoskeletal armor immediately collecting the charged particles that swirled around them. Within minutes, the pristine surfaces acquire a rusty patina as the abrasive sand etches microscopic patterns into protective plating. Joints become the first vulnerability, fine particles infiltrating servo mechanisms, interfering with movement calibration, and transforming smooth combat motions into jerky, unpredictable actions.

Their helmet visors fare a little better. The specialized polycarbonate surfaces, designed to withstand energy weapon impacts, succumb to the relentless friction of billions of electrically charged particles. Vision systems degrade from crystal clarity to hazy approximation within the first hour of exposure. Communication systems fail intermittently as electromagnetic interference disrupts standard frequencies, forcing squad leaders to resort to hand signals that become useless in the limited visibility.

"Standard defensive perimeter," orders the Battalion commander through momentarily clear communication channels. "Deploy sensor beacons at ten-meter intervals. Establish hardened communication relays."

The soldiers implement these instructions with characteristic discipline despite the hostile environment. Their movements, though increasingly labored as their exoskeletons accumulate damage, maintain the precision that defines Battalion operations. They establish a circular defense pattern, weapons facing outward, and sensor equipment deployed to maximum range despite degraded functionality.

This textbook response proves useless against Bardes' unique defensive strategy. The sensor beacons register nothing but electromagnetic static, their detection algorithms overwhelmed by the storm's consistent interference patterns. Communication relays establish temporary connections before succumbing to power fluctuations caused by irregular discharge patterns across their external components.

Through this chaos, Sidia's warriors approach with predatory patience. They move through the storm like phantoms, their stone bodies naturally resistant to the abrasive particles that devastate Battalion equipment. The electrical charge that disrupts enemy systems actually enhances their own capabilities, their weapons drawing power directly from the ambient electromagnetic field.

"Western quadrant," Sidia signals, her massive hand gestures visible to warriors adapted to Bardes' storm conditions. "Converge on their sensor array."

Her warriors spread out, their movements synchronized through years of training in these precise conditions. They don't fight against the storm, but with it, they use current patterns to enhance movement speed, letting electromagnetic flows guide projectile weapons with greater accuracy than mechanical systems could provide. Their armor, infused with conductive minerals harvested from Bardes' deepest caverns, creates localized field distortions that render them nearly invisible to what remains of Battalion detection equipment.

The first squad of Battalion soldiers falls without firing an effective shot. Bardesian warriors emerge from swirling amber clouds, attack with devastating precision, and then disappear back into the maelstrom before reinforcements can respond. The pattern repeats across the perimeter: surgical strikes against communication equipment, weapons systems, and command personnel, each attack lasting seconds before the responsible warriors vanish into the storm they've navigated since childhood.

From orbit, Caelus tracks these engagements through his Aetheris perception. The metal bands around his fingers have grown hot enough to leave burn marks on adjacent digits, the price of maintaining such extended awareness. Blood streams freely from his nose now, spattering the tactical console with crimson droplets that evaporate in the ship's environmental controls.

"Battalion attempting to regroup at these coordinates," he relays to Selenea, transmitting precise positioning data. "Their remaining functional ships are consolidating to cover the fire."

Selenea receives this intelligence with a sharp nod, her attention never leaving the weapons control surface. "Target locked," she confirms, initiating the firing sequence. "Executing precision strike."

The ship's main batteries discharge with calculated intensity. The energy beams cut through the upper atmosphere, and their trajectories adjust in real-time to compensate for electromagnetic interference. They connect with the consolidating Battalion vessels, targeting propulsion and weapons systems rather than attempting outright destruction.

"Rear flank neutralized," she reports, already shifting focus to secondary targets. "Target their rear flank, Selenea. Cut off their retreat."

In the hidden command center, Kiran Tritus monitors battlefield developments with methodical attention despite their perpetually anxious movements. Their stone fingers tap against control surfaces, each touch initiating different aspects of Bardes' defensive systems. The crystalline displays before them show the storm's progress, Battalion positions, and warrior deployments, all rendered in three-dimensional clarity despite the chaos engulfing the actual battlefield.

"Initiating resonance lure deployment," they announce, activating devices that represent the culmination of decades of research.

Across the battlefield, small cylindrical objects activate within the storm. These resonance lures emit precise electromagnetic signatures that mimic Battalion communication protocols. Each lure broadcasts tactical data that would appear legitimate to Battalion systems, false retreat coordinates, phantom reinforcement locations, and counterfeit command overrides. The devices don't merely transmit static signals but adapt based on Battalion response patterns, creating increasingly convincing deceptions.

"They're falling for it," Kiran reports, flicking sand from a console with nervous fingers as they track Battalion movement patterns. "Three squads redirecting to false coordinates. Command unit responding to phantom distress signals."

The lures draw Battalion forces into prepared ambush zones, areas where the storm's electromagnetic properties have been specifically enhanced to maximize interference with their equipment. As they enter these zones, their already compromised systems experience cascading failures. Exoskeletons lock mid-motion, rendering soldiers immobile. Communication systems emit painful feedback loops directly into helmet audio systems. Weapons discharge randomly as control circuits fail under intense electromagnetic pressure.

The battalion commander, a veteran of seventeen planetary conquests with an unbroken record of success, recognizes that the strategic collapse was too late. His attempt to establish a centralized fallback position fails as communication channels collapse entirely. The precise coordination that defines Battalion effectiveness dissolves into isolated units fighting for survival rather than victory.

"All units, emergency protocol seven," he broadcasts, using his command vessel's enhanced transmitter to momentarily cut through interference. "Converge on my position. Prepare for orbital extraction."

The order reaches fewer than thirty percent of deployed forces, the rest already cut off by communication failures or engaged in hopeless combat against enemies they can barely detect. Those who receive the command attempt to comply, abandoning equipment too damaged to transport, supporting wounded comrades through the blinding storm toward coordinates that represent their final hope of survival.

Sidia intercepts this communication through Bardesian monitoring systems. She stands atop a dune ridge, her massive stone form silhouetted against the amber-lit storm clouds. The electromagnetic discharge creates luminous patterns across her crystalline skin, sigils carved into her exterior glowing with absorbed energy.

"They're converging for extraction," she informs her warriors through Bardes' native communication network, a system that uses the planet's electromagnetic field as its transmission medium. "Final engagement protocol. No survivors."

She leads the charge across the dunes, her warriors moving in perfect formation through conditions that have reduced Battalion soldiers to stumbling, disoriented targets. The Bardesians don't merely navigate the storm, and they become extensions of it, their movements amplified by electromagnetic currents, their weapons charged by the same energy that disables their enemies' defenses.

The sandstorm reaches peak intensity as the final assault begins. The air itself becomes a weapon, charged particles achieving densities that interfere with standard respiration equipment. Electrical discharges create electromagnetic pulses that render the remaining Battalion technology useless. The abrasive particles no longer merely damage equipment but strip it away entirely, reducing advanced combat systems to useless scrap.

Through this apocalyptic environment, flashes of weapons fire create brief illumination, stuttering glimpses of Bardesian warriors overwhelming the remaining Battalion forces. The crimson light of the twin suns filters through the maelstrom in blood-red patterns that transform the battlefield into a hellscape of amber clouds and vermillion shadows. Each lightning-like discharge reveals another moment of the Battalion's final collapse: soldiers falling, equipment failing, the perfect military machine reduced to individual lives ending in a storm they never understood.

Caelus tracks the battle's conclusion through increasingly fragmented Aetheris perception. His ability, taxed beyond sustainable limits, now provides only glimpses rather than comprehensive awareness. Still, these fragments tell the same story: total Battalion defeat across all engagement zones.

"It's over," he announces to Selenea, his voice hoarse from strain. "No surviving Battalion ships detected. Ground forces eliminated or captured."

Selenea powers down weapons systems with methodical precision, her movements displaying none of the fatigue that might be expected after such intense combat. "Confirm with Sidia."

The confirmation comes minutes later as the storm begins its controlled dissipation. The resonance towers adjust their output frequencies, and electromagnetic fields shift from combat parameters to standard containment patterns. The glowing particles begin to settle, guided by precise field manipulations back to the planet's surface.

"Battalion neutralized," Sidia reports, her voice carrying the flat certainty of absolute victory. "Minimal Bardesian casualties. Collection teams recovering salvageable technology."

As the storm subsides, the battlefield reveals the extent of the Battalion's defeat. Their vessels lie half-buried in sand drifts, once-gleaming hulls now stripped to bare metal by the abrasive particles. Exoskeletons stand in frozen poses like macabre sculptures, their occupants eliminated by weapons they never saw coming. Equipment meant to conquer a planet has been reduced to scrap by the very environment it sought to control.

The resonance towers power down to standby levels, their vibrations decreasing from combat intensity to the standard frequencies that maintain Bardes' everyday defensive readiness. The twin suns emerge from thinning storm clouds, their crimson light illuminating a landscape transformed by battle yet fundamentally unchanged, a desert planet that has once again survived through the perfect integration of natural forces and defender determination.

In the command center, Kiran runs final diagnostics on defense systems, their nervous energy returning as the immediate threat subsides. "Camouflage systems reactivating," they report. "Fleet returning to asteroid configuration. Resonance towers at standard output."

The battle for Bardes concludes not with dramatic last stands or heroic final charges but with the simple, inevitable victory of a world defended by those who understand its nature against those who seek to impose their will upon it. The Fourth Battalion, like the Third before it, discovers too late that Orpheus's conquest faces its greatest challenge not from the comparable military force but from worlds whose defenses transcend conventional warfare through perfect adaptation to their unique environments.

Chapter 14

Orpheus's Gambit

The hidden chamber beneath Zathira's primary meditation hall exists in perfect darkness until Orpheus enters. Light responds to his presence, not flooding the space but emerging in precise patterns that illuminate only what he wishes to see. Ancient technology, preserved from civilizations long extinct, activates beneath his fingertips as he approaches the central platform where decisions that shift the fate of worlds take form.

The chamber itself defies conventional architecture. Its walls curve inward at impossible angles, creating spaces that seem to extend beyond physical dimensions. Embedded sigils, older than the monastery itself, pulse with a subtle energy that reacts to Orpheus's proximity. They don't merely generate light but bend reality slightly, creating pockets where surveillance cannot penetrate and communications remain undetectable. Here, the boundary between material existence and the void between realities leads to imperceptible margins.

"Display tactical overview," he commands.

The chamber responds. Light coalesces above the platform, forming a three-dimensional map of nearby systems. Planets appear as spheres of varying sizes and colors, their surfaces rendered with perfect topographical accuracy despite the miniature scale. Fractals, the controlled tears in space-time that allow interstellar travel, appear as crystalline connections between worlds, their stability indicated by color intensity.

Orpheus studies this cosmic display with practiced efficiency, his eyes revealing nothing of the calculations occurring behind them. His fingers move through the hologram with deliberate precision, dismissing certain worlds with casual flicks while enlarging others for closer inspection. Eventually, only two planets remain highlighted, Mordia and Marinami.

"Access Fifth Battalion deployment protocols," he continues, voice carrying those distinctive harmonic undertones that no human vocal cords should produce. "Display current vector calculations."

A red line appears, connecting a Valthorim outpost to Mordia, the officially sanctioned target for the Fifth Battalion's next "pacification" mission. Orpheus studies this trajectory briefly before his mouth forms what might technically qualify as a smile, though the expression contains no warmth.

"Now access communication interception array."

New holographic windows materialize around him, and dozens of intercepted transmissions are captured from Caelus's network. Text streams, voice recordings, and navigational data are collected through specialized Fractal harmonics that allow him to monitor communications without detection. His fingers sort through these with expert precision, selecting specific elements that serve his purpose.

"Begin sequence manipulation," he says. "Redirect Battalion priority targeting from Mordia to Marinami."

The chamber's technology responds to his command with subtle efficiency. The intercepted data transforms beneath his guidance, coordinates shift, priority assessments rearrange, and threat analyses recalibrate. All with such perfect precision that even the most sophisticated verification protocols would detect no tampering. The red trajectory line on the holographic display wavers for a moment, then reforms with Marinami as its endpoint.

"Transmit falsified intelligence package to Fifth Battalion command using Valthorim override protocols."

Authentication codes appear briefly before dissolving into the transmission stream. These access keys, reserved for the highest Valthorim authority, ensure the altered orders will be implemented without question. The battalion will never know they're being redirected from their official target to serve Orpheus's hidden agenda.

He turns his attention to Marinami's holographic representation, enlarging it until the water planet fills the center of the chamber. His fingers trace the blue sphere's surface, analyzing defensive capabilities with analytical detachment. The planet rotates slowly beneath his touch, revealing underwater cities protected by manipulated current systems and bioluminescent warning networks.

"Access Fifth Battalion pre-launch status," he commands.

A new display forms, showing a Valthorim outpost where ships prepare for departure. Troops board assault vessels with characteristic discipline. Equipment specifically designed for jungle warfare, appropriate for Mordia but useless against Marinami's oceanic defenses, loads into cargo holds. The battalion remains completely unaware that their carefully planned operation now targets an entirely different world.

Orpheus watches these preparations with cold satisfaction. His hand passes through Marinami's holographic representation, fingers curling as if physically grasping the planet. The blue light casts his face in ghostly illumination, creating shadows that seem to shift independently of his movements.

"Planetary analysis indicates ninety-seven percent success probability against Mordia," he says, though no one else is present to hear. "Against Marinami, with current equipment configurations, success probability drops to forty-three percent."

This statistical disadvantage doesn't concern him. In fact, the subtle curve of his lips suggests it may be precisely what he intended. His fingers trace patterns through Marinami's holographic oceans with proprietary familiarity.

"Caelus tracks Battalion movements through Aetheris with impressive accuracy," he continues, his voice still carrying those unsettling harmonics. "But Aetheris follows intent patterns, not physical trajectories. The Battalion embarks believing they target Mordia, and their intent remains aligned with that destination until the final approach."

He steps back, watching as the falsified coordinates complete their transmission. Battalion vessels begin final launch preparations, their commanders reviewing tactical briefings that now contain subtle contradictions they're unlikely to notice until too late.

"By the time Aetheris's perception detects the redirect, the Fifth Battalion will have already engaged Marinami," Orpheus observes. "Caelus can't track what commanders themselves don't yet know."

The chamber responds to his satisfaction, lights dimming except for the pulsing blue glow of Marinami's hologram. This selective illumination casts Orpheus's face in eerie patterns that emphasize the unnatural stillness of his features. He makes a subtle gesture that enlarges several regions of the water planet, defensive installations, population centers, and critical infrastructure.

"Let's see how quickly your Aetheris adapts to this, Caelus," he murmurs, expression calculating rather than malicious.

The words aren't born from personal vendetta but from strategic necessity. Each world that falls, whether through direct conquest or exhaustion from defensive efforts, weakens the growing resistance against Valthorim's authority. Each battle forces Caelus to expend precious resources, stretch his abilities beyond sustainable limits, and reveal more of his tactical approach.

Orpheus steps back from the platform, allowing the holographic display to continue its rotation. Battalion ships complete final preparations, their drives igniting in sequence as launch protocols initiate. He watches this with the patient satisfaction of someone who has orchestrated countless such deceptions across centuries of careful manipulation.

"Begin the countdown to Fractal formation," he commands.

Numeric indicators appear beside the Battalion fleet, tracking time until their departure. As these numbers decrease, Orpheus turns away from the display, moving toward the chamber's exit with unhurried confidence. The light recedes with his departure, darkness flowing back into spaces no longer requiring illumination.

The last image visible before complete darkness returns is Marinami's blue sphere, rotating in perfect ignorance of the fate now directed toward it, casting eerie shadows across the empty chamber where decisions affecting millions have been made by a single entity pursuing goals beyond conventional understanding.

Caelus stands at the center of the bridge, hands extended before him with fingers spread wide. The metal enhancement bands circling each digit pulse with blue energy as he channels his Aetheris ability. To the crew, he appears to be manipulating empty air, but through his perception, a complex web of glowing threads stretches across the void, cosmic connections that reveal the movements of Battalion forces through the fabric of space-time itself.

The ship hums around him, environmental systems adjusting automatically to compensate for the heat generated by his exertion. Holographic displays surround his position, translating his Aetheris readings into data the crew can interpret. Star charts, vessel trajectories, and probability matrices cascade across screens in flowing patterns that mirror the cosmic threads only he can see.

"Fifth Battalion moving through expected vectors," he reports, voices tight with concentration. "Formation consistent with approach to Mordia. Trajectory aligns with previous intelligence."

The sigils tattooed across his skin warm beneath his uniform, responding to the energy flowing through his nervous system. Small capillaries have begun to burst in his left eye, creating a starburst pattern of red against white. A thin trickle of blood forms at his nostril, the physical price of pushing Aetheri's perception beyond normal limitations.

The navigation officer glances up from her station, concern evident in her expression but discipline preventing comment. She's witnessed this toll before, the gradual deterioration that accompanies extended Aetheris use. Instead of speaking, she adjusts the environmental temperature downward two degrees, a small mercy for his overheating system.

Caelus narrows his focus, tracking the primary command vessel of the Fifth Battalion. The cosmic thread connecting it to Mordia should be the strongest, its energy signature reflecting the intent patterns of those directing the vessel. But something shifts, subtle at first, then with increasing dissonance. The thread flickers, weakens, and then abruptly redirects.

"Wait," he says, brow furrowing. "Something's wrong."

His fingers move with greater urgency now, enhancement bands glowing brighter as he channels more energy. The threads, visible only to him as glowing strands of cosmic connection, begin to shift, their patterns reorganizing toward an entirely different vector. Where they had stretched toward Mordia's jungle world, they now reorient toward the oceanic sphere of Marinami.

"This doesn't make sense," he mutters, pushing his perception further.

The effort costs him immediately. Blood vessels rupture in his right eye now, matching the left. The trickle from his nose becomes a steady flow that he absently wipes away, leaving a crimson streak across his cheek. His breathing becomes labored, each inhalation carrying audible strain.

"Sir?" The systems officer approaches cautiously. "Your biometrics are reaching critical thresholds."

Caelus ignores the warning, focusing instead on the sensor logs displayed to his right. His fingers leave the cosmic threads momentarily, moving to manipulate physical data screens. The enhancement bands leave traces of blue light hanging in the air as he sorts through information too complex for standard analysis algorithms.

"Run a trajectory comparison," he commands, voices rough with effort. "Fifth Battalion's scheduled course versus actual position. Full spectrum analysis."

The system responds immediately, and holographic displays shift to show overlapping flight paths. The scheduled route, approved by Valthorim command protocols, extends toward Mordia in a perfect arc that optimizes fuel consumption and tactical positioning. The actual trajectory, compiled from passive sensor readings and Aetheris tracking, begins identically but gradually diverges toward Marinami's sector.

"Divergence confirmed," the systems officer reports, surprise evident in her tone. "Five degrees initially, widening to twenty-three degrees at the current position. The projected endpoint now aligns with Marinami rather than Mordia."

Caelus grips the navigation console, knuckles whitening around the enhancement bands. His body trembles slightly, the consequence of maintaining Aetheris perception far beyond safe duration. The sigils beneath his uniform now burn hot enough to be visible through the fabric, creating patterns of amber light that pulse with his elevated heartbeat.

Selenea approaches from the tactical station, her movements carrying the measured precision of someone evaluating a rapidly evolving threat. She stops beside him, close enough to provide support without interfering with his concentration. Her presence creates a momentary stillness within the urgency, the eye of a storm gathering force around them.

"You're pushing too hard," she says quietly, observation rather than criticism.

"I need to be certain." Caelus wipes more blood from his nose, leaving another streak across his hand. "The Battalion thinks they're heading to Mordia. Their intent patterns still align with jungle warfare. But their actual course, "

"Marinami," Selenea concludes, already reviewing the tactical implications. Her fingers move across her own console, calculating defense scenarios against this unexpected development. "A water planet against a battalion equipped for jungle engagement."

"Exactly." Caelus's eyes remain fixed on the diverging trajectories. "They're configured for the wrong environment. This wasn't a tactical decision, and it's manipulation."

The realization crystallizes within him, bringing both clarity and renewed urgency. His fingers trace the air as he follows the cosmic threads back to their origin point, seeking the moment of divergence. The enhancement bands flare bright enough to cast shadows as he pushes his ability to its limit.

"Orpheus," he says, the name carrying both understanding and accusation. "He's intercepted communications and falsified coordinates. The Fifth Battalion commanders still believe they're heading to Mordia."

Selenea's expression hardens as tactical considerations flow through her mind. "When will they realize the discrepancy?"

"Only upon final approach," Caelus responds, finally releasing his Aetheris perception. The glowing threads fade from his awareness, leaving ordinary reality that seems flat and limited by comparison. He staggers slightly, exhaustion washing through him as the enhancement bands cool to dull metal. "By then, they'll be committed to engagement."

"And Marinami is unprepared." Selenea moves immediately to the communications station. "They're expecting no attack."

Caelus steadies himself against the console, wiping blood from his face with practiced efficiency that suggests this is far from the first time. The sigils beneath his uniform gradually cool, their glow fading as his system begins recovery processes.

"We need to redirect immediately," he announces to the bridge crew. "Plot the fastest course to Marinami through the nearest Fractal."

The navigation officer responds without hesitation, fingers dancing across control surfaces to calculate optimal approach vectors. "Nearest viable Fractal is in the Altari sector. Transit time to Fractal: fourteen hours. Estimated arrival at Marinami: twenty-six hours if the Fractal remains stable."

"The Battalion will reach them in thirty," Caelus notes, calculating timeline advantages with mathematical precision despite his physical exhaustion. "Narrow margin, but workable."

The bridge erupts into coordinated activity. The propulsion officer initiates drive recalibration for maximum sustainable output. Tactical systems run contingency simulations for various arrival scenarios. Communications establish encrypted channels to alert Marinami's defense network without triggering Battalion intercept protocols.

Selenea returns to her tactical station, already planning defense strategies suitable for Marinami's oceanic environment. "We should contact Lyra Mareen directly," she suggests. "Marinami's defense systems rely on synchronized water manipulation. They'll need time to configure current patterns."

Caelus nods in agreement, moving toward the command chair with careful steps that betray his lingering exhaustion. "Establish a secure connection as soon as we're within range. Priority alert protocols."

The ship's engines shift tone as power redirects to propulsion systems. The subtle change in ambient vibration signals acceleration beyond standard parameters. Through the main viewport, stars begin to elongate slightly as the vessel increases velocity toward the Altari Fractal.

Caelus settles into the command chair, his posture betraying none of the exhaustion evident in his bloodshot eyes and pallid complexion. The enhancement bands around his fingers have cooled completely, temporarily drained of energy, yet his mind calculates possibilities with undiminished clarity.

"Orpheus is getting desperate," he observes, more to himself than the crew. "Changing tactics, manipulating perception rather than confronting directly."

Selenea meets his gaze across the bridge, understanding the passing between siblings without the need for elaboration. They've entered a new phase of this conflict, one where deception becomes as dangerous as direct assault, where anticipating Orpheus's strategies becomes as crucial as countering his forces.

The navigation officer confirms their course with quiet efficiency, and the ship accelerates toward a desperate race against deliberately falsified time.

Chapter 15

Perils of the Living Planet

The ship breaks through Mordia's upper atmosphere, parting a golden haze of spores that clings to the hull like hungry microorganisms. Through the viewport, the landscape unfolds in impossible configurations, massive fungal structures that shouldn't support their own weight reaching hundreds of meters skyward, creating a canopy that pulses with internal light. Caelus studies the readings on his console, frowning as the instruments flicker, struggling against the planet's natural interference patterns.

"Descent thrusters compensating for atmospheric density," the pilot announces, fingers dancing across controls that spark with intermittent static. "Landing coordinates locked, though the surface topology keeps... shifting."

Ven Diona stands behind them, and her eyes narrowed in concentration as she absorbs every detail of the terrain below. Her fingers trace patterns in the air, cataloging environmental variables with practiced precision. "Adjust three degrees starboard," she instructs. "That clearing isn't stable. See how the edges pulse faster than the center?"

The pilot complies without question. No one argues with Ven when it comes to environmental navigation, not after she saved them from the acidic fog pits on Vescit Three. The ship banks slightly, approaching a different landing zone where the bioluminescent activity maintains consistent rhythmic patterns.

"The Battalion will find this place challenging," Selenea observes from the tactical station. "Their jungle warfare configurations won't translate well to fungal terrain."

Caelus nods, though his attention remains fixed on the final approach. "That's precisely why Orpheus redirected them to Marinami. But we need to understand what they were originally targeting here. Mordia holds something he wants."

The ship settles onto the landing zone with a gentle shudder, suspension systems compensating for ground that doesn't behave like solid matter should. Through the hull, they feel a subtle rhythm, rise and fall, rise and fall, as if they've landed on the chest of a sleeping giant.

"Atmosphere analysis complete," the environmental officer reports. "Oxygen levels sustainable but high spore count. Filtration masks are recommended. Temperature twenty-six degrees, humidity ninety-three percent."

Caelus secures the enhancement bands around his fingers, checking each connection with methodical care. The metal feels unusually cool against his skin, almost resistant to his touch. "Full environmental suits," he orders. "Nothing exposed. We don't know what these spores might do to human tissue."

The crew, six in total, including Caelus, Selenea, and Ven, prepares with practiced efficiency. They secure weapons in easily accessible positions, check communication devices, and don transparent helmets that seal with a soft hiss. Each movement flows from years of experience on hostile worlds, though none quite like Mordia.

"I'll take the point," Ven says, securing specialized sensors to her wrists. The devices, her own design, measure subtle environmental fluctuations that most equipment can't detect. "Standard formation. Step exactly where I step. The ground here... it remembers."

The loading ramp extends, opening to a world that assaults their senses despite the protection of their suits. The air carries visible particles that swirl in currents that are too organized to be random. Light pulses through vegetation in sequences that almost suggest language, amber to blue to violet and back again in patterns just complex enough to seem intentional.

Ven Diona pauses at the bottom of the ramp, kneeling to examine the surface. She presses one hand against the ground, feeling its subtle rise and fall. "The breathing is normal," she announces. "Consistent rhythm indicates we haven't triggered defensive mechanisms yet."

She stands, eyes scanning the perimeter where fungal structures create a natural enclosure around the landing zone. "The path is there," she points toward a narrow opening where the bioluminescence flows in a distinctive current. "Follow single file. Minimum two-meter spacing."

They move with cautious precision, Ven setting a deliberately slow pace. Each step requires assessment, watching how the ground responds, noting changes in light patterns, and sensing shifts in air current. The path leads them between towering fungal trunks that creak with internal pressure, releasing spores in controlled bursts that drift through their artificial corridor.

Caelus walks third in line, behind Selenea. The sigils on his skin prickle beneath his suit, a sensation he's come to recognize as a warning. He extends his awareness, enhancement bands glowing as he attempts to utilize his Aetheris perception. Instead of the familiar expansion of consciousness, he encounters resistance, like trying to see through turbulent water.

"Something's blocking me," he mutters, frustration evident in his voice. The enhancement bands flicker, their blue light struggling against interference patterns that seem to originate from the planet itself. "The cosmic threads are... distorted here."

Selenea glances back. "The planet has its own electromagnetic field. Probably interacts with the fungal network."

"It's more than that," Caelus insists, wincing as feedback pulses through the enhancement bands. "It feels deliberate. Like something is actively counteracting the perception."

Ven halts abruptly, raising one hand. The crew freezes in practiced response. She kneels again, studying the ground with enhanced visors that reveal spectrum layers invisible to normal sight. "The path is changing," she announces. "Structural modifications occurring at the molecular level."

As if responding to her observation, the fungal walls around them shift slightly. New growth emerges to their right, a corridor that hadn't existed moments before, its floor smoother, its bioluminescence brighter and more inviting than their current path.

"Ignore that," Ven commands, pointing to the deceptive trail. "It's a trap. See how the light pulses faster? Luring patterns. The planet uses them to direct prey toward digestive zones."

The security officer, a veteran of seventeen hostile world expeditions, steps closer to examining the false path. "Impressive adaptation. Almost beautiful in its execution."

"Step back," Ven snaps. "Observation distance only. The transition boundaries trigger on proximity."

The officer complies immediately, though Caelus notes the reluctance in his movement. The planet's lure affects them despite their awareness of its nature. The light patterns contain something hypnotically attractive, a visual harmony that bypasses rational thought.

They continue forward, the original path narrowing as fungal walls press closer. The air grows heavier with spores that swirl around their helmets, testing seams and connections with seemingly purposeful movement. Condensation forms on their visors, not from humidity but from contact with microscopic filaments that emerge and retreat from the fungal surfaces around them.

"The planet is watching us," Ven observes, studying a pattern of light that follows their movement through the fungal wall. "These networks transmit information. Every step we take is being communicated through the entire organism."

"Organism? Singular?" Selenea asks, hand resting on her weapon.

Ven nods without turning. "Current research suggests all visible growth connects to a single massive mycelium network. One entity with distributed consciousness."

The ground beneath them trembles slightly, different from the steady breathing rhythm. Caelus feels it through his boots, a reaction, perhaps even a response to Ven's assessment. The fungal corridor ahead splits into three identical paths, each displaying the same light patterns and the same structural composition.

Ven studies them for a long moment, her body perfectly still except for her eyes, which track subtle differences invisible to the others. She points to the leftmost path. "This one. The spore discharge pattern is consistent with stable growth."

She turns to face the crew, her expression serious even through the helmet visor. "From here, the navigation grows more complex. The planet will create multiple false paths. It learns our decision patterns and adapts accordingly." Her eyes move from face to face, emphasizing her next words. "Follow exactly where I step. No deviations. No matter what you see or think, you understand."

They nod in acknowledgment, professionals who recognize expertise when they encounter it. Ven turns back to the path, shoulders set with the burden of responsibility. She steps forward, and the fungal walls seem to lean inward as if the planet itself holds its breath in anticipation.

The fungal forest thickens as they progress, ceiling structures drooping lower while floor organisms grow taller, creating a narrowing tunnel effect that forces them into a tighter formation. Light patterns shift from the steady pulses of the landing zone to erratic flashes that seem deliberately designed to disorient. The air grows thicker, each breath drawing moisture that condenses inside their helmets, requiring periodic clearing of visors that fog with unnatural speed.

Ven moves with increasing focus, her steps precise and deliberate as she tests each section of ground before committing her weight. The others follow her example, matching her movements with military discipline. Their progress slows to an almost ritualistic pace: step, test, wait, advance.

"The growth patterns are accelerating," Ven observes, voice calm despite the implication. "Normal adaptation cycles take hours. These changes are occurring in minutes."

A sudden movement flashes at ankle height. Crystalline thorns snap from carnivorous vines embedded in the fungal wall, their transparent surfaces catching light in prismatic bursts. The security officer reacts instantly, freezing mid-step as the thorn misses his suit by millimeters.

"Don't react," Ven warns, not turning back. "They track motion. Slow, steady movements only."

The thorns retract into the wall, leaving small holes that ooze clear liquid. Seconds later, new growth covers these wounds, the fungal structure repairing itself with visible efficiency. The vines remain partially visible beneath the surface, moving like muscles tensing beneath the skin.

"Fascinating defense mechanism," Caelus observes, studying the wall with a scientific detachment that masks his growing unease. The enhancement bands around his fingers continue to pulse erratically, and his Aetheris ability is still compromised by the planet's interference. "The thorns appear silicon-based rather than carbon. Probably condenses from mineral solutions transported through the mycelium network."

"Save the analysis for when we're not surrounded by them," Selenea suggests, eyes continuously scanning for movement ahead and above.

They continue forward, the path narrowing further until they must proceed single file with shoulders brushing against fungal walls that react to their touch with subtle recoiling movements. The bioluminescence intensifies around points of contact, creating trailing patterns of light that follow their progress.

The environmental officer, fourth in line, steps slightly off Ven's established path. His boot connects with a patch of seemingly identical ground just centimeters from where Ven had placed her foot. The reaction is immediate and alarming, and a cascade of bioluminescent warnings erupts across the vegetation in all directions, with light patterns flowing away from the contact point like neural signals transmitting information.

"Stay focused," Ven hisses, reaching back to pull him onto the correct path. "The planet is watching us." She emphasizes each word, her usual methodical tone sharpening with urgency. "Every deviation is recorded and analyzed. It learns our patterns and adapts to our behaviors."

The officer nods, the motion barely perceptible in the confined space. "Sorry. The path looked identical."

"That's intentional," Ven responds, already turning back to continue navigation. "Visual mimicry is this planet's specialty. Trust your foot placement, not your eyes."

The passage widens suddenly into a small clearing where multiple paths converge. Here, the ground displays complex patterns of fungal growth, creating a deceptive mosaic of safe zones and danger areas indistinguishable from untrained observation. Ven pauses, her body language betraying uncharacteristic hesitation as she studies the options.

"We need to cross this section to reach the central spore forest," she explains, gesturing toward a particularly dense collection of fungal towers visible beyond the clearing. "That's where the unusual mineral concentrations appear in our scans."

Caelus steps forward, careful to remain within the safe zone Ven has identified. "The Battalion was targeting those mineral formations. Whatever Orpheus wants from Mordia, it's there."

Ven points to several innocent-looking pools scattered across their path. The liquid appears clear and still, reflecting the bioluminescence from surrounding structures with mirror-like perfection. "Digestive enzymes," she explains without breaking her assessing stance. "One drop dissolves flesh. The pools form at path intersections to catch creatures that hesitate or choose incorrectly."

She studies the pattern for several more seconds before pointing to a seemingly arbitrary route through the clearing. "Follow exactly three steps behind me. The ground tests weight distribution and timing. Too close or too far disrupts the safe sequence."

They proceed with agonizing slowness, each step precisely measured and timed. The pools remain still as they pass, though Caelus notices subtle ripples forming on the surfaces furthest from their path as if something beneath is responding to their presence, preparing for potential opportunity.

Halfway across the clearing, the fungal canopy above them shifts with sudden, coordinated movement. Massive structures rotate and interlock, blocking their view of the sky and, more significantly, their ship. The change brings immediate, oppressive darkness relieved only by the bioluminescence that now provides their sole illumination.

"They're cutting us off," the security officer observes, hand moving to his weapon.

"Don't," Selenea warns. "Weapon discharge might trigger further defensive responses."

Ven continues forward, though her steps now display minute hesitations invisible to anyone who hasn't worked closely with her. She stops again at the edge of another junction, studying the path options with increasingly intense concentration.

"The patterns are changing faster than I can read them," she admits, the confession clearly costing her professional pride. Her fingers move through the air, tracing flow patterns in the bioluminescence that only her trained eye can detect. "This isn't consistent with documented behavior."

"The planet feels threatened," Caelus suggests, watching how the fungal walls around them pulse with increased intensity. "Our presence might register as an invasion."

Ven shakes her head, kneeling to examine growth patterns at the junction. "This isn't natural. Even stress responses follow established parameters. This is..." she pauses, searching for the appropriate term, "accelerated. Directed. Something's actively manipulating the normal defense systems."

The communications officer checks his equipment with growing concern. "Signal to the ship is completely blocked. The fungal growth must contain signal-dampening compounds."

"Or it's deliberately jamming us," Selenea suggests, her tactical mind already calculating escape routes and defensive positions.

Ven rises, having made her determination. "This path," she indicates a narrow opening to their right where the bioluminescence flows in subtle currents. "The substrate compression patterns suggest recent use by something heavy. Possibly natural wildlife."

They follow her lead, the passage narrowing further until they must turn sideways to progress. The fungal walls press closer, their texture changing from the relatively dry, fibrous surface encountered earlier to a moister, almost mucous-covered membrane that reacts to touch with visible contractions.

"The biological activity is increasing," Ven notes, her scientific detachment returning despite the increasingly threatening environment. "We're approaching a high-energy node in the network."

The ground suddenly trembles beneath them, not with the gentle rhythm of breathing but with violent, seismic intensity. The movement throws them off balance, forcing contact with walls that immediately respond with brightening bioluminescence.

"This isn't right," Ven's voice carries genuine alarm now. "The vibration pattern isn't consistent with natural movement cycles."

A sound travels through the fungal network, not airborne but conducted through the structures themselves. The sensation resembles distant machinery powering up, a deep thrumming that they feel through their boots more than hear.

Caelus turns to check their retreat path and finds it gone. Fungal growth has sealed the passage behind them, and a thick wall of intertwined structures continues to thicken as he watches. "We're being herded," he announces, drawing his cutting tool while knowing it will prove inadequate against the rapidly growing barrier.

Ven's expression hardens into grim determination. "Something's accelerating the changes," she admits, eyes scanning the passage ahead where the bioluminescence has intensified to almost painful brightness. "This isn't natural. The planet doesn't behave this way without direction."

The trembling intensifies, the passage walls bulging inward and then pulling back in peristaltic waves that propel them forward despite their resistance. The floor tilts subtly, creating a downward slope that grows steeper with each step.

"It's a trap," Selenea states, drawing her weapon despite the potential consequences. "And we're already inside it."

The fungal structures ahead part to reveal a large chamber filled with intensely bright bioluminescence. The light pulses in complex patterns that suggest communication rather than random energy discharge. The slope increases, and their controlled movement becomes a desperate struggle to maintain balance as the living corridor delivers them toward whatever waits within the glowing chamber.

The crystalline vines erupt without warning, bursting from the walls and floor with explosive force. They move with metallic precision rather than plant-like growth, targeting joints and limbs with tactical intelligence no natural organism should possess. The security officer fires a single shot that shatters one vine before three more wraps around his arm, immobilizing his weapon. Bioluminescence surges through the tendrils, flowing toward their source like information traveling through circuits.

"Defensive positions!" Selenea shouts, slashing at vines that curl around her legs. Her blade connects with crystalline fibers that part momentarily before sealing themselves, and the damage is repaired almost instantly.

The ground beneath them tilts sharply, becoming a living slide that propels them forward despite their resistance. Fungal structures along the walls extend to form channels that guide their descent, preventing escape while allowing the vines to maintain their grip. They tumble toward a central clearing where the fungal growth forms a massive structure, unlike anything they've encountered, a bulbous, pulsing formation that resembles a flower bud scaled to impossible proportions.

Caelus manages to free one arm, enhancement bands glowing as he attempts to channel Aetheris energy into the vines restraining him. The metal grows hot against his fingers but produces no effect on the crystalline restraints. "The interference is complete," he grunts, switching to physical resistance. "Can't establish any cosmic connection."

"Cut yourselves free!" Ven shouts, her normally composed voice tight and urgent. "The thorns aren't poisonous! They're communication conduits, not weapons!"

She demonstrates, slicing through the vines around her wrist with a vibration blade calibrated to match the crystalline frequency. The severed tendrils twitch and retreat, leaking clear fluid that hisses against the fungal floor.

Caelus follows her example, activating his own blade to sever the restraints. The momentary freedom allows him to reach the enhancement band controls, adjusting their frequency to create a localized disruption field. The vines nearest him recoil from the interference pattern, creating a bubble of temporary safety.

"They're learning," he warns as new vines approach, these with thicker crystalline structures resistant to the frequency he's emitting. "Each attack teaches them about our defenses."

For each vine they sever, two more take its place, emerging from the walls with increased speed and tensile strength. The crystalline structures evolve visibly, adapting to counter their resistance with each generation. Newer tendrils feature barbed tips that catch in clothing and equipment, while others secrete adhesive compounds that bind to exposed surfaces.

The central bloom structure shudders, and the massive petals that form its exterior are slowly parting. Light spills from within, not the ambient bioluminescence that illuminates the passages but a concentrated, almost solar intensity that forces them to activate helmet filters. A heavy, sweet scent penetrates even their sealed suits, carrying complex compounds that make their thoughts momentarily sluggish.

"Pheromone defenses," Ven identifies, adjusting her mask's filtration settings. "Cognitive disruptors. Maximum filter density."

The massive bloom completes its opening sequence, petals extending outward to reveal Vorax Vunes in all its alien magnificence. The entity towers three meters tall at the center of the chamber, its primary form resembling a colossal flytrap with deep purple-black leaves edged in complex bioluminescent patterns. Multiple smaller auxiliary traps surround its base, each moving independently to track different crew members.

Most striking is the entity's central mass, a pulsing, iridescent core visible through partially transparent tissues that shift between solid and liquid states. The colors flow in patterns too complex to track, creating an almost hypnotic effect that draws and holds attention. The mouth-like trap at its crown features intricate sensory tendrils that wave gently in air currents that shouldn't exist this deep within the fungal forest.

"Trespassers," Vorax Vunes speaks its voice, not a sound but a vibration that resonates through the fungal network surrounding them. The sensation travels through their bodies, bones conducting the message directly to inner ears, bypassing normal auditory pathways. "You violate the sanctity of Mordia."

The crew hangs suspended in crystalline restraints, their struggles diminishing as they confront this manifestation of the planet's consciousness. Vorax's auxiliary traps snap at the air around them, not striking but clearly demonstrating capability.

The entity's primary trap extends toward Caelus, tendrils wrapping around his suspended form. They lift him from the ground with surprising gentleness, bringing him face-to-face with the pulsing core. At this proximity, Caelus sees patterns within the iridescent mass that suggest neural activity and thought processes visualized through biochemical reactions.

"Your purpose here?" Vorax demands, tendrils tightening just enough to emphasize the question. The bioluminescent patterns at its edges intensify, creating a corona effect that frames its massive form.

Caelus struggles against the grip, not in panic but seeking to establish a less vulnerable position. "We came to protect Mordia," he explains, his voice steady despite his predicament. "Orpheus sends battalions to subjugate worlds. We tracked their planned assault on your planet."

The enhancement bands around his fingers pulse weakly, still attempting to establish Aetheris's connection despite the interference. "We fight against those who would destroy your world, not with them."

Vorax's auxiliary traps snap closed and open in sequence, creating a rhythmic sound like stone striking stone. The entity's root system, visible through the transparent floor beneath them, glows with subtle patterns, communication with the broader mycelium network that spans the planet.

"Lies," Vorax declares, its vibration carrying harmonic undertones that suggest multiple voices speaking simultaneously. "The living planet has witnessed your kind before. Destroyers. Consumers."

The tendrils around Caelus constrict further, not enough to cause injury but to establish dominance. The massive primary trap inclines toward him, sensory appendages brushing against his helmet with delicate precision.

"Your weapons. Your technology. Your disruptive energies." Each phrase resonates with increasing intensity. "All identical to those who came before. Those who harvested our essence for their wars."

Selenea strains against her restraints, managing to establish eye contact with the entity. "We're not with the Battalion. We fight against them. Check our ship; there are no battalion markings or Valthorim symbols."

Vorax's attention shifts momentarily, auxiliary traps turning toward her with cold assessment. "All off-worlders claim distinction without difference. All seek Mordia's secrets. Our biological compounds. Our communication network. Our spore synthesis."

The tendrils holding Caelus withdraw slightly, allowing him to see his crew suspended in similar grasps. Each hangs immobilized, weapons useless, at the mercy of an entity that evolved specifically to capture and process organic matter.

"You arrived ahead of the others," Vorax continues, its central mass pulsing with colors that shift toward deeper purples. "A tactical advantage. The first hunters claim the territory."

"We came to warn you," Caelus insists. "The Battalion planned an attack on Mordia. We have evidence."

"Evidence," Vorax repeats, the vibration now carrying something resembling bitter amusement. "Data. Transmissions. Records. More abstractions used to justify extraction."

The crystalline vines tighten around all crew members simultaneously, drawing them closer to Vorax's central mass. The floor beneath them transforms, converting from solid fungal matter to a semi-liquid state that begins to rise around their legs.

"Mordia protects itself," Vorax declares. "Through absorption. Through understanding. Through incorporation."

The meaning becomes horrifyingly clear as the liquid floor rises further, the consistency suggesting digestive properties. Ven struggles against both the crystalline restraints and the rising fluid, her analytical mind still processing options.

"The Battalion use thermal lances," she shouts to Vorax. "Heat-based weapons that would burn through your network. We carry no such devices. Scan our equipment!"

Vorax pauses, the rising fluid halting at knee level. An auxiliary trap extends toward their equipment packs, sensory tendrils exploring with methodical thoroughness. The iridescent colors in its core shift again, patches of blue appearing within the purple dominant tones.

"Different tools," it acknowledges. "But purpose remains unproven."

"The Battalion redirected to Marinami," Caelus explains, seizing the moment of hesitation. "But they will come here eventually. Orpheus wants something from Mordia, something in your central spore forest. We need to understand what before they return in force."

Vorax's primary trap fully opens, revealing rows of crystalline structures that resemble teeth only in function, not form. The display creates an unmistakable threat gesture as the entity processes this information.

"Knowledge is absorption," Vorax states, the fluid around their legs beginning to move again, creating gentle currents that draw them deeper into its central mass. "To understand your truth or falsehood, Mordia must incorporate your consciousness."

The crew hangs suspended in Vorax's grasp, crystalline vines ensuring no escape as the digestive fluid rises with inexorable patience. The entity's bioluminescent patterns intensify, creating a pulsing rhythm that seems to count down the moments until incorporation begins.

"The process is not painful," Vorax assures them, auxiliary traps positioning themselves beneath each crew member. "Your knowledge becomes Mordia's knowledge. Your purpose becomes transparent. Truth separates from deception through the complete dissolution of barriers."

The enhancement bands around Caelus's fingers flicker one final time, a desperate attempt to establish a cosmic connection. For an instant, so brief he might have imagined it, a thread forms, connecting him not to distant stars but to the entity before him. In that fractional moment, information flows not through conventional senses but through the same network Vorax uses to communicate with the planet.

The image forms in both their minds simultaneously: Battalion ships descending through golden spore clouds, thermal lances cutting through fungal forests, and collection vehicles harvesting crystalline structures for transport to waiting vessels. The vision carries not words but pure meaning; Orpheus seeks Mordia's communication compounds, the unique crystalline structures that allow thought to travel through biological networks with perfect fidelity.

The connection breaks as quickly as it formed, leaving Caelus gasping and Vorax's central mass pulsing with rapid color shifts. The crew remains suspended, caught between understanding and oblivion as Vorax processes this unexpected communion.

Chapter 16

Rescue and Revelation

The bridge bathes Selenea in blue-white light from a dozen holographic displays, each showing a different aspect of Mordia's writhing surface. Her eyes dart between readouts, fingers dancing across control surfaces with precise, efficient movements. Six hours since the crew's last check-in, five hours and forty-two minutes longer than the communication blackout protocol allows. She feels a tightness in her chest, an uncomfortable pressure that she recognizes as fear, but her hands remain steady as she calibrates the sensors for another planetary scan.

"Reconfigure bio-trace parameters," she tells the ship's systems. "Focus on human metabolic signatures within fungal density zones."

The holographic displays shift, data reorganizing itself into more specialized search patterns. The view of Mordia's surface transforms from general topography to a complex web of life-force indicators. Massive fungal structures pulse with internal energy, creating patterns that confuse standard scanning protocols. What appears solid one moment flows like liquid the next, a planet-wide organism constantly reshaping itself according to stimulus patterns invisible to human perception.

"Filter out standard mycelium network activity," Selenea continues, adjusting sensitivity thresholds with methodical precision. "Isolate anomalous metabolic clusters."

She should have gone with them. The thought cuts through her tactical focus, sharp and unwelcome. However, the mission parameters were clear, and someone needed to maintain orbital security while the ground team investigated the mineral formations. Battalion forces could arrive at any moment, despite Caelus's Aetheris tracking suggesting they'd diverted to Marinami. Orpheus plays deeper games than they anticipate. She knows this from bitter experience.

The scan completes its fifth iteration, producing the same frustrating results: nothing. Mordia's biological interference blocks conventional life-sign detection, the planet's electromagnetic field creating false positives that multiply with each scanning pass. She needs a different approach.

"Access non-standard detection protocols," she orders, entering her command authorization. "Execute program sequence: Diona-7."

The ship acknowledges with a soft tone. Ven Diona programmed this specialized detection algorithm herself, designed specifically for planetary environments that defy standard sensing technology. It doesn't search for human life signs directly but for the discontinuities they create within natural biological systems, gaps in the pattern, and disruptions in the flow.

New data cascades across the displays. Mordia's surface reimagines itself through Ven's unique analytical framework. The fungal structures now appear as data currents, flowing in complex but predictable patterns, except for one location, where the currents bend around an anomalous obstruction like water flowing around a submerged stone.

"There," Selenea whispers, fingers already inputting coordinate locks.

The ship's sensors focus on the anomaly, a massive bioluminescent structure, unlike the surrounding fungal towers. Where other formations pulse with steady rhythms, this entity exhibits complex, organized patterns that suggest higher neural activity. The structure resembles an enormous carnivorous plant, its central mass surrounded by trap-like appendages.

"Magnify central zone, spectral analysis."

The display zooms in, penetrating the outer layers of the plant structure through specialized scanning frequencies. Within the iridescent mass, six small heat signatures register human metabolic patterns, their clarity disrupted by the entity's biological interference.

Selenea's hands freeze momentarily, her throat tightening. Then training reasserts itself, emotions locked away behind tactical necessity. She inputs commands with renewed intensity, initiating targeted scans of the entity's biological composition.

"Analyze neural network density and distribution."

The results confirm her fears. The plant entity possesses a central nervous system with complexity approaching sentient parameters. More concerning, this network extends beyond its physical structure, connecting to the surrounding fungal forest through filaments that branch outward for kilometers. It doesn't just exist within the forest; it controls it, using the broader mycelium network as an extended sensory and defensive system.

"Calculate minimum safe approach trajectory," she instructs the navigation system, already moving to the weapons station. "Avoid primary neural pathways and major nutrient channels."

The ship responds, plotting a winding path through Mordia's canopy that minimizes contact with living structures capable of reporting their presence to the central entity. The trajectory appears on the main display, a narrow, twisting route that requires precision flying through gaps barely wider than the ship itself.

"Activate defensive systems," Selenea continues, checking power allocation levels. "Configuration D-7, non-lethal botanical protocols."

Weapon systems come online with soft hums that vibrate through the deck plates. Unlike standard combat configurations designed for Battalion engagements, these settings utilize specialized disruptors that temporarily paralyze plant neural systems without causing permanent damage. The weapons can't destroy the entity, not without potentially killing her brother and his crew trapped inside, but they can create brief windows of opportunity.

Selenea moves to the equipment locker, extracting a specialized extraction kit while the ship continues its preparations. The device, compact enough to fit in her palm when collapsed, expands into a complex apparatus designed specifically for hostile biological environments.

"Pressurize extraction cables with neutralizing compound C-22," she instructs, connecting the device to a chemical synthesizer. "Double standard concentration."

The compound, developed after three crew members were lost on Vescit Three, counteracts most known forms of digestive enzymes. If the plant entity follows standard carnivorous biology, the crew's environmental suits won't hold against its digestive processes for long. Every minute increases the risk of a catastrophic breach.

Back at the command station, Selenea straps herself into the pilot's chair. Her movements remain methodical despite the urgency burning in her chest. Rushing leads to errors; errors lead to additional casualties.

"Initiate atmospheric entry sequence," she commands. "Maintain stealth protocols until the final approach phase."

The ship acknowledges environmental shields engaging as they prepare to penetrate Mordia's spore-laden atmosphere. Descent thrusters adjust to compensate for the planet's unusual gravitational fluctuations caused by the massive biomass concentrated in its fungal forests.

Selenea reviews the final approach path one last time, committing each turn and obstacle to memory. If the ship's systems fail under Mordia's electromagnetic interference, she'll navigate manually. Her fingers tightened around the controls, and the subtle tremor in them was visible only to herself.

"Hold position," she whispers, though there's no way for Caelus to hear. "We're coming."

The ship tilts forward, beginning its controlled fall toward the writhing surface below. Atmospheric entry warnings flash across displays as they breach the outer layer of golden spores. The hull heats, environmental shields straining against particulate matter dense enough to qualify as solid rather than gas.

Through the viewport, Mordia opens before her an alien landscape of impossible structures that defy conventional biological understanding. The ship descends into this living maze, and its engines muted to minimize detection as it glides toward the heart of Vorax Vunes's territory.

Inside Vorax Vunes, reality bends according to plant consciousness. The massive chamber pulses with bioluminescent light that shifts between blue and violet wavelengths, creating shadows that move independently of their sources. The curved walls ripple with fluid movement, tissues that exist somewhere between solid and liquid states, designed by evolution to process organic matter with perfect efficiency. Within this living stomach, the crew hangs suspended in crystalline vines that have been shaped by centuries of predatory refinement, each tendril positioned to maximize enzyme exposure while preventing escape.

Caelus struggles against the crystalline restraints, their transparency belying impossible strength. The vines tighten in response to his movement, adapting their pressure to his precise musculature. Beside him, the security officer's environmental suit shows the first signs of degradation, the knee sections bubbling as digestive enzymes work through the specialized fabric designed to withstand conventional hazards. Nothing about Vorax qualifies as conventional.

"Don't move," Ven whispers, her voice barely carrying through their helmet communications. "Motion triggers increased enzyme production."

The digestive fluid rises with methodical patience, now reaching mid-thigh on most crew members. Its surface tension creates an almost perfect meniscus against their suits, maximizing contact area. Where it touches, it doesn't merely rest but actively works, microscopic filaments extending from the liquid to probe for weaknesses in their protective gear.

"The chemical composition is changing," the environmental officer reports, checking readings on his wrist display before the screen flickers and dies. "Becoming more specifically calibrated to our suit materials."

Ven Diona turns her attention to Vorax's central mass, where colors pulse through patterns she recognizes as information exchange. Her years studying xenobiology give her a framework for understanding, if not the specific content.

"Vorax," she addresses the entity directly, keeping her voice calm despite their predicament. "We seek only passage, not conquest. Your world holds knowledge we need to protect other planets from the Battalion."

The response comes not as sound but as vibration, a physical sensation that travels through the fluid and into their bodies, bypassing audio systems entirely. The sensation resolves into meaning that manifests directly in their minds.

"Your kind always claims peaceful intent before destruction follows," Vorax communicates, auxiliary traps snapping in agitation around the chamber's perimeter. "Mordia remembers. Each intrusion leaves scars in the network. Each extraction diminishes us."

"We're not like the others," Ven insists, deliberately slowing her respiratory rate to project calmness. "Scan our biological signatures. Compare them to those who harvested before. Different genetics. Different technology."

The digestive fluid rises another centimeter, now approaching the connection points where their suit sections join. These junctions, necessarily more complex than the surrounding material, provide easier entry points for the enzyme's probing filaments.

Caelus closes his eyes, focusing inward. The enhancement bands around his fingers pulse weakly as he attempts to establish an Aetheris connection. The metal grows warm against his skin, drawing on his body's energy reserves to compensate for external interference. For a brief moment, cosmic threads form in his perception, faint, distorted, but present. Then, they shatter as Vorax's neural network emits counter frequencies specifically designed to disrupt the connection.

"It's blocking me," he grunts, blood vessels rupturing in his left eye from the strain. "Actively targeting the Aetheris wavelengths."

The communications officer, suspended near the chamber's far wall, gestures toward his helmet, where small ruptures have allowed fluid to seep inside. "My systems are failing," he reports, voices tight with controlled panic. "Respirator functionality at thirty percent and dropping."

Vorax's auxiliary traps move closer, surrounding the suspended crew in a circle of watching, waiting mouths. The sensory tendrils extend further, delicately examining each crew member with scientific curiosity that does nothing to diminish their predatory purpose.

"Your respiration increases. Your cardiovascular systems accelerate." The vibration carries clinical detachment. "Fear responses identical to previous specimen classifications. Deception patterns consistent with prior extraction teams."

The security officer's suit breaches at the knee, digestive enzymes making direct contact with the skin beneath. His face contorts in pain, disciplined control briefly fracturing before reasserting itself. "Burns," he reports through clenched teeth. "Chemical, not thermal. Progressive tissue breakdown."

Ven Diona changes tactics, her analytical mind racing through communication options. "The Battalion that follows us they seeks your crystalline communication compounds. Specifically, the structures that allow thought transmission through biological networks."

This produces a visible reaction in Vorax's central mass, colors shifting rapidly through patterns that suggest alarm or perhaps recognition. The fluid level stabilizes temporarily, neither rising nor receding.

"How do you possess this knowledge?" The vibration carries new harmonic tones; suspicion layered with curiosity.

"My brother saw it," Ven explains, nodding toward Caelus. "Through Aetheris perception. Orpheus plans to harvest your network components for his own communication systems. To control minds across vast distances."

The environmental officer's suit develops multiple small breaches along the seams, the material dissolving faster as Vorax's enzymes adapt to its specific molecular structure. He struggles to maintain composure as the fluid enters, creating burning sensations wherever it touches exposed skin.

"Lies disguised with partial truths," Vorax responds after apparent consideration. "A more sophisticated deception pattern than previously documented."

Caelus makes another attempt, channeling what remains of his strength into the enhancement bands. Blood now streams from both nostrils as he forces energy through pathways partially blocked by Vorax's interference. "I can show you, I can prove, "

The attempt fails catastrophically. The bands overheat, burning his fingers beneath his quickly deteriorating gloves. The neural feedback knocks his consciousness sideways, leaving him hanging limply in the crystalline restraints, eyes unfocused.

The fluid rises with renewed purpose, now reaching the lower edges of their helmets. Where it touches, the transparent material clouds immediately, visibility degrading with alarming speed. The security officer's exposed skin develops painful welts that spread outward from the initial contact points, the digestive process accelerating as it adapts to human cellular structure.

"We don't seek to harvest," Ven tries again, desperation entering her voice despite her efforts to maintain scientific detachment. "We fight to prevent harvest. To protect worlds like yours from consumption by Orpheus and the Valthorim."

"All consumers claim to fight consumption," Vorax responds, the chamber walls contracting slightly, bringing them closer to the central mass. "All harvesters proclaim protection. Mordia has evolved beyond such simple deceptions."

The primary trap above them begins to close, massive leaves folding inward to create a smaller, more concentrated digestive chamber. The bioluminescence intensifies, focusing on wavelengths that penetrate their visors more effectively, allowing Vorax to observe their reactions with greater clarity.

"Your biological responses to imminent dissolution contain valuable data," Vorax explains, scientific curiosity evident in the vibration patterns. "The network will absorb your knowledge directly. No deception survives molecular integration."

The communications officer's helmet fills halfway with fluid, forcing him to tilt his head back to maintain airspace. "System breach imminent," he reports with remarkable composure given the circumstances. "Full suit failure estimated in three minutes."

Ven makes a final attempt, switching to a completely different communication approach. Instead of words, she forces her body to emit specific pheromone patterns through her suit's degrading fabric, chemical signals that mimic distress indicators common to plant species across multiple worlds.

"Please," she says, simultaneously releasing the chemical message that transcends linguistic barriers. "We are not your enemy."

Vorax's response pauses and sensory tendrils are suddenly alert to this new information channel. The auxiliary traps cease their rhythmic movements, focusing entirely on the unexpected chemical signals.

The digestive fluid reaches their helmet seals, beginning to work through the final barrier separating them from complete immersion. The chamber walls contract further, compressing the space around them as Vorax prepares for the final phase of absorption.

"Dissolution begins," Vorax announces, the vibration now containing harmonics that might, in another species, indicate anticipation. "Your knowledge becomes Mordia's knowledge. Your purpose becomes transparent."

The primary trap closes further, reducing the chamber to half its original size. In the concentrated space, the enzyme concentration intensifies, accelerating the degradation of their protective gear. The crew hangs suspended in this living stomach, equipment failing, hope fading, as Vorax Vunes prepares to convert their bodies and minds into information for Mordia's vast network.

The ship screams through Mordia's outer atmosphere, its hull plates glowing orange-red from friction. Selenea grips the controls with white-knuckled intensity, her body straining against harness restraints as the vessel shudders through layers of spore-dense air. Warning indicators flash across every display, structural integrity is at eighty-seven percent, environmental shields fail in sections three and four, and navigation sensors are disrupted by electromagnetic interference from the fungal canopy below. She ignores these, eyes locked on the trajectory path that leads to Vorax Vunes's position, mentally calculating contingencies for each potential point of failure.

"Engaging secondary shielding," she mutters to herself, redirecting power from non-critical systems. "Compensating for atmospheric density."

The ship breaks through the golden spore layer, plunging into Mordia's middle atmosphere, where massive fungal structures reach skyward like the fingers of buried giants. These towers, some nearly a kilometer tall, sway with deceptive languor, their movements slow enough to appear stationary until the moment they suddenly shift position to intercept passing objects.

Selenea banks hard to port, narrowly avoiding a fungal spire that rotates thirty degrees without warning. The maneuver sends them skimming along the structure's side, close enough that sensors register the microscopic filaments extending from its surface, seeking, testing, and learning from the brief contact.

"Adaptive defense system engaging," the ship's AI warns. "Fungal network redistributing resources to intercept flight path."

The warning proves immediate as previously separate towers begin bending toward one another, creating a lattice pattern designed to entrap the ship. Selenea dives beneath the forming barrier, threading through a gap barely wider than the vessel itself. The ship's outer hull scrapes against fungal matter and sensor readings show immediate chemical reactions where contact occurs.

"Hull integrity compromised in section six," the AI reports. "Corrosive compounds detected."

"Seal affected segments," Selenea orders, already calculating a new approach vector. "Reroute atmospheric controls."

She pushes the ship into a spiraling descent that follows the natural energy currents flowing through Mordia's fungal network. By matching these patterns, the vessel mimics natural movement, temporarily confusing the planet's defensive responses. Through the viewport, the landscape blurs into a whirling pattern of bioluminescent structures, each pulsing with internal light that communicates its presence to the broader network.

Carnivorous vines snap at the ship as they descend further, their crystalline thorns scraping against the hull with sounds that vibrate through the entire structure. The targeting system struggles to maintain the lock on Vorax's position as the surrounding biological mass constantly shifts, changing relative positions and interfering with conventional navigation parameters.

"Manual targeting mode," Selenea decides, switching to direct control. Her fingers dance across the weapons console, programming specific frequencies for the ion burst emitters. "Setting neural disruption pattern Delta-Seven."

The ship breaks through the final layer of the fungal canopy, emerging into a clearing dominated by Vorax Vunes's massive form. The plant entity has contracted into attack configuration; its primary trap is partially closed around what must be the crew's position, and digestive processes are visibly accelerating as bioluminescent patterns flow faster through its tissues.

"Target lock established," Selenea confirms, the crosshairs on her display centering on specific neural clusters within Vorax's central mass. "Firing."

The ship's ion emitters discharge with surgical precision, releasing concentrated energy bursts calibrated to the exact frequency that disrupts plant neural transmission without causing permanent damage. The beams connect with Vorax's primary ganglia, energy cascading through its neural network in visible patterns that cause immediate paralysis of specific functions.

Vorax's primary trap freezes mid-contraction, and the massive leaves suddenly become rigid as the paralyzing energy disrupts its motor control systems. The auxiliary traps snap reflexively before similarly freezing, caught in various stages of movement. The bioluminescent patterns throughout its structure flicker erratically as communication pathways temporarily fail.

"Deploying extraction equipment," Selenea announces to no one, activating the specialized system prepared earlier. The ship's underside opens, extending mechanical arms that terminate in the extraction cables. Each cable, no wider than her finger but capable of supporting enormous weight, contains microscopic delivery systems for the neutralizing compound that will counteract Vorax's digestive enzymes.

She positions the ship directly above Vorax's now-paralyzed primary trap, hovering just high enough to avoid the still-dangerous thorns that line its outer surface. The targeting system reconfigures, now focusing on the crew's life signs within the digestive chamber.

"Penetration sequence initiated."

The extraction cables fire downward with pneumatic force, easily puncturing Vorax's outer membrane. They drive through layers of increasingly dense tissue, their specialized tips navigating through the plant's internal structure toward the specific chamber holding the crew. The neutralizing compound is released continuously during penetration, creating protected pathways through the otherwise corrosive interior.

Inside Vorax, the crew perceives the attack as a sudden stillness followed by six metallic projectiles punching through the chamber ceiling. The penetrating cables spray clear liquid that creates expanding zones of neutralized digestive enzymes. Where the cables reach the fluid's surface, the corrosive substance hisses and turns inert, changing from acidic green to harmless transparent.

"Grab the cables!" Selenea's voice crackles through their partially functional communication systems. "Now!"

The crystalline vines holding the crew remain rigid from the neural disruption, but the paralysis effect won't last long. Already, subsidiary neural pathways are rerouting control signals, bypassing damaged sections. The cables whip through the digestive fluid, seeking human contact.

Caelus recovers consciousness just as a cable strikes his chest, its tip automatically adhering to his suit material. Without hesitation, he grabs it with both hands as the other cables find their targets among the remaining crew members.

"Cable lock confirmed," Selenea acknowledges, watching status indicators switch from red to green as each crew member secures the connection. "Extraction in three... two... one..."

The cables retract with violent suddenness, yanking the crew upward through Vorax's digestive system. The neutralizing compound creates temporary tunnels through the plant's interior, but these collapse almost immediately behind them, forcing them through narrowing passages of living tissue. Suit material tears against partially neutralized internal structures, the remaining digestive enzymes burning exposed skin as they're dragged upward.

The extraction proves brutally efficient; six human forms ripped through Vorax Vunes's body and into the waiting ship. They arrive in the cargo bay gasping and disoriented, covered in partially neutralized digestive fluids that continue to eat through what remains of their protective gear.

Vorax recovers from the neural disruption just as the last crew member clears its outer membrane. The plant entity's rage transmits through the entire fungal network in waves of bioluminescent fury. Its primary trap snaps closed on empty space, auxiliary mouths extending upward toward the hovering ship. The ground beneath it heaves as its root system drives deeper, connecting to the planet's broader mycelium network to draw additional resources.

"Massive energy spike detected," the ship's AI warns as Selenea banks hard, narrowly avoiding a tendril thick as her torso punches upward through the space they occupied seconds before.

"Full thrust, vertical ascent!" Selenea commands, dumping emergency power into the engines. The ship leaps upward, but not before three massive thorned tendrils connect with its underside, penetrating the hull in multiple locations.

Warning alarms shriek through the bridge as pressure sensors report breaches in the cargo bay and lower maintenance sections. Indicator lights flash from green to amber to red as systems fail under the biological assault. The tendrils convulse, attempting to drag the ship back down toward Vorax's waiting traps.

"Emergency severance protocol," Selenea orders, activating a rarely-used defense system. Superheated plasma discharges along the ship's underside, burning through the organic matter with molecular precision. The tendrils separate, their remaining segments thrashing in the cargo bay before secondary containment fields activate, isolating the breach zones.

The ship rockets upward, engines straining against both Mordia's gravity and the fungal towers that bend inward, trying to intercept their escape. Selenea weaves through the narrowing gaps, the hull scraping against biological matter with sounds like fingernails on metal. Structural integrity warnings intensify as the strain exceeds design parameters.

"Recalculating atmospheric exit vector," the AI announces, its normally even tone carrying urgency indicators. "Recommend immediate course correction."

Selenea ignores the suggestion, pushing the ship through a gap that closes behind them with whip-like speed. The final fungal barrier, a massive canopy of interconnected structures, looms ahead, already shifting to seal potential escape routes.

"Brace for impact," she warns the crew through internal communications, then rams the throttle forward.

The ship hits the biological barrier at maximum thrust, the reinforced prow crumpling slightly under impact forces. For one terrible moment, they hang suspended, caught in living matter that wraps around the hull with predatory intention. Then, the engines surge with emergency power, burning through the final resistance.

They break free into Mordia's upper atmosphere, trailing fragments of fungal matter that continue to writhe with independent purpose. The ship shudders as auto-repair systems activate, sealing the worst breaches while environmental controls struggle to compensate for the damage.

"Hull integrity at sixty-four percent," the AI reports as they climb toward the safety of orbit. "Atmospheric contamination detected in sections seven through twelve. Initiating containment and decontamination protocols."

Through the viewport, Mordia recedes beneath them, its golden spore layer now visibly disturbed by their passage, swirling patterns spreading outward from their exit point as the planet's defense system communicates the intrusion. The ship breaks free of the atmosphere entirely, the rattling vibrations finally subsiding as they reach the relative calm of orbit.

Selenea releases her white-knuckled grip on the controls, allowing herself three deep breaths before unbuckling to check on the rescued crew. Behind them, sensors detect increased activity in Mordia's fungal network, but they're beyond its reach now, safe, if not unscathed, from the living planet's fury.

The decontamination chamber hisses with automated medical systems, bathing the rescued crew in neutralizing mist that smells of antiseptic and artificial mint. Blue-white sterilization fields flicker across exposed skin, targeting microscopic traces of Vorax's digestive enzymes that continue to eat through organic matter. Caelus sits with his back against the chamber wall, environment suit cut away in sections to reveal angry red chemical burns where the enzymes penetrated. His enhancement bands lie beside him, metal surfaces partially corroded, the intricate circuitry exposed in places where the protective casing dissolved.

"Hold still," the medical unit instructs, applying regenerative compound to the security officer's more severe wounds. The skin around his knees has sloughed away entirely, exposing raw tissue beneath that pulses an alarming deep red. He doesn't flinch as the spray contacts the wound, though the slight whitening around his lips betrays the pain.

Ven Diona examines what remains of her specialized sensors, now reduced to corroded components barely recognizable as technology. "Completely degraded," she notes, her scientific detachment returning despite her own injuries, a series of burns along her left arm where her suit split at the elbow. "The enzyme adapted its molecular structure specifically to target our materials."

The communications officer sits with his helmet beside him, the once-transparent visor now clouded and pitted with microscopic holes. His face bears a latticework of superficial burns where digestive fluid seeped through these same openings, a record of the helmet's failure mapped directly onto his skin.

The chamber door slides open with a pneumatic hiss, admitting Selenea. She steps through the sanitization field without breaking stride, her focus entirely on the crew. Her eyes find Caelus immediately, relief momentarily softening her tactical composure.

"The ship's structural integrity is holding," she reports, maintaining professional distance despite the personal connection. "Auto-repair systems are sealing the major breaches. We'll need extensive retrofitting at the next outpost, but we'll make it."

She kneels beside Caelus, finally allowing herself to touch his shoulder, a brief gesture of comfort quickly withdrawn. Her fingers leave a smear in the neutralizing compound coating his skin. "You look terrible," she says, the simple observation carrying layers of concern beneath.

Caelus manages a weak smile that pulls at the chemical burn extending from his right cheek to his jaw. "How did you find us?" he asks, voice hoarse from exposure to spores that penetrated his respirator. "The planet's interference blocked all standard communications."

"Ven's detection algorithm," Selenea explains, nodding toward the scientist. "It doesn't search for you directly, and it looks for the disruptions you create in natural systems. You were the discontinuity in Mordia's patterns."

The medical unit moves between crew members with mechanical efficiency, deploying specialized treatments calibrated to each person's specific injuries. Synthetic skin spray seals the worst chemical burns, while tissue regeneration compounds accelerate healing processes. Pain suppressors activate automatically when biometric sensors detect threshold readings, their delivery causing momentary cloudiness in the recipients' eyes before clarity returns.

"The digestive compounds are neutralized," the unit announces after completing its fifth scan. "No remaining active enzymes detected in tissue samples. Beginning secondary treatment phase."

Caelus examines his enhancement bands; testing connection points with careful fingers. "Damaged but repairable," he determines, the assessment applying equally to the technology and himself. The metal feels cool against his burned fingertips, and the sensation is both painful and reassuring, a reminder that some things survive even in the most hostile environments.

"What about Vorax?" Ven asks, scientific curiosity overriding personal discomfort. "The neural disruption pattern, was it temporary as designed?"

Selenea nods, checking the data on her wrist display. "Sensors indicate normal activity resuming in the fungal network. No permanent damage to primary neural structures. The neutralizing compound will break down into harmless components within their system."

The environmental officer attempts to stand, and the medical unit immediately adjusts his support harness to compensate for weakened leg muscles. "We need to warn other worlds about Mordia's defensive capabilities," he says. "The Battalion won't be prepared for, "

His statement cuts off as emergency signals flash across all active displays. The ship's communication system activates without command input, with indicators showing maximum priority override.

"Incoming transmission," the ship announces. "Emergency bandwidth. Origin: Marinami."

The main screen activates, filling with images that momentarily silence the entire crew. Marinami's ocean surface churns with controlled violence, massive water spouts rising hundreds of meters into the air before collapsing with tactical precision onto Battalion vessels below. These aren't natural formations but weapons manipulated by Marinamian controllers visible as small figures riding the water columns themselves.

The footage shifts perspective, diving beneath the waves to reveal the full scale of the battle. Fifth Battalion vessels, designed for jungle warfare, not oceanic combat, struggle against currents that suddenly reverse direction, trapping them in vortexes that tear at hull plating. Marinamian defenders move through these same waters with perfect adaptation, their bodies enhanced with technological modifications that allow them to manipulate their environment with unprecedented control.

"That's the Fifth Battalion," Caelus whispers, recognition dawning with terrible clarity. "They were supposed to target Mordia."

The transmission focus changes again, showing a crystalline command center constructed from coral and advanced alloys. At its center stands Lyra Mareen, her iridescent scales catching the light as she directs defense operations with fluid hand gestures that manipulate holographic displays. Water moves around her in miniature versions of the massive weapons deployed across the planet's surface, responding to her commands with living precision.

"Status report," she demands, voice carrying despite the water flowing around her. "Eastern defense grid."

"Holding," responds an officer whose webbed hands make adjustments to current patterns with practiced expertise. "The Battalion's thermal lances lose fifty-seven percent effectiveness at our operating depth. Their jungle configuration works against them."

Lyra nods, satisfaction evident in the subtle color shift of her hair that ripples like seaweed in response to her emotional state. "Maintain pressure on their command vessels. They expected surrender, not organized resistance."

The crew watches in stunned silence as the battle unfolds, a conflict they should have been present for had Orpheus not diverted them to Mordia. The realization spreads across their faces in waves of dawning comprehension.

"He split his forces," Caelus says finally, struggling to his feet despite the medical unit's protests. "Orpheus knew we'd detect the Battalion movement. He wanted us to follow them to Mordia while he simultaneously attacked Marinami."

Selenea's expression hardens as tactical implications cascade through her mind. "The false intelligence about targeting Mordia. The sudden redirection to Marinami. He played us perfectly."

"Neither force is at full strength," Ven observes, analyzing the battle footage with professional detachment. "The Fifth Battalion configuration is wrong for oceanic engagement. They're fighting at reduced effectiveness."

"That's deliberate," Caelus concludes, the enhancement bands warming slightly as his Aetheris perception partially returns, free from Vorax's interference. "He doesn't need to win decisively. He just needs to drain resources and force defensive responses on multiple fronts simultaneously."

The security officer tests his injured legs, grimacing as regenerated tissue protests the movement. "Divide and exhaust. Basic tactical doctrine. While we rescue one world, another falls."

The transmission from Marinami continues, showing that the battalion forces are regrouping for a secondary assault. Despite their inappropriate configuration, they adapt with professional efficiency, transforming jungle warfare equipment into makeshift underwater weapons. The Marinamians respond with increased water manipulation, creating defense barriers of pressurized liquid that shreds incoming projectiles.

"Can the Marinamians hold?" the communications officer asks, voice rough from chemical exposure.

"For now," Selenea responds, already calculating transit possibilities. "But they weren't prepared. No warning, no reinforcements."

Caelus picks up the damaged enhancement bands, fitting them over his burned fingers despite the pain the contact causes. "We need to redirect immediately. Calculate the fastest route to Marinami."

"Already done," Selenea confirms. "But we're seventeen hours away at maximum sustainable speed. The battle will be decided before we arrive."

The transmission abruptly terminates as Battalion forces target Marinami's communication array, and the screen fills with static before switching to ship diagnostics. The sudden silence feels accusatory, highlighting their absence from a conflict they should have anticipated.

"This is just the beginning," Caelus says quietly, the enhancement bands pulsing weakly as his Aetheris sense expands beyond the ship. "I can feel disturbances forming near other allied worlds. Orpheus is implementing coordinated attacks across multiple systems simultaneously."

He meets Selenea's gaze, and both siblings recognize the magnitude of the strategic challenge before them. Where they had fought individual Battalions on single worlds, now they face a coordinated offensive across multiple fronts, each carefully calibrated to divide their attention and resources.

"We need to warn them all," Selenea states, already moving toward the bridge. "And we need to make choices about which battles we can fight directly."

Caelus follows, his injuries temporarily forgotten as larger concerns take precedence. The deadly calculus of triage, which worlds they might save and which they must leave to fend for themselves, hangs unspoken between them as they prepare to counter Orpheus's expanded strategy.

Behind them, the medical unit continues treating the remaining crew, preparing them for battles yet to come as the ship accelerates toward a conflict they've already missed, leaving Mordia's golden spore clouds far behind.

Chapter 17

Clash of Titans

Reality shatters above Mordia's bioluminescent canopy, the Fractal opening not with chaos but with mathematical precision. The tear begins as a crystalline point of light that expands into a perfect geometric pattern, its edges cutting through space-time with surgical efficiency. Golden spores swirl into the rift, drawn by pressure differentials that create hypnotic spiral patterns against the void beyond.

Orpheus's flagship emerges first, its angular hull slicing through the dimensional tear like a blade through flesh. Behind it, battalion vessels follow in perfect formation, their engines disrupting the spore clouds into undulating waves of amber light. The ships hover above the fungal forest, their metallic undersides reflecting bioluminescence in cold, mechanical patterns that stand in stark contrast to the organic pulses below.

On the command deck, Orpheus stands motionless before the primary viewport. His form blurs at the edges, as if he exists partially in shadow, his tall silhouette rendered in stark relief against flickering tactical displays that cast his face in alternating patterns of light and darkness. The mask covering his features catches these illuminations, ancient sigils etched into its surface seeming to shift and move with each flicker.

"Preliminary scan complete," reports an officer, voice steady despite the unease that Orpheus's presence always inspires. "Primary neural networks identified. Strongest connections located in sector seven."

Orpheus doesn't turn, his attention fixed on the living landscape below. "Secure the neural pathways first," he orders, his voice carrying those impossible harmonic undertones that no human vocal cords should produce. "Cut off their communication."

The order propagates through command channels with mechanical efficiency. Battalion officers direct their vessels into predetermined configurations, splitting their forces with practiced precision. Tactics developed across dozens of conquered worlds now deploy against Mordia's unique defenses, each movement calculated to maximize efficiency while minimizing resistance.

"Deploy harvesters to primary extraction points," Orpheus continues, fingers extending toward the tactical display. Where he touches, the holographic images shift, focusing on specific fungal structures that pulse with greater intensity than their surroundings. "These nodes contain the highest concentration of communication compounds."

Kilometers below crouched at the edge of a crystalline grove, Caelus presses his palm against a pulsating root. The recovery dermal patches on his skin have barely finished their work, and the pink new tissue is still sensitive, where Vorax's digestive enzymes burned through his flesh days earlier. The enhancement bands around his fingers, repaired but still bearing corrosion marks from their previous encounter with Mordia, pulse with blue-white energy as he establishes a connection with the planet's neural network.

His amber irises, rimmed with red from ruptured vessels that haven't fully healed, widen as information flows through the connection. The sigils tattooed across his body flare beneath his environment suit, creating patterns of light visible through the fabric. Blood vessels dilate along his temples and the price of maintaining Aetheris connection after his system has already been pushed beyond sustainable limits.

"They're splitting into three groups," he reports, voice clipped with exhaustion. "Targeting the main fungal nodes. Precision deployment, not full-scale invasion. They're after specific compounds."

Selenea nods, checking the tactical display on her wrist. Her own injuries have mostly healed, though she still favors her right side, where a thorned tendril punctured her suit during their escape from Vorax. "Battalion configuration suggests mineral extraction priority. Heavy harvesting equipment, minimal ground troops."

The security officer scans the perimeter, his movements slightly stiff from regenerated tissue that hasn't fully integrated with the original knee structures. "Four-kilometer radius. Three primary approach vectors. Sensor array still shows interference patterns from the fungal network."

Ven Diona kneels beside another root formation, her environmental sensors, which have been hastily rebuilt after their destruction, still showing offline status. Without her specialized equipment, she relies on more direct methods of information gathering. Her fingers trace the root's surface, feeling subtle vibrations that most would miss entirely.

"The spore production has increased fifteen percent since our arrival," she notes, eyes tracking microscopic color shifts in the bioluminescent patterns. "Response to external stimulus. The Mordians are aware. They're preparing defenses."

The fungal forest around them reacts to the battalion's arrival, light patterns flowing through connected structures in warning sequences that spread outward from the initial contact points. The ground itself seems to tense, micro-movements rippling through the substrate as mycelium networks reconfigure in response to the threat. Where battalion ships pass overhead, the bioluminescence dims momentarily before intensifying to almost painful brightness.

"Vorax is mobilizing defensive structures three kilometers east," Ven continues, her scientific detachment returning despite the imminent danger. "Crystalline thorn production accelerating. Digestive pools forming at likely ground troop deployment zones."

The communications officer adjusts his rebuilt equipment, compensating for the increasing electromagnetic interference generated by the fungal network's heightened activity. "Signal from orbit," he reports. "Selenea's team has visual confirmation on battalion deployment."

Her voice crackles through their comms, the slight distortion unable to mask the tactical calm that defines her under pressure. "Five primary extraction vessels moving to the southern node. Heavy armor support. Two secondary vessels approaching from the east with what looks like specialized cutting equipment."

Caelus winces as a spike of pain shoots through his temple, blood vessels straining under the continued Aetheris connection. "Orpheus is on the primary vessel. Northwestern quadrant." He presses his other hand against his forehead, trying to maintain focus through the building pressure behind his eyes. "He's searching for something specific. I can feel it through the cosmic threads."

"Targeting data received," Selenea acknowledges. "Positioning orbital support vessels to counter their primary extraction points. Limited effectiveness without ground coordination."

The environmental officer checks atmospheric readings, frowning at the results. "Spore density increasing exponentially. Oxygen-to-particulate ratio shifting toward hazardous levels. Suit filters will reach capacity in approximately four hours."

"That's deliberate," Ven observes. "The fungal network is increasing spore production to interfere with battalion breathing apparatus. They're turning the atmosphere itself into a weapon."

Caelus rises slowly, disconnecting from the root with visible effort. His hand trembles slightly as he checks weapon systems and communication equipment. "We need to disrupt their extraction before they sever the main neural connections. If they isolate segments of the network, Mordia loses its primary defense coordination."

The security officer distributes specialized charges designed to interfere with battalion harvesting equipment. "Targeting priorities?"

"Primary extractors first," Caelus decides. "Then communication jammers. The fungal network can recover from physical damage, but if they collect enough of the communication compounds, they'll reverse-engineer the technology."

Overhead, the battalion vessels complete their initial deployment phase. Extraction equipment descends on mechanical arms, specialized cutting tools already glowing with activation energy. The first incisions into the fungal canopy release clouds of golden spores that swirl around the intrusion point like blood in the water.

Selenea's voice returns through the communication network, her tone shifting from information gathering to operational command. "All orbital support units in position. Ground teams confirmed at secondary interception points. For the primary strike team, you have tactical command. We'll follow your lead."

Caelus looks at his team, each member bearing the marks of their previous encounter with Mordia, each understanding exactly what failure means for this living world and countless others. The enhancement bands around his fingers pulse with renewed determination as he establishes their path forward.

"Move out," he orders, turning toward the nearest extraction point where battalion harvesters have begun their destructive work. "Stay connected, stay aware. Mordia fights with us now."

The fungal forest responds to their movement, bioluminescent pathways brightening to guide their advance while dangerous zones dim in warning. The planet, having tested its intentions once before, now accepts them as allies against a common threat that cuts into its living flesh with cold, mechanical precision.

The harvester machines descend from battalion vessels on hydraulic arms, their cutting surfaces glowing orange-white with concentrated heat. They pierce the fungal canopy like surgical instruments, releasing fountains of golden spores that hang suspended for a moment before being sucked into collection chambers. Where the cutters connect with living tissue, the fungal structures emit high-frequency vibrations that travel through the entire network, a planetary scream that needs no sound to convey its agony.

Battalion engineers in white exoskeletal armor deploy alongside the harvesters, establishing perimeters with practiced efficiency. They set up field generators that create containment bubbles around extraction sites, preventing the increasingly aggressive spore clouds from interfering with their work. Inside these protected zones, the harvesting intensifies, precision tools extracting specific compounds from the fungal structures while leaving surrounding tissue deliberately intact.

The fungal network responds with unexpected coordination. Mordia's defensive systems, which evolved over millennia to counter natural threats, now adapt to this artificial invasion. Specialized spore sacs rupture near battalion positions, releasing corrosive compounds that eat through protective coatings and respiratory filters. The golden particles transform into biological weapons, each microscopic spore carrying enzymes calibrated to break down synthetic materials.

"Filters at sixty percent capacity," the environmental officer warns as their team moves through dense undergrowth where bioluminescent patterns pulse with increased urgency. "The spores are changing composition faster than our systems can adapt."

Caelus leads them through terrain that shifts beneath their feet, the living ground responding to their presence with subtle adjustments that create safer passages while collapsing potential escape routes for battalion forces. His enhancement bands glow with sustained energy as his Aetheris perception guides their movement through the chaotic landscape, following cosmic threads that reveal paths invisible to normal senses.

"The network is learning," he observes, stepping carefully over a root structure that pulses with amber light. "It's allowing us passage while actively working against battalion movement. Watch your step, and the safe zones change every few seconds."

The security officer follows closely, weapon ready. "Movement at two o'clock. Battalion scout team."

They freeze as a patrol passes twenty meters to their right, the soldiers fighting against terrain that seems deliberately designed to impede their progress. The fungal growth thickens around their legs, slowing movement, while bioluminescent patterns shift to create disorienting visual effects that make standard navigation systems useless.

Ven studies these defensive adaptations with scientific admiration. "The network is deploying targeted responses. It's identifying individual battalion soldiers and customizing obstacles based on their equipment configurations."

Caelus presses forward as soon as the patrol passes, his Aetheris perception stretching ahead to identify their primary target. The enhancement bands burn hot against his fingers, the strain of sustained use causing blood vessels to dilate across his temples. Fresh beads of blood form at his nostrils, but he maintains the connection despite the physical cost.

His perception suddenly locks onto a massive structure rising from the fungal forest two kilometers ahead, a towering formation that pulses with intensified bioluminescence, its patterns complex and organized in ways the surrounding growths aren't. Cosmic threads converge on this location, revealing its significance within the planetary network.

"There, the command node!" Caelus points, excitement momentarily overriding the pain of extended perception. "That's where the neural pathways converge. The battalion is targeting it specifically."

Through his Aetheris vision, he sees battalion forces already converging on the structure, heavy extraction equipment moving into position while combat units establish defensive perimeters. At the center of this activity, a distinctive vessel hovers, its design clearly setting it apart from standard battalion craft.

"Orpheus is there," Caelus confirms, wiping blood from his upper lip. "He's overseeing the extraction personally."

The communications officer adjusts their approach coordinates. "Orbital team updated. Selenea is repositioning for support."

They increase the pace, following paths that the fungal network creates specifically for them, routes that open and close behind their passage, preventing battalion forces from tracking their movement. The bioluminescence guides them through natural choke points, where the terrain provides tactical advantages against numerically superior forces.

As they approach the command node, the entire landscape trembles. The vibration builds from deep underground, traveling through connected root systems and resonating within the massive fungal structures. Battalion soldiers pause in their extraction efforts, scanning for the source of the disturbance.

The ground erupts beneath a primary harvester machine. Vorax Vunes surges from below, its massive form unfolding with terrifying speed. The primary trap extends upward, engulfing the lower portion of the harvester while crystalline thorns punch through metal plating with the precision of armor-piercing rounds. The machine crumples, its hydraulic systems hissing as the pressurized fluid escapes through dozens of puncture points.

"Biological counterattack initiated," Ven observes, her scientific detachment momentarily broken by something resembling satisfaction. "Vorax is targeting their extraction equipment first."

The entity's massive form towers above the battlefield, its deep purple-black leaves now edged with intensified bioluminescent patterns that pulse with unmistakable hostility. Battalion soldiers open fire, thermal lances cutting through the air with orange brilliance. Where they connect with Vorax's exterior, the energy weapons leave scorched trails that seal almost immediately as the plant entity's regenerative systems activate.

Auxiliary traps emerge from the ground around battalion positions, snapping closed around soldiers with mechanical precision. Neural vines whip through the air, wrapping around engineers and dragging them toward spore pits that have opened strategically throughout the extraction zone. The victims' screams cut off abruptly as they disappear beneath golden surfaces that bubble with digestive activity.

"The fungal network is coordinating defense through Vorax," Caelus explains, observing the tactical patterns in the entity's attacks. "It's not random, and it's prioritizing threats according to their impact on the neural pathways."

Ven guides their team around the main battle zone, identifying safer approaches through increasingly hazardous terrain. "Stay three meters to my left," she instructs as they encounter a field of what appear to be shallow puddles with mirror-like surfaces. "Don't touch the amber pools, digestive enzymes!"

The environmental officer scans the pools with the remaining functional sensors. "Concentrated version of what we encountered inside Vorax. Would dissolve environmental suits in seconds."

They navigate the treacherous ground with painstaking care, following Ven's guidance as she reads subtle indicators in the surrounding vegetation that signal safe passage. Meanwhile, the battle intensifies around the command node, battalion forces regrouping after Vorax's initial assault to establish defensive positions with overlapping fields of fire.

Selenea's voice cuts through their comms, her tone precise and focused. "In position for orbital support. Designate primary targets."

Caelus marks the largest extraction vehicles on their tactical display. "Targeting data transmitted. Priority on harvesting equipment, secondary on troop concentrations."

Seconds later, energy beams lance from above, cutting through the fungal canopy with surgical precision. The orbital strikes tear open gaps in the living ceiling, shafts of unfiltered sunlight penetrating the perpetual amber twilight of the forest floor. The sudden illumination creates stark contrasts, battalion equipment casting long shadows across the churned landscape.

The strikes connect with designated targets, harvesting machines erupting in controlled explosions that minimize collateral damage to the surrounding network.

Battalion soldiers scatter, defensive formations dissolving temporarily as they seek cover from the unexpected attack.

On the command vessel, Orpheus observes these developments with cold calculation. His form remains absolutely still while chaos erupts around him, officers rushing to implement defensive protocols and redirect resources. When he finally moves, it's with deliberate purpose, fingers extending toward a specialized control surface.

"Bring in the Fractal cutters," he orders, his voice carrying those unsettling harmonic undertones that seem to vibrate the air itself. "Sever their neural network at the source."

The order transmits through battalion command channels, triggering the deployment of equipment unlike any previously utilized. From specialized vessels, mechanical arms extend, bearing devices that appear similar to standard cutting tools but emit crystalline light patterns identical to the Fractal dimensions themselves.

"New threat detected," the security officer warns, pointing toward the devices now positioning themselves around the command node. "Unknown technology."

Caelus recognizes the danger immediately, enhancement bands flaring as his Aetheris perception identifies the fundamental threat these devices pose. "Fractal cutters," he explains, alarm evident despite his exhaustion. "They don't just sever physical connections, and they cut through the dimensional fabric that allows the network to function as a unified consciousness."

The cutters activate, creating miniature Fractal tears that slice through neural pathways with horrifying efficiency. Where they cut, the bioluminescent connections don't merely go dark; they cease to exist in conventional space-time, and the severed ends are unable to reconnect through normal biological processes.

Vorax Vunes shudders, auxiliary traps convulsing as sections of its extended awareness suddenly vanish. The entity redirects its attacks toward these new threats, but the cutters operate from protected positions, their work continuing despite the plant's increasingly desperate counterattacks.

"We need to disable those cutters," Caelus determines, adjusting their approach vector toward the nearest device. "If they sever enough pathways, the entire network fragments into isolated sections. Mordia loses its unified defense capability."

The fungal forest around them trembles as these fundamental connections begin to fail, the living planet fighting for its consciousness against weapons designed to destroy the very fabric of its being.

Fifth Battalion ships punch through Marinami's surface tension like metallic predators breaching for air. Water cascades from their hulls in silver sheets, catching the sunlight in patterns that might be beautiful if not for their violent purpose. The vessels hover momentarily, water still draining from specialized hull compartments, before formation computers align them in perfect attack configuration, twelve vessels in a three-dimensional array designed to maximize firing solutions against defensive targets while minimizing exposure to counterattack.

Their thermal lances, designed for cutting through jungle vegetation, now recalibrate for aquatic engagement, power levels adjusting to compensate for water's higher heat dispersion properties. The weapons emerge from protective housing, and tracking systems are already identifying priority targets beneath the rolling surface.

Standing on a floating platform that rises and falls with the gentle rhythm of Marinami's waves, Meridia Flux watches the invasion unfold through eyes that shift between deep blue and violet as her emotions fluctuate. Her iridescent scales catch the morning light, refracting it in patterns that match the water's surface. The guilt she carries from past battles briefly surfaces, a moment of hesitation at the violence to come before her training reasserts itself, hands steadying as she extends them toward the control interface.

"Hydrokinetic grid online," reports a technician, gills pulsing with increased respiration rate. "All nodes responsive."

Meridia nods once, fingers moving through the interface with practiced precision. The motion, elegant despite its martial purpose, activates defense protocols developed through generations of protecting Marinami's waters. "Redirect power to the eastern quadrant," she orders, voice carrying the slight resonant echo common to deep-water Marinamians. "Form primary containment pattern."

The ocean responds to her command, not through mystical connection but by precise technological manipulation. Beneath the surface, thousands of hydrokinetic nodes activate simultaneously, their energy signatures creating interference patterns that shape water molecules according to predetermined configurations. The seemingly natural process results from decades of engineering refinement and technology that works with Marinami's environment rather than against it.

Water spouts rise around the battalion formation, not with the chaotic energy of natural phenomena but with the controlled precision of weaponized architecture. They tower fifty meters high, their surfaces smooth as polished glass, internal currents flowing in complex patterns that allow Marinamian defenders to ride within while remaining invisible to external observation.

The spouts weave together, forming a maze of liquid walls that encircle the invading vessels. Battalion pilots recognize the danger immediately, engines flaring as they attempt evasive maneuvers. Their ships, configured for jungle insertion rather than oceanic combat, respond sluggishly to atmospheric controls, their movement hampered by water still clogging thrust vectors and cooling systems.

"Defensive maze established," Meridia confirms, fingers continuing their complex dance above the interface. Her white facial markings glow faintly as she channels more power through the system. "Initiating sequence two."

Beneath the surface, Lyra Mareen leads aquatic warriors through shimmering currents that would disorient land-dwellers but provide perfect navigational references for those born to Marinami's depths. Her hair, resembling flowing seaweed, changes from deep blue to aggressive crimson as she shifts to combat readiness. The transformation spreads through her troops, their bodies adapting to battle configurations as specialized fins extend along forearms and calves, increasing maneuverability in combat currents.

"Form the undertow pattern," she commands, her voice traveling through the water with perfect clarity, carried by acoustic properties unique to Marinamian physiology. "Target their submersible deployment bays."

Her warriors respond with synchronized movement, bodies arranged in formations that enhance the natural flow patterns they now manipulate. They don't fight against the water's current but with it, using their technology to amplify forces already present in the environment. Where they move, the water moves with them, not following but complementing, an extension of their tactical intent.

Bioluminescent fish swirl at the boundaries between currents, their movements appearing random to untrained observers but actually following precise mathematical distributions calculated to disrupt Battalion targeting systems. Each fish serves as a living decoy, its light signature mimicking Marinamian warriors while creating false targeting solutions that waste Battalion resources.

The defense platforms, floating structures that appear fragile against the massive Battalion vessels, activate secondary systems as the attack intensifies. Beneath their seemingly vulnerable exteriors lie technological cores developed specifically to counter invasion, their capabilities hidden until needed. Energy fields extend outward, manipulating water pressure to create barriers invisible to standard sensors.

In the lead Battalion vessel, the commander scans tactical displays with growing frustration. What should have been a straightforward subjugation has transformed into a complex engagement against an enemy using the environment itself as both a weapon and shield.

"Deploy depth charges," he orders his voice sharp and with contained anger. "Target their underwater infrastructure."

Weapon bays open along the vessels' undersides, releasing spherical devices that drop toward the ocean surface. They break through with minimal splash, and their density is calibrated to carry them to specific depths before detonation. Battalion engineers designed these weapons specifically for the mission, explosive force contained and directed to maximize underwater pressure waves while minimizing collateral dispersion.

Lyra detects the deployment through defense sensors embedded throughout Marinami's water column. "Depth charges inbound," she reports through the communication network. "Activating countermeasures."

The protective bubbles form before the charges reach their target depths, not simple air pockets but complex pressure differentials created by hydrokinetic technology. These spherical zones redirect explosive force along predetermined vectors, channeling destructive energy away from vital infrastructure while dissipating pressure waves that would otherwise cause catastrophic damage.

The charges detonate in sequence, creating underwater thunder that travels for kilometers. Where battalion commanders expect structural collapse and system failure, they find instead minimal effect, their weapons' power redirected and wasted against Marinami's defensive adaptations.

On her command platform, Meridia monitors these developments through sensory inputs that combine traditional displays with direct hydrological feedback. Her fingers adjust water flow patterns in real-time, compensating for battalion tactical shifts while establishing new defensive configurations.

"They're attempting to breach the southern quadrant," she notes, scales shifting to deeper blue as she concentrates. "Diverting additional power to containment spouts three through seven."

The water walls respond, thickening where battalion vessels attempt penetration. The liquid barriers don't simply block physical movement but actively interfere with sensor systems, creating false readings that make navigation increasingly hazardous. Battalion pilots find themselves trapped in a three-dimensional maze that continuously reconfigures according to their own movement patterns, learning and adapting to each attempted escape.

"Their thermal lances lose effectiveness with each firing cycle," Lyra reports from beneath the surface, where her warriors continue to harass battalion deployment systems.

"Hull integrity on their lead vessel shows increasing compromise from water pressure fluctuations."

The battalion commander recognizes the deteriorating tactical situation. His vessels, designed for atmospheric operations with limited aquatic capability, face an enemy evolved specifically for this environment. The jungle configuration that should have been deployed against Mordia now works against them, systems struggling to adapt to conditions they weren't designed to counter.

"Recalibrate thermal lances for maximum dispersion," he orders, searching for any advantage. "Target their command platform directly."

The weapons adjust, focusing energy in wider patterns designed to overcome water's dispersive properties. The attack momentarily overwhelms localized defenses, steam erupting where energy connects with water spouts protecting Meridia's position. For a few seconds, the defensive pattern falters, gaps appearing in the liquid maze.

Meridia feels the platform beneath her shudder as peripheral systems overload. Her gills pulse with increased respiration, but her hands remain steady, fingers already implementing countermeasures. "Reinforce northern approach vectors," she commands. "Deploy sonic disruptors."

Beneath the surface, Lyra receives this command and signals her warriors to activate specialized equipment carried for precisely this contingency. The devices, small enough to fit in a Marinamian palm, generate focused acoustic pulses that travel through water with devastating efficiency. The waves target battalion hull structures, creating resonance patterns that stress metal along microscopic fault lines invisible to standard inspection protocols.

The battalion vessels shudder as these sonic attacks connect, vibrations traveling through their structures with increasing amplitude. Warning systems activate throughout their command centers, and structural integrity monitors show progressive failure patterns that will, if unchecked, lead to a catastrophic hull breach.

"Hydrostatic pressure increasing along all vectors," Lyra reports, satisfaction evident in her tone despite the professional delivery. "Their jungle configuration lacks sufficient reinforcement for sustained underwater engagement."

The battalion commander watches his tactical advantage dissolve, vessels now fighting against both Marinamian defenders and the environment itself. Water infiltration systems are not designed for prolonged submersion, while pressure fluctuations stress hull sections are configured for atmospheric conditions. What began as a precisely calculated attack has devolved into a desperate struggle against an enemy perfectly adapted to turn his own forces' specifications against them.

Caelus kneels at the center of the battlefield, enhancement bands burning white-hot against his fingers. The fungal forest around him pulses with synchronized bioluminescence, channeling energy into his Aetheris connection. Blood vessels spider across his temples, rupturing in tiny starbursts beneath his skin as he forces his perception beyond physical limitations, cosmic threads stretching through the chaos of battle to locate his target.

"I need more," he whispers, not to his team but to Mordia itself.

The planet responds. Fungal structures bend toward him, their surfaces connecting with his environment suit at precise points where the sigils tattoo his skin beneath. The connection burns – not with heat but with raw information transfer, neural patterns flowing between human consciousness and planetary network. The sigils beneath his suit illuminate, their amber glow intensifying until light seeps through the fabric in geometric patterns that match Mordia's native communication compounds.

Selenea's voice crackles through his helmet comm. "Status update. We're holding position at grid seven, but battalion harvesters have breached the secondary neural cluster."

Caelus can't spare the energy to respond. His consciousness expands beyond conventional sensory limits, following cosmic threads that connect all conscious entities within his range. Each battalion soldier appears as a knot of intention and action, their movements predicted seconds before physical execution. The harvester machines register differently – not as consciousness but as voids in the pattern, artificial constructs cutting through the living tapestry of Mordia's network.

The enhancement bands around his fingers glow brighter, metal heating to a near-melting point against his skin. He feels nothing – nerve endings temporarily overwhelmed by the Aetheris connection – but smells burning flesh as the bands sear into finger tissue. Blood flows freely from his nose now, spattering the ground beneath him where fungal structures immediately absorb it, analyzing his biological composition in real-time.

"Protecting," Vorax Vunes communicates, not through sound but through a direct neural connection to Caelus's expanded consciousness. The entity rises from the ground around him, massive purple-black leaves unfurling to create a living fortress. Crystalline thorns extend outward, forming defensive barriers against approaching battalion forces while the primary trap remains open above, allowing his Aetheris perception an unobstructed connection to the cosmic threads.

Ven crouches beside him, monitoring his deteriorating physical condition with growing concern. "His core temperature is rising," she reports to the team. "Vascular system showing stress patterns consistent with extreme Aetheris extension."

The security officer positions himself at the perimeter of Vorax's protective formation, weapon ready. "Battalion approaching from the northeast. Heavy weapons configuration."

Through Caelus's expanded perception, the battalion movements appear as predictable patterns flowing through predetermined paths. His consciousness traces their trajectories backward, seeking the source of their coordination, the center from which their orders emanate. Cosmic threads lead him through layers of command structure, past field officers and tactical coordinators, toward a presence that distorts the very fabric of perception around it.

His body convulses suddenly, back arching as blood vessels rupture in both eyes simultaneously. The sigils across his skin pulse with blinding intensity, now fully visible through his environment suit as if the material has become transparent to their energy. His mouth opens in a silent scream as his perception finally locks onto the source of the invasion.

"There," he gasps, voice barely audible. "Northeast quadrant. Command vessel."

The words cost him enormously, each syllable forcing his consciousness to contract momentarily from its expanded state. Blood bubbles between his lips, internal hemorrhaging accelerating as his body pays the physical price for sustained Aetheris perception.

"Coordinates confirmed," Selenea acknowledges through the comm system. "Moving into position now."

Above the fungal canopy, her ship dives through battalion defensive fire, engines pushing beyond sustainable parameters. The vessel's underside glows red from thermal discharge as weapon systems activate, energy beams lancing toward the coordinates Caelus provided.

The command vessel – sleeker than standard battalion craft, with angular surfaces that suggest both functionality and status – attempts evasive maneuvers too late. Selenea's attack connects with precision, energy beams slicing through defensive shields calibrated for ground-based threats rather than aerial assault. Secondary explosions cascade along the vessel's port side as damaged systems fail in sequence.

On the forest floor, battalion forces respond to the attack on their command structure with immediate tactical adjustment. Extraction teams abandon harvesting operations, redeploying to defensive positions around key equipment. The Fractal cutters – still severing neural pathways with methodical efficiency – receive additional protection, specialized shields extending to ensure their critical work continues despite the shifting battle conditions.

Vorax Vunes extends further, with auxiliary traps connecting with other fungal entities to form a living network around Caelus. The cooperative defense creates not merely physical protection but a channeling system that amplifies his Aetheris connection, fungal network intelligence supplementing his fading strength. Where his perception weakens, planetary awareness compensates, maintaining the cosmic threads that track battalion movements.

"The command vessel is damaged but operational," Caelus reports, each word forced through gritted teeth. His body trembles with exhaustion, muscles spasming as his nervous system struggles under the continued Aetheris strain. "Orpheus is redirecting resources."

Through his expanded perception, he witnesses Orpheus on the command deck – the figure's edges blurring as if he exists partially in shadow, mask catching light in patterns that suggest awareness beyond human limitations. The cosmic threads connecting Orpheus to reality itself appear distorted, unlike any consciousness Caelus has encountered through Aetheris perception.

Selenea's ship pivots for another attack run, evading defensive fire with tight maneuvers that compress her crew against harness restraints. "Secondary target lock established," she reports. "Engaging harvester concentration at the southern neural junction."

Her weapons discharge again, energy beams cutting through the fungal canopy to strike battalion extraction equipment below. The precision attack avoids critical neural pathways while destroying the machines attempting to sever them, creating moments of tactical reversal as Mordia's defenses surge into gaps created by the aerial assault.

The fungal network responds with a coordinated counterattack. Crystalline vines erupt from the ground beneath battalion positions, thorns targeting vulnerable joint sections in exoskeletal armor. Digestive pools expand beneath damaged equipment, consuming metal and synthetic materials with the same efficiency previously directed against organic matter. Bioluminescent patterns shift to disorienting frequencies that interfere with battalion targeting systems, creating false signatures that waste precious ammunition.

Caelus's perception narrows suddenly, cosmic threads collapsing as his system approaches complete failure. The enhancement bands dim, metal cooling as his body can no longer maintain the energy required for expanded awareness. With his remaining strength, he focuses entirely on Orpheus's command vessel, watching as the battalion leader makes his decision.

Orpheus stands motionless amid the chaos of his damaged command center, officers rushing to implement emergency protocols around him. When he finally speaks, his voice carries those impossible harmonic undertones that resonate through the comm systems intercepted by Caelus's team.

"Fall back to the Fractal point," Orpheus commands, the order propagating through battalion channels with immediate effect. "We'll regroup at the secondary location."

The battalion responds with disciplined efficiency despite its tactical disadvantage. Extraction teams disconnect from partially harvested neural pathways, securing collected samples before beginning the coordinated withdrawal. The Fractal cutters – their work incomplete but substantial – retract into protective housing as support teams establish covering positions for the retreat.

Through the fungal network, Caelus feels Mordia's response – not triumph but a combination of relief and continued vigilance. The network has survived, though damaged in ways that will require extensive regeneration. Severed neural pathways pulse with residual energy, their ends seeking reconnection points that no longer exist in conventional space-time.

In orbit above Mordia, the Fractal reopens – not with the controlled precision of the initial invasion but with the hurried distortion of emergency extraction. Battalion vessels rise through the fungal canopy, abandoning equipment that is too damaged to recover and prioritizing personnel and harvested samples over material assets. Their formation, perfect during arrival, now displays gaps where vessels have been lost to Mordian defenses and Selenea's attacks.

Caelus collapses as the last of his strength fades, enhancement bands completely dark against his burned fingers. Vorax's protective structure contracts slightly, with auxiliary traps repositioning to maintain defensive coverage despite reduced threat levels. The fungal network continues to support his failing body, specialized compounds flowing through the connections established earlier, stabilizing critical systems while his consciousness retreats from expanded awareness.

"Battalion forces entering the Fractal," Selenea confirms through the comm system. "Eighty-seven percent of their remaining vessels accounted for. They're withdrawing."

On the ground where Fractal cutters operated, the neural network displays permanent damage – not the temporary disruption of physical injury but fundamental severance from the dimensional fabric that allows thought to propagate through biological systems. The forest floor around these wounds darkens, bioluminescence failing as connection patterns collapse into isolated segments, unable to rejoin the greater consciousness.

The Fractal closes behind the last battalion vessel, dimensional tear sealing with crystalline finality. The golden spore clouds, agitated during battle, begin to settle into normal patterns, though their density remains elevated – a lingering defense mechanism that will persist until the network confirms the threat has truly passed.

Ven kneels beside Caelus and medical equipment has already been deployed to assess his condition. "Extreme physiological stress," she reports, voice maintaining scientific precision despite her concern. "Multiple internal hemorrhages. Enhancement band interface shows third-degree burns at all contact points."

Through cracked lips, Caelus manages a single question before unconsciousness claims him. "How much did they take?"

The environmental officer scans nearby neural pathways, measuring bioluminescent intensity against baseline readings. "Approximately twelve percent of the communication compounds from the primary cluster. Enough for analysis, not for large-scale replication."

Caelus processes this information with grim satisfaction as darkness closes around him. They've prevented complete harvest, preserved Mordia's neural network integrity, and forced Orpheus to retreat with partial results. A tactical victory within the larger strategic conflict, bought with blood and pain and permanent scars – both his and Mordia's – that will never fully heal.

Meridia Flux stands on the command platform, gills flaring with controlled rage as she surveys the battlefield. The Fifth Battalion vessels - disoriented but still dangerous - attempt to regroup into a defensive formation above Marinami's churning surface. Her iridescent scales shift from deep blue to electric violet as she makes her decision, hands extending outward with fingers splayed like a conductor before an orchestra of destruction. The water around the platform responds immediately, currents redirecting themselves according to patterns she's rehearsed countless times but never deployed at full capacity.

"Prepare final convergence sequence," she commands, voice carrying that distinctive, resonant echo that travels through the water more efficiently than air. Her prominent gill structures pulse with bioluminescence that matches her emotional intensity. "All hydrokinetic nodes to maximum output."

The technicians around her, their own scales reflecting the tension in rapid color shifts, implement her orders with practiced precision. Their webbed hands dance across control interfaces, each movement triggering responses from underwater nodes positioned strategically throughout Marinami's defense grid. Energy readings spike across monitoring displays, the entire system drawing power from thermal vents that tap the planet's molten core.

"Integrity of eastern defense platforms deteriorating," reports an officer, fingers pressed against a sensory pad that transmits structural data directly through skin contact. "Hull breaches detected in platforms seven and nine."

Meridia acknowledges with a slight nod, calculation rather than concern crossing her features. "Those platforms have served their purpose. Redirect their remaining power to the primary vortex system."

She steps to the edge of the command platform, the structure rising and falling beneath her with the increasingly agitated ocean surface. Below, the water darkens as deeper currents rise in response to her commands, carrying cold from abyssal depths to the surface combat zone. Her white facial markings begin to glow with increased intensity, not mere bioluminescence but an active interface with the hydrokinetic systems she's about to unleash.

"Focus on the outer hull," she calls, the command traveling through the communication network to scattered defenders. Her hands weave complex patterns in the air before her, not simply gesturing but actively molding energy fields that shape water molecules according to mathematical formulas refined through generations of Marinamian defense engineering.

The ocean responds.

What begins isn't a chaotic eruption but a precisely calculated sequencing of pressure differentials and thermal gradients. Water columns rise in synchronized patterns, creating a vast circular formation around the struggling Battalion vessels. Each column twists at identical rotation rates, their surfaces revealing the mathematical precision that differs so dramatically from natural phenomena. This isn't nature-unleashed but nature-harnessed, water responding to technological direction with an efficiency that makes it more formidable than any conventional weapon.

The columns bend inward as they rise higher, their upper portions arcing toward the center of the formation. Battalion pilots recognize the imminent danger, engines flaring as they attempt evasive maneuvers. Their ships, already compromised from earlier attacks, respond sluggishly, water-clogged systems struggling against Marinami's environment.

"Containment pattern established," Meridia confirms, fingers continuing their dance above the interface. Her movements become more fluid now, mimicking the water itself as she directs the transition from formation to activation. "Initiating primary vortex convergence."

The water columns merge at precisely calculated intersection points, creating a spiraling vortex that pulls inward with inexorable force. The rotation accelerates, and surface tension creates an almost glass-like exterior that distorts light into prismatic patterns across its surface. Within this forming maelstrom, Battalion vessels find themselves fighting against currents that increase exponentially with each second, hydraulic forces beyond their thrust capacity to overcome.

Kilometers away, Lyra Mareen propels herself through underwater currents with powerful strokes of her webbed limbs. Her hair, resembling flowing seaweed, streams behind her in crimson tendrils that signal combat readiness to all Marinamian defenders. She navigates between defense nodes with practiced efficiency, and her body adapted through evolution and technological enhancement for optimal movement through her native environment.

"Intensify pressure gradient in section four," she commands as she reaches a spherical structure anchored to the ocean floor. Her hands connect with the control interface, and the technology responds to her touch with immediate recalibration. "Direct excess energy to the surface convergence."

The node pulses with blue-white light as it implements her adjustments, power flowing through conduits that extend outward like nerve fibers through the surrounding water. Where these energy lines intersect, protective bubbles form, not simple air pockets but complex pressure differentials that create defensive barriers against Battalion weaponry.

Lyra launches herself toward the next node, and her body is streamlined for maximum speed through the water column. Around her, Marinamian warriors move in coordinated patterns, their formations enhancing the effectiveness of both defensive systems and individual combatants. They don't fight as isolated units but as an integrated force that uses the environment itself as a weapon and shield simultaneously.

"Eastern defense grid reconfigured," she reports through the communication network, voice traveling through the water with perfect clarity. "Protective bubbles at one hundred and twenty percent capacity."

Meridia receives this confirmation through her direct neural connection to the defense system. "Acknowledged. Maintain position for final convergence support."

The vortex above reaches critical momentum, its circumference now encompassing all remaining Battalion vessels. Water pressure increases against their hulls, and metal groans under forces it wasn't designed to withstand. Internal bulkheads buckle on the most damaged ships, and compartments flood as seal integrity fails under the relentless compression.

Around and through this destructive spiral, schools of bioluminescent fish move in complex formations that only appear random. Each fish, genetically enhanced through centuries of selective breeding, emits light patterns calibrated to specific frequencies that interfere with Battalion targeting systems. Their movements create shifting visual landscapes that make accurate weapon deployment nearly impossible, sensors returning contradictory data that renders automated targeting useless.

The fish swirl in tightening patterns that mirror the larger vortex, their collective light creating a disorienting environment where water and energy become indistinguishable. Battalion gunners fire blindly into these illuminated clouds, energy weapons dissipating harmlessly through schools that separate and reform with fluid intelligence, gaps closing instantly around the projectiles' paths.

Inside the lead Battalion vessel, the commander grips the edge of the tactical display as warning indicators flash across every system. Hull integrity monitors show progressive failure across multiple sections and structural support beams approaching critical stress thresholds. The ship shudders as another pressure wave strikes its port side, metal screaming as molecular bonds begin to fail.

"Thirty-seven percent power remaining in maneuvering thrusters," reports an officer, voice steady despite the chaos surrounding them. "Primary weapons systems offline. Defensive shields failing."

The commander studies the tactical display with cold calculation, watching as his carefully planned invasion dissolves into imminent destruction. The Marinamian defenses, initially underestimated due to incomplete intelligence, have proven not merely adequate but overwhelmingly superior against forces configured for jungle warfare.

"Retreat through the Fractal now!" he orders, voice cutting through the command center with desperate authority. "All vessels, maximum thrust toward extraction coordinates."

The order propagates through remaining communication channels, and battalion discipline maintains cohesion even in defeat. Engines push beyond safety parameters, and ships strain toward the designated coordinates, where their entry Fractal can be reopened for emergency extraction.

Below the surface, Lyra detects the energy signatures of Battalion systems reconfiguring for escape. "They're preparing for Fractal reentry," she reports, already moving to intercept. "Southeastern quadrant."

Meridia adjusts the vortex parameters not to prevent escape but to ensure maximum damage during withdrawal. "Let them run," she responds, fingers recalibrating pressure distributions. "But make them remember why they should never return."

The water vortex shifts, creating a high-pressure corridor that channels the retreating vessels toward their extraction point while continuing to compress hull structures and interfere with stabilization systems. The pathway simultaneously guides and punishes, allowing escape while ensuring lasting damage.

At the designated coordinates, reality splits beneath the water, the Fractal reopening with crystalline precision despite the aquatic environment. The dimensional tear forms not in the air but through the water itself, creating a phenomenon where the ocean seems to fold inward upon itself, liquid flowing into spaces that shouldn't exist within conventional physics.

Battalion vessels enter this water-borne rift in desperate sequence, their damaged hulls trailing debris and leaking fluids that disperse instantly in the surrounding currents. The ships that arrived with perfect military precision now flee in staggered disarray, formation discipline abandoned in favor of simple survival.

The commander's vessel enters last, its external sensors capturing final images of Marinami's defenses, data that will inform future tactical assessments. The Fractal closes behind them, reality resealing with rippling distortion that sends concentric waves across the ocean surface.

The sudden silence feels almost physical as Meridia releases her control stance, hands dropping to her sides with exhausted finality. The defense platforms, those that survived, settle into recovery configuration, and automated systems are already beginning repair sequences. The vortex dissipates gradually rather than collapsing, with controlled deactivation preventing destructive aftershocks that would damage Marinami's own structures.

"Battalion forces have withdrawn through the Fractal," confirms a sensor operator, gill structures relaxing as the immediate danger passes. "No signs of remaining vessels within detection range."

Meridia exhales slowly, bubbles rising from her gill slits in a visible sign of physical and emotional release. Her scales shift from combat-ready violet back toward their natural blue as she surveys the aftermath. The defense platforms, damaged but operational, float on the now-calming surface like wounded sentinels that have fulfilled their purpose despite the cost.

Beneath the surface, Lyra Mareen signals her warriors to stand down from immediate combat readiness while maintaining vigilance against possible return. The protective bubbles remain active, though scaled back to conservation levels that can be maintained indefinitely. Bioluminescent fish disperse into more natural patterns, and their defensive formations are no longer required.

Marinami has survived, not unscathed, but unconquered. The water bears witness to their victory, currents already beginning to cleanse the battlefield of debris, erasing physical evidence of conflict while the defenders' memories preserve the lessons learned for inevitable next encounters.

Chapter 18

The Fall of Aetheris

The command deck bathes Orpheus in the cold light of defeat. Holographic displays surround him in a perfect circle, each projection showing a different aspect of the simultaneous failures of Mordia and Marinami. His form remains absolutely still at the center of this technological observatory, the edges of his silhouette blurring slightly against the backdrop of tactical data. The ornate mask covering his features reflects fragmented images of battles lost, its ancient sigils seemingly alive in the shifting light.

"Fifth Battalion sustained eighty-three percent casualties on Marinami," reports a commander, her voice steady despite delivering catastrophic news. "Remaining vessels show critical structural damage. Seventeen percent of harvested materials secured."

Orpheus doesn't acknowledge the report. His attention fixes on the largest display where Mordia's fungal defenses continue their assault on retreating battalion forces. Bioluminescent patterns pulse through connected structures, coordinating attacks with an intelligence that exceeds mere biological reactions. Crystalline thorns punch through exoskeletal armor with surgical precision, targeting joint sections where protection is the thinnest. Battalion soldiers fall in synchronized waves, their tactical formations dissolving into desperate individual survival attempts.

At the center of this combat choreography stands Caelus, enhancement bands glowing blue-white against his fingers. The holographic capture shows him directing the defense through his Aetheris perception, cosmic threads visible only to him determining where and when Mordian defenses strike. Blood streams from his nose and eyes, the physical cost of maintaining extended perception, yet his concentration never wavers.

Orpheus tilts his head slightly, the first movement he's made in seventeen minutes. "Magnify quadrant seven."

The display shifts, focusing on Caelus's hands where the enhancement bands burn against his skin. The metal edges have begun to melt from sustained energy output, fusing with flesh beneath in places. Still, the Aetheris connection holds cosmic threads extending outward to track battalion movements with perfect accuracy.

Another display flares with sudden activity, drawing Orpheus's attention to Marinami. The oceanic battlefield presents an entirely different yet equally devastating defeat. Water spouts rise with architectural precision, forming liquid walls that crush battalion vessels caught within their convergence. Hydrokinetic technology manipulates pressure differentials with mathematical perfection, creating underwater force vectors that tear through hulls designed for atmospheric operations.

Meridia Flux appears briefly in the footage, her iridescent scales shifting from deep blue to electric violet as she directs the defense with fluid hand movements. Water responds to her commands, currents redirecting to form complex attack patterns beyond conventional military countermeasures. Nearby, Lyra Mareen leads underwater warriors through coordinated strikes against vulnerable battalion deployment systems.

"Marinami losses?" Orpheus asks, his voice carrying those distinctive harmonic undertones that vibrate the air unnaturally.

"Two defense platforms destroyed. Four damaged but operational," another commander responds, consulting data streaming across his personal display. "Civilian casualties minimal. Their water manipulation technology exceeds our intelligence assessments by approximately forty-seven percent effectiveness."

"And the communication compounds from Mordia?"

"Twelve percent secured before extraction. Insufficient for large-scale replication. The Fractal cutters severed approximately twenty-two percent of their neural network before we were forced to withdraw."

The commanders await a reaction, perhaps anger, strategic reassessment, or even concern, but Orpheus displays none. His stillness transcends human behavioral patterns, suggesting consciousness operates according to fundamentally different parameters. When he finally moves, the motion appears unnaturally smooth, as if his form transitions through space without intervening positions.

"These are not failures," he states, mask turning toward his commanders. "They are data points."

The dark matter energy around him pulses briefly, responding to fluctuations in his true form contained beneath the physical appearance he maintains. For a moment, his edges blur completely, the substance becoming a shadow before resolidifying with a subtle rippling effect.

"The Mordian neural network functions as predicted. Their communication compounds can be harvested and synthesized." He approaches the central display, fingers extending toward Caelus's image. "But the Aetheris ability remains the critical variable. Without it, our opponents are reactive rather than predictive."

The commanders exchange glances, and uncertainty is evident despite their disciplined exteriors. One step forwards, her posture conveying respect tinged with apprehension.

"The Solaris siblings have coordinated defense on seventeen worlds now," she notes. "Their effectiveness exceeds standard tactical parameters. Perhaps alternative approaches, "

"Alternative approaches are unnecessary," Orpheus interrupts, his tone unchanged yet somehow carrying finality that silences further discussion. "The sister is tactical. Competent but conventional. The brother is the true asset."

His fingers trace patterns in the air before him, activating deeper system functions through gesture interfaces calibrated to his specific energy signature. A new display forms a three-dimensional map of nearby systems with Fractal pathways marked as crystalline connections between worlds. One location pulses with greater intensity, its position marked by complex sigils that match those on Orpheus's mask.

"Zathira contains chambers designed specifically for Aetheris containment," he continues, focus unwavering from the tactical displays. "The monastery's position at the cosmic convergence point provides unique properties for isolation and study."

The dark matter around him intensifies, shadows deepening as his form briefly exists in multiple dimensional states simultaneously. The effect lasts mere seconds before he stabilizes, though the commanders instinctively step back during the fluctuation.

"Without the Aetheris, they are blind," Orpheus states, certainty carrying through his harmonic voice. "Their resistance becomes predictable. Manageable."

He approaches a specialized console set apart from standard command systems. The interface, composed of materials that appear partially crystalline and partially organic, responds to his proximity with soft illumination that matches his energy signature. His hands move through activation sequences too complex for conventional observation, accessing communication channels that exist partially within normal space-time and partially within the void between realities.

"Activate Fractal communicator," he commands. "Secure channel to special operations unit seven."

The system acknowledges a tone that resonates at frequencies technically beyond human auditory range yet is somehow perceived by all present. A projection forms before him, not a standard hologram but a dimensional tear that reveals masked figures waiting in a chamber constructed from materials identical to Zathira's architecture.

"New operational parameters," Orpheus states, transmitting precise coordinates that appear as crystalline data formations within the tear. "Target: Caelus Solaris. Extraction priority alpha. Delivery destination: Zathira, inner sanctum."

The figures acknowledge synchronized movements that suggest both military discipline and something fundamentally inhuman in their coordination. Orpheus continues by stating that his instructions are explicit and unambiguous.

"The target must be secured alive and unharmed," he emphasizes, the harmonic undertones in his voice intensifying. "Damage to his consciousness or Aetheris capacity is unacceptable. Secondary targets are irrelevant. Collateral impact unrestricted."

His form shifts again, darkness briefly consuming his outline before he resolidifies. The effect coincides with increased energy readings throughout the command deck, systems responding to power fluctuations that originate from his presence rather than technological sources.

"His ability is all that matters," Orpheus concludes. "Prepare extraction team for immediate deployment."

The communication terminates, dimensional tear sealing with crystalline precision. Orpheus returns to his position at the center of the command deck, resuming his perfect stillness as the holographic displays continue showing the aftermath of battles fought and lost. Yet his posture now contains something new, not quite an anticipation, but a focused intensity directed toward events not yet unfolded.

Around him, the commanders return to their duties, reorganizing battalion remnants and calculating resource allocations for future operations. No question about the strategic pivot or the resources being diverted to a single extraction operation. They've served under Orpheus long enough to understand that his perspective encompasses calculations beyond conventional military doctrine, a vision that measures victories and defeats according to metrics they cannot fully comprehend.

Caelus's hands tremble as he adjusts the enhancement bands, their metal surfaces still warm against his raw, blistered skin. Golden spores drift around him, catching the fading daylight filtering through Mordia's fungal canopy. Each breath pulls the metallic-sweet tang of spores into his lungs despite the respirator, a lingering reminder of how alien this world remains even after they fought together against Orpheus's forces. The sigils tattooed across his body ache with a dull persistence, overtaxed neural pathways protesting the extended Aetheris use that turned the tide of battle.

He stands at the edge of a clearing where the fungal forest recedes, giving way to a field of shorter growth that pulses with gentle bioluminescence. The patterns have changed since the battle; they are no longer the frantic warning signals of combat but slower, more regular sequences that suggest recovery and reorganization. Mordian defenses gradually power down, crystalline thorns retracting into protective sheaths while digestive pools shrink to minimal operational size.

Blood vessels have burst in both eyes, filling the whites with crimson webs that make his amber irises seem to float in pools of blood. Fresh trails of red trace paths from his nostrils to his upper lip, dried now but telling of the strain his body has endured. The enhancement bands, repaired after their previous encounter with Vorax Vunes, now show new damage, metal warped from energy overload, and fusion points where extreme heat briefly melted connections together.

"Eastern perimeter secure," he reports to his communicator, his voice rough from breathing spore-laden air for hours. "Battalion stragglers neutralized. Vorax is containing any remaining extraction equipment."

The response comes through with static interference, and Mordia's electromagnetic field is still disrupting standard communications. "Copy that. Northern teams report a similar status. Preliminary assessment suggests ninety-four percent of neural network remains viable despite Fractal cutter damage."

Caelus scans the horizon where the last battalion vessels disappeared through the Fractal hours earlier. His Aetheris perception lies dormant now, enhancement bands cool against his fingers, the cosmic threads invisible without the energy he can no longer safely channel. This blindness, returning to conventional sensory limits after expanded awareness, always leaves him feeling uncomfortably confined, as if his consciousness has been compressed into too small a container.

"Ground teams should prioritize damaged neural pathways," he continues, fingers absently tracing one of the sigils on his forearm that burns hotter than the others. "Vorax indicated the network can regenerate if connection points remain viable. The Fractal cutter damage is permanent, but they can isolate those sections to prevent cascade failure."

He steps forward, legs unsteady beneath him. The fungal ground adjusts subtly to support his weight, a small courtesy from a world that hours ago fought alongside him against common enemies. The bioluminescent patterns shift in response to his movement, creating a soft path that guides him toward the rendezvous point where Selenea's shuttle will extract the ground teams.

A sound fractures the relative quiet, not loud but fundamentally wrong like reality itself being torn along mathematical seams. Caelus turns, instincts firing warning signals through his depleted system. Behind him, air splits vertically, a line of absolute darkness rimmed with electric blue energy. The tear expands with precise geometry, widening into a Fractal opening large enough for human passage.

His hand moves to his weapon, fingers wrapping around the grip with practiced automaticity. The movement feels abnormally slow, with muscles responding with a syrup-thick delay. The enhancement bands remain dark against his skin, and Aetheris's perception is unavailable after hours of overuse.

Figures emerge from the Fractal tear with fluid, synchronized movement. They wear masks similar to Orpheus's, though simpler in design, the sigils etched into their surfaces glowing with the same blue energy that rims the dimensional opening. Their forms blur at the edges, suggesting beings not fully materialized in conventional reality.

"Identify yourselves!" Caelus commands, weapon raised despite the tremor in his arm. The fungal forest around him responds to his alarm, bioluminescent patterns accelerating as defensive systems begin to reactivate. Crystalline thorns emerge from nearby structures, sensing threat patterns similar to those recently defeated.

The figures don't respond. They spread out in a semicircle, movements displaying inhuman coordination, not merely practiced but fundamentally different, as if their bodies operate according to physics beyond conventional understanding. No communication passes between them, yet they move with perfect tactical synchronization, closing distance with methodical efficiency.

Caelus fires a warning shot, an energy beam passing through the space where one figure stood milliseconds before. The target has shifted position without transitioning through intervening space, simply existing in one location and then another with no movement between states.

"Selenea," he says into his communicator, backing toward the fungal structures that now pulse with increasing defensive energy. "Fractal breach at my position. Unknown hostiles. Request immediate, "

The first attacker reaches him with impossible speed, moving from ten meters distance to direct contact in less than a heartbeat. A precise strike targets the nerve cluster in Caelus's right shoulder, temporarily paralyzing his weapon arm. The second attacker arrives simultaneously from the opposite direction, sweeping his legs with perfect mechanical efficiency.

Caelus lands hard, combat training asserting itself despite his exhaustion. He rolls, converting momentum into a recovery movement that brings him back to his feet. His left hand connects with an attacker's midsection, delivering a strike that would incapacitate a normal opponent. The figure absorbs the impact without reaction, and its form briefly destabilizes around the contact point before resolidifying.

Fungal defenses respond to the conflict, crystalline thorns launching from surrounding structures toward the intruders. The projectiles pass harmlessly through their targets, suggesting the figures exist partially in another dimensional state, present enough to affect physical reality but not fully subject to it.

Three attackers converge simultaneously, their movements forming a perfect geometric pattern that leaves no escape route. Caelus blocks the first strike but misses the second, a precision blow to his solar plexus forcing air from his lungs in an explosive gasp. The third attacker sweeps his legs again, this time successfully bringing him to the ground.

His communicator skitters across the fungal surface as a calculated strike knocks it from his hand. "Selenea!" he shouts, voice carrying through the device's open channel before it slides beyond reach. The forest floor beneath him vibrates with increasing intensity as Mordian defenses escalate their response, the planet attempting to protect its ally despite limited comprehension of the dimensional nature of these attackers.

Caelus lands a solid kick to an attacker's knee joint, the impact producing a momentary ripple effect through the figure's form rather than structural damage. He attempts to rise, muscles burning with fatigue, sigils across his skin flaring with final reserves of energy. The enhancement bands flicker weakly, attempting to establish Aetheris's connection despite his depleted state.

The attackers adjust their approach, movements becoming faster and more precise. They target specific nerve clusters and pressure points with surgical accuracy, and each strike is calculated to disable without causing permanent damage. Caelus feels his body responding less effectively with each passing second, neural pathways temporarily blocked by perfectly placed impacts.

One attacker produces restraints, metallic bands inscribed with sigils that match those on their masks. The material catches the blue light from the Fractal, suggesting properties beyond standard containment technology. With synchronized efficiency, two attackers secure his wrists while a third produces an injector device from within its blurred form.

"Wait," Caelus gasps, still struggling despite the futility. The needle pierces his neck with clinical precision, the injection hissing as it delivers its contents directly into his bloodstream.

The effect is immediate. His muscles lose coherent control, though consciousness remains. The world blurs around the edges, and sensory input becomes confused and disjointed. The fungal forest's defensive response reaches full activation too late, crystalline thorns and neural vines converging on the position only to find their targets already retreating toward the Fractal tear.

Caelus feels himself being lifted, carried between two attackers with perfect weight distribution. His body floats through their coordinated movement, approaching the vertical tear in reality that still pulses with electric blue energy. His vision tunnels, darkness encroaching from the periphery as the sedative spreads through his system.

The last thing he sees is the Fractal's blue light engulfing them, reality folding around his consciousness as they pass through the dimensional tear. Behind them, Mordia's defenses strike empty air, the planet's response arriving seconds too late to prevent the extraction of its ally. The Fractal seals closed with crystalline precision, leaving only disturbed spores swirling where combatants stood moments before.

Selenea stands before the primary viewport, hands clasped behind her back as Mordia rotates slowly beneath the ship. The golden spore layer that envelops the planet ripples with lingering disturbances from the battle, currents spreading outward from points where battalion vessels tore through atmospheric layers during their retreat. Status reports flow through nearby displays, cataloging victory with cold numerical efficiency: enemy casualties, equipment losses, and neural pathway damage assessments. Her reflection in the viewport's surface appears ghostly against the planet below, a hollow-eyed specter with dried blood still crusted at her hairline from a wound sustained during the orbital engagement.

"Final ground teams reporting extraction complete," announces the communications officer, fingers moving across his console with practiced precision. "Fungal defense systems returning to standard parameters. Battalion presence eliminated from all monitored sectors."

Selenea nods without turning, attention fixed on a single data point among dozens, Caelus's locator signal, pulsing with reassuring regularity from the eastern perimeter where fungal growth recedes into more manageable terrain. The signal provides silent confirmation of her brother's safety, a digital heartbeat she's grown accustomed to monitoring during their separations.

"Maintain position until all teams are aboard," she orders, finally turning from the viewport. Her movement reveals the full extent of her battle fatigue, uniform torn at the shoulder where emergency patches seal a pressure breach, dark circles beneath eyes that retain their tactical focus despite exhaustion. "Prepare for departure to rendezvous coordinates once, "

"Commander!" The sensor officer interrupts, an unprecedented breach of bridge protocol that immediately claims Selenea's full attention. "Caelus's signal is gone."

The words hang in the recycled air, their meaning requiring several seconds to penetrate her combat-fatigued mind. Selenea moves to the sensor station with three quick strides, leaning over the console where Caelus's signal pulsed steadily moments before. The display shows only empty terrain, and his identifier code is absent from the monitoring grid.

"Sensor malfunction?" she asks, voice maintaining professional calm that contradicts the sudden tightness in her chest.

The officer shakes his head, fingers already implementing diagnostic protocols with urgent efficiency. "Negative. All systems function within parameters. The signal terminated abruptly at coordinates 47-82-03. No degradation pattern consistent with equipment failure."

Selenea takes control of the console, and personal command codes override standard protocols to access deeper scanning systems. "Recalibrate for bio-signature detection. Ignore spore interference patterns. Focus on human metabolic readings."

The display shifts and terrain mapping is temporarily replaced by energy distribution patterns that reveal life signatures throughout the scanning grid. Fungal structures pulse with their distinctive biological rhythms, while smaller concentrations indicate ground team members moving toward extraction points. No signal appears at Caelus's last known position.

"Expand scanning parameters," she orders, fingers moving with increasing urgency. "Full spectrum analysis. Check for residual Aetheris energy signatures."

New data cascades across the display; specialized detection algorithms search for the unique energy patterns generated by Caelus's enhancement bands. These frequencies, recognizable even when dormant, leave trace signatures in surrounding environments for hours after use. The scan completes in seconds, returning empty results from the target coordinates.

"Deploy search drone," Selenea commands, abandoning the sensor station to access the tactical console. "Priority override. Maximum speed to last known coordinates."

The ship acknowledges with a soft tone, deployment systems activating as a specialized reconnaissance drone detaches from the ventral hull. The small craft accelerates toward the planet's surface, its trajectory forming a golden trail across tactical displays as it penetrates the spore layer.

"Last communication?" Selenea demands, attention fixed on the drone's descent path.

The communications officer reviews recent transmissions, isolating the relevant data stream. "Final communication received seven minutes ago. Standard status report. Eastern perimeter secure, battalion stragglers neutralized." He pauses, attention caught by an anomaly in the transmission log. "Wait, there's a partial transmission. Extremely brief. Time index matches signal disappearance."

"Play it," Selenea orders, moving to the communications station.

The system responds, audio filling the bridge with Caelus's voice, strained, urgent, cut short: "Selenea! Fractal breach at my position. Unknown hostiles. Request immediate,"

The transmission ends with jarring abruptness, leaving unnatural silence in its wake. The bridge crew freezes, each person processing the implications of those few words. Fractal breach. Unknown hostiles.

Selenea stands motionless for three heartbeats, the tactical part of her mind calculating possibilities while something deeper, more primal, screams for immediate action. When she moves again, it's with explosive force directed at the sensor console, her fist connecting with the display surface hard enough to crack the outer shell. The impact leaves a smear of blood across the screen, and knuckles split from the connection.

"Find him!" she shouts, voice cracking with an emotion her crew has never heard from her. "Full planetary scan. Check every, " She stops mid-sentence, disciplined control reasserting itself through force of will. Her next breath comes slower, deeper, as she steps back from the console.

The sensor officer stares at the blood on his display, uncertain how to respond to this unprecedented behavior from his commander. The drone reaches Caelus's last coordinates, and the visual feed shows empty terrain with fungal structures still displaying agitated bioluminescent patterns consistent with recent disturbance.

Selenea watches this feed, blood dripping from her knuckles onto the deck plates in slow, measured drops. Her back straightens imperceptibly, and her shoulders square as command discipline replaces momentary vulnerability. When she speaks again, her voice carries the flat, controlled tone her crew recognizes from critical combat situations.

"Set course for Marinami," she orders, returning to the command chair. "Maximum sustainable speed."

The navigation officer turns, confusion evident despite professional restraint. "Commander? Shouldn't we maintain the position for search operations?"

"He's not here," Selenea responds, certainty hardening her voice. "A Fractal breach means targeted extraction. Orpheus took him." Her fingers enter command sequences with methodical precision despite the blood still seeping from her injured hand. "We need allies. Set course now."

The navigation officer complies without further question, understanding dawning as tactical logic reasserts itself. The ship's engines shift tone as power redirects to propulsion systems, the subtle change in ambient vibration signaling acceleration toward their new destination.

Selenea activates the ship-wide communication system, her voice reaching every compartment and corridor. "This is Commander Selenea. My brother has been taken." She pauses, allowing the information to register before continuing. "I need all senior crew in the strategy room immediately. Prepare for full tactical assessment and response planning. This is not a recovery operation, and this is a rescue mission."

She deactivates the comm system, rising from the command chair with renewed purpose. Blood continues to drip from her injured hand, but she makes no move to treat the wound, its physical pain providing focus against the larger, more dangerous emotions threatening her tactical clarity.

"You have the bridge," she tells the second officer, already moving toward the exit. "Maintain course to Marinami. Estimated arrival time?"

"Four hours, seventeen minutes at maximum sustainable speed," the navigation officer responds.

Selenea nods once, acknowledgment and dismissal combined in a single efficient motion. The bridge doors slide open before her, then close with a soft pneumatic hiss as she disappears into the corridor beyond.

Alone in the turbolift that will carry her to the strategy room, Selenea finally allows herself three seconds of complete vulnerability. Her hands tremble violently, breath catching in her throat as the reality of Caelus's abduction fully registers. The moment passes exactly as she allows it to, precisely three seconds, before control returns, fingers steadying as she accesses preliminary planning protocols on her personal device.

"I'm coming, Caelus," she whispers to the empty lift, the words carrying absolute certainty rather than desperate hope. It was not a prayer but a promise, one sealed in blood and still drying on her knuckles.

The strategy room hums with tightly controlled energy as four women face each other across the holographic table. Selenea stands with military rigidity, the medical patch on her hand already soaking through with blood she refuses to acknowledge. Ven Diona remains near the doorway, Mordian spores still clinging to her environment suit in golden constellations that shift with each movement. Lyra Mareen and Meridia Flux, newly arrived from Marinami, create small puddles beneath their feet as seawater drips from their forms, their scales catching the harsh light in iridescent patterns that send colored reflections dancing across tactical displays.

"Orpheus took him," Selenea states without preamble, her voice flat and controlled. She activates the central projector with a quick gesture from her uninjured hand. "Twenty-three minutes ago. Fractal breach at these coordinates."

The hologram materializes above the table, and Mordia's surface is rendered in perfect topographical detail, focusing on the eastern perimeter where fungal forests thin into more navigable terrain. A pulsing red marker indicates Caelus's last known position.

"He managed one transmission before they cut him off." Selenea's finger hovers over control and then presses with deliberate pressure. The room fills with Caelus's voice, the same partial message that shattered the bridge's composure minutes earlier: "Selenea! Fractal breach at my position. Unknown hostiles. Request immediate, "

Meridia Flux's gill structures flutter with increased respiration, the only outward sign of her emotional response. "Battalion reinforcements?"

"No." Selenea shakes her head once, a sharp military negation. "Specialized extraction team. Precise. Efficient." Her finger swipes across the display, bringing up new data. "Sensor readings detected a Fractal energy signature consistent with controlled formation rather than combat deployment. This was planned."

The hologram shifts, displaying a spectral analysis of the dimensional tear's unique energy pattern. Complex mathematical formulas scroll alongside the visual representation, and algorithms attempt to identify distinct characteristics that might reveal the Fractal's destination.

"Without Caelus's Aetheris, we can't track battalion movements," Selenea continues, her tactical training evident in how she presents critical information first. "We're blind to their next targets. This wasn't just an attack on my brother, and it's a strategic move against our entire defense network."

Ven Diona steps forward, her methodical mind already analyzing environmental patterns within the data. Her fingers, still stained with Mordian biochemicals that resist standard decontamination, trace particular energy signatures within the Fractal analysis.

"These harmonics are distinctive," she notes, isolating specific frequency ranges within the display. "The crystalline structure shows precision formation consistent with established dimensional coordinates rather than ad hoc generation." She magnifies a particular section of the energy pattern. "The Fractal signature suggests Zathira. It's the only place with enough power to contain Aetheris."

The name hangs in the air between them, carrying weight beyond its syllables. Zathira, the space monastery, the cosmic nexus where multiple Fractal pathways naturally intersect. Their occasional ally, now potentially their greatest obstacle.

"That makes tactical sense," Selenea acknowledges, manipulating the display to show Zathira's known layout, incomplete intelligence gathered through years of limited cooperation and careful observation. "The monastery exists partially in normal space and partially in the void between realities. Perfect for containing abilities that transcend conventional physics."

Lyra Mareen moves closer to the table, her graceful swimmer's movements slightly awkward on dry land. Her hair, resembling flowing seaweed, has shifted from its natural blue to a deeper indigo that indicates tactical consideration. Her webbed hands spread across the edge of the table, fingers extending toward the holographic representation of Zathira.

"The monastery sits at a cosmic convergence point," she notes, eyes tracking the Fractal pathways that naturally intersect at Zathira's location. "If I can access their water reservoirs, every habitat requires hydration systems, and I can create a distraction at their defenses. Manipulate pressure points within their life support infrastructure."

Her fingers mimic the movements that would direct such manipulation, small currents forming in the puddles at her feet as her abilities unconsciously respond to her strategic thinking. "Their outer defenses rely heavily on conventional technology despite their spiritual appearances. Water circulates through cooling systems, environmental controls, and waste management."

Meridia Flux paces with restless energy, scales shifting between deep blue and violet as she processes the tactical challenge. Unlike Lyra's awkward land movement, Meridia carries herself with aggressive precision, her Marinami Defense Corps training evident in every motion.

"And I can disrupt their energy shields," she adds, stopping to face the others. Her white facial markings glow faintly with increased focus. "Marinami developed countermeasures against electromagnetic barriers during the Third Battalion incursion. The principles should transfer to Zathira's defensive systems."

She approaches the hologram, manipulating the display to highlight what intelligence suggests are Zathira's shield generators. "These nodes operate on resonance principles similar to Fractal harmonics. Targeted hydrokinetic pulses at precisely calculated frequencies will create disruption windows, temporary but sufficient for insertion."

The four women study the projection in momentary silence, each processing elements relevant to their specialties. The hologram rotates slowly, revealing Zathira's impossible architecture, structures that follow sacred geometric patterns mirroring the crystalline structure of Fractals themselves.

"We'll need precise timing," Selenea notes, as well as tactical mind-calculating approach vectors and coordination requirements. "Zathira's unique position means conventional assault strategies won't work. We'll have one opportunity before their adaptive defenses reconfigure."

Her fingers manipulate the display, creating a three-dimensional timeline with color-coded insertion points and coordination markers. "Lyra disrupts water systems here, creating resource allocation conflicts in their defense grid. Meridia targets shield generators during the resulting power fluctuations. Theinsertion team enters through this maintenance access point, which is lightly defended but requires specialized environmental equipment for void exposure."

Ven studies these plans with characteristic methodical attention. "Zathira's environmental systems are highly specialized. The pocket of stabilized space-time they maintain requires constant adjustment. If we introduce specific compounds derived from Mordian fungal structures..." She manipulates a section of the display, calculating chemical reactions with practiced precision. "We can temporarily destabilize their atmospheric regulators without risking catastrophic failure."

Selenea nods, incorporating this suggestion into the evolving tactical display. "That gives us a three-minute window before their adaptive systems compensate. Enough time to locate and extract Caelus if our intelligence is correct."

"And if he's not there?" Meridia asks the question directly rather than doubtfully.

"He's there." Selenea's certainty carries absolute conviction. "Orpheus wants his Aetheris ability. Zathira contains chambers designed specifically for ability containment and study. It's the logical destination."

She zooms the holographic display to focus on Zathira's central sanctuary. "We won't get a second attempt. This operation requires perfect execution from all teams, synchronized down to fifteen-second intervals."

Her fingers trace paths through the projected structure, mapping extraction routes with the efficiency of someone who converts fear into operational parameters. "Orpheus won't keep him alive long once he realizes Caelus won't cooperate with whatever he has planned."

The timeline expands to include phase two, extraction pathways and emergency contingencies for various scenarios. The women study these with a professional focus, mentally rehearsing their roles within the complex operation.

"Once we breach the inner sanctuary, communication may become impossible," Selenea warns. "Zathira's core chambers exist partially in the void between realities. Standard transmission protocols fail under those conditions."

Lyra nods, understanding. "Marinamian bioluminescent signaling can function in void conditions. We've tested it in deep-space environments." Her hair shifts slightly, demonstrating subtle color changes that constitute an alternative communication system. "I can adapt our emergency protocols for the team."

"Prepare for immediate departure," Selenea concludes, straightening to her full height as the planning phase transitions to implementation. "We launch in ten minutes. This is a volunteer mission, and the risks extend beyond standard operational parameters."

The statement is a formality rather than a genuine option. No one moves to leave. Ven Diona begins calculating final adjustments to her environmental compounds. Lyra and Meridia exchange brief glances that confirm the shared commitment, their Marinamian defense training creating wordless tactical understanding.

The women disperse with practiced efficiency, each moving to prepare specialized equipment and review their mission parameters. Selenea remains at the holographic table, manipulating controls to display one final image, Caelus's last known location, the Fractal energy signature still visible as fading traces in the sensor data.

Her fingers hover over the hologram, not quite touching the projection of her brother's last known position. The medical patch on her hand has soaked completely through with blood, yet she shows no sign of discomfort. For a brief moment, with no witnesses present, her expression shifts from tactical determination to something more vulnerable, more raw.

"I'm coming, Caelus," she whispers, then switches off the display with a single decisive motion. The hologram dissipates into nothingness, leaving only empty air where, moments before, her brother's last coordinates glowed with fading hope.

She turns and leaves the strategy room, back straight, steps measured, every movement projecting the confidence her crew needs to see. Behind her, the blood from her injured hand leaves a single drop on the floor, the only evidence of the fear she refuses to acknowledge, even to herself.

Chapter 19

Return to Zathira

The ship cuts through the asteroid field surrounding Zathira, engines whispering against the void. Selenea guides it with precise movements, her injured hand leaving smears of blood on the controls. The space monastery looms ahead, an impossible structure of ancient stone and crystalline formations that pulse with internal light, existing partially in normal space and partially somewhere else entirely. Its geometric patterns mirror the crystalline structure of Fractals themselves, pathways of light connecting sections that shouldn't physically align yet somehow form a cohesive whole.

"Defensive systems active but not targeting," reports the sensor officer, voice tight with tension. "They know we're here."

Selenea nods once, eyes never leaving the approaching structure. The bioluminescent crystals studding Zathira's exterior flare briefly as the ship passes certain thresholds, ancient warning systems acknowledging their presence without yet determining the threat level. Behind her, the bridge crew maintains disciplined silence, each person armed but with weapons concealed beneath standard uniforms. The plan requires subtlety until the final moment.

"Lyra, Meridia, status?" Selenea asks, guiding the ship through a particularly narrow gap between asteroids that drift in mathematically precise orbits around the monastery.

"Hydro-disruption systems primed," Lyra confirms from her position near the environmental controls. Her hair has shifted to combat-ready crimson, webbed fingers resting on specialized equipment designed for the mission. "Ready to target their water reservoirs once we establish access."

Meridia stands beside her, scales shifting between deep blue and violet as she monitors shield frequencies. "Countermeasures calibrated to their resonance patterns. First disruption window estimated at thirty seconds after initiation."

Ven Diona completes final adjustments to the canisters containing Mordian compounds, her movements methodical despite the tension permeating the bridge. "Atmospheric destabilizers ready. Three-minute window once deployed."

The ship approaches the designated docking port, a seemingly minor access point that intelligence suggests connects to maintenance corridors less heavily monitored than primary entrances. Selenea engages in docking procedures with deliberate care, her injured hand throbbing beneath the blood-soaked medical patch. She feels nothing from the wound, and her focus is narrowed entirely to the mission parameters. The pain registers as distant information, relevant only as a potential limitation to combat effectiveness.

"Docking sequence initiated," she announces as magnetic clamps engage with soft metallic sounds that reverberate through the hull. "Prepare for insertion."

The airlock cycles with ancient precision, mechanisms that have operated for centuries, adjusting to connect with their ship's more modern systems. Through the viewport, Zathira's crystalline structures emit pulses of light that create shadows where none should exist, effects of the monastery's partial existence in the void between realities.

The crew moves toward the airlock, Selenea leading with Ven close behind. Lyra and Meridia take flanking positions, and their Marinamian combat stances are adapted to the artificial gravity environment. Each step brings them closer to the point of no return, the moment when their presence will transition from unexpected visitors to hostile intrusion.

The airlock completes its cycle with a hiss of equalizing pressure. The door slides open to reveal the stone corridor beyond, but the passage isn't empty.

Reality tears open before them, multiple vertical rifts forming with crystalline precision. Blue energy rims each Fractal opening as massive figures materialize in perfect geometric positioning that blocks all approaches to the monastery's interior. The Valthorim guardians step through these dimensional breaches with a fluid grace that belies their imposing size.

Their forms shift between solid presence and void absence, making it impossible to focus on them directly. Hooded in deep black cloaks that seem to absorb light rather than merely block it, they tower over the crew by at least a meter. Where faces should be, only darkness shows beneath their hoods, occasionally punctuated by points of light like distant stars glimpsed through cosmic dust.

"Trespassers at the cosmic nexus," they speak in perfect unison, their voices carrying harmonic undertones that seem to originate from everywhere simultaneously. The sound vibrates not just through the air but through the molecular structure of the corridor itself, resonating in ways that trigger primal recognition of something fundamentally beyond human comprehension. "Your presence disrupts the universal balance."

Selenea steps forward, favoring her uninjured side with a subtlety that only trained observers would notice. Her stance projects authority despite facing entities that existed before stars formed.

"I come for my brother," she states, voice clear and unwavering. "Caelus Solaris, taken against his will from Mordia through unauthorized Fractal breach. His abduction violates cosmic law."

The Valthorim shift positions with perfect synchronization, their movements suggesting communication occurring at levels beyond conventional perception. The crystalline structures embedded in the corridor walls pulse with increased frequency, responding to the guardians' presence.

"The balance requires adjustment," they respond, voices layering in complex harmonics that create meaning beyond the words themselves. "Orpheus works to restore cosmic equilibrium. Your brother's ability serves universal necessity."

Selenea takes another step forward, entering the space between worlds where the Valthorim partially exists. The air here feels thinner, charged with energies that prickle against exposed skin and raise the fine hairs on her arms. The scent of ancient incense mingles with a metallic tang unique to Zathira, and the smell of reality itself is wearing thin at the boundaries.

"Kidnapping isn't equilibrium," she counters, entering the monastery proper now. Behind her, the crew remains at the threshold, weapons still concealed but hands positioned for immediate access. "Orpheus violates the Valthorim's own principles of non-interference."

The corridor stretches before them, illuminated by pulsing crystals embedded in ornate archways carved with sigils that match those tattooed on Caelus's skin. The stone beneath their feet, actual stone in this age of synthetic materials, bears the patina of countless footsteps over millennia, worn smooth by the passage of entities whose nature defies conventional understanding.

The Valthorim move closer, their forms rippling like shadow and light intermingling. "You understand nothing of cosmic principles," they state, the harmonics in their voices taking on a deeper, more ominous tone. "Orpheus serves purposes beyond your comprehension."

"I understand my brother was taken by force," Selenea responds, her hand moving to her side, where her weapon remains hidden beneath her uniform. The medical patch has soaked completely through now, fresh blood seeping between her fingers. "I understand Orpheus fears what Caelus can perceive through Aetheris. I understand that fear suggests guilt."

The statement hangs in the space between them, its implications rippling through the corridor like the pulse of distant stars. The crystalline structures react, their light patterns shifting to faster, more agitated sequences that cast dancing shadows across the ancient stone walls.

The Valthorim confer in frequencies beyond human hearing, their cloaks rippling with energy discharges that manifest as brief flickers of cosmic imagery, nebulae forming and collapsing, stars birthing and dying, all in fractions of seconds.

"Your interference risks more than you comprehend," they finally respond. "Universal balance hangs by threads you cannot perceive."

"Then let me speak with Orpheus directly," Selenea demands, refusing to retreat despite the overwhelming presence of beings that could erase her existence with a thought. "If his purpose serves cosmic law, he should welcome witnesses."

The standoff intensifies, energy building in the narrow space between human determination and cosmic power. The monastery itself seems to respond, structural vibrations traveling through stone and crystal alike, creating harmonies that resonate with the Valthorim's presence.

Finally, one guardian steps forward, its form solidifying slightly as it focuses its attention entirely on Selenea.

"You may enter alone," it pronounces, voice now distinct from the unified chorus. "The others remain here. Interference with Orpheus's work will bring consequences beyond your comprehension. The void awaits those who disrupt cosmic necessity."

Selenea nods once, a soldier's acknowledgment of terms accepted. She turns to her crew, eyes meeting each person briefly before settling on Ven.

"Begin the countdown," she says quietly, the words carrying meaning beyond their surface instruction. "I'll find him."

She turns back to the Valthorim, straightening to her full height despite the pain that flares through her injured side with the movement.

"Lead on," she commands, stepping fully into Zathira's domain, leaving bloody footprints on the stone that has witnessed the birth and death of galaxies.

Caelus sits cross-legged in the center of the meditation chamber, enhancement bands cold and dark against his raw fingers. The room exists partially in the void, its boundaries shifting between solid stone and transparent nothingness that reveals the raw fabric of reality beyond. Fractal windows surround him in perfect geometric alignment, each one showing a different cosmic vista, a star collapsing into itself, a nebula birthing new solar systems, and a black hole devouring light at the edge of a galaxy. The blood in his eyes has dried to rusty crescents, but new ruptures form as he strains to maintain awareness against the sedative still coursing through his system.

His sigils glow faintly beneath his tattered environment suit, responding to the cosmic energies permeating the chamber despite his inability to channel them. Each breath draws air that tastes like the space between stars, impossibly cold yet somehow burning in his lungs, carrying particles that shouldn't exist in conventional reality.

Orpheus circles him with measured steps, his tall form occasionally rippling like shadow poured over light. His movements produce no sound against the ancient stone floor as if he is treading on the concept of the surface rather than the physical structure itself. The ornate mask concealing his features catches light from the Fractal windows, its intricate sigils shifting slightly with each passing moment, rearranging themselves in subtle patterns that strain the eye to follow.

"Why didn't I sense you?" Caelus asks, voice rough from disuse. He focuses on the enhancement bands, willing them to activate despite knowing they've been dampened by Zathira's unique properties. "Aetheris connects to everything composed of stardust. Everything has a cosmic origin. You should have appeared in the threads."

Orpheus completes another circuit around him, unhurried, considering. His cloak moves with unnatural fluidity, edges blurring as if constantly recalculating their position in space-time.

"You cannot sense what predates sensing itself," Orpheus responds, those harmonic undertones more pronounced in this chamber that amplifies cosmic frequencies. "Your perception extends only to that which emerged after the division. After the error."

Caelus's brow furrows, analytical mind working despite the sedative fog. "What division?"

Orpheus stops directly before him, towering over his seated form. His hands, if they can be called hands, rise slowly to the edges of his mask. "The division that created your universe. The mistake we have come to correct."

The mask detaches with a sound like reality tearing. Orpheus removes it with ceremonial slowness, revealing not flesh or even alien features but a swirling vortex of dark matter, particles that exist primarily through their gravitational effects rather than conventional physical properties. Where a face should be, cosmic winds shape and reshape patterns that resemble eyes, mouths, and expressions before dissolving back into primal chaos. Stars twinkle within the swirling mass, captured or perhaps born there, struggling against the darkness that contains them.

Caelus recoils instinctively, their body recognizing something fundamentally wrong before his mind can process it. The sigils across his skin flare brighter in warning, ancient protection mechanisms activating against a threat older than the symbols themselves.

"What are you?" he whispers, the question emerging unbidden.

The darkness shifts, approximating a smile with terrible precision. "I am Valthorim. The original state. Before the schism that created your stars, your worlds, your limited perception of existence."

The Fractal windows pulse in response to these words, their vistas shifting to show earlier cosmic states, the universe as it was forming, galaxies coalescing from primordial matter, the first stars igniting in the darkness.

"The Valthorim was unified once," Orpheus continues dark matter swirling faster as he speaks. "A single consciousness existing in perfect harmony with the void. Then came the division, those who wished to create, to fill the emptiness with matter and energy and eventually life." His form ripples with what might be disgust. "And those, like myself, who understood that creation was contamination. Complexity where simplicity reigned. Chaos where order once existed."

Understanding dawns in Caelus, pieces connecting across years of observations. The Valthorim's mysterious appearances throughout history, their manipulation of Fractal pathways, and their seemingly contradictory interventions in cosmic affairs. The enhancement bands warm slightly against his fingers, responding to his accelerating thoughts even without an active connection.

"The monastery," he says, gaze sweeping across the chamber's impossible architecture. "Zathira exists where both factions can meet. A neutral ground between creation and void."

"A compromise," Orpheus confirms, the darkness within him momentarily revealing glimpses of entire galaxies swirling in miniature. "One that has allowed the contamination to spread unchecked for too long. Your stars multiply. Your life forms evolve. The original perfection recedes with each passing eon."

Caelus's mind races ahead, connecting implications with horrifying clarity. "The Battalions. The attacks on worlds with unique defense capabilities. You've been eliminating resistance."

"Systematic reduction of complexity," Orpheus corrects, moving closer. The temperature drops precipitously with his approach, frost forming along the edges of Caelus's environment suit. "Returning chaotic systems to ordered states. Preparing the universe for its restoration."

Horror spreads through Caelus, a cold more penetrating than the chamber's void-touched atmosphere. "You've been using me," he realizes, memories realigning with new context. "My Aetheris ability, tracking planetary defenders, finding resistance leaders, I've been helping you target them."

"Your perception exceeds conventional limitations," Orpheus acknowledges. "You see the threads that connect all stardust-born entities. You find those our sensors cannot detect. Those who might otherwise have escaped the cleansing."

The revelation strikes Caelus with physical force, stealing his breath. His hands clench into fists despite the pain from raw, blistered skin. Blood vessels ruptured in his left eye as the implications cascaded through his consciousness: every mission, every target he tracked, every "victory" against Battalion forces suddenly recontextualized as moves in a game he didn't know he was playing.

"The people who died fighting the Battalions," he says softly, "they were the ones who could have stopped you."

"Some," Orpheus confirms, dark matter swirling with increased velocity. "Others merely presented inefficiencies to be eliminated. The universe returns to darkness one light at a time."

Caelus struggles to rise, legs unsteady beneath him after hours in the meditation position. The sigils across his body pulse with increasing urgency, responding to both his emotional state and the proximity of Orpheus's true form.

"There are still defenders," he challenges, finding strength in defiance despite his physical weakness. "My sister, "

"Your sister's rebellion was unexpected," Orpheus interrupts, the darkness within his form briefly constricting around the captured stars, "but ultimately irrelevant. She delays the inevitable. The universe will return to its perfect state."

Orpheus moves to the chamber's center, hands extending toward control interfaces that respond to his proximity with soft illumination. The Fractal windows shift in response, their vistas accelerating through cosmic time, showing stars dying, galaxies cooling, and energy dissipating into the void.

"You will aid in the final stages," he states, not a request but a declaration of cosmic certainty. "Your Aetheris will locate the remaining resistance leaders. Those who still fight against universal entropy. Those who perpetuate the contamination of existence with their persistent order."

Caelus backs away until he meets the chamber's wall, solid stone one moment, void-touched emptiness the next. The enhancement bands remain dark against his fingers, but the sigils across his body burn brighter, responding to his desperation with the ancient power that predates their current forms.

"I won't help you," he states, voice finding strength in absolute certainty. "I'll die first."

"Death is irrelevant," Orpheus responds, dark matter rippling with what might be amusement. "Your consciousness will be extracted. Your perception is harnessed. Your cooperation is preferred but not required."

He approaches a specialized apparatus that rises from the chamber floor with sinuous mechanical movement. Its design suggests both ancient craftsmanship and technology beyond current understanding, crystalline components merging with materials that shift between solid and energy states without clear transition.

"The process begins now," Orpheus states, activating sequences with precise gestures. "Your sister approaches through the outer corridors, as predicted. Her presence will provide additional motivation for your compliance."

Caelus feels a surge of both hope and terror at this revelation; Selenea is coming, but walking into a trap Orpheus has anticipated from the beginning. The enhancement bands warm slightly against his fingers as his determination crystalizes. He must resist. Must delay. Must give Selenea any possible advantage in the confrontation to come.

"The universe chose creation," he says, straightening despite the pain that courses through his depleted body. "The stars exist because your faction lost the original argument. Life emerged because it was meant to emerge."

"A temporary anomaly," Orpheus dismisses, the dark matter within him consuming another tiny star. "The void awaits us all."

Selenea moves through Zathira's labyrinthine corridors, each step leaving faint bloody footprints on ancient stone. The monastery guides her despite itself, floating platforms materializing beneath her feet when pathways suddenly end at void-space, doorways shifting into alignment as she approaches junctions that should lead nowhere. The air grows thinner as she penetrates deeper into the structure, carrying scents of incense and ozone that burn in her lungs. Her injured hand throbs with each heartbeat, pain providing clarity against the disorienting effects of a place that exists partially beyond conventional reality.

Massive archways carved with ancient sigils pulse with energy as she passes, their patterns matching those tattooed on Caelus's body, connections to cosmic forces established millennia before either of them existed. Some symbols brighten at her proximity, responding to the blood seeping through her medical patch, recognizing its connection to someone who bears their permanent marks.

"Brother," she whispers, the word carrying no sound but still traveling through whatever bond connects them despite Zathira's interference. She feels him, not with standard senses but through something deeper, more primal. The same connection that always helped her find him when they played among hologram museums as children now draw her through impossible architecture toward the monastery's heart.

A corridor ends abruptly at a vertical shaft that plunges both upward and downward into darkness. No visible means of traversal presents itself, yet as Selenea approaches, a platform detaches from the wall, floating toward her with deliberate intent. She steps onto it without hesitation, and the balance is perfect despite her injuries. The platform moves immediately, accelerating downward into depths where the boundary between physical space and void grows increasingly permeable.

The descent terminates at a circular chamber where multiple corridors converge like spokes on a wheel. At the chamber's center hovers a three-dimensional projection of the entire monastery complex, an accurate model showing both its physical structure and the void-spaces between areas that exist in dimensional states conventional sensors cannot detect.

Selenea moves toward the projection, her reflection distorted on the polished stone floor. Her injured hand passes through the holographic representation, and blood droplets fall through the image to connect with specific locations. The model responds, certain sections illuminating with increased intensity, creating a path through the monastery's most heavily protected regions, a route that shouldn't be accessible to unauthorized visitors.

She follows this newly revealed path through corridors that narrow progressively, walls pressing closer with each turn until she must move sideways through certain passages. The stone itself seems alive here, warm beneath her touch, vibrating with subtle frequencies that resonate with the sigils carved into its surface.

Voices echo ahead, one familiar despite its weakness, the other carrying those unsettling harmonic undertones she recognizes from the Valthorim guardians, but somehow deeper, more fundamentally wrong. Selenea presses against the wall beside a doorway, listening to the exchange within.

"The Valthorim created life for a reason," Caelus argues, his voice strained but determined. "Even your faction must have seen purpose in consciousness, or you would have destroyed it immediately."

"Purpose?" The harmonic voice responds with what might be amusement. "The purpose of an infection is to spread. The purpose of a disorder is to grow. These are not virtues but flaws in the cosmic structure, errors we have tolerated too long out of misplaced curiosity."

Selenea peers around the doorway's edge. The chamber beyond exists partially in void space, its boundaries fluid rather than fixed. Fractal windows surround its perimeter, showing cosmic vistas that are impossible to view from conventional space-time. At its center stands Caelus, sigils glowing beneath his tattered environment suit, facing a figure whose edges blur into shadow.

The figure, Orpheus, with his mask removed, consists of not flesh but swirling dark matter, particles that exist primarily through gravitational effects rather than conventional physical properties. Stars twinkle within the cosmic vortex of his form, captured or perhaps born there, struggling against the darkness that contains them.

"Your sister approaches," Orpheus states, turning toward an apparatus that rises from the chamber floor. "Her presence proves useful. The severance of familial bonds provides excellent motivation for Aetheris cooperation."

The apparatus activates crystalline components connecting with materials that shift between solid and energy states. It extends toward Caelus, focusing on the enhancement bands around his fingers. Energy begins to flow, not into the bands but from them, drawing out the Aetheris connection that defines his unique perception.

Selenea moves without conscious decision, and tactical training converts observation to action in microseconds. She emerges from the doorway at full sprint, weapon drawn, injured hand forgotten as adrenaline overrides pain receptors. Three precise shots strike the apparatus, disrupting its energy flow and sending crystalline components shattering across the chamber floor.

"Step away from my brother," she commands, voice carrying the absolute authority she normally reserves for combat operations. Her weapon remains trained on Orpheus's dark matter form, though instinct tells her conventional energy weapons will have minimal effect against something so fundamentally different from normal matter.

"Selenea!" Caelus's face transforms, exhaustion momentarily eclipsed by desperate relief. Blood vessels have burst in both his eyes, filling the whites with crimson webs. His hands, blistered and raw where the enhancement bands connect, reach toward her with the instinctive need for contact.

She crosses to him in four quick strides, one hand maintaining a weapon target on Orpheus while the other clasps her brother's shoulder. The touch grounds them both, a physical confirmation of survival against impossible odds. Their eyes meet, volumes of information exchanged in that brief contact, his warning, her determination, shared understanding of what they face.

"He's not human," Caelus says urgently, words rushing out as precious seconds tick away. "He's Valthorim, the original faction that opposed creation itself. The Battalions, the attacks on defensive worlds, all part of his plan to return the universe to darkness."

Orpheus's dark matter form expands, filling more of the chamber with cold void energy that drops ambient temperature precipitously. Frost forms along the edge of Selenea's uniform, crystallizing her exhaled breath before it fully leaves her lungs.

"The sister arrives as predicted," Orpheus notes, his harmonic voice resonating through the chamber's structure itself. "Your tactical approach was calculated to ninety-seven percent accuracy. Even your weapon choice matches our behavioral models."

Selenea positions herself partially in front of Caelus, creating a defensive stance that protects her injured brother while maintaining offensive capability. "Your models didn't predict Mordia," she counters. "Or Marinami. Worlds fighting back doesn't fit your calculations."

"Temporary anomalies," Orpheus dismisses, dark matter swirling faster around the captured stars within his form. "Statistical noise in the inevitable progression toward entropy."

The Fractal windows surrounding the chamber pulse with sudden increased energy, not responding to controls but to something happening throughout the monastery itself. Reality tears at the edges, small Fractal openings appearing along the chamber's perimeter, each one revealing glimpses of distant space-time locations connected through dimensional mathematics too complex for human comprehension.

The Valthorim guardians materialize through these openings, their hooded forms solidifying as they step into the chamber with synchronized movements. Unlike Orpheus, they maintain a humanoid shape, though their edges still blur into shadow where conventional reality struggles to contain their true nature.

"Orpheus," the guardians speak in a unified voice, "you violate the compact. Zathira remains neutral ground between factions. Your actions threaten the balance."

"Balance?" Orpheus's form expands further, darkness flowing like liquid into the corners of the chamber. "Your faction's experiment has reached its conclusion. The data is clear: creation leads only to disorder, suffering, and extinction. The original state beckons."

The chamber trembles, architectural components shifting as the partial void-space responds to conflicting cosmic entities within its boundaries. More Fractals begin opening throughout the structure, not controlled pathways but tears. In reality, dimensional mathematics is destabilizing under the strain of opposed Valthorim's presence.

Through one such tear, Selenea glimpses the bridge of her ship, where Ven, Lyra, and Meridia monitor tactical displays with growing concern. The countdown they initiated earlier approaches critical thresholds, and their sabotage of Zathira's environmental systems is progressing despite the escalating cosmic confrontation.

"The compact preserved both approaches," the guardians counter, moving to form a living barrier between Orpheus and the siblings. "Creation and void, balanced in eternal coexistence."

"A failed experiment," Orpheus responds, the dark matter now filling half the chamber, temperature dropping to levels that burn human skin on contact. "The void is the natural state. Stars die. Planets cool. Energy dissipates. All returns to darkness eventually; we merely accelerate the inevitable."

Caelus struggles to stand straighter, enhancement bands flickering weakly as they attempt to reestablish Aetheris connection. "You fear what we've become," he challenges. "Life adapting, evolving, connecting. You fear we'll reach your level eventually."

The dark matter surrounding Orpheus contracts suddenly, stars within his form dimming as if squeezed by an invisible force. When it expands again, the cold intensifies, freezing the very air molecules in sections of the chamber.

"Your interference ends now," Orpheus declares, his form losing all pretense of humanoid shape as it expands toward the ceiling in a column of pure dark matter. The Fractal tears widen throughout the monastery, reality itself straining under the pressure of cosmic forces in opposition. "The void awaits us all."

Selenea grips her brother's arm, calculating their increasingly limited options as the temperature continues to plummet and reality fragments around them. The guardians maintain their position between Orpheus and the siblings, their own forms shifting more rapidly between states as the conflict escalates toward physical manifestation.

The chamber shudders again, more violently this time, as Zathira's very foundations respond to the cosmic discord within its walls. Through the widening Fractal tears, the void beyond conventional reality becomes increasingly visible, not merely emptiness but something alive with potential and threat in equal measure, the original state from which all creation emerged and to which Orpheus believes it must return.

Chapter 20

Orpheus Unmasked

Selenea crouches in the shadow of a crystalline outcropping, studying Zathira's outer perimeter through narrowed eyes. The space monastery hangs impossibly against the void, defying conventional physics as portions of its structure fade in and out of reality. Blood pulses beneath the tight grip of her fingers around her weapon, adrenaline pushing back the exhaustion of the journey. She has one chance to find Caelus before the Valthorim realize she's not where they think she is.

The Valthorim guardian who escorted her inside believes she's following the designated path to meet Orpheus. They don't know about the secondary plan, Ven's environmental compounds already seeping through Zathira's atmospheric systems, and Lyra and Meridia's sabotage of the water and power infrastructure. The countdown has begun. She has eighteen minutes before those systems fail.

A security panel glows with soft blue light beside an unmarked doorway. Selenea studies its crystalline interface, recognizing sigils similar to those tattooed across Caelus's skin. Her fingers hover over the patterns, recalling her brother's explanations of their meaning, cosmic anchors, dimensional keystones, and paths between realities. She presses them in the sequence she's seen him use during Aetheris connection.

The panel flashes red. A crystalline needle extends with sudden speed, piercing her palm before she can withdraw. Selenea suppresses a gasp, watching as the device draws blood through microscopic channels in the crystal. The security measure isn't designed to injure but to verify, to confirm that her blood carries the same cosmic markers as the authorized user it seeks.

"Blood recognition protocol," she whispers, remembering Caelus's offhand comment about Zathira's unconventional security. "They're testing for Solari's lineage."

The panel shifts from red to amber as it analyzes the sample. Selenea pulls her hand free, blood welling from the small puncture to join the partially dried stains from her earlier injury. She tears a strip from her undertunic, wrapping it hastily around her palm. The makeshift bandage soaks through immediately, blood continuing to seep between her fingers.

The panel finally shifts to green. The door slides open with a sound like distant chimes, revealing a corridor that shouldn't exist according to any schematic. Selenea slips through, the door sealing behind her with the same musical tone.

The passage beyond pulses with bioluminescent light. Crystals embedded in the walls react to her presence, brightening as she passes before dimming once more. The floor beneath her feet isn't stone but something that gives slightly with each step, as if testing her weight against some cosmic standard. The air carries the scent of incense mixed with an electrical tang that reminds her of lightning strikes on Solarune, ozone and potential.

Selenea follows the corridor's gentle curve, staying low where the ceiling dips toward the void space. Blood drips from her wrapped hand, leaving a trail of dark droplets that the floor absorbs without a trace. The monastery seems alive around her; its very structure is aware of her presence but allows her passage, perhaps curious about her purpose, perhaps recognizing her connection to someone already within its walls.

Voices echo ahead. Selenea freezes, pressing herself against the wall as two Valthorim guardians pass through an intersecting corridor. Their hooded forms drift rather than walk, edges blurring into the surrounding air as if they exist partially in another dimension. Where their cloaks brush the crystal walls, the bioluminescence dims momentarily, responding to whatever void-energy comprises their true nature.

She holds her breath until they pass, not certain if they need conventional senses to detect intruders. The blood from her injured hand trickles down her wrist, collecting at her elbow before falling to the floor in perfectly timed drops that match her heartbeat. Each drop disappears into the living surface, the monastery consuming this offering without comment.

A Fractal window materializes in the wall beside her, opening without warning to reveal a vista of distant space where stars collapse into themselves. The cosmic view shifts as she watches, focusing on a particular system where planets orbit a dying sun. Within seconds, the window closes again, leaving only a smooth crystal where it appeared. She can't be certain which is a test or a message.

Selenea continues forward, finding a maintenance shaft that drops vertically through multiple levels of the monastery. Unlike the polished corridors, this passage shows signs of conventional use: handholds worn smooth by centuries of grip, tool marks on access panels, and the faint residue of oil from mechanical systems. She descends quickly, using her uninjured hand to control her speed while scanning for patrols below.

The void-touched spaces grow more frequent as she penetrates deeper into Zathira's structure. Patches of corridor simply cease to exist in normal space-time, requiring her to step through dimensional fluctuations that pull at her molecular structure. Each transition burns like static electricity against her skin, leaving behind a lingering numbness that spreads with each passage.

Her tactical training keeps her oriented despite the monastery's impossible geometry. She maintains a mental map as corridors branch and rejoin in patterns that defy conventional architecture. The blood trail she leaves becomes her most reliable reference point, a molecule-thin connection to normal physics in a place where reality itself is negotiable.

A subtle vibration travels through the structure, growing stronger as she approaches the monastery's core. Not mechanical but harmonic, a resonance created by powerful energies contained within specific chambers. Selenea recognizes the pattern from her brother's description of Aetheris connections, the distinctive frequency generated when cosmic perception bridges dimensional boundaries.

"Close," she whispers to herself, following the vibration to its source.

She reaches a circular chamber where multiple corridors converge. At its center floats a holographic representation of the entire monastery, showing both physical structures and void spaces that conventional sensors cannot detect. Selenea approaches cautiously, watching as the projection responds to her presence, certain sections illuminating to create a path through Zathira's most heavily protected regions.

The monastery guides her, whether out of recognition of her blood connection to Caelus or for purposes of its own, she cannot determine. She follows the indicated route, moving through increasingly narrow passages until she reaches an ornate doorway inscribed with sigils that match those on her brother's skin. The symbols glow with soft amber light as she approaches, responding to the blood still dripping from her injured hand.

Selenea touches the door with blood-slick fingers. It dissolves rather than opens, matter transitioning to energy before reassembling behind her as she steps through. The central sanctuary spreads before her, a vast chamber that exists simultaneously in normal space and the void between realities.

Fractal windows surround the room's perimeter, each opening to a different cosmic vista impossible to view from conventional space-time. A massive holographic star map dominates the ceiling, tracking disturbances across multiple galaxies with crystalline precision. Ancient sigils carved into stone walls pulse with ethereal energy, their patterns shifting subtly as if communicating in a language too complex for human comprehension.

In the chamber's center, Caelus kneels within a containment field of dark energy. Bands of void-force suppress his Aetheris ability, wrapping around his throat and wrists like a living shadow. His enhancement bands, burned and damaged from the escape on Mordia, lie dormant against his raw fingers. Blood has dried in rusty crescents beneath his eyes, evidence of ruptured vessels from pushing his perception beyond sustainable limits.

The apparatus generating the containment field rises from the floor with sinuous mechanical movement, its design suggesting technology beyond current understanding, crystalline components merging with materials that shift between solid and energy states without clear transition. It hums with a frequency that sets Selenea's teeth on edge, a sound that exists partially beyond conventional hearing.

Selenea steps forward, and the weapon is drawn, blood still dripping from her injured hand. The star map above flickers momentarily, cosmic patterns adjusting to her presence in the sanctuary. Behind Caelus, partially concealed in shadows that bend impossibly around his form, stands Orpheus, watching, waiting, his mask concealing whatever passes for a face on a being older than stars themselves.

The moment of infiltration ends. The confrontation begins.

Selenea assesses the containment apparatus with a soldier's precision, identifying power nodes where the dark energy converges. Her weapon, designed for ship-to-ship combat rather than precision work, feels suddenly inadequate against technology that predates human civilization. She adjusts the settings anyway, cranking the energy output to a maximum while narrowing the beam focus to its most concentrated point. Blood from her injured hand makes the grip slick, but her aim remains steady as she sights down the barrel.

"Step away from the containment field," she calls, voice echoing through the sanctuary's impossible architecture. The command serves as both warning and distraction, drawing attention as she shifts position for optimal firing angle.

Orpheus turns, mask catching the light from the Fractal windows in patterns that strain human vision. "The sister arrives as predicted," he says, harmonic undertones in his voice setting the crystalline components vibrating at molecular levels. "Your tactical approach matches our models to ninety-seven percent accuracy."

Selenea fires three shots in rapid succession, ignoring his words entirely. The energy beams, modified to penetrate ship hull plating, strike the containment apparatus at precisely calculated weak points where power conduits connect to stabilization nodes. The first shot severs the primary energy loop, unleashing a cascade of purple-white sparks that dance across the sanctuary floor. The second disrupts the temporal stabilizer that prevents Caelus from accessing the Aetheris. The third destroys the neural interface attempting to extract his consciousness patterns.

The containment field flickers, dark energy bands wavering like disturbed water before dissipating entirely. Caelus collapses forward, enhancement bands clattering against the stone floor. The sound echoes through the chamber, harmonizing briefly with vibrations still traveling through the crystalline structures from Orpheus's voice.

Selenea closes the distance in three quick strides, dropping to one knee beside her brother. Her hand, the uninjured one, grips his shoulder, finding it thinner than she remembers, muscle mass already diminishing from whatever extraction process Orpheus initiated. Caelus looks up, blood-filled eyes struggling to focus on her face. Recognition dawns slowly, fighting through layers of sedatives and neural suppression.

"You came," he whispers, voice rough from disuse. His fingers, raw and blistered where the enhancement bands connect, reach for her with a desperate need for confirmation that she's real, not another hallucination induced by void exposure.

"Always," she responds, the word carrying years of shared history, promises made and kept through childhood and beyond. Her eyes scan him for additional injuries, cataloging each burn, each ruptured blood vessel, each sign of void-touched exposure for later retribution.

Caelus struggles to his knees, leaning heavily against her as his body remembers how to function without the containment field's suppression. "You need to go," he urges, words slurring slightly. "He's not what we thought. The Battalions, the attacks on defensive worlds, it's all part of something bigger."

"I know," Selenea says, supporting his weight while maintaining weapon readiness with her other hand. Blood from her injured palm leaves stark crimson prints on his tattered environment suit. "Ven figured out most of it. The others are now targeting Zathira's infrastructure. We have, " she checks her internal chronometer, "twelve minutes before systems fail."

The holographic star map above them flickers, cosmic patterns shifting as if responding to their exchange. Caelus follows her gaze upward, his Aetheris perception returning in fragments as the sedatives slowly metabolize out of his system. "The map," he says, recognition spreading across his features. "It's showing Battalion movements across seventeen systems simultaneously. Coordinated attacks against every world with unique defensive capabilities."

Before Selenea can respond, the air between them and the containment apparatus ripples like heat waves rising from sun-baked stone. Light bends around a focal point that emerges from shadow, creating distortions in visual space that strain the eye to follow. Objects near this disturbance, fragments of shattered crystal specks of dust in the sanctuary air, begin to orbit the point as if affected by localized gravity.

"Your interference changes nothing," Orpheus states, his form materializing fully from the distortion. He no longer stands but hovers slightly above the floor, the bottom edge of his cloak ending in tendrils of darkness that never quite touches the stone beneath. "The process has already begun across multiple systems. The reduction to original state proceeds as calculated."

A small metal component from the destroyed apparatus lifts from the floor unbidden, accelerating toward Orpheus before beginning to orbit his form at increasing speed. Other debris follows: crystal fragments, dust particles, even droplets of Selenea's blood that had fallen from her injured hand, all captured by whatever gravitational anomaly surrounds him.

Selenea shifts position, placing herself more fully between Orpheus and her brother. Her weapon remains trained on the figure, though she recognizes with cold clarity that conventional energy weapons likely have minimal effect against something exhibiting such fundamental control over physical forces.

"Your weapon is designed for matter," Orpheus observes, moving closer without seeming to walk, his form gliding through space with unnatural smoothness. "I am not composed of matter as you understand it."

He raises his hands to the edges of his mask, fingers disappearing into shadow where they touch the ornate surface. The mask detaches with a sound like reality tearing, revealing not a face but a swirling vortex of dark matter, particles that exist primarily through gravitational effects rather than conventional physical properties. Where features should be, cosmic winds shape and reshape patterns that momentarily resemble eyes, mouths, and expressions before dissolving back into primal chaos.

Caelus tenses beside her, enhancement bands flickering weakly against his raw fingers. "This is why I couldn't track him through Aetheris," he explains, voice steadying as awareness returns. "Aetheris only works on beings composed of stardust, cosmic matter formed after the Big Bang. He exists from before."

Tiny stars twinkle within the swirling mass of Orpheus's true form, captured or perhaps born there, struggling against the darkness that contains them. As he moves closer, the temperature drops precipitously, frost forming along the edges of their environment suits. The air itself seems too thin as if whatever comprises his true nature consumes conventional matter simply by proximity.

"I am what existed before stars," Orpheus confirms, his voice now unfiltered by the mask, harmonic undertones intensifying until they create visible wave patterns in the crystalline structures throughout the sanctuary. "Before the contamination of order upon perfect chaos. Before light polluted the purity of dark energy."

Incense smoke from ceremonial burners placed throughout the sanctuary responds to his voice, swirling into complex geometric patterns that mirror the sigils carved into the stone walls. The smoke doesn't rise naturally but moves as if alive, forming momentary images of cosmic events, stars collapsing, galaxies forming, and matter and energy separating from original unity.

Selenea watches these patterns with tactical awareness, recognizing them as more than aesthetic displays; they form a visual language that communicates concepts beyond conventional understanding. She adjusts her grip on her weapon, knowing its inadequacy yet unwilling to relinquish the only physical advantage they possess.

"You're Valthorim," Caelus states, enhancement bands warming slightly as his Aetheris perception continues to recover. "But different from the guardians. Older. More fundamental."

"The original state," Orpheus confirms, dark matter swirling faster at this recognition. The stars within his form dim slightly, compressed by the intensifying darkness. "Before the division that created your limited reality."

The Fractal windows surrounding the sanctuary pulse with sudden increased energy, their cosmic vistas shifting to show earlier universal states, matter coalescing from primordial energy, the first separation of forces that allowed conventional physics to emerge. The holographic star map above flickers between current reality and something other, a representation of existence before conventional matter, when dark energy comprised the totality of being.

"Your gift only works on beings of stardust," Orpheus continues, moving in a circular pattern that forces the siblings to rotate to maintain defensive positioning. "You cannot sense what predates sensing itself. Cannot track what existed before tracking became possible. Your cosmic threads only connect to what emerged after the division."

His voice creates harmonic resonance throughout the sanctuary, crystal components vibrating at frequencies that border on shattering. The incense smoke continues its unnatural movement, now forming miniature galaxies that rotate briefly before collapsing back into formlessness, a visual demonstration of the cycle Orpheus describes.

Caelus manages to stand fully now, enhancement bands glowing with increasing strength as his connection to Aetheris rebuilds. Beside him, Selenea maintains her weapon's aim despite knowing its futility, her injured hand leaving fresh blood droplets on the floor that immediately begin orbiting Orpheus's gravitational field.

"What do you want?" she demands, voice steady despite the cosmic horror materializing before them.

The dark matter shifts, approximating a smile with terrible precision. Stars disappear within the swirling void as Orpheus answers:

"The end of your contamination. The return to purity."

Orpheus's dark matter form expands, filling more of the sanctuary with cold void energy. The temperature plummets further, frost forming in geometric patterns across the stone floor that mirror the ancient sigils carved into the walls. Stars trapped within his swirling mass struggle against their imprisonment, their light dimming and brightening in distress patterns that Caelus recognizes from studying dying solar systems. This isn't merely an alien being; and it's a fragment of the universe's original state, a living embodiment of what existed before conventional reality formed.

"The Valthorim were wrong to create stars and life," Orpheus states, his harmonics deepening until they resonate through bone and tissue. "The universe was perfect in its original dark matter state. Pure. Unified. Complete."

The Fractal windows surrounding the sanctuary ripple violently, their cosmic vistas shifting between present reality and increasingly distant past states. One window shows a galaxy in mid-formation, stars coalescing from cosmic dust, then flickers to reveal the same region before stellar ignition, when only potential existed in dark matter clouds. Another displays a nebula birthing planetary systems before transitioning to show that same space as an empty void, untouched by creation's contamination.

"There was a schism," Orpheus continues, dark tendrils extending from his main form to trace patterns in the frost-covered floor. "Some Valthorim believed complexity held value. They introduced energy differentials into perfect uniformity. Created the first stars, the first matter, the first contamination of ordered systems within chaos."

The massive holographic star map suspended above them flickers between representations, the current universe with its billions of galaxies alternating with a void of nothingness punctuated only by dark matter concentrations. The transitions between states accelerate, creating a visual argument between existence and non-existence, between the cosmos as it is and as Orpheus believes it should be.

"Others of us understood this was an error," he explains, voice creating crystalline resonance throughout the sanctuary. "The perfect state needed no addition, no complexity, no life. We withdrew to observe the experiment, certain it would fail. Certain entropy would reclaim all created systems naturally."

Selenea shifts position, maintaining her protective stance before Caelus while scanning for any tactical advantage in their surroundings. Her injured hand leaves fresh blood droplets on the floor, and each one is immediately caught in Orpheus's gravitational field to orbit his expanding form.

"But some systems persisted," Orpheus continues, dark matter contracting momentarily around the captured stars within him, causing them to dim further. "Life emerged. Consciousness developed. Worse, a connection formed between consciousness and the underlying fabric of reality itself. Abilities like Aetheris appeared, bridging created matter with primal forces."

Caelus's enhancement bands warm against his fingers, responding to the cosmic energies permeating the sanctuary. The sigils tattooed across his body begin to glow beneath his tattered environment suit, amber light seeping through the fabric in patterns that mirror those carved into the walls around them. Not coincidence, connection, the same primal language written in flesh and stone.

"That's why you need me," Caelus realizes, perception extending beyond conventional limits as his Aetheris ability gradually returns. "You're tracking every being with cosmic connection. Eliminating those who could detect your true purpose."

Orpheus's form ripples with what might be satisfaction. "The Battalions serve as instruments of reduction. Targeting worlds with unique defensive capabilities, harvesting their technologies, and eliminating potential resistance. Preparing the universe for its restoration to purity."

Selenea's tactical mind processes these revelations with cold precision, recalculating the conflict's true scale. It is not merely territorial expansion or resource acquisition, extinction at a cosmic level, or the unmaking of existence itself. Her finger tightens slightly on her weapon's trigger, the gesture more reflexive than a rational response to a threat beyond conventional physics.

"The Aetheris users were the greatest threat," Orpheus acknowledges dark tendrils extending further across the sanctuary floor. "Those who could perceive cosmic threads, track our movements between realities, potentially interfere with the restoration process. They were eliminated first."

"Except me," Caelus states, enhancement bands now glowing steadily against his raw fingers. The sigils across his body pulse with increasing brightness, responding to both his returning abilities and the sanctuary's ancient energies. "You kept me alive because I was tracking your enemies for you. Finding the resistance leaders without realizing what they were resisting."

The revelation burns through him, worse than any physical pain, the understanding that his gift was weaponized against those fighting to preserve existence itself. Blood vessels rupture in his left eye as emotion overrides physical limitation, fresh crimson filling the white until his amber iris seems to float in a sea of blood.

Selenea feels her brother's anguish without turning to see it, their connection transcending conventional senses. Her own sigils, smaller and fewer than his but present since childhood, begin to glow beneath her uniform, responding to both the sanctuary's energy and her brother's activated state.

"How many worlds?" she demands, the tactical officer seeking to target data even in cosmic horror. "How many systems are targeted for 'reduction'?"

"All of them," Orpheus answers simply, dark matter expanding to touch the ceiling now, stars within his form compressed to mere pinpoints of struggling light. "Creation was the error. Restoration requires complete reversal."

The siblings process this information silently, tactical and analytical minds converging on the same conclusion from different paths. The Fractal windows continue their violent rippling, cosmic vistas shifting between states of existence and void. The holographic star map accelerates its alternating display, the universe blinking in and out of being above their heads.

"We won't let you," Caelus states, voice finding strength in absolute moral certainty. The enhancement bands around his fingers pulse with blue-white energy, cosmic threads becoming visible to his perception once more. Not merely connections between stardust entities but the underlying fabric of reality itself, the patterns Orpheus seeks to unravel.

"Your permission is irrelevant," Orpheus responds, his form beginning to expand beyond conventional limitations. Dark tendrils reach toward the siblings from multiple directions simultaneously, moving with mathematical precision through three-dimensional space. "The process has already begun across seventeen systems. Critical defense worlds fall as we speak. The reduction accelerates with each collapse."

Selenea steps back, maintaining position before her brother while calculating trajectory angles for the approaching tendrils. Her weapon may prove ineffective against dark matter, but her tactical mind refuses to surrender to inevitability. Her blood-soaked bandage leaves crimson prints on her weapon grip, physical pain providing focus against cosmic dread.

"You cannot stop what has already begun," Orpheus warns as his form continues expanding, dark matter filling more of the sanctuary with each passing second. The temperature drops further, and frost patterns thicken across all surfaces. "The void awaits us all."

Caelus places his hand on Selenea's shoulder, enhancement bands connecting with her glowing sigils through the fabric of her uniform. Energy transfers between them, and his Aetheris perception extends to include her tactical awareness. Their strengths combine, his ability to see cosmic connections merging with her capacity to identify vulnerability in seemingly impenetrable defenses.

"He's wrong," Caelus says quietly, the words meant only for her. "Dark matter requires normal matter to exist. Perfect void is a fantasy. Even original chaos contained the potential for order."

Selenea nods once, understanding flowing between them without the need for further explanation. Their sigils pulse in synchronized patterns now, ambient energy from the sanctuary flowing through the ancient symbols tattooed on their bodies. Whatever the sigils were designed for millennia ago, they activate now in response to primal threats.

"The system targeting," she responds equally quietly. "If we can disrupt it at the source, "

"The star map," Caelus finishes, eyes tracking upward to the holographic display still alternating between existence and void. "It's not just showing the Battle coordination, it's directing it. Cut the head, the body fails."

Orpheus's dark tendrils reach the edge of their defensive position, voiding energy and creating microfractures on the stone floor where it touches. The sanctuary vibrates with increasing intensity as reality itself strains under opposing cosmic forces.

"You face what existed before existence," Orpheus states, the dark matter now filling two-thirds of the chamber, captured stars completely extinguished within his expanded form. "Your resistance is a mathematical impossibility."

The siblings stand together, blood and sigils and determination creating something Orpheus's perfect calculations failed to anticipate, a connection forged in the messy complexity of life itself, the very contamination he seeks to erase. Their bond strengthened not despite the revelation but because of it, understanding of cosmic stakes crystallizing their resolve.

"We are what comes after stars," Selenea responds, weapon raised toward the holographic star map rather than Orpheus himself. "The next evolution you never accounted for."

The dark tendrils reach for them as Fractal energy pulses through the chamber, reality trembling at its foundations as cosmic forces prepare for confrontation.

Chapter 21

Battle in the Void

The dark tendrils reach for the siblings as reality fractures around them. The stone beneath their feet rumbles, ancient foundations groaning under forces they were never designed to contain. Selenea's weapon remains aimed at the holographic star map while Caelus's sigils pulse with increasing intensity, the siblings standing as the last barrier between Orpheus's void and the universe of light they defend.

The air splits open with crystalline precision as multiple Fractals tear through the fabric of the chamber. Not the controlled pathways used for travel but raw, jagged rifts in reality itself. Through these dimensional wounds, step figures previously scattered across the stars arrive with perfect synchronicity at the moment of greatest need.

Ven Diona materializes near the eastern columns, her methodical mind already analyzing the sanctuary's structural weaknesses. The Mordian compounds she released into Zathira's atmosphere have destabilized the monastery's environmental regulators right on schedule. Her movements carry the careful precision of someone who reads environments like others read text, each step placed with deliberate purpose.

"Atmospheric disruption at sixty-three percent," she reports, voice maintaining scientific detachment despite the cosmic horror unfolding before her. "The monastery's integrity is failing at multiple junction points."

Water molecules pulled from distant reservoirs coalesce into humanoid forms as Lyra Mareen and Meridia Flux position themselves beside ornate basins where ceremonial water once flowed. Their iridescent scales catch the chaotic light of fluctuating Fractals, reflecting distorted patterns across stone walls. Their webbed hands already manipulate invisible currents, preparing hydrokinetic countermeasures against Orpheus's expanding form.

"Water systems compromised," Meridia confirms, her facial markings glowing with increased intensity. "Shield generators destabilizing on our command."

From a Fractal rimmed with frost appears Skif Zar, the temperature around him plummeting further as his tactical mind instantly assesses battlefield positions. Ice crystals form in geometric patterns where his feet touch the ground, spreading outward in calculated defensive formations that mirror the ancient sigils carved into the walls.

"Thermal countermeasures ready," he states, his pragmatic voice carrying the dry cold of deep space. "Targeting dark matter condensation points."

The stone floor cracks as magma seeps through previously imperceptible faults, rising into Neous Dera's massive, semi-solid form. His core glows with white-hot intensity, casting stark shadows across the increasingly unstable chamber. Where his magma-form touches the monastery's ancient stone, material states shift and transform, molecular bonds reconfiguring under extreme heat.

"The void cannot stand against the fire of creation," he rumbles, voice like stone grinding against stone. "Even darkness burns."

Orpheus's dark matter expands exponentially, his form abandoning all pretense of humanoid shape as it rises toward the vaulted ceiling. Stars previously trapped within his essence have been completely extinguished, their light absorbed into nothingness. Tendrils of absolute darkness extend in mathematical patterns across the chamber, targeting each newcomer with calculated precision.

"The universe was perfect before stars," he declares, his voice resonating at multiple frequencies simultaneously, creating destructive harmonics that crack crystalline structures throughout the sanctuary. "We will return it to darkness."

The temperature plummets as gravity shifts erratically. Objects not secured to the floor, fragments of the destroyed apparatus, ancient texts, and ceremonial implements begin to float, orbiting invisible focal points as fundamental forces rewrite themselves in the presence of primal energies. Blood droplets from Selenea's wounded hand suspend in mid-air, forming a constellation of crimson spheres that trace her movement through the distorted space.

"Battalion forces still active across seventeen systems," Caelus warns, enhancement bands now burning white-hot against his raw fingers. Cosmic threads of blue-white light materialize around him as his Aetheris perception extends beyond conventional limits, connecting to each ally with luminous strands that pulse in time with their heartbeats. "They're attacking defensive worlds according to patterns directed from this chamber."

Selenea moves with tactical precision, her injured hand leaving traces of blood that float rather than fall. "Ven, Skif, target the structural weak points where Fractals are forming. Lyra, Meridia, counter his gravitational distortions. Neous, prepare thermal disruption along his primary mass."

Reality tears further as massive cloaked entities materialize throughout the chamber, the loyal Valthorim stepping through dimensional boundaries with a fluid grace that belies their imposing size. Their hooded forms tower over even Neous, edges blurring as they exist simultaneously in conventional space and the void beyond. Where their cloaks brush against walls or floor, matter seems to both exist and not exist simultaneously, quantum states collapsing and reforming in their wake.

"The compact is broken," they intone in a unified voice, creating harmonic overtones that stabilize the chamber's disintegrating architecture. "Balance must be restored."

Orpheus's dark matter form contracts suddenly, density increasing as he focuses his essence into a more concentrated state. "You failed to maintain the purity," he accuses the Valthorim, his harmonics shifting to frequencies that make human ears bleed, and crystalline structures resonate at near-shattering pitch. "Creation was the original contamination."

His attack comes with mathematical precision, tendrils of void energy striking multiple targets simultaneously. Where they connect with physical matter, objects don't merely break but cease to exist, their fundamental particles unraveling as if they never formed in the first place. A column beside Ven dissolves into nothingness, the stone returning to the pre-matter state in seconds.

The Valthorim respond with gestures that bend light around their massive forms. Reality ripples outward from their movements, creating zones where Orpheus's dark energy cannot penetrate, pockets of protected space-time where conventional physics temporarily reasserts itself.

Caelus drops to one knee, hands pressed against the vibrating floor as his Aetheris perception expands beyond sustainable limits. Blood vessels rupture across his forehead, crimson rivulets tracing paths down his face that mirror the ancient sigils tattooed across his skin. The enhancement bands burn against his fingers, metal edges beginning to melt into the flesh beneath.

"I can see the pattern," he gasps, voice strained from the effort of comprehension beyond human capacity. "The Battalion attacks aren't random; they're creating a geometric configuration across all seventeen systems. A cosmic fractal that, when complete, will allow void energy to flow through normal space."

Selenea repositions her weapon, targeting points where Orpheus's form appears most concentrated. Her tactical mind calculates angles and energy requirements even as gravity fluctuates around her. "Where's the control node? The central point directing the pattern?"

"There, " Caelus points toward the holographic star map, still alternating between existence and void. "It's not just showing the Battalion coordination. It's directing it. The map connects to Fractal pathways across all targeted systems."

Neous launches the first counterattack, his magma form extending with explosive force toward Orpheus's central mass. Where fire meets void, impossible physics manifests, and heat transfers to nothingness, creating boundary states that shouldn't exist in conventional reality. Steam hisses from the contact points, not from water but from reality itself, boiling at the edges.

Skif Zar creates ice formations that climb the walls in geometric patterns mirroring Orpheus's dark tendrils. The crystalline structures refract light from the Fractals, creating interference patterns that temporarily disrupt the void energy's expansion. "His form responds to thermal differentials," Skif observes, his methodical mind tracking effectiveness with clinical precision. "Coordinated temperature variations create structural weaknesses."

Lyra and Meridia move in synchronized patterns, their evolved bodies shifting into combat configurations as they manipulate water molecules that shouldn't exist in the destabilized environment. Their hydrokinetic abilities create pressure differentials that counter Orpheus's gravitational distortions, forcing his dark matter to expend energy maintaining cohesion rather than attacking.

Ancient sigils embedded in the monastery walls begin to glow in response to the cosmic forces being unleashed. Their patterns, dormant for millennia, activate in sequences that mirror the tattoos across Caelus's skin. The symbols pulse with amber light that spreads along mortar lines between stones, transforming the entire chamber into a massive containment system designed eons ago for precisely this confrontation.

"The monastery knew," Caelus realizes, watching as the sigils brighten in perfect harmony with those on his body. "Zathira was built as a failsafe, a cosmic prison in case the void ever attempted to reclaim created space."

Selenea's blood-soaked bandage unravels as she moves, droplets forming patterns in the air that match specific sigil configurations on the walls. The crimson constellation orbits her like a personal galaxy, each droplet finding a position in a mathematical formula written in blood and light and ancient knowledge.

"Then let's use it," she states, directing her weapon's energy beam not at Orpheus directly but at specific sigils around the chamber. Where the energy connects, symbols flare with blinding intensity, activating sequences dormant since the monastery's creation.

The chamber trembles as cosmic forces collide, the battle for existence itself unfolding in a space designed as the final battleground between creation and void.

The sigils flare with blinding intensity as reality gives way completely. Fractals tear wider across the chamber, their crystalline edges no longer containing the void but surrendering to it. The monastery's ancient stone, designed to exist at the boundary between realities, can no longer maintain its integrity against such fundamental forces. Walls, columns, and floors fragment into islands of matter, floating in absolute nothingness as combatants are pulled into the starless void beyond physical space.

Selenea feels her body lighten, blood from her wounded hand no longer falling but extending outward in frozen tendrils that trace her movement through dimensionless space. The void presses against her senses, not darkness as humans understand it, but the absolute absence of everything, including the concept of absence itself. Her lungs burn briefly before Caelus's Aetheris web connects with her, creating a pocket of sustained existence around her form.

The monastery disintegrates around them, not crumbling but separating into perfectly geometric sections that orbit invisible focal points. Ancient stone, crystalline structures, and metal components drift in mathematical patterns, forming a three-dimensional constellation of architectural fragments. The holographic star map, untethered from its housing, expands across the void, its representation of battling universes now surrounding the combatants in all directions.

Caelus floats at the center of a luminous web, enhancement bands burning white-hot against his flesh. The metal has partially fused with his fingers, creating a permanent connection that both empowers and damages him with each pulse of energy. Blood suspended around his face catches the light of his Aetheris strands, creating a crimson mask that highlights the determination in his amber eyes.

"Stay connected!" he calls his voice somehow carrying through the vacuum as Aetheris strands extend from his body toward each ally. Where the strands connect, protective bubbles of sustained reality form, not the atmosphere but the fundamental conditions necessary for existence itself. "The threads will maintain your molecular cohesion!"

The luminous web expands as Caelus channels more power through his enhancement bands, creating a network that links all allies despite the increasing distances between them as the void expands. Each strand pulses with the combined lifeforce of those it connects, their consciousness partially merged through the Aetheris bond.

Orpheus's dark matter form expands exponentially in this native environment, no longer constrained by the physical limitations of normal space-time. His essence spreads across the void like a liquid shadow, flowing between fragments of the monastery with fluid grace impossible in conventional physics. Stars previously extinguished within his form reappear briefly before being consumed again, their death throes visible as miniature supernovas within his expanding darkness.

"You see now," his voice resonates through the void itself, creating ripples in nothingness that shouldn't be possible. "This is the natural state, perfect emptiness. Your existence is the contamination."

The Valthorim grow to their true cosmic scale, their hooded forms expanding until they tower over the battlefield like sentient constellations. Their cloaks drift open, revealing glimpses of impossible geometries beneath, structures that exist in dimensions beyond human comprehension, and shapes that follow mathematical rules from before the universe settled on its physical constants. Where their true forms partially manifest, reality itself bends and warps around them, creating boundary zones where void and matter negotiate their coexistence.

"The compact maintained balance," they intone, their unified voice creating visible harmonics that ripple through the nothingness. "Neither void nor matter supreme, but existing in equilibrium."

Selenea adapts to the impossible battlefield with a soldier's pragmatism, her tactical mind calculating trajectories in three-dimensional space where conventional physics no longer apply. Her weapon, designed for ship-to-ship combat in normal space, should be useless here, yet when she fires, precision shots briefly disrupt Orpheus's form where his darkness appears most concentrated.

"The energy signatures are inconsistent," she calls to her allies, each word connecting through Caelus's Aetheris web rather than sound waves. "Target the points where his form intersects with monastery fragments!"

Neous Dera's magma body should be impossible in the vacuum of void space, yet his essence burns with concentrated force as he hurls portions of himself toward Orpheus's expanding darkness. Where magma meets void, both substances briefly flicker in and out of existence, matter and nothingness negotiating their fundamental incompatibility. The heat of creation burns against the cold of non-being, creating boundary zones where new physics write themselves into existence.

"Even here, fire defies emptiness," Neous rumbles, his voice traveling through Aetheris connections rather than conventional medium. "The void fears heat because it remembers creation's first spark."

Skif Zar manipulates ice formations that shouldn't exist without atmosphere or pressure, yet his tactical mind has already adapted to the void's strange properties. The ice structures he creates refract energy from the Fractals, splitting their dimensional light into precise beams that momentarily force Orpheus's darkness to contract where they connect.

"His form maintains coherence through gravitational differentials," Skif observes, methodical even in impossible space. "Targeting these variations disrupts his ability to maintain unified consciousness."

Lyra and Meridia move through the void with the grace of beings evolved for three-dimensional navigation. Water molecules that should instantly vaporize in a vacuum instead form complex structures around them, manipulated by hydrokinetic abilities that transcend conventional limitations. They create pressure waves through the nothingness, distortions in space-time that push against Orpheus's expanding form.

"Water remembers its origins in stellar formation," Meridia states, her gills pulsing with bioluminescence that traces patterns through the void. "Hydrogen and oxygen, the first children of stars."

"You cannot destroy what came before creation itself," Orpheus taunts, his essence flowing around their attacks with fluid adaptability. Dark tendrils extend toward the Aetheris strands, connecting the allies, testing for weaknesses in the network and keeping them coherent in the void.

Caelus channels more power through his enhancement bands, fresh blood vessels rupturing across his face as he pushes his perception beyond human limitations. "We're not trying to destroy it," he counters, each word costing him physically as oxygen molecules within his protected bubble deplete with each syllable. "We're preventing you from destroying everything else."

Monastery fragments continue their orbital dance through the void, ancient stone-carrying sigils that pulse with increasing urgency. The symbols respond to the battle surrounding them, centuries of dormant purpose activating in the presence of the conflict they were designed to contain. The stone that once formed walls and columns now realigns itself, creating new configurations that channel energy through precisely calculated vectors.

A tendril of darkness wraps around one of Caelus's Aetheris strands, void energy attempting to sever the connection to Ven Diona. The methodical scientist doesn't panic but instead releases a concentrated burst of Mordian compounds that shouldn't function without the atmosphere to carry them. The golden spores float through nothingness in precise formations, carrying with them the memory of a world that evolved specifically to counter void intrusion.

"Spore structures contain sigil patterns at the molecular level," Ven explains, her scientific detachment undiminished by the cosmic battle. "They recognize void energy as a fundamental threat to biological existence."

The void itself begins to respond to the conflict, harmonic undertones pulsing through the nothingness as reality strains under the cosmic forces being unleashed. What begins as subtle vibration grows into visible distortions, ripples in emptiness that shouldn't be possible yet manifest as opposing forces reach their critical threshold. The very concept of non-existence begins to acknowledge the battle for existence taking place within it.

Selenea fires again, her weapon's energy beam refracted through Skif's ice formations to strike Orpheus from multiple angles simultaneously. Where the modified beams connect with his darkness, tiny points of light briefly spark, matter momentarily asserting itself within void essence.

"The battalion targeting is still active," she warns, eye tracking the expanded holographic star map surrounding them. "Seventeen systems still under coordinated attack."

Caelus strains against the limits of human comprehension, enhancement bands now permanently fused to his fingers as his Aetheris perception extends to its absolute limit. Through the cosmic threads, he perceives not just the physical battlefield but the mathematical patterns underlying reality itself, the code determining whether existence or non-existence predominates.

"The map," he gasps, blood from ruptured vessels floating around his face in crimson constellations. "It's not just directing the attacks, and it's calculating the optimal pattern for void propagation. If the battalions complete their coordinated strikes, they create a geometric structure that allows void energy to flow through normal space like water through a broken dam."

Orpheus's darkness contracts suddenly, concentrating into a more defined form as he focuses his essence on a singular purpose. "The contamination ends," he declares, his harmonics creating destructive interference patterns that threaten to unravel the Aetheris web. "The geometric key is nearly complete."

The loyal Valthorim responds with gestures that bend dimensions around their massive forms, creating boundary zones where void energy cannot penetrate. Their movements follow patterns established at the universe's birth, the original compromise between creation and entropy, between existence and nothingness.

As the battle reaches new intensity, reality itself trembles at its foundations. The void, supposedly empty, fills with the mathematical echoes of conflict, harmonic patterns rippling through nothingness as cosmic forces struggle for supremacy. What began in Zathira's sanctuary has expanded to the scale of universal principles, fundamental forces themselves taking sides in the battle between creation and oblivion.

Caelus's blood floats in perfect spheres around his head, each droplet catching light from the Aetheris strands extending from his body. He sees beyond physical limitations now, and perception has expanded to the very edge of human comprehension. The cosmic threads connecting all stardust entities reveal themselves not as individual strands but as a unified field, the underlying mathematics of existence itself. And within those equations, he finally sees how to bind something that predates binding.

"I need to channel everything," he calls through the Aetheris web connecting their group. His voice sounds distant in his own ears; and consciousness is stretched thin across dimensional boundaries. "Every connection, every thread, focused on a single pattern."

The enhancement bands have fused completely with his fingers now; metal merged with flesh at the molecular level. Blood vessels burst in a cascading wave across his face and chest as he drew more power than his body had been designed to channel. The sigils tattooed across his skin burn with white-hot intensity, no longer merely glowing but transforming into conduits of pure cosmic energy.

"Whatever you're doing, do it fast," Selenea responds, firing precise shots that momentarily disrupt Orpheus's expanding darkness. "Battalion attacks have reached a critical threshold in twelve systems already."

Caelus extends his hands and fingers splayed in a gesture that resembles both supplication and command. The Aetheris web around them shifts, luminous strands detaching from the allies to reorient toward Orpheus's dark matter form. Each thread moves with mathematical precision, forming geometric patterns that mirror the ancient sigils fragmented across the floating monastery stones.

"I need to invert his own mathematics," Caelus explains, words coming with increasing difficulty as more of his consciousness transfers into the Aetheris field. "Void exists through negative definition, the absence of something else. If I create a pattern of presence that exactly contradicts his absence..."

The cosmic threads converge on Orpheus's form, not attacking but encircling, creating a network of light that traces the exact boundaries of his darkness. Where the luminous strands intersect, they create nodes of intensified reality, points where existence itself becomes concentrated, pushing back against the void energy with equivalent force.

Selenea recognizes the pattern forming around Orpheus, a multidimensional cage constructed from pure Aetheris energy. She positions herself at a crucial junction point where multiple threads converge, her tactical mind instantly identifying the structural weakness in the forming network. Blood from her injured hand flows along the nearest thread, strengthening the connection with something uniquely hers, life essence freely given rather than forcibly taken.

"The binding needs anchors," she calls to the others. "Living conduits at each major intersection."

The allies respond with immediate understanding, each moving to position themselves at critical junctions in the expanding Aetheris network. Neous Dera extends his magma form along three converging strands, his core temperature intensifying to strengthen the light where darkness appears most concentrated. Skif Zar creates crystalline formations that refract the energy through precise angles, multiplying its effect through mathematical amplification. Lyra and Meridia position themselves where the network appears most tenuous, their hydrokinetic abilities creating pressure differentials that stabilize the dimensional fluctuations.

Orpheus's dark matter form ripples with increasing agitation as the Aetheris cage tightens around him. His essence fluctuates between solid and gaseous states, tendrils of void energy probing for weaknesses in the binding pattern.

"Your mathematics are flawed," he snarls, voice creating dissonant harmonics that threaten to shatter the Aetheris strands at their weakest points. "You cannot contain what existed before containers themselves were conceived."

Yet the network holds, reinforced by the conscious determination of beings whose very existence Orpheus seeks to erase. The Aetheris strands pulse with combined life force, each heartbeat strengthening the pattern that Caelus has woven into a cosmic prison.

The toll on Caelus grows visible with each passing moment. His body appears increasingly translucent as more of his essence transfers into the Aetheris field. Blood no longer flows but simply appears, materializing from ruptured vessels to float in expanding constellations around his fading form. The enhancement bands glow with blinding intensity, metal and flesh and cosmic energy becoming indistinguishable at their junction points.

"I can't hold this long," he warns, voice barely audible through the Aetheris connection. "The pattern requires more energy than I can channel alone."

The Valthorim entities respond to this admission, their massive forms converging on the trapped dark matter apparition. They move with synchronized precision, positioning themselves at equidistant points around the Aetheris cage. Their hooded forms begin to merge, individual entities flowing together into a unified consciousness that exists simultaneously across multiple points in space-time.

"The balance must be maintained," they speak in perfect unison, their voices creating visible ripples through the void. "Neither void nor matter supreme, but existing in eternal equilibrium."

Their merged form contracts, compressing the space containing Orpheus and the Aetheris cage. Reality bends around this focal point, dimensions folding inward as the Valthorim apply pressure not through physical force but through manipulation of fundamental cosmic principles. The void itself responds to their authority, nothingness compressing around Orpheus's essence.

"This universe was never meant for light," Orpheus struggles against the compression, his form alternating between states as parts of his essence begin to dissipate under combined pressure from Aetheris binding and Valthorim compression. "There will be others who see the truth."

His consciousness fragments under the increasing pressure, portions of his dark matter essence seeking escape through microscopic fluctuations in the Aetheris pattern. Each attempt is countered by precise adjustments from the allies, their combined awareness tracking and responding to his desperate maneuvers.

"The void doesn't fear existence," Caelus states, understanding flowing through him as his consciousness merges more completely with the cosmic mathematics he's channeling. "It fears being forgotten. Being irrelevant. The nothing that doesn't matter."

This truth strikes at the core of Orpheus's being. His form fluctuates more violently, darkness condensing into a singularity of pure void essence. "My followers are legion," he warns as the compression reaches a critical threshold. "More battalions are coming. What I began cannot be stopped by temporary setbacks."

The Valthorim apply final pressure, their merged consciousness creating a perfect sphere of containment around Orpheus's compressed form. "Your actions violated the compact," they declare. "The punishment is dissolution and redistribution."

Caelus channels the last of his strength into the Aetheris binding, enhancement bands now burning with energy that consumes his flesh as fuel. His sigils activate their final purpose, not merely a connection to cosmic forces but the sacrifice of self to power the pattern that contains primordial darkness.

Orpheus's form collapses inward, his essence compressed by combined Aetheris binding and Valthorim pressure until he implodes into nothingness. The implosion creates a shockwave that ripples through the void, causing the Fractals to pulse violently as dimensional mathematics recalibrate to accommodate the removal of a fundamental cosmic force.

The shockwave expands outward, passing through the allies like a wind composed of pure mathematical concepts rather than matter. Monastery fragments vibrate with harmonic frequencies, ancient stone responding to forces they were designed to withstand. The holographic star map flickers, its representation of battalion attacks freezing in mid-coordination as the directing consciousness vanishes.

As quickly as it began, the implosion concludes. Orpheus's essence compresses to the point of infinite density before disappearing completely, redistributed across dimensional boundaries by Valthorim's decree. His consciousness, or something that approximated consciousness in void terms, fades from perception, leaving only mathematical echoes in the fabric of reality itself.

The void begins to stabilize, nothingness gradually yielding to the reassertion of conventional physics. Fragments of Zathira drift together with increasing purpose, ancient stones recognizing their original configurations through patterns embedded in their molecular structure. Walls reform, columns reconnect, and floors reestablish themselves as the monastery gradually reconstructs its physical form around the combatants.

Caelus's Aetheris web contracts, luminous strands returning to their creator as the immediate threat dissipates. His body materializes more fully as his consciousness flows back into physical form, but the damage is evident. The enhancement bands have burned permanent channels into his fingers, metal and flesh inseparable after channeling cosmic energy beyond sustainable limits. Blood vessels have ruptured throughout his system, creating patterns of internal bleeding that trace the path of power flowing through his body.

As the final stones lock into place, reality stabilizes around them. The sanctuary reforms, damaged but intact, its ancient architecture bearing new scars from cosmic conflict. The Fractals seal closed with crystalline finality, dimensional tears healing as the monastery asserts its primary purpose as the boundary between realities.

Caelus collapses, limbs giving way as conscious control fails. Selenea catches him before he strikes the stone floor, her injured hand leaving fresh blood on his tattered environment suit. The siblings connect through more than physical contact, a bond forged in a shared struggle against cosmic horror, in combined sacrifice for existence itself.

"Did we win?" he whispers, consciousness fading as his body demands rest to process the damage sustained.

Selenea looks up at the Valthorim entities, which have now diminished to a more conventional scale but are still imposing in their hooded forms. They hover silently at the sanctuary's perimeter, their presence acknowledgment of what has transpired rather than the promise of the future alliance.

"For now," she answers, tactical mind already processing Orpheus's final warning. More battalions are coming. Followers legion. The battle was won, but the war continued across stars, worlds and dimensions beyond current understanding.

The monastery settles into uneasy stability, ancient stone bearing witness to a conflict as old as the universe itself, the eternal tension between creation and void, between light and darkness, between existence and nothingness that both precedes and awaits it. Balance was maintained, but temporarily, precariously, requiring constant vigilance against forces that existed before vigilance itself was possible.

Chapter 22

The Price of Victory

The Valthorim converge around Orpheus in a perfect circle, their massive cloaked forms drifting through the void like sentient constellations. Their edges ripple against the nothingness, reality itself straining to accommodate beings that exist partially beyond its boundaries. Orpheus floats at the center of their formation, his dark matter essence fluctuating between states, one moment a humanoid silhouette outlined in negative space, the next a formless cloud of cosmic darkness interrupted only by the faint pinpricks of dying stars trapped within his being.

Caelus and Selenea witness this final confrontation from a fragment of Zathira that now drifts through the void like a raft on cosmic currents. The stone beneath them, once part of the sanctuary floor, bears ancient sigils that pulse with amber light, providing a small island of stability amid universal chaos. The monastery slowly reforms around them, shattered pieces finding their original positions through some innate architectural memory, but the process remains incomplete. Walls reconnect in impossible configurations, and doorways lead to void-space, columns rise toward ceilings that haven't yet materialized.

Caelus leans heavily against his sister, enhancement bands still fused to his fingers, metal and flesh inseparable after channeling energies beyond human tolerance. Blood vessels have burst across his face, creating patterns that mirror the sigils tattooed on his skin. Each breath comes with visible effort, his body struggling to contain a consciousness that briefly expanded to touch the mathematical foundations of reality itself.

"Look at them," he whispers, voice raw from strain. "The oldest conflict in existence."

Selenea supports her brother's weight, her own injured hand leaving fresh blood on his tattered environment suit. The crimson droplets float upward rather than fall, forming a small constellation between them before dispersing into the void. Her tactical mind continues analyzing their position, calculating escape routes should the cosmic confrontation turn against them.

Orpheus's dark matter form pulses with renewed intensity, his essence struggling against the Valthorim's containment. Where their energies connect, reality itself flickers, space-time straining under opposed cosmic forces. The dying stars within his form dim further, their light consumed as he draws on his final reserves of power.

Then, impossibly, Orpheus laughs.

The sound carries no acoustic waves through the void but manifests directly in the consciousness of all present, a harmonic disruption that creates visible ripples through nothingness. His form solidifies briefly into a rough approximation of his masked appearance, dark matter condensing into recognizable features before dissolving back into chaos.

"You think this ends with me?" he taunts, voice resonating at frequencies that crack the monastery fragments still drifting through the void. "My followers are legion. More battalions await my signal across the galaxies."

His form expands suddenly, tendrils of darkness extending toward the Valthorim circle. When they touch the ancient guardians, their cloaks momentarily dissolve, revealing glimpses of their true forms, impossible geometries that exist in dimensions beyond conventional comprehension.

"The cleansing continues without me," Orpheus continues, his voice creating destructive harmonics that threaten to shatter the platform beneath the siblings. "The void remembers what came before stars. Before light. Before your failed experiment with creation."

Selenea tightens her grip on Caelus as their platform trembles beneath them. Her weapon, depleted but still clutched in her blood-slick hand, rises instinctively toward Orpheus, tactical training asserting itself despite the futility.

"He's lying," she says, though doubt edges her voice. "Without him coordinating, the Battalions will fragment. Lose cohesion."

Caelus shakes his head slowly, enhancement bands flickering weakly as residual Aetheris energy pulses through them. "He planned for this. Created redundancies." Each word costs him visibly, breath coming in shorter gasps. "I saw it in the star map, nested command structures, and backup coordination points. The pattern continues even if the source dies."

Orpheus's form ripples with what might be satisfaction. "The sister understands tactics. The brother sees patterns. Yet neither comprehends the scale of what comes." Dark tendrils withdraw from the Valthorim, coiling back toward his central mass. "My essence may disperse, but my purpose endures. The universe returns to darkness one light at a time."

The Valthorim respond as one, their massive forms shifting position with mathematical precision. They do not speak but communicate through pure concepts, ideas flowing between them as visible currents of energy that create complex interference patterns in the void. Their decision forms as consensus emerges from these patterns, not democracy but unified understanding transcending individual comprehension.

The circle contracts, closing the distance around Orpheus's fluctuating form. Their cloaks extend inward, edges merging to create a sealed sphere of containment. Within this boundary, reality itself answers to Valthorim authority rather than universal constants, physics rewritten according to rules established at the cosmos's birth.

Orpheus's dark matter essence reacts violently, tendrils lashing against the containment sphere with increasing desperation. "You cannot erase what came before erasure itself," he snarls, harmonics intensifying until they manifest as visible wave patterns through the void. "The pattern is set. The return inevitable."

The Valthorim concentrate their collective will, energies flowing between them in synchronized pulses. Light builds within their circle, not conventional electromagnetic radiation but something more fundamental, a force that existed in the first moments of creation when reality itself was still defining its parameters. The brilliance intensifies, transitioning through spectrums visible and invisible to human perception, frequencies impossible to register with conventional senses yet somehow perceived by the siblings through means beyond explanation.

"Close your eyes," Caelus warns, arm rising weakly to shield his sister. "This is how stars were born."

The light explodes outward in a silent, perfect sphere of pure creative force. Orpheus's dark matter form disperses under this assault, not merely damaged but fundamentally unmade. His essence disintegrates into particles of primordial darkness, scattered across dimensions as the Valthorim assert their collective authority over even that which predates their own existence.

The blast washes over the siblings in a wave of heat that burns without temperature, energy that transfers without medium, and power that transforms without physical contact. Their sigils flare in response, ancient symbols recognizing the forces that first inscribed them into cosmic understanding.

When vision returns, slowly, painfully, reality reasserting itself in fragments, Orpheus is gone. Where his form once fluctuated, only void remains, emptiness distinguished from surrounding emptiness only by the faint mathematical echo of what existed there moments before.

The dark matter particles that once comprised his essence drift through the void like cosmic dust, each speck containing some infinitesimal fragment of the consciousness that sought to return all existence to primordial darkness. They disperse with apparent randomness, yet Caelus perceives a pattern in their movement purpose rather than chaos guiding their trajectories toward distant points across the universe.

The Valthorim remain in their circle, though their forms appear diminished after channeling such fundamental energies. Their cloaks no longer ripple with the same vitality, edges fraying into wisps of cosmic energy that dissolve into surrounding nothingness. The cost of their victory is written in their reduced presence, power expended to contain a threat as old as existence itself.

"He's gone," Selenea states, tactical mind confirming absence through multiple observational vectors. Her fingers relax slightly on her weapon, though they don't release it entirely.

"His form is gone," Caelus corrects, eyes tracking the dispersing particles of dark matter with concern. "But his warning remains." His gaze shifts to the fractured holographic star map still floating amid monastery fragments, its display frozen in mid-coordination as Orpheus's directing consciousness vanishes. "Seventeen systems still under attack. Battalions still executing their programmed objectives."

The implications settle between them as the monastery continues its slow reformation around their floating platform. The battle was won, but the war continued across stars and, worlds and dimensions. The victory was achieved, but at a cost they've yet to fully calculate.

The Valthorim drift toward the siblings, their massive forms no longer dominating the void but seeming to shrink with each passing moment. Their cloaks, once absolute in their darkness, now hang in tatters around formless centers, cosmic energy leaking from tears in the fabric of their existence. The entities move with visible effort as if the confrontation with Orpheus has drained some fundamental essence from their ancient being. They approach the fractured platform where Caelus and Selenea stand, the void between them feeling suddenly small against the weight of what has transpired.

Around them, the monastery continues its gradual reconstruction. Fractals that tore reality apart now seal themselves with crystalline precision, dimensional rifts closing like wounds healing across the face of existence itself. Stone fragments drift through the void with increasing purpose, finding their original positions through some architectural memory embedded in their molecular structure. Walls reconnect, ceilings reform and corridors realign as Zathira slowly reclaims its function as the boundary between realities.

Caelus sways slightly, enhancement bands still fused to his fingers, now cooling from white-hot to dull red as residual energies dissipate. Blood has dried in complex patterns across his face, mapping the pathways where vessels ruptured during his connection to cosmic forces beyond human tolerance. His breathing remains shallow but steadies as the immediate danger passes.

Selenea maintains her supportive grip on her brother, her own injuries momentarily forgotten as she watches the approaching Valthorim with wary attention. Her tactical mind calculates their changed demeanor, noting the diminished presence, the fraying edges, the reduced scale of beings that minutes ago commanded the very fabric of reality itself.

The lead Valthorim stops before them, hovering at a distance that suggests respect rather than threat. No sound passes through the void, yet words form directly in the siblings' minds:

"The balance of the universe has been threatened."

The communication carries no acoustic properties but creates a resonance within their consciousness, concepts transferring with perfect fidelity across the barrier between the cosmic entity and human understanding. The Valthorim's mental voice carries exhaustion beneath its power, the cost of their victory evident in diminished harmonic overtones.

"We cannot maintain it alone any longer."

Each word manifests not merely as language but as direct experience; they don't simply hear about balance but perceive it, witnessing the delicate equilibrium between creation and entropy, between matter and void, between light and darkness that has defined universal existence since its inception. This knowledge settles into their awareness not as an abstract concept but as fundamental understanding, as intrinsic to their perception now as color or sound.

A second Valthorim moves forward, its form even more diminished than the first, where its cloak has torn completely away, glimpses of its true nature become briefly visible, geometries existing in dimensions beyond conventional space-time, mathematical patterns that define reality rather than existing within it. Its communication forms in their minds with quieter resonance but equal clarity:

"Orpheus's warning is true. His followers will continue his work."

As these words settle in their consciousness, visions accompany them, and Battalion forces continue coordinated attacks across multiple systems, void-touched entities direct operations from shadow positions, dark matter manipulators spreading Orpheus's philosophy of cosmic reduction throughout susceptible civilizations. The scale of the threat unfolds in their minds, not as tactical data but as lived reality, as if they simultaneously witness conflicts occurring across seventeen systems in real-time.

Caelus and Selenea exchange glances, wordless communication passing between them with the efficiency of siblings who have faced countless dangers together. In his sister's eyes, Caelus sees the tactical officer already calculating response scenarios, prioritizing threats, and identifying critical intervention points. In his gaze, she reads the pattern-recognition specialist mapping connections between seemingly disparate events, tracing lines of influence back to their sources.

"We're not equipped for this scale," Selenea thinks but doesn't say, the thought forming and dissolving in seconds as her military training asserts itself against momentary doubt.

"No one ever is," Caelus responds aloud to her unspoken concern, enhancement bands flickering briefly as residual Aetheris energy responds to his emotional state. "That's why they chose us anyway."

The lead Valthorim responds to this exchange with what might be approval, a subtle shift in their cosmic presence that creates momentary warmth in the surrounding void. Its form stabilizes slightly, edges firming as it summons remaining strength for what comes next.

"We entrust you with this task," it communicates, concepts flowing directly into their minds. "You have proven yourselves worthy guardians."

The entity extends what appears to be a tendril of pure energy, not physical matter but conceptual force given temporary visibility in conventional space-time. The appendage glows with soft amber light that matches the color of the siblings' sigils, suggesting a connection to the same primal forces that marked them at birth.

"The cosmic balance requires conscious maintenance," the Valthorim continues, its mental voice creating ripples of understanding through their awareness. "Orpheus disrupted patterns established at creation's dawn. These must be restored through deliberate intervention rather than natural processes."

The tendril moves toward them with gentle purpose, hovering momentarily before them as if seeking permission. Selenea straightens her posture, soldier's discipline asserting itself before cosmic authority. Beside her, Caelus manages to stand more fully upright, drawing strength from his sister's unwavering presence.

"What does this mean for us?" he asks, voice barely above a whisper yet somehow carrying through the void.

"Transformation," the Valthorim answers simply. "Knowledge. Responsibility."

The tendril splits into twin filaments of pure energy, each moving with precise intent toward the siblings. They touch simultaneously, one to Caelus's forehead, directly above his bloodied eyes, the other to Selenea's brow, just above her determined gaze. The contact creates no physical sensation but an immediate cognitive response as if libraries of information suddenly open within their minds.

They gasp in unison as cosmic knowledge floods their consciousness. Star maps unfold with perfect detail, showing not merely the physical location of celestial bodies but their interconnections through Fractal pathways, their energy signatures, and their vulnerability to void manipulation. They perceive Fractal networks spanning galaxies, dimensional shortcuts connecting systems that conventional space travel would require centuries to reach. They see the names of Orpheus's known followers written not in language but, in essence, void-touched entities identified by the unique signature of their corruption.

More than mere data transfers through this connection. They receive an understanding of cosmic balances maintained since creation's first moments, the delicate equilibrium between fundamental forces, and the mathematical harmony that allows reality to sustain itself against entropy's constant pressure. They comprehend why Orpheus's philosophy represents an existential threat rather than merely a technological or military challenge; his "reduction" would unravel reality's foundational equations, returning all existence to a pre-creation void.

The knowledge settles into their consciousness not as foreign information but as remembered truth, as if they have always known these cosmic principles but temporarily forgot them during human incarnation. Their sigils respond to this awakening, glowing with renewed intensity beneath skin and clothing, ancient symbols recognizing their original purpose as conduits for universal understanding.

When the tendrils finally withdraw, the siblings stand straighter despite physical exhaustion. Something has changed within them; not merely knowledge has been added, but perspective has shifted, and awareness has expanded beyond conventional human limitations without losing human connection.

"You understand now," the Valthorim observes, not a question but recognition of transformed consciousness. "The task before you."

Selenea nods, tactical mind already applying this cosmic knowledge to immediate strategic concerns. "The Battalion attacks follow specific geometric patterns," she states, information flowing through newly opened mental pathways. "If we disrupt key nodes, the entire coordination collapses."

"And Orpheus's followers gather on specific worlds," Caelus adds, enhancement bands glowing with renewed purpose as his Aetheris perception integrates with the transferred knowledge. "I can track them now, even without a direct connection. Their void-touch leaves traces in the cosmic fabric."

The Valthorim begin to withdraw, their forms diminishing further as they prepare to retreat from direct intervention. Their final communication reaches the siblings with fading resonance:

"The compact requires our withdrawal. Direct involvement violated cosmic law. The balance now depends on those who exist within creation rather than before it."

They drift backward, ancient guardians returning to observation rather than action, to the role they maintained for eons before Orpheus forced direct intervention. As they recede, the monastery completes its reformation around the siblings, with stone walls solidifying, crystal components realigning, and reality stabilizing into recognizable structures once more.

Caelus and Selenea stand in the restored sanctuary, no longer drifting on void currents but firmly anchored in reconstituted space-time. The knowledge transferred by the Valthorim continues to integrate with their consciousness, cosmic understanding merging with human perspective to create something new, guardians with feet planted in created reality but minds open to forces beyond.

The central chamber of Zathira still bears the scars of cosmic conflict. Scorched patterns mark the ancient stone where void energy touched physical matter, leaving mathematical burns that follow precise geometric formulas rather than chaotic flame damage. Fractured crystals catch the light at odd angles, refracting it through dimensional microfissures that create prismatic patterns impossible in normal space-time. The ceiling continues its final stages of self-repair, pieces drifting into position with deliberate slowness, stone remembering stone across the void that temporarily separated them. Around the central table, crew members gather with varying degrees of caution, each processing the aftermath of a battle fought at the edge of comprehension itself.

Neous Dera paces the perimeter, his massive semi-solid form of living magma leaving small scorch marks with each step. His core pulses with fluctuating intensity, bright white-orange when his thoughts turn to the battle just ended, cooling to deeper red as he contemplates what comes next. Each circuit around the chamber traces a perfect geometric path, his methodical mind finding comfort in mathematical precision amid cosmic uncertainty.

"The monastery's structural integrity concerns me," he rumbles, voice like stones grinding together. "Core temperature variations suggest dimensional stress points remain active beneath the surface."

Skif Zar stands perfectly still near an eastern column, and his pragmatic nature is expressed through an absolute economy of movement. Ice crystals form and reform at his feet in complex patterns that reflect his tactical calculations, spreading outward in fractals that mirror the mathematical burns on nearby walls. His gaze shifts between crew members with dry assessment, measuring capabilities against the scale of threat now understood.

"Conserve energy," he advises Neous with characteristic directness. "Further conflicts await. Temperature regulation takes priority over structural analysis."

At the far side of the chamber, Ven Diona examines damaged murals with methodical precision. Her fingers trace ancient sigils with scientific curiosity, collecting trace elements on specialized equipment designed to analyze dimensional residue. Golden Mordian spores still cling to her environment suit, creating tiny constellations that shift position with each careful movement.

"Fascinating," she murmurs, more to herself than others. "The sigil pattern modifications suggest deliberate adaptation to void energy. The monastery learned from the conflict."

Near the entrance, Sidia Lith maintains a vigilant watch, her massive rock form positioned with perfect defensive geometry. She says nothing, her stoic discipline expressing itself through attentive silence rather than unnecessary communication. Her crystalline eyes scan continuously for threats, prioritizing crew safety over idle curiosity about their cosmic surroundings.

At the center of it all, Caelus spreads a star map across the ancient table. It is not the holographic projection that directed battalion attacks but something more fundamental: a physical representation created directly from the knowledge transferred by the Valthorim. The map glows with soft amber light that matches his sigils, information flowing from his consciousness through the enhancement bands still fused to his fingers. His face remains marked with dried blood from ruptured vessels, but his eyes now burn with renewed purpose, amber irises reflecting starlight from the map before him.

"Orpheus had followers everywhere," he explains, fingers tracing luminous pathways between systems. Each touch creates ripples through the map, stars brightening or dimming as connections between them are revealed. "And battalions ready to continue his work even without his direct guidance."

The map expands as he speaks, growing to encompass seventeen systems currently under coordinated attack. Miniature representations of Battalion forces move between planets, their formations following precise geometric patterns now visible to the enhanced perception granted by Valthorim knowledge.

"These aren't random military targets," Caelus continues, voice stronger than it was during the battle but still carrying the strain of recent trauma. "Each attack location corresponds to a dimensional weak point, places where the boundary between normal space and void is naturally thinner."

Selenea moves to stand opposite her brother, and the siblings frame the map between them like cosmic bookends. Her tactical mind processes the strategic implications with military efficiency, identifying critical intervention points with the precision of an officer born to command. The blood-soaked bandage around her hand has been replaced with a proper medical wrap, though fresh red spots already show through the clean material.

"If these attacks succeed," she explains, gesturing to specific formations, "they create a geometric configuration across all seventeen systems. A cosmic fractal that will allow void energy to flow through normal space even without direct manipulation."

"Like Orpheus did with the Fractal network," Ven observes, moving closer to study the pattern. "But on a galactic scale rather than local."

"Precisely," Caelus confirms, enhancement bands glowing softly as they interact with the map. "His physical form is gone, but his strategy continues through his followers."

Neous Dera stops his pacing, massive form turning toward the map with renewed focus. "Can we disrupt all seventeen simultaneously? My thermal capabilities could potentially destabilize three, perhaps four nodes if deployed strategically."

Selenea shakes her head, tactician's precision cutting through hopeful speculation. "We don't have the resources for simultaneous intervention across all systems." Her finger moves decisively to a specific location near the map's center, touching a planet rendered in deeper shadows than those surrounding it. "We target the keystone, Gloam."

The dark planet pulses beneath her touch, its representation shifting to reveal details previously hidden. Vast crystalline formations jutting from terrain perpetually shrouded in darkness. Fields of bioluminescent vegetation that pulse with soft, ethereal colors. Ancient structures were made of light-absorbing material that matched the dark matter signature of Orpheus's true form.

"The dark planet," Skif Zar notes, ice crystals at his feet rearranging into a geometric approximation of Gloam's surface features. "Strategic selection. Its natural darkness provides optimal conditions for void energy manipulation."

"Orpheus's followers gather there in numbers that suggest critical operations," Selenea confirms. "According to the Valthorim knowledge, Gloam sits at a dimensional crossroads where multiple Fractal pathways naturally intersect, similar to Zathira but with opposite properties."

"Where Zathira exists to maintain boundaries between realities," Caelus adds, "Gloam naturally erodes them. If the void-followers gain full control of its properties..."

He doesn't finish the sentence. He doesn't need to. The implication hangs in the chamber's repaired air with the weight of existential threat, of reality itself unraveling should they fail.

Around the table, crew members exchange glances, calculating odds and measuring their diverse abilities against cosmic-scale challenges. They've faced impossible situations before: Battalion forces overwhelming planetary defenses, extraction missions through hostile territory, and survival against technologies designed specifically to counter their unique physiologies. But never with these stakes, never with existence itself balanced on their success or failure.

"We've stopped them before," Neous Dera finally states, flames flickering across his shoulders with renewed intensity. His voice carries absolute certainty despite the odds arrayed against them. "We'll do it again."

The simple declaration breaks the tension, not through false optimism but through the sheer pragmatic determination it represents. One by one, other crew members nod their agreement, Ven with methodical assessment, Skif with practical acknowledgment, Sidia with stoic commitment.

Selenea surveys them all, her command presence filling the ancient chamber despite her physical exhaustion. "The Valthorim have entrusted us with maintaining the cosmic balance," she says, voice steady with the weight of newly accepted responsibility. "We can't let them down."

Her gaze meets her brother's across the glowing map between them. In his eyes, she sees the same determination that burns in her own, the shared understanding that they've crossed a threshold from which there is no return. They are no longer merely siblings fighting a war they stumbled into but conscious guardians of principles that predate their existence, entrusted with the knowledge that transforms perception itself.

Caelus closes the map with a decisive gesture, the glowing representation folding inward until it concentrates into a small crystalline device that fits in his palm. The movement carries finality; the debate is concluded, the decision is made, and the course is set.

"To Gloam, then," he states simply, pocketing the crystal with care despite his injured hands. "We have a universe to protect."

The words echo briefly in the ancient chamber, bouncing from newly repaired walls with strange harmonics that suggest the monastery itself acknowledges its purpose. The battle against Orpheus may have ended, but the war for existence itself has only just begun.

Chapter 23

Defenders of the Dark

The ship cuts through Gloam's dense atmosphere, sensors struggling against the perpetual twilight that gives the planet its name. Caelus leans forward in the command chair, enhancement bands still fused to his raw fingers, their metal edges catching the light from the navigation display. Below, vast fields of bioluminescent vegetation pulse with blues and purples that ripple across the landscape like heartbeats in the darkness, revealing glimpses of the battalion transports already descending toward the planet's surface.

"Multiple battalion signatures," the sensor officer reports, voice tight with tension. "Deployment patterns suggest standard occupation protocol. They're establishing a perimeter around the central crystal formations."

Caelus nods, then winces as pain lances through his temples. The Aetheris web flickers at the edges of his perception, threads connecting to the crew members around him growing momentarily thin before stabilizing. Ever since Zathira, maintaining focus has required increasingly painful effort. Blood vessels in his left eye, still healing from previous ruptures, throb with each heartbeat.

"Can you track their commanders?" Selenea asks, moving to stand beside her brother. Her own hand, freshly bandaged but still seeping blood at the edges, rests on the console between them.

Caelus closes his eyes, enhancement bands warming against his damaged fingers. The cosmic threads extend outward, seeking the unique signatures of void-touched officers among the battalion forces. Images flash through his mind, dark matter troops deploying in geometric patterns across Gloam's shadowy terrain, their movements following precise mathematical formulas that trace sigils of containment and control across the landscape.

"Seven command units," he manages, voice strained. "They're establishing a focal point at the largest crystal formation. The one that, " His voice cuts off as his vision blurs, the Aetheris connection wavering under his physical weakness.

Selenea's hand moves to his shoulder, steadying him without comment on his deteriorating condition. "Tactical," she calls instead, turning toward the bridge officers. "Give me terrain analysis. What's our best approach vector?"

The main display shifts and topographical data replaces the visual feed. Massive crystal formations jut from the dark soil like jagged teeth, their structures refracting what little light exists on Gloam into disorienting patterns. Between these formations, ravines cut through the landscape, most filled with light-absorbing vegetation that registers as void space on conventional sensors.

"South approach offers minimal exposure," the tactical officer suggests, highlighting a winding ravine system. "Battalion sensors will struggle with the crystal interference patterns, and the light-absorbing flora provides additional concealment."

Selenea studies the proposed route, using a tactical mind to calculate risks against the battalions' known detection capabilities. "Confirmed. Take us in. Minimal power signature, full stealth protocols." Her fingers trace a path through the ravine system, adding markers at strategic points. "Primary landing zone here. A secondary extraction point is here if we need an emergency emergency evac."

The ship banks sharply, descending toward the southern hemisphere where the crystal formations grow denser. The bioluminescent plains continue their rhythmic pulses, colors shifting subtly as the ship passes overhead. A constant low humming fills the cabin, vibrations from the crystal structures creating sound waves that penetrate even the ship's shielded hull.

Caelus forces himself to stand, legs unsteady beneath him. The enhancement bands glow with fitful energy, responding to his fluctuating focus. "I need to be on the ground," he states, determination masking exhaustion. "Aetheris connection is stronger with direct contact."

No one argues, though concerned glances pass between crew members at his obvious weakness. They've all seen the toll that is channeling cosmic forces at Zathira has taken on him: the permanently fused enhancement bands, the blood vessels that rupture with each extended use of his abilities, the tremors that course through his hands when he thinks no one is watching.

The ship settles into the designated ravine with barely a tremor, landing struts adjusting automatically to the uneven terrain. Outside, light-absorbing vegetation forms a natural canopy that shields them from orbital detection. The plants don't merely block light but consume it, creating patches of absolute darkness between the softly glowing fungal clusters that cling to the ravine walls.

"Environmental readings suggest breathable atmosphere," Ven Diona reports, her methodical mind already analyzing the botanical structures visible through the viewports. "Though atmospheric density fluctuates in proximity to the crystal formations. Suggest breather units as a precaution."

Neous Dera moves toward the exit hatch, his massive form flowing with volcanic grace despite the confined space. "The temperature gradients are unstable," he notes, core temperature adjusting in preparation for the external conditions. "Suggests recent energy discharge consistent with battalion weapon signatures."

Selenea activates the ship-wide communication system. "All teams, final equipment check. We deploy in three minutes. Maintain communication discipline and stick to assigned tactical groups." She turns to Caelus, voice lowering. "Are you sure about this? You could coordinate from here."

Caelus shakes his head once, a decision already made. "I need direct contact with Gloam's surface. The planetary signatures might help stabilize my Aetheris connection."

The hatch opens with a soft hiss of equalizing pressure. The air that enters carries a metallic tang mixed with something like ozone, the scent of crystal formations vibrating at frequencies just beyond human hearing. The constant humming intensifies as they step onto Gloam's surface, the sound seeming to originate from within the planet itself rather than any specific source.

Caelus exits first, enhancement bands flaring briefly as they touch Gloam's atmosphere. The sigils tattooed across his body respond with answering pulses, their amber light visible through the tears in his partially repaired environment suit. His breath catches as the planet's unique energy signatures wash over him, not hostile but alien, complex harmonics that interact with his Aetheris perception in unexpected ways.

The crew follows in tactical formation, weapons ready but not yet drawn. They spread outward from the ship with practiced efficiency, establishing a perimeter that encompasses both their vessel and the shadow-filled ravine beyond. The light-absorbing plants shift subtly as they pass, not with the wind but with what appears to be a conscious response to their presence.

Selenea pauses at the edge of the ravine, gaze tracking upward to where crystal formations tower overhead, their structures creating natural amplifiers for Gloam's constant harmonic vibrations. The battalion transports are no longer visible from their position, but distant flashes of energy weapons paint momentary constellations against the twilight sky.

The darkness beside her shifts deepens and then separates from the surrounding shadows. The movement draws all eyes, instinctively orienting toward the disturbance as reality tears open in a vertical rift of absolute blackness. The shadow-wound in space resolves into a humanoid figure that never quite solidifies, edges constantly blurring, form shifting between solid and vapor states with each subtle movement.

"You're late," Barum Voyd states, voicing a resonant whisper that seems to come from multiple directions simultaneously. Their form ripples with what might be amusement, points of deep purple light where eyes might be focusing on each crew member in turn. "The shadows have been restless for hours."

Caelus approaches without hesitation, extending a hand that passes partially through Barum's semi-corporeal form. The sensation sends cold electricity up his arm, enhancement bands flaring in response to contact with a being composed partially of void energy. "We came as soon as we could," he responds, withdrawing his hand with a subtle shiver. "What defenses does Gloam have?"

Barum solidifies slightly, edges becoming marginally more defined as they focus their attention fully on the newcomers. "More than the battalion realizes," they answer, voices warming with something like pride. "Less than we'll need if their work continues unchallenged."

Their gaze shifts to Selenea, points of purple light narrowing with assessment. "The shadows speak of your battle at Zathira. They say you faced the void itself and survived." A pause, their form shifting slightly toward Caelus. "They say you carry its marks still."

Caelus's hand rises unconsciously to his face, fingers tracing the patterns where blood vessels ruptured during his confrontation with Orpheus. "We faced something that existed before existence," he acknowledges. "But its followers remain, and they've chosen your world as their focal point."

Barum's form expands slightly, darkness flowing outward before contracting once more into a roughly humanoid shape. "Then we have much to discuss," they state, turning toward a narrow path that winds deeper into the ravine system. "The shadows know all the places the battalion cannot see. And Gloam has secrets even the void has forgotten."

Barum glides through the bioluminescent fungi fields, their form occasionally merging with patches of deeper shadow before reconstituting steps ahead. The crew follows in tactical formation, boots sinking slightly into soil that absorbs sound as readily as it absorbs light. All around them, mushroom caps larger than human torsos pulse with blue-green light that creates moving patterns across the dark ground, while crystal formations rising between fungal clusters catch and amplify these illuminations into geometric displays that shift with each passing moment.

"Gloam exists in perpetual twilight," Barum explains, voice resonating at frequencies that harmonize with the constant humming from surrounding crystal formations. "The atmospheric composition filters most of our star's light, creating conditions where shadow is the natural state rather than the exception."

They paused beside a particularly tall crystal spire, points of purple light where eyes might be tracking upward along its jagged length. The crystal seems to respond to their proximity, internal facets shifting to create new refraction patterns that cast momentary star-like points across the landscape.

"The planet itself fights back when threatened," they continue, one shadow-hand passing through the crystal's surface without resistance. "These formations are not merely geological curiosities but sensory organs. They detect disturbances in Gloam's natural harmonics and respond accordingly."

Selenea studies the crystal with tactical interest, noting how its base connects to what appears to be a network of root-like structures just beneath the soil surface. "Connected systems," she observes. "Natural defense network."

"More than that," Barum confirms. Their form shifts, expanding slightly to encompass a nearby shadow before contracting once more. "The crystals amplify certain frequencies that disrupt Battalion technology. The shadow nets, " they gesture toward nearly invisible webbing stretched between crystal spires, "can disorient invaders by separating them from their own shadows."

Caelus extends a hand toward the nearest shadow net, enhancement bands warming as they detect the void-adjacent energy signature. "Dimensional interference," he notes, wincing as his Aetheris perception pulses painfully behind his eyes. "Similar to Fractal harmonics but inverted."

"Gloam has evolved to exist at the boundary between conventional reality and void space," Barum acknowledges. "The light-absorbing flora doesn't merely block illumination; it processes it, converts it, uses it to strengthen the planetary defense network."

The explanation is complete, and Selenea's command presence reasserts itself. "We need to incorporate these natural defenses into our strategy," she decides, turning to address the crew now gathered in a loose semicircle. "Tactical squads, specific assignments. We amplify what Gloam already provides."

The crew divides with practiced efficiency, each member moving to their specialized role without the need for detailed instruction. They've fought together enough to understand their complementary functions, each bringing unique abilities that form a comprehensive whole.

Ven Diona kneels beside a cluster of fungi, specialized collection equipment already extracting spores with methodical precision. "These bioluminescent patterns aren't random," she observes, her scientific detachment undiminished by the alien surroundings. "They respond to specific harmonic frequencies with predetermined light sequences."

Her fingers move across portable analysis equipment, mapping fungal response patterns with mathematical accuracy. "I can prime specific spore clusters to bloom in phosphorescent patterns that will confuse Battalion sensors," she explains, already extracting catalysts from her equipment pouch. "Their targeting systems won't be able to distinguish natural illumination from biological signatures."

Nearby, Skif Zar circulates among the crystal outcroppings, and his pragmatic assessment identifies optimal amplification points. Ice forms at his touch, not through external manipulation but as a direct extension of his tactical thinking. The crystalline patterns he creates complement the natural formations, reinforcing their structure while subtly altering their resonance properties.

"These fissures will amplify the disorienting hum by approximately forty-three percent," he states, with no pride in his voice, merely clinical accuracy. "Battalion neural implants are particularly vulnerable to frequencies in this range."

Neous Dera moves with surprising delicacy for his massive form, magma-core temperature regulated to prevent premature ignition of the devices he plants at strategic intervals throughout the fungi field. His hands sink into the dark soil, leaving momentary glowing traces before the light-absorbing properties of the ground consume the illumination.

"Magma bombs positioned along likely approach vectors," he reports, the volcanic scent of his weapons barely detectable beneath the metallic tang of Gloam's atmosphere. "Triggered remotely or by proximity, depending on tactical necessity."

At the edge of a narrow ravine, Lyra and Meridia work in synchronized harmony, their Marinamian physiology adapting to Gloam's unusual atmospheric conditions. Water extracted from their specialized equipment flows under their precise control, forming hydro-wells at points where the terrain naturally channels movement.

"Battalion troops favor linear assault patterns," Lyra notes, hair shifting to tactical crimson as she concentrates. "These wells will create disorienting mist patterns when activated, breaking visual contact between their advance units."

Meridia's scaled hands move in complex gestures that shape water molecules into predetermined formations. "The mist interacts with crystal harmonics to create spatial distortion effects," she adds, white facial markings glowing faintly with focused effort. "Similar to deep-water hunting techniques on Marinami."

Throughout these preparations, Caelus moves from position to position, enhancement bands flaring with fitful energy as he extends his Aetheris perception across Gloam's twilight landscape. Each effort brings fresh pain, blood vessels visibly throbbing beneath the skin of his temples, yet he pushes through with determined focus.

"They're converging on the central crystal field," he reports, voices tight with controlled suffering. A vision flashes through his mind, dark matter troops advancing in perfect geometric patterns, their movements creating void-energy sigils across Gloam's surface. "Seven command units, each leading a battalion section. They're establishing a perimeter that matches Orpheus's reductionist pattern."

He straightens with visible effort, eyes momentarily unfocusing as he tracks energies beyond conventional perception. "They're attempting to create a focal point where multiple Fractal pathways intersect naturally. If they succeed, void energy will flow through unchecked."

Selenea approaches her brother, placing a steadying hand on his shoulder. The contact grounds him, Aetheris threads momentarily stabilizing through their sibling connection. Her tactical mind processes his information immediately, stratographic images forming behind her eyes as she visualizes the battlefield.

"Ven, concentrate spore distributions along these coordinates," she instructs, transmitting location data through their shared communication system. "Skif, ice formations to channel their approach toward Neous's primary detonation zone. Lyra, Meridia, hydro-wells active when they reach this perimeter."

Her instructions continue, precise and economical, each word carrying the authority of someone born to command. The crew responds with immediate compliance, respecting both her tactical acumen and her unwavering certainty.

Throughout this activity, Barum observes from the edge of the fungi field, their form occasionally merging with nearby shadows before reconstituting with slightly altered dimensions. Their purple eye-lights follow each crew member in turn, assessment evident in the intensity of their gaze.

"Curious," they finally mutter, voice carrying that resonant quality that seems to originate from multiple positions simultaneously. "How you fight for a world not your own."

The observation draws Caelus's attention despite his focus on tracking battalion movements. "After Zathira," he responds, enhancement bands flickering with the effort of maintaining dual awareness, "all worlds are our concern. The void threatens existence itself, not just individual planets."

Barum's form shifts in what might be acknowledgment. "Gloam exists at the boundary between light and darkness," they note. "We understand better than most the necessity of both. The void-followers would eliminate the balance entirely."

They move closer to Caelus, their shadowy essence temporarily cooling the air between them. "Your Aetheris perception reaches further than you realize," they observe. "But at great cost. The shadows whisper that you burn your own life essence as fuel."

Caelus doesn't deny this observation, enhancement bands glowing against his damaged fingers with an intensity that mirrors the surrounding crystal formations. "Some prices are worth paying," he states simply, then winces as fresh pain lances through his temples. "They're accelerating their approach. We have minutes, not hours."

Selenea immediately shifts from planning to execution mode, her command presence expanding to encompass the entire field of operations. "All units, final positions. Communication discipline from this point forward." Her gaze sweeps across the assembled crew, meeting each person's eyes with calm certainty. "We've faced worse odds than this."

As the crew disperses to their assigned positions, Barum's form expands slightly, edges blurring further into the surrounding twilight. "You haven't faced Gloam's shadows yet," they note, something like anticipation coloring their resonant voice. "Neither have they."

The first battalion scouts step into Ven's phosphorescent trap field, their dark-matter armor absorbing light in hungry gulps that create moving voids against the bioluminescent backdrop. Fungal spores activate on contact, blooming in brilliantly coordinated patterns that pulse at frequencies specifically calibrated to disrupt battalion sensors. The scouts freeze, neural implants overwhelmed by contradictory data as biological signatures seem to materialize and vanish around them in impossible configurations. Behind them, the main force advances in perfect geometric formation, shadow-tech weapons drawn and humming with void energy that creates pockets of absolute darkness wherever it touches Gloam's twilight atmosphere.

"First contact established," Ven reports through the tactical communication network, her voice maintaining scientific detachment despite the tension evident in her precise movements. "Spore response exceeding predicted parameters. Effectiveness at eighty-seven percent and increasing."

The battalion troops press forward despite their scouts' disorientation, void-touched officers directing their movements with cold precision. Their weapons activate in synchronized bursts, firing concentrated packets of shadow-energy that absorb all light they encounter. Where these projectiles strike, patches of absolute darkness bloom, creating expanding zones where even Gloam's bioluminescent flora temporarily cease to function.

"Shadow-tech null fields," Skif observes from his position behind a crystalline outcropping. "Latest generation void weaponry. Designed specifically for light-manipulation environments."

The battalion's advantage proves temporary. As they advance through the fungal fields, Barum's form suddenly expands, stretching upward into a towering pillar of concentrated darkness that somehow remains distinct from the surrounding twilight. Their purple eye-lights multiply, dozens appearing throughout their elongated form, each focusing on different sections of the advancing force.

"You mistake borrowed darkness for true shadow," their voice resonates across the battlefield, creating vibration patterns that harmonize with the crystal formations. "Gloam remembers what existed before void-touch. Before battalion corruption."

Barum raises what might be arms, appendages of pure shadow extending from their central mass, and makes a gesture both summoning and commanding. Across the battlefield, natural shadows respond, detaching from surfaces with fluid grace. The darkness beneath fungi clusters, crystal formations, and light-absorbing flora rises, separating from the objects that cast them to form autonomous entities that flow across the terrain with predatory purpose.

"The shadows remember," Barum intones, voice echoing from multiple directions simultaneously, creating disorienting acoustic patterns that disorient battalion communication systems. "They've fought this battle before."

Battalion troops falter as shadows envelop their flanks, creating confusion in their perfect geometric formation. Void-tech weapons fire wildly, creating more dark patches that Barum immediately incorporates into their growing shadow army. The invaders' tactical advantage dissolves as Gloam itself rises against them.

Ancient sigil-carved spires, previously dormant and indistinguishable from natural crystal formations, activate in sequence across the battlefield. Each one pulses with energy that matches the patterns tattooed across Caelus's skin, suggesting a connection to the same cosmic forces manipulated by his Aetheris ability, where these energies touch battalion equipment, systems fail, void-tech weapons shutter, neural implants cycle through emergency reboot protocols, and tactical overlays dissolve into meaningless static.

Caelus coordinates from atop a central crystal outcropping, enhancement bands burning hot against his fused fingers. Blood vessels have burst across his forehead, creating fresh patterns that trace the flow of power through his system, yet he maintains focus with grim determination. The Aetheris web extends from his position, luminous threads connecting to each crew member while simultaneously mapping battalion movements across Gloam's surface.

"Command node at sector seven exposed," he calls through the tactical network, voice strained but steady. "Coordination disrupted between northern and eastern battalion sections. Priority target is void-tech amplifier at these coordinates."

His consciousness extends beyond physical limitations, perceiving both the immediate battlefield and the cosmic threads connecting to distant points across the galaxy. Through these connections, he senses the wider pattern, how this conflict on Gloam forms one node in a seventeen-system assault still progressing according to Orpheus's final plan. The enhancement bands pulse with renewed intensity as he channels this awareness into tactical advantage, identifying vulnerabilities that conventional sensors cannot detect.

The crew executes their combined strategy with synchronized precision. Skif activates his ice fissures along crystalline outcrops, the formations resonating at frequencies that amplify Gloam's natural harmonics into painful waves that penetrate battalion neural implants. Soldiers stagger, equilibrium disrupted as their inner ear functions struggle against oscillations designed to target their specific biology.

"Disruption at optimal efficiency," Skif reports, no emotion coloring his voice despite the effectiveness of his contribution. Ice continues forming in geometric patterns that mirror the ancient sigils, creating reflection points that scatter battalion targeting systems.

Neous triggers his magma bombs in sequential detonation, timing each explosion to coincide with battalion movement patterns. The dark soil erupts in brilliant orange flares that blind void-adjusted vision systems while simultaneously releasing mineral compounds that interact with battalion armor at the molecular level, compromising its integrity through rapid temperature fluctuations.

"Thermal disruption complete," Neous confirms, his own core temperature intensifying as he channels additional energy into secondary detonation sequences. "Eastern flank contained. Proceeding to the secondary target zone."

Lyra and Meridia activate their hydro-wells with perfect synchronicity, releasing precisely calculated moisture into Gloam's dry atmosphere. The water molecules, manipulated through their hydrokinetic abilities, form disorienting mist patterns that distort spatial perception while simultaneously conducting electrical charges between crystal formations. Battalion communication systems fail as signals scatter through the charged particles, and command structure fragments as orders fail to reach front-line troops.

"Hydro-disruption at maximum effectiveness," Meridia reports, scale shifting between deep blue and violet as she manipulates increasingly complex water formations. "Creating sensory isolation zones at key junction points."

The battalion troops find themselves caught in a perfect trap, a bioluminescent maze where shadows move independently, crystal harmonics disrupt neural functions, fungal spores create false targeting data, and mist patterns destroy formation integrity. Their advance stalls, perfect geometric patterns breaking into isolated clusters as command coordination fails across multiple sectors.

Barum leads the final assault, their shadow form expanding to encompass multiple enemies simultaneously. Where their darkness touches battalion soldiers, void-tech temporarily fails, protective systems shuttering as they encounter shadow energy fundamentally different from the void-touch that powers them. Barum flows between enemy formations with impossible fluidity, seemingly everywhere at once, coordinating Gloam's shadow defenders with instinctive precision.

They confront a battalion commander directly, their form towering over the void-touched officer whose armor bears sigils reminiscent of Orpheus's mask. Barum's darkness engulfs the commander entirely, purple eye-lights multiplying to observe from every angle simultaneously.

"Your darkness is borrowed," they state, voice resonating through the commander's neural implants directly rather than traveling through a conventional atmospheric medium. "Ours is eternal."

The commander's systems fail completely, void-tech armor seizing as contradictory energy signatures overwhelm its processing capabilities. Around them, battalion troops retreat in disarray, tactical cohesion shattered by the combined assault of crew abilities and Gloam's natural defenses.

A Fractal tears open at the battalion's rear position, its edges jagged and unstable compared to the precise dimensional mathematics of controlled passages. The retreating forces pour through this emergency extraction point, abandoning equipment and wounded comrades in their desperate withdrawal. The Fractal fluctuates wildly, dimensional integrity compromised by the conflicting energies permeating Gloam's atmosphere, before finally collapsing with a silent implosion that briefly distorts reality in its immediate vicinity.

Silence settles across the battlefield as the last battalion troops disappear through the fractured Fractal. Bioluminescent fungi resume their natural patterns, crystal formations return to their baseline harmonic frequencies, and shadows gradually reattach to their corresponding objects. Only scattered battalion equipment remains as evidence of the conflict, void-tech devices already being reclaimed by Gloam's light-absorbing soil.

Barum contracts to more human dimensions, though their form remains fluid at the edges, never quite settling into fixed boundaries. The shadow entities they commanded disperse, flowing back to their natural positions across Gloam's landscape. Their purple eye-lights dim slightly, the expenditure of power evident in their reduced luminosity.

"They'll return," Barum warns as the crew gathers at the center of the now-quiet battlefield. Their form solidifies slightly, perhaps in an unconscious effort to appear more substantial when delivering critical information. "This was merely a probing attack, testing Gloam's defenses before committing their main force."

Gloam's shadows settle back into place, resuming their natural positions yet somehow changed by the experience of autonomy. Something has awakened in the planet's ecosystem, a defensive awareness that persists even as immediate threat recedes. The crystal formations continue to pulse with subtle energy, maintaining vigilance through harmonics that connect to cosmic forces beyond conventional understanding.

"But Gloam remembers its defenders," Barum adds, their resonant voice carrying something like pride beneath its usual detachment. "The shadows do not forget those who stand with them against the void."

Caelus nods, enhancement bands finally cooling as he releases the Aetheris connections maintained throughout the battle. Fresh blood traces path down his face, yet his amber eyes remain clear, focused on a point in the distance where his perception has located the last retreating battalion ship. The cosmic threads connecting all seventeen systems under attack remain visible to his expanded awareness, the pattern still progressing despite this localized victory.

"And so will we," he states with quiet certainty, the words carrying weight beyond their simple syllables. A promise not just to Barum and Gloam but to existence itself that the fight against those who would return all to darkness continues, one world at a time, one battle at a time, for as long as necessary.

Chapter 24

The Cosmic Concordance

The central chamber of Gloam opens before them like a wound, in reality, itself, a vast space where fragments of Zathira's ancient monastery have fused with the planet's natural crystal formations to create something that shouldn't exist yet undeniably does. Bioluminescent light pulses in waves of deep blue and violet, casting ever-shifting shadows across the battle-worn faces of Caelus's crew as they step cautiously into this impossible nexus.

Caelus winces as his enhancement bands pull at tender flesh, the metal still fused to his fingers from channeling cosmic forces beyond human tolerance. Blood vessels throb visibly beneath the skin of his temples, mapping paths of pain across his face. Each pulse of the chamber's light sends fresh needles behind his eyes, yet he maintains his focus, scanning the chamber with the determination that has carried him through impossible odds.

"This place exists in multiple dimensions simultaneously," he notes, voices soft but steady despite his evident pain. "Like Zathira, but inverted, extending into void-space rather than creating boundaries against it."

Selenea moves protectively to her brother's side, her stance never relaxing despite their victory against the Battalion forces. Her hand rests near her weapon, bandages still seeping blood where she grips the holster. Her eyes track every shadow and every crystalline surface, and her tactical mind calculates defensible positions and escape routes with unconscious efficiency.

"Something's watching us," she murmurs, gaze-catching momentary reflections in crystal facets that shouldn't exist from their current angle.

The chamber floor bears evidence of ancient conflicts and scorch marks that follow precise geometric patterns rather than chaotic blast radii as if energy itself had been directed through mathematical formulas rather than conventional physics. Scattered Battalion debris litters the periphery where the retreating forces abandoned equipment during their hasty extraction. Void-tech weapons lie dormant, their shadow-energy cores flickering weakly as they're gradually reclaimed by Gloam's light-absorbing soil.

"The architecture maintains wound memory," Ven Diona observes, her analytical mind cataloging structural anomalies even in this alien environment. She kneels briefly, fingers hovering just above a particularly intricate scorch pattern. "These marks date from multiple time periods. The chamber has witnessed similar conflicts repeatedly."

As they advance deeper, crystal formations emit a low harmonic hum that intensifies with each step. The sound begins at the edge of perception, a vibration felt rather than heard, before gradually resolving into complex harmonics that resonate at frequencies just beyond human comfort. The crew feels it in their teeth, in the small bones of their inner ears, in the marrow of their skeletons.

Caelus's sigils respond to these harmonics, the tattoos across his skin pulsing with amber light that creates counterpoint rhythms to the chamber's blue-violet illumination. His enhancement bands warm against his damaged fingers, not with the painful heat of Aetheris channeling but with recognition, metal and flesh and cosmic energy finding equilibrium in this strange dimensional junction point.

"The monastery fragments recognize me," he whispers, watching as sigils carved into crystal walls pulse in perfect synchronization with those tattooed on his body. "They remember their purpose."

The air in the center of the chamber thickens, density increasing as reality folds inward upon itself. Shadows detach from surfaces with fluid grace, coalescing into forms that drift with deliberate slowness toward the chamber's core. The darkness deepens, not as the absence of light but as the presence of something more fundamental, entities that exist primarily in the spaces between conventional matter.

The ancient Valthorim materialised from these gathered shadows; their cloaked forms diminished from the cosmic scale they achieved during the battle with Orpheus, yet still imposing in their otherworldly presence. They hover slightly above the chamber floor, the edges of their robes never quite settling into fixed boundaries as they exist simultaneously in normal space and the void beyond. Where their cloaks brush against crystal surfaces, bioluminescent light dims momentarily, creating moving zones of deeper twilight that trace their positions.

The crew forms a semicircle before these ancient entities, each member's posture reflecting both respect and readiness. Neous Dera stands with clenched fists, his magma core still glowing with residual heat from the battle. His massive form shifts subtly, maintaining optimal temperature against the chamber's fluctuating energy fields, each micro-adjustment betraying his continued combat readiness despite the apparent peace.

Beside him, Skif Zar maintains perfect stillness, his pragmatic mind calculating probabilities with cold precision. Ice crystals form and reform at his feet in complex patterns that mirror the sigils carved into nearby walls. His gaze shifts methodically between the Valthorim entities, assessing each with tactician's detachment, seeing not cosmic beings but strategic variables to be incorporated into contingency planning.

Ven Diona's attention is divided between the ancient entities and the living energy of the chamber itself. Her fingers twitch occasionally with scientific curiosity, clearly longing to collect samples from this impossible fusion of monastery architecture and planetary crystal. The golden Mordian spores still clinging to her equipment glow faintly in response to the chamber's harmonics, creating miniature constellations that orbit her slim form.

Sidia Lith stands with characteristic stoicism, her massive rock form positioned with perfect defensive geometry. She says nothing, her crystalline eyes unreadable as they reflect the chamber's shifting illumination. Her silence carries more weight than words, communicating an absolute commitment to her crew's protection regardless of what cosmic forces confront them.

At the edge of their formation, Barum Voyd exists in a state of partial materialization, their shadow-essence melding with the chamber's natural darkness while maintaining a distinct identity. Their purple eye-lights pulse with recognition as they regard the Valthorim, not as strangers but as entities somehow familiar despite never having been directly encountered before.

"The shadows remember you," Barum notes, voice resonating at frequencies that harmonize with the chamber's hum. "They speak of battles fought before stars existed."

The Valthorim regard the assembled crew with what might be assessment, though no features are visible within their hooded forms. Their presence creates pressure against reality itself, the air becoming dense around them as dimensional mathematics adjusts to accommodate beings that exist partially beyond conventional physics.

Caelus steps forward despite Selenea's subtle gesture of caution. Blood vessels rupture afresh across his forehead as he pushes his Aetheris perception to identify what these diminished yet still powerful entities want from them. The enhancement bands glow against his fingers, creating connections to cosmic threads that reveal glimpses of the Valthorim's true nature, beings that existed before the universe settled on its current physical constants, custodians of balance between forces more fundamental than gravity or light.

"We've done what you asked," he states, voice steady despite the fresh blood tracing patterns down his face. "We've prevented Orpheus's followers from using Gloam as a focal point. What more do you want from us?"

The question hangs in the chamber's crystalline air, creating momentary distortions in the bioluminescent patterns as reality itself waits for the Valthorim's response.

The Valthorim bow in perfect unison, their synchronized movement creating ripples in the chamber's dim light as if reality itself bends in acknowledgment. The gesture carries weight beyond its simple execution; ancient entities show respect not through words but through deliberate motion that transcends language barriers. The chamber responds to this cosmic courtesy, bioluminescent patterns shifting to create momentary constellations that trace paths between the cloaked figures and the assembled crew.

"You have done what many thought impossible," they speak in a unified voice that seems to originate from everywhere and nowhere simultaneously. The sound resonates through the crystal floor, vibrating up through the crew's bodies with physical force. "The balance teeters but holds."

The harmonics of their voice interact with the chamber's natural frequencies, creating interference patterns that manifest as visible waves rippling through the bioluminescent light. These waves carry emotional content rather than mere sound, conveying recognition, relief, and something like gratitude from beings who exist partially beyond conventional emotion.

"The void threatened to reclaim what was never intended for darkness," the Valthorim continue, their hoods tilting slightly to regard each crew member in turn. "You stood where even we could not directly intervene."

The crew exchanges glances, their expressions a complex mixture of relief and lingering tension. Neous Dera's core temperature fluctuates subtly, betraying emotional responses his stoic face attempts to conceal. Skif Zar maintains his characteristic detachment, though the ice patterns forming at his feet arrange themselves in more organized configurations, a subconscious indication of reduced threat assessment. Ven Diona's scientific curiosity overtakes her caution, eyes widening as she studies the light patterns created by Valthorim's speech.

Caelus steps forward, his movements careful and deliberate. Fresh blood has dried in rusty crescents beneath his eyes, evidence of ruptured vessels from pushing his Aetheris perception beyond sustainable limits. He gestures toward the sigils carved into the crystal walls, precise geometric patterns that match those tattooed across his forearms where his tattered environment suit no longer covers them.

"These were here before I was born," he observes, voice carrying the weight of recent understanding. "Yet they match what's written on my body exactly. Not similar, identical."

The sigils pulse in perfect synchronization with his heartbeat, amber light flowing between wall and skin like a current through a closed circuit. The connection creates visible energy pathways that trace three-dimensional patterns through the chamber's air, mathematical formulas written in light rather than symbols.

"My father never explained where he found these designs," Caelus continues, enhancement bands warming as they interact with the active sigils. "He only said they were meant to contain something that existed before containers themselves were conceived."

Selenea steps beside her brother, her steady presence supporting him physically and emotionally. The bandage around her hand has been freshly changed, though blood already seeps through its edges. Her posture remains alert despite exhaustion, which shows in the tight lines around her eyes.

"We united against Orpheus's forces," she recounts, her voice steady but carrying the fatigue of recent battle. "The Battalion troops came in standard occupation formation, establishing perimeter control around Gloam's central crystal field. They were attempting to create a focal point where multiple Fractal pathways naturally intersect."

Her tactical mind reconstructs the battle with precise clarity, identifying key moments in the conflict without unnecessary embellishment. "Barum commanded Gloam's natural shadows, creating confusion in their perfect geometric formations. Neous deployed thermal countermeasures while Skif amplified the crystal harmonics to disrupt their neural implants. Ven's phosphorescent traps overwhelmed their sensors, and hydrokinetic interference from Lyra and Meridia isolated their command structure."

She doesn't mention her own role, the precision shots that disrupted key command nodes, or the tactical coordination that unified their disparate abilities into a cohesive defense. Her focus remains on results rather than individual contributions.

"When their formation broke, they attempted emergency extraction through an unstable Fractal," she concludes. "The withdrawal was disorganized, suggesting their command structure has been significantly compromised."

"Not destroyed," one Valthorim notes, voice separating briefly from their unified chorus. "Merely fragmented. Temporarily weakened."

The Valthorim extend shadowy appendages toward the center of the chamber, their movements creating trails of deeper darkness that hang momentarily in the air before dissolving back into ambient twilight. Where these trails intersect, reality shimmers, dimensional mathematics recalculating as space-time folds inward upon itself.

Fractal windows materialize in the chamber's air, geometric tears in reality that emerge with crystalline precision rather than jagged ruptures. Each window opens to a different cosmic vista, offering glimpses of distant stars and void simultaneously, as if all points in space-time exist concurrently from Valthorim's perspective.

Unlike the Fractals used for transportation, these windows remain static, offering observation without transition. Their edges glitter with multidimensional complexity, reality folding into itself at mathematical angles that strain human comprehension. Through these apertures, the crew glimpses cosmic landscapes impossible to view from conventional space, the filamentary structure of dark matter webs connecting galaxy clusters, the precise boundary where conventional physics yields to void mathematics, the birth of stars from cosmic dust clouds illuminated from perspectives no human has witnessed.

"What you have preserved is more ancient than stars themselves," the Valthorim explain, their unified voice creating harmonic overtones that interact with the fractal edges, causing them to pulse with each syllable. "Before your universe settled on its current physical constants, balance existed between opposing forces."

The fractals shift in unison, their vistas transitioning to show the birth of the universe, swirling energies coalescing into primal forms that precede matter itself. Light and darkness separate, distinct forces emerging from the original unity. The crew watches in stunned silence as stars ignite across the newly formed void, only to abruptly collapse back into darkness as some fundamental equation shifts. Then the cycle repeats: creation, dissolution, recreation, an endless pattern of cosmic birth and death playing out across microseconds that represent billions of years in compressed time.

"The universe you know is not the first attempt," a Valthorim observes, hood tilting toward a particular fractal showing matter coalescing from void energy. "Merely the most stable configuration discovered through countless iterations."

The fractal windows expand further, surrounding the crew with visions of cosmic history unfolding from perspectives impossible to achieve through conventional observation. Galaxies form and dissolve, stars ignite and perish, and planetary systems emerge and collapse, all following mathematical patterns that suggest purpose rather than random chance.

Caelus stares into these cosmic vistas with growing comprehension, the enhancement bands around his fingers pulsing in synchronization with the fractal edges. The sigils across his skin respond to specific cosmic events shown in the windows, suggesting a connection more fundamental than mere symbolic representation.

"The sigils aren't just designs," he realizes, voice barely above a whisper. "They're mathematical formulas that help stabilize this version of reality against void intrusion."

The Valthorim's unity ripples with what might be approval. "You begin to understand what was written upon you before birth," they acknowledge, their combined voice creating new harmonic patterns. "Why you were chosen as a vessel for such knowledge."

The fractal windows pulse more intensely, their edges brightening as they prepare to reveal deeper cosmic secrets to those now ready to receive them.

The fractal windows expand with geometric precision, their edges extending until they merge into a continuous panorama of cosmic vision that surrounds the crew completely. Reality beyond the chamber ceases to exist from their perspective, replaced by views into spaces and times no human was meant to witness. Stars birth and die in compressed time, galaxies spin through eons in seconds and are woven through it all, and darker patterns move with deliberate purpose, conscious entities that predate conventional matter itself.

"Before light, there was void," the Valthorim intone, their unified voice creating ripples through the cosmic vistas surrounding the crew. "Before stars, there was darkness. We are the custodians of both."

Their words manifest visually in the fractal display, darkness that isn't merely the absence of light but something more fundamental, a presence with properties and purpose that existed before conventional physics established its current parameters. This primal darkness writhes with potential, mathematical patterns forming and dissolving within it like thoughts within a cosmic mind.

"Darkness is not evil," one Valthorim clarifies, voice separating briefly from their chorus. "Void is not emptiness. Both are states of existence as valid as the light and matter you perceive more readily."

Their hooded forms drift in slow circles around the crew, each movement creating trails through the fractal displays that alter the cosmic visions slightly, subtle adjustments to the perspective that reveal new aspects of universal history. Where their cloaks brush against the fractals, images shift to show deeper layers of reality, dimensions that exist perpendicular to conventional space-time.

The windows flicker between images of creation and entropy, galaxies forming from void energy only to eventually dissolve back into darkness, stars igniting in brilliant fusion only to collapse under their own gravity, planets cooling from molten states into habitable worlds only to eventually freeze as their stars die. The cycle repeats across billions of simulated years, compressed into moments of observation that nonetheless convey the weight of cosmic time.

"Some among us believed the universe should remain in darkness," the Valthorim continue, their unified voice creating harmonic patterns that match specific cosmic events displayed in the surrounding fractals. "Others sought to create light and life. The conflict between these philosophies is as old as consciousness itself."

The crew watches in stunned silence as the fractals shift to show ancient Valthorim entities engaged in cosmic battle, massive beings of pure energy manipulating forces more fundamental than gravity or light. These primordial entities tear reality apart and reform it according to competing visions, their conflict playing out across dimensional boundaries that human language lacks words to describe.

Some Valthorim gather void energy, compressing it into patterns that resist illumination. Others ignite stars from cosmic dust, creating galaxies that push back against the darkness. Neither side destroys the other completely, instead, their conflict establishes boundaries, creates rules, and defines the parameters that eventually allow a stable universe to emerge.

"Balance was our compromise," the Valthorim explain, shadows beneath their hoods deepening as they recall events from before time itself had meaning. "Neither void nor matter supreme, but coexisting in equilibrium. This universe, your universe, exists because neither philosophy completely dominated."

Caelus reaches toward one fractal, showing Orpheus's final moments, dark matter essence dispersing across dimensional boundaries and consciousness fragmented but not completely destroyed. His fingers pass through the image, creating momentary distortions as present reality intersects with recorded history. The enhancement bands around his fingers pulse with recognition, metal and flesh responding to energies similar to those they channeled during the confrontation at Zathira.

"He believed void was the natural state," Caelus observes, understanding flowing through him as cosmic visions connect to his Aetheris perception. "That creation itself was contamination."

"Not merely believed," a Valthorim corrects, hood tilting toward the fractal Caelus touches. "Remembered. Orpheus existed before the current universal configuration stabilized. His essence recalled a time when void dominated all."

The fractals shift again, cosmic history accelerating as eons pass in eyeblinks. The crew glimpses conflicts across countless worlds, battles between void-followers and creation-guardians playing out in endless variations throughout universal history.

Different faces, different forms, but the same fundamental struggle repeating in cosmic cycles beyond counting.

"Orpheus was not the first to seek the void's return," the Valthorim continued, their voices growing heavier with each word. "Nor will he be the last."

The surrounding fractals coalesce into a single window, dominating the chamber's center. The image shifts, cosmic dust swirling to form a figure wreathed in shadow but different from Orpheus in subtle ways. Where Orpheus manifested as barely contained chaos, this entity demonstrates precise control. Where Orpheus commanded through force, this being suggests influence through subtlety. Its form never fully materializes, existing at the edge of perception, yet somehow more present in its restraint than Orpheus ever was in his excess.

"Umbraeth waits," the Valthorim warn, their unified voice creating visible distortions in the crystalline air. "Where Orpheus sought to destroy, Umbraeth seeks to corrupt. Where Orpheus commanded, Umbraeth persuades."

The figure in the fractal turns slightly as if aware of being observed across dimensional boundaries. Its face remains hidden in shadow, yet the crew feels its attention focusing on them with uncomfortable precision. Caelus's sigils pulse with a warning, amber light flaring against his skin as ancient protections activate in response to this distant observation.

"They were scholars together at Zathira," a Valthorim explains. "Seekers of knowledge about universal origins. Where Orpheus found justification for destruction, Umbraeth discovered methods for subtler manipulation."

The fractal window shows glimpses of this method, void energy flowing through complicated sigil structures, corrupting matter from within rather than opposing it from without. Stars that don't explode but slowly dim, their fusion processes gradually converting to void reactions. Planets that don't shatter but transform, their fundamental atomic structures shifting toward dark matter configurations that exist adjacent to conventional physics.

"Patience is their strategy," the Valthorim continued. "Conversion rather than confrontation. The slow persuasion of reality itself to accept darkness as its final state."

The fractal window closes with a sound like shattering glass, crystalline edges folding inward until they vanish completely. The chamber plunges into deeper darkness, illuminated only by the pulsing bioluminescence of Gloam's natural flora and the glow of Caelus's sigils.

The crew stands in resolute silence, their faces showing the weight of comprehension. Neous Dera's core temperature burns with renewed purpose, creating a corona of heat around his massive form. Skif Zar's ice patterns shift from defensive to offensive configurations, and calculations are already adapting to this new threat assessment. Ven Diona's fingers move in subtle patterns, cataloging information for later analysis. Sidia Lith's crystalline eyes reflect determination undiminished by cosmic scale. Barum Voyd solidifies slightly, their shadow-essence separating more distinctly from the chamber's darkness as if to emphasize their allegiance to balance rather than void dominance.

Selenea steps forward, her military bearing undiminished by exhaustion or cosmic revelation. "How do we find them?" she asks, her tactical mind already converting abstract threats to concrete objectives. "How do we stop something that corrupts rather than confronts?"

The Valthorim turn toward her in unison, hoods tilting with what might be approval. "You already possess the means to detect void corruption," they respond, shadowy appendages gesturing toward Caelus's enhancement bands. "The Aetheris connection can trace manipulation of cosmic threads, identify patterns of subtle void intrusion."

Caelus nods slowly, enhancement bands warming against his damaged fingers. Fresh understanding flows through him, not merely of threat but of purpose, of why he carries these abilities and the sigils that define their use. The connection between his personal struggle and universal stakes crystallizes in perfect clarity.

"And we have the means to counter it," he states, voice finding strength in certainty. "Not alone, but together. Each ability complements the others."

The Valthorim draw back slightly, their forms diminishing as they prepare to withdraw from direct intervention. Their final words echo through the chamber with the weight of cosmic authority:

"The war for the universe's nature continues. You are now its defenders."

The proclamation settles into the crystalline air, not merely sound but investiture, recognition of role, acceptance of duty, and acknowledgment of the battle lines drawn across stars and worlds and dimensions. The crew stands united in the chamber's bioluminescent glow, defenders named by forces that existed before stars themselves took light.

Chapter 25

A New Dawn

Caelus and Selenea step through the threshold into the nexus chamber, where Zathira's ancient monastic architecture impossibly fuses with Gloam's natural crystal formations. The walls curve upward in geometries that defy conventional physics, monastery stone seamlessly flowing into a translucent crystal that pulses with inner light. Caelus staggers slightly, enhancement bands glowing hot against the raw flesh of his fingers, metal and skin now permanently bonded from channeling forces beyond human tolerance. Blood vessels map intricate patterns beneath his skin, visible evidence of power that continues to exact its price.

"Steady," Selenea murmurs, her hand finding his elbow. The fresh bandage wrapped around her palm already shows crimson seepage where her wounds have reopened. Her touch anchors him as the chamber's energies wash over them both in waves that disturb more than just their physical senses.

Caelus nods once, jaw tight against the pain he refuses to acknowledge. His amber eyes scan the impossible space, cataloging details with the precision that kept him alive through countless tracking missions. "This place exists in multiple states simultaneously," he whispers, voice rough from exertion. "The architecture shouldn't be stable, yet it persists."

The chamber expands before them, circular yet somehow containing angles that shouldn't connect. Sections of Zathira's ancient stone walls, carved with sigils identical to those marked across Caelus's skin, stand alongside Gloam's crystalline growths, the two materials neither competing nor fully integrated but coexisting in defiance of structural logic. Overhead, a vaulted ceiling opens to a view that isn't Gloam's perpetual twilight but something deeper, as if space itself has folded inward to allow glimpses beyond conventional reality.

Bioluminescent fungi clusters line the lower walls, pulsing in blues and violets that create moving patterns across the floor. Each pulse corresponds to a harmonic note that vibrates through the chamber, sound becoming almost visible as crystal surfaces resonate in response. The frequency settles into bones and teeth, creating uncomfortable awareness of skeletal structure, as if the sound intends to remind visitors of their physical impermanence.

Caelus winces as a particularly strong harmonic vibrate through him. The amber sigils tattooed across his body respond with answering pulses, creating counterpoint rhythms that briefly ease his pain before intensifying it again. The enhancement bands around his fingers flare with each cycle, metal edges catching light from the chamber's bioluminescence.

"Something's responding to you," Selenea observes, her tactical mind analyzing pattern recognition even as she scans for potential threats. Her injured hand rests near her weapon, fingers maintaining readiness despite the bandage restricting her grip.

The deeper they advance into the chamber, the more pronounced the harmonic vibrations become. Crystal formations emit tones that shift in response to their proximity, creating a composition that seems deliberately calibrated to human nervous systems. The sound exists at the boundary between discomfort and revelation, pushing perception toward thresholds usually closed to conscious awareness.

The air density changes suddenly, pressure increasing as if the chamber has descended deep underwater. Shadows along the walls detach from their sources, moving with deliberate purpose toward the central area. These aren't the natural shadows that Barum commanded during the battle but something more fundamental: the darkness that predates light itself, moving with conscious intent across dimensional boundaries.

Neous Dera shifts position, his massive form flowing with volcanic precision toward a defensive stance. His core temperature increases reflexively, casting orange-red illumination that creates a stark contrast against the chamber's blue-violet light. Tiny fissures open across his surface as internal pressure rises, preparing for conflict even as his tactical mind registers the absence of a direct threat.

Skif Zar remains perfectly still, only the ice formations at his feet betraying his heightened alertness. The crystalline patterns spread outward in geometric configurations that mirror the ancient sigils on the walls, his unconscious mind recognizing and reproducing mathematical formulas beyond his conscious understanding. His breath emerges as visible vapor despite the chamber's neutral temperature, evidence of internal cooling processes activating in response to the energy shift.

Ven Diona's fingers twitch with scientific curiosity, eyes widening as she catalogs environmental changes with methodical precision. The Mordian spores still clinging to her equipment glow with increased intensity, responding to energies her instruments fail to measure. Her posture shifts subtly from defensive caution to analytical interest, prioritizing observation over retreat.

Barum Voyd exists in a state of partial integration with the moving shadows, their form blurring at the edges as they simultaneously maintain individual identity while connecting to the chamber's primordial darkness. Their purple eye-lights pulse with recognition, as if encountering distant relatives after a long separation.

The shadows converge at the chamber's center, darkness pooling into depths that shouldn't be possible in physical space. From this concentrated void, three massive forms materialize with deliberate slowness. Their emergence follows a precise mathematical progression, first outline, then volume, and finally, a presence that exerts a gravitational influence on the surrounding reality. The Valthorim hovers slightly above the floor, and cloaked forms gradually solidify, though never achieving complete physical definition.

Their hoods tilt in perfect unison, a synchronized movement that suggests collective consciousness rather than individual entities. Where their cloaks brush against crystal formations, the bioluminescence dims momentarily, creating moving zones of deeper twilight that trace their positions through the chamber. No features are visible within their hoods, only darkness deeper than the void that spawned them.

"You have succeeded where many would falter," they speak, the voice emanating not from their forms but from the chamber itself. The words vibrate through stone and crystal simultaneously, creating harmonic overtones that correspond to specific sigil patterns on the surrounding walls. "The balance persists because of your actions."

Their unified voice creates pressure against reality itself, the air between words becoming dense with mathematical concepts that translate imperfectly into human language. The crew feels their proclamation as much as hear it, meaning settling directly into consciousness without full auditory processing.

Selenea stands straighter, military bearing, asserting itself even as her tactical mind calculates its position relative to these cosmic entities. Blood seeps through her bandage onto the floor, droplets hovering momentarily before settling in patterns that mirror constellations visible through the chamber's vaulted ceiling.

Caelus meets the darkness within the central Valthorim's hood, amber eyes steady despite the fresh blood tracing paths from ruptured vessels near his temples. The enhancement bands burn against his fused fingers, metal and flesh, responding to energies that recognize their origin in the entities before them.

"What happens now?" he asks, voice steady despite his physical deterioration. The question carries weight beyond its simple syllables, acknowledgment of transformed purpose, of battles fought and sacrifices made, of cosmic understanding that cannot be unlearned.

The Valthorim entities drift closer, their movements creating ripples in the chamber's bioluminescent patterns. The crystal formations respond with an intensified humming that vibrates through bone and stone alike. The air between them and the crew shimmers with potential, reality preparing to reveal knowledge kept hidden since stars first ignited across the primitive void.

The air between the Valthorim and the crew crystalizes with mathematical precision, reality folding along invisible seams. Static fractal windows materialize around the chamber, their edges catching light that shouldn't exist in this spectrum. Each window opens to a different cosmic vista, the birth of stars, the collision of galaxies, and the silent expansion of void between structured matter. The crew stands transfixed as primordial history displays itself in perfect fidelity, events that predate human existence by billions of years playing out in compressed time across dimensional apertures that shouldn't be stable in conventional space.

"Before your consciousness," the Valthorim intone in perfect unison, their cloaks rippling with subtle movement that distorts nearby fractal edges, "before your stars ignited, before matter separated from energy, only void existed."

The windows shift in synchronized movement, showing the universe in its pre-creation state, not emptiness but potential, darkness alive with patterns that suggest consciousness without form. The void pulses with mathematical precision, quantum fluctuations creating momentary structures that dissolve back into darkness without achieving permanence.

"Some among us preferred this purity," one Valthorim states, voice separating briefly from their chorus. "The perfect state, unified, uncontaminated by differentiation."

The central fractal expands, revealing darkness interrupted by the first spark of creation. Light emerges not as an explosion but as a decision, a conscious choice rather than a random chance. The spark expands, separating into distinct energies that establish the fundamental forces. Gravity, electromagnetism, and nuclear interactions all emerge from original unity with deliberate purpose.

"Others sought complexity," another Valthorim continues, hood tilting toward the expanding light. "Creation rather than perfect void. Structure rather than unlimited potential."

The fractals shift again, revealing cosmic battles beyond human comprehension, massive entities of pure energy manipulating forces more fundamental than gravity or light. Some gather darkness, compressing it into patterns that resist illumination. Others ignite stars from cosmic dust, creating galaxies that push back against the void. Neither side destroys the other completely, instead, their conflict establishes boundaries, creates rules, and defines the parameters for a stable universe.

"Balance became our compromise," the Valthorim explain, shadows beneath their hoods deepening as they recall events from before time itself had meaning. "Neither void nor matter supreme, but coexisting in equilibrium."

Caelus watches these cosmic vistas with growing comprehension, enhancement bands pulsing against his damaged fingers. The sigils across his skin respond to specific cosmic events shown in the fractals, suggesting a connection more fundamental than mere symbolic representation. Fresh blood traces the path from his temples as vessels rupture under the strain of processing information beyond the human scale.

"Orpheus was brother to us all," the Valthorim continue, their unified voice creating harmonic patterns that match the crystal formations surrounding them. "Scholar of cosmic origins. Keeper of void knowledge."

A fractal window shifts to show Orpheus in his original form before corruption distorts his essence. The image reveals not the dark matter entity they confronted at Zathira but a cloaked figure similar to the Valthorim themselves, distinguished only by subtle patterns along the edges of his robes.

"He believed creation itself was an error," they explain, their tone carrying something like sorrow beneath its cosmic detachment. "That complexity contaminated perfect simplicity. That all should return to original void-state."

The window expands to show Orpheus's transformation, his gradual separation from the Valthorim consensus, his experiments with void manipulation, and his eventual embrace of dark matter as his preferred physical state. The progression follows mathematical inevitability, each step flowing from the previous with terrible logic.

"His corruption spread through battalion forces," the central Valthorim states, gesturing toward fractal images showing void-touched soldiers advancing across multiple worlds. "Military precision serving cosmic dissolution. Direct confrontation forcing an immediate choice."

The fractals ripple suddenly, their edges distorting as new images replace the historical record. A figure wreathed in shadow emerges, similar to Orpheus yet distinct in crucial aspects. Where Orpheus manifested as barely contained chaos, this entity demonstrates perfect control. Where Orpheus commanded through force, this being suggests influence through subtle manipulations. Its form never fully materializes, existing at the edge of perception, yet somehow more present in its restraint than Orpheus ever was in his excess.

"Umbraeth follows a different path," the Valthorim warn, their unified voice creating visible distortions in the crystalline air. "Subtlety where Orpheus used force. Corruption rather than destruction. The slow persuasion of reality itself to accept darkness as its final state."

The name strikes Caelus like a physical blow. His knees buckle as his Aetheris connection deepens involuntarily, cosmic awareness flooding senses already strained beyond human tolerance. The enhancement bands flare with blinding intensity, metal edges cutting deeper into flesh that no longer registers pain. His amber sigils pulse in perfect resonance with the fractal edges, creating feedback loops of information that bypass conscious processing to map connections across galaxies directly into his awareness.

Selenea catches him before he falls, her strength supporting his suddenly weightless form. Blood from her reopened hand wounds mingles with his where their skin touches, creating momentary sparks that trace patterns matching specific sigils on the chamber walls.

"What you're showing us," she states, military directness cutting through cosmic awe, "is another war. A different front. An enemy we haven't faced before."

Her tactical mind already processes strategic implications and calculates probable approaches to identifying potential vulnerabilities. Her posture shifts subtly from reactive defense to proactive planning, with her shoulders squaring with unconscious authority that makes others follow without question.

"How do we locate and stop Umbraeth?" she demands, a question directed not from desperation but from the need for operational parameters. "What resources do we have? What weaknesses can we exploit?"

The Valthorim hover closer, their massive forms creating gravity wells that pull at the edges of perception. Their hoods tilt in perfect unison, acknowledging her questions with respect due to a commander accepting impossible odds.

"You are defenders now," they respond, voices merging into harmonic resonance that vibrates through the crystal chamber. "The shell of eternal duty passes to you. Where we cannot directly intervene, you will stand as guardians of balance."

The space between them shimmers as air molecules reorganize with impossible precision. A crystalline device materializes, its structure more complex than simple geometry allows, angles connecting in configurations that shouldn't be stable in three-dimensional space. Within its translucent depths, miniature fractal pulses with contained energy create a map of cosmic pathways visible only from perspectives beyond conventional space-time.

"This will guide your path," the Valthorim explained as the device drifted toward Caelus with deliberate slowness. "It contains knowledge gathered across eons, Umbraeth's known movements, void-touched locations, and protective sigils for your continued defense."

Caelus recovers enough strength to extend his hand, enhancement bands responding to the approaching crystal with renewed illumination. The device settles against his palm with a perfect fit, as if designed specifically for his grasp. Where it touches his skin, information transfers directly into his consciousness, not as data but as understanding, knowledge becoming part of his awareness rather than simply accessible to it.

The crew exchanges glances, Neous's core glowing with intensified purpose, Skif's pragmatic assessment accepting new parameters without visible reaction, Ven's scientific curiosity already calculating how to analyze the crystalline device, Barum's shadow-form rippling with what might be anticipation. In each face, determination overshadows fear; duty transcends personal concern.

"We accept," Selenea states simply, speaking for all of them with the authority they've collectively granted her. Her injured hand rests briefly on her brother's shoulder, a blood-soaked bandage leaving a crimson mark on his tattered uniform. The gesture carries years of shared history, promises made and kept through childhood and beyond, and trust forged in countless dangers survived together.

The Valthorim bow in acknowledgment, their synchronized movement creating ripples in the chamber's bioluminescent patterns. The fractals begin to fold inward upon themselves, cosmic vistas disappearing as reality reestablishes conventional parameters. The chamber's crystals pulse with renewed intensity, humming at frequencies that settle into the crew's awareness like forgotten memories suddenly recalled.

"The void waits," the Valthorim warn as their forms begin to dissipate back into shadow. "But so does light."